D1462442

The Bohemians

The Bohemians

A Novel

Anne Gédéon Lafitte, Marquis de Pelleport

Translated by
Vivian Folkenflik

With an Introduction by
Robert Darnton

PENN

University of Pennsylvania Press
Philadelphia

Cet ouvrage, publié dans le cadre d'un programme d'aide à la publication, bénéficie du soutien du Ministère des Affaires étrangères et du Service Culturel de l'Ambassade de France aux Etats-Unis. This work, published as part of a program of aid for publication, received support from the French Ministry of Foreign Affairs and the Cultural Services of the French Embassy in the United States.

Published by
University of Pennsylvania Press
Philadelphia, Pennsylvania 19104-4112

Printed in the United States of America on acid-free paper
10 9 8 7 6 5 4 3 2 1

Library of Congress Cataloging-in-Publication Data
La Fitte, Anne-Gédéon, marquis de Pelleport, 1755?–1810?
    The Bohemians : a novel / Anne Gédéon Lafitte, Marquis de Pelleport ; translated by Vivian Folkenflik ; with an introduction by Robert Darnton.
    [Bohémiens. English.]
    p. cm.
    ISBN 978-0-8122-4194-5 (alk. paper)
Includes bibliographical references.
    1. Bohemianism—France—History—18th century—Fiction. 2. Libertines (French philosophers)—Fiction.
PQ1993.L27 B613 2010
843'.5 22

Contents

INTRODUCTION

Robert Darnton

While the marquis de Sade was drafting *The 120 Days of Sodom* in the Bastille, another libertine marquis in a nearby cell was writing another novel—one equally outrageous, full of sex and slander, and more revealing for what it had to say about the conditions of writers and writing itself. Yet Sade's neighbor, the marquis de Pelleport, is completely unknown today, and his novel, *Les Bohémiens*, has nearly vanished. Only a half-dozen copies are available in libraries throughout the world. This edition, the first since 1790, makes a major work of eighteenth-century libertinism accessible, and it also opens a window into the world of garret poets, literary adventurers, down-and-out philosophers, and Grub Street hacks. More than a century before *La Bohème*, it shows how bohemianism came into being.

Bohemianism belongs to the Belle Epoque. Puccini set it to music and fixed it firmly in late nineteenth-century Paris. But *La Bohème*, first performed in 1896, looked back to an earlier era, the pre-Haussmann Paris of Henry Murger's *Scènes de la vie de Bohème* (*Scenes from Life in Bohemia*) first published in 1848. Murger drew on themes that echoed from the Paris of Balzac's *Illusions perdues* (*Lost Illusions*, first part published in 1837), and Balzac's imagination stretched back to the Ancien Régime, where it all began. But how did it begin? The earliest bohemians inhabited a rich cultural landscape, which has never been explored.

In the eighteenth century, the term *Bohémiens* generally referred to the inhabitants of Bohemia or, by extension, to Gypsies (Romany), but it had begun to acquire a figurative meaning, which denoted drifters who lived by their wits.[1] Many pretended to be men of letters.[2] In fact, by 1789, France had developed an enormous population of indigent authors—672 poets alone, according to one contemporary estimate.[3] Most of them lived down and out in Paris, surviving as best they could by hack work and scraps of patronage. Although they crossed paths with grisettes like Manon Lescaut, there was nothing romantic or operatic about their lives. They lived like Rameau's nephew, not Rameau. Their world was bounded by Grub Street.

Of course, Grub Street, both as an expression and as a milieu, refers to London. The street itself, which ran through the miserable, crime-infested ward of Cripplegate, had attracted hack writers since Elizabethan times. By the eighteenth century, the hacks had moved to other addresses, most of them closer to the bookshops, coffeehouses, and theaters of St. Paul's Churchyard, Fleet Street, Drury Lane, and Covent Garden. But the *Grub-Street Journal* (1730–1737) perpetuated a mythical version of the milieu, and the myth continued to spread through works like Alexander Pope's *Dunciad*, John Gay's *Beggar's Opera*, Daniel Defoe's *Moll Flanders*, Jonathan Swift's *Tale of a Tub*, and Samuel Johnson's *Life of Mr. Richard Savage*. Did nothing comparable exist in Paris? Certainly—Paris had an even larger population of scribblers, but they were scattered in garrets throughout the city, not in any distinct neighborhood, and they never dramatized or satirized their lot in works that captured the imagination of posterity.[4] True, Diderot's *Neveu de Rameau* (*Rameau's Nephew*), Voltaire's *Pauvre Diable* (*Poor Devil*), and parts of Rousseau's *Confessions* evoked the life of Grub Street, Paris, and Paris's Scriblerian culture permeates less-known works such as Mercier's *Tableau de Paris*.[5]

Yet not before Balzac and Murger did any writer bring *la Bohème* to life—no one, that is, except the marquis de Pelleport. His novel, published in two volumes in 1790, deserves to be rescued from oblivion, because it provides an inside tour of the most colorful but least familiar zones of literary life. It is also a very good read. I believe it deserves a place next to, or on a shelf just below, the masterpieces that inspired it: *Don Quixote* and *Tristram Shandy*—and I would place it several shelves above the works of Sade. But readers will judge for themselves. Thanks to a superb translation by Vivian Folkenflik, they now have access to Pelleport's novel in an English version that conveys all the wit and brio of the original.

But first, a warning: in recommending *The Bohemians*, I may be succumbing to a case of biographical enthusiasm. I stumbled upon the book while trying to reconstruct the life of its author, one of the most interesting characters that I have encountered during many years of digging in archives. Anne Gédéon Lafitte, marquis de Pelleport, was, according to everyone who met him, a scoundrel, a reprobate, a rogue, a thoroughly bad hat. He charmed and seduced wherever he went, and left a trail of misery behind him. He lived miserably himself, because he was disowned by his family and relied on his wits and his pen to escape destitution. He was an adventurer who spent most of his life on the road. His itinerary led him along the routes that connected Grub Street, Paris, with Grub Street, London, and his novel provides a picaresque account of them. So whether or not it qualifies as great literature, it deserves to be studied as a guidebook to a world that lies off the beaten track of sociocultural history.

Grub Street, Paris, had many had exits. They led to Brussels, Amsterdam, Berlin, Stockholm, St. Petersburg, and other cities with Grub Street cultures of their own. When Parisian writers found their careers blocked, their rent due, or a *lettre de cachet* hanging over their heads, they took to the road and sought their fortune wherever they could exploit the fascination for all things French. They tutored, translated, peddled pamphlets, directed plays, dabbled in journalism, speculated in publishing, and spread Parisian fashions in everything from bonnets to books.[6] The largest colony of expatriates existed in London, which had welcomed refugees since the persecution of the Huguenots and the adventures of the young Voltaire. The city also had developed its own style of mud-slinging journalism, first during the pamphlet wars of the Walpole ministry, then during the press and parliamentary battles provoked by John Wilkes.[7] The French refugees picked up tricks from the British press, but they also perfected a genre of their own: the *libelle* or libel, a scandalous account of private life among the great figures of the court and capital. The term does not get much use in modern French, but it belonged to common parlance in the book trade of the Ancien Régime; the authors of such works went down in the files of the police as *libellistes*.

The libelers of London learned to survive in the Grub Streets of both capitals. Most of them had received their basic training as hack writers in the literary underground of Paris and crossed the Channel in order to escape the Bastille. After their arrival, they cobbled together a living by teaching, translating, and providing copy for the English presses that tried to satisfy the demand for illegal literature in France. Several expatriates took up journalism, particularly as contributors to the *Courrier de l'Europe*, a biweekly published in London and reprinted in Boulogne-sur-Mer, which provided the fullest reports about the American Revolution and British politics that were available to French readers during the 1770s and 1780s. Others lived from libels. Thanks to information supplied by secret informants in Paris and Versailles, they churned out books and pamphlets that slandered everyone from the king and his ministers down to boulevardiers and actresses. Their works circulated throughout the clandestine book trade in France and sold openly in London, above all in a bookshop in St. James Street operated by a Genevan expatriate named Boissière.[8]

The French reading public had enjoyed revelations about the private lives of public figures for decades without turning against the government, but the libels published after 1770 looked unusually threatening to the authorities, because they appeared at a time of acute political crisis. After crushing the parlements in 1771, the ministry led by Chancellor René Nicolas Charles Augustin de Maupeou ruled with such arbitrary power that many Frenchmen believed the monarchy had degenerated into despotism. Calm returned with the accession of Louis XVI in May 1774, but ministerial intrigues and scandals climaxed by the Diamond Necklace Affair of 1785 brought public opinion back to a boil on the eve of the Revolution. Throughout this period, government officials learned to be wary of the power of public opinion—not that they expected anyone to storm the Bastille but because well-placed slander could damage relations within the delicate system of protection and clientage at the heart of politics in Versailles.

A great deal of the slander came from London. One of the first and most notorious libels, *Le Gazetier cuirassé* (*The Armor-Plated Gazetteer*, 1771), was written by the leading libeler in the colony of expatriates, Charles Théveneau de Morande. It took Chancellor Maupeou as its main target and sullied reputations throughout the court and capital with such effect that when Morande announced a sequel, an attack on Mme du Barry entitled *Mémoires secrets d'une femme publique* (*Secret Memoirs of a Public Woman*), the government resorted to extreme measures. At first it attempted to kidnap or assassinate Morande. When that plot failed, it decided to buy him off. It sent Beaumarchais, who at that time was more active as a secret agent than a playwright, to negotiate; and after a series of baroque intrigues worthy of Figaro, Morande agreed to suppress the entire edition for the princely sum of 32,000 livres and an annuity of 4,800 livres. The other libelers soon followed his example. Instead of merely writing to satisfy the demand in France for scandalous literature, they transformed the manufacture of libels into a blackmail operation. Morande retired from the field, taking up an even more lucrative career as a spy for the French government, which gave him an opportunity to denounce his former colleagues.

Morande's main successor was Pelleport, an equally unscrupulous but far more talented writer. Using Boissière as a middleman, he invited the French government to bid on a series of libels, which he promised to destroy if the price were right. They included *Les Passe-temps d'Antoinette* (*Antoinette's Pastime*), an account of the queen's sex life; *Les Amours du visir de Vergennes* (*The Love Affairs of the Vizir Vergennes*), a similar attack on the foreign minister; and *Les Petits Soupers et les nuits de l'Hôtel Bouillon* (*Intimate Suppers and Nights in the Hôtel Bouillon*), revelations about orgies conducted by the princesse de Bouillon and her servants with her sometime partner, the marquis de Castries, France's naval minister during the American war. No copy of the first two works has survived, perhaps because Pelleport only invented the titles, intending to compose the texts if the French government came up with enough money. But he ran off an edition of *Les Petits Soupers* and used it as bait in blackmail negotiations with an inspector from the Paris police named Receveur, who arrived in London in 1783 on a secret mission to eradicate libels and, if possible, their authors. With Receveur disguised as a "baron de Livermont" and Pelleport hiding behind Boissière, the bidding got up to 150 louis d'or (3,600 livres, the equivalent of ten years' wages for an unskilled laborer). But Pelleport held out for 175 louis (4,200 livres). Receveur was not authorized to go that high; he finally returned to Paris, confounded by his inability to cope with the tricks of the libelers (they led him on a merry chase through pubs and bookshops) and the customs of the English (they spoke an impossible language and had strange notions such as habeas corpus, trial by jury, and freedom of the press). Pelleport proceeded to market *Les Petits Soupers* and followed it up with a far more damaging work, *Le Diable dans un bénitier* (*The Devil in the Holy Water*), a libel about the mission to suppress libels. While avoiding names and compromising information, Pelleport celebrated the expatriate writers as champions of liberty and mocked Receveur and his superiors as agents of despotism, who had attempted to establish a secret branch of the Parisian police in London. The cast of villains included the lieutenant general of police in Paris, the most powerful ministers in Versailles, and their main undercover agent in London: Morande.

Morande triumphed in the end, however, because he procured some proofs of *Le Diable dans un bénitier* with corrections in Pelleport's handwriting. He sent them to the French authorities as evidence for the argument that he had advocated as a secret advisor to Receveur: Pelleport had become the chief of operations among London's libelers. If the government could get its hands on him, while abandoning its policy of agreeing to pay blackmail, it might shut the whole industry down. Using Samuel Swinton, the owner of the *Courrier de l'Europe*, as an intermediary, the police lured Pelleport to Boulogne-sur-Mer and promptly arrested him. They locked him up in the Bastille on July 11, 1784, and on the next day imprisoned his close friend, Jacques-Pierre Brissot de Warville, the future leader of the Girondists during the French Revolution. Brissot had joined the expatriates in London, where he attempted to found a philosophic club (or "Licée") and to support himself by journalism. But his projects threatened to collapse into bankruptcy, and when he traveled to Paris to raise money from some potential backers, the police arrested him on suspicion of collaborating with Pelleport.

Brissot remained in the Bastille for four months; Pelleport stayed four years and three months, an unusually long term. The few documents that survive from this period in the archives of the Bastille suggest that the police considered Pelleport a big catch, the source of the most outrageous attacks on the French court, and correspondence from the archives of the ministry of foreign affairs confirms this impression. The comte de Vergennes, foreign minister at the time of Pelleport's arrest, intervened actively in the attempts of the Paris police to repress the libelers in London. Despite repeated entreaties, Pelleport had no hope of being released from the Bastille until after Vergennes's death on February 13, 1787. Even then, he remained confined for another year and a half—until October 3, 1788—when a new minister with jurisdiction over the Bastille, Laurent de Villedeuil, finally agreed to his release. By that time, the campaign against the libelers no longer interested anyone in Versailles, and the public's attention had shifted to the debates about the Estates General.[9]

While Brissot went on to become one of the leaders of the French Revolution, Pelleport disappeared into obscurity. Perhaps he should be permitted to remain there. Only one scholar has ever devoted even a minor article to him. In the *Bulletin du bibliophile* of 1851, Paul Lacroix, an authority on eighteenth-century French literature, wrote a brief notice about *Les Bohémiens*, a "philosophical and satirical novel, which is completely unknown and of which nearly every copy was destroyed by the printer." Lacroix described it as follows:

> Here is an admirable, here is an abominable book. It deserves to be placed next to the novels of Voltaire and Diderot for the wit, the verve, the prodigious talent that one is astonished to find in it. It also should have a place next to the infamies of the marquis de Sade and the gross obscenities of the abbé Dulaurens [an allusion to Dulaurens's bawdy and very popular novels such as *Le Compère Mathieu* (*Old Boy Mathieu*)]. As

soon as this singular work will have aroused the curiosity of book lovers, it will certainly be much sought after.[10]

Despite Lacroix's prediction, no student of French literature has ever taken up this extraordinary novel, a kind of "Chef-d'oeuvre d'un inconnu" (masterpiece by an unknown author), wittier and wickeder than the book published under that title by Thémiseul de Saint-Hyacinthe in 1714. Like Saint-Hyacinthe, Pelleport satirized pedantry, but his pedants were *philosophes*, and he grouped them with other hack writers under a category that constituted a new literary theme, one proclaimed by the title of his book: *Les Bohémiens*.

Pelleport's Bohemians do not yet have an "ism" attached to them, but they are not simply gypsies or vagabonds, as in the earlier usage of the word. Pelleport plays on that association, because he describes them as a troupe of drifters who wander across northern France, living off the land—for the most part by stealing chickens from peasants. But his Bohemians are marginal men of letters, the same Grub-Street characters who had collaborated with him in the colony of French expatriates in London. Instead of appearing in a relatively favorable light, as in *Le Diable dans un bénitier*, they now are a pack of rogues. They deliver endless philosophic harangues, one more absurd than the other, bawl and brawl like schoolchildren, and pause only to gobble up whatever they can poach from the barnyards along their route. Pelleport disguises their names and even changes the disguises, so the characters reappear under different pseudonyms as the scene shifts and the narrator leads the reader through a succession of extravagant episodes.

The narrator also interrupts the action by stepping out of the story and addressing the reader directly, sometimes with comments on the action, sometimes with digressions, sometimes even with a dialogue in which reader and narrator match wits, disagree, quarrel, and make up. The digressions account for more than half the text. They are essays on all sorts of subjects, whatever suits the narrator's fancy—travel, military tactics, poverty, women, and especially the hard lot of authors. The principal author is the narrator himself, an anonymous voice in the first person singular. His last digression turns into a full-fledged autobiography, which gives him an opportunity to insert himself into the action under a disguise of his own—he is a wandering poet just released from the Bastille—and to bring the book to an end, though hardly to closure, by joining the bohemians for a meal in his favorite tavern in the town where he was born.

Full of lively prose, parody, dialogue, double entendre, humor, irreligion, social commentary, outrageous incidents, and obscenity (but no vulgar language), *Les Bohémiens* is a tour de force. It belongs to several genres, for it can be read as a picaresque novel, a roman à clé, a collection of essays, a libertine tract, and an autobiography, all at the same time. In style and tone it evokes *Don Quixote*, which Pelleport cites as a main source of inspiration. But it also bears comparison with *Jacques le fataliste* (which Pelleport could not have read because it was not published until 1796), *Candide*, *Gil Blas*, *Le Compère Matthieu*, and *Tristram Shandy*. That such a work should have no place at all in literary history seems remarkable, but its nonexistence in the corpus of French literature may be explained by the circumstances of its publication. It appeared in 1790, anonymously, without the name of a printer, and under an address that might have been false: "A Paris, rue des Poitevins, hôtel Bouthillier."[11] At this time, French readers were devouring so much material related to the Revolution that they had little appetite for anything else. Pelleport's novel contains no allusions to politics or current events beyond 1788. It takes place in a world that seems firmly fixed, not about to explode in a social upheaval. Pelleport must have composed the narrative—a complex, well-wrought text that runs to 451 pages in duodecimo format—during his confinement in the Bastille, when he had plenty of time and an adequate supply of writing materials. But it was already out of date when it appeared in print. As far as I can tell, no journal mentioned it after its publication, and only a half-dozen copies of it have survived, in six different countries.[12]

Whether or not *Les Bohémiens* will be recognized for its literary qualities, it deserves to be studied as a source of information about life in Grub Street during the 1780s. To do so, however, requires some familiarity with Pelleport's career and his relations with the other hack writers in London, especially Brissot. A police report, which dates from some time shortly before his arrest in 1784, provides some information about Pelleport's origins:

> He is the son of a gentleman in the household of Monsieur [the king's elder brother.] He was expelled from two regiments in which he served, Beauce and Isle-de-France, in India, and was imprisoned four or five times at the request of his family for dishonorable atrocities. He spent two years wandering through Switzerland, where he got married and got to know Brissot de Warville. He was a student at the Ecole militaire, not the best one it ever turned out. He has two brothers who also

were trained there and who were discharged dishonorably, just like him, from the regiments in which they were placed.[13]

In short, Pelleport was a déclassé. Born into an aristocratic family, he had sunk into the ranks of the libelers after an unsuccessful career in the army and enough dishonorable conduct to have done time in prison at the request of his family.

Some additional material culled from other sources fills out the picture. According to a summary of Pelleport's dossier in the archives of the Bastille published in *La Bastille dévoilée* (*The Bastille Unveiled*, 1789), he was born in Stenay, a small town near Verdun. When he migrated to Switzerland in the late 1770s, he married a chambermaid to the wife of Pierre-Alexandre DuPeyrou, Rousseau's protector in Neuchâtel. They settled in the Jura mountain town of Le Locle, where she bore him at least two children and he found employment as a tutor in the household of a local manufacturer. By 1783, Pelleport had left his family in order to seek his fortune in London. That led to libeling and the four years in the Bastille. During his imprisonment, Pelleport's wife, who had been supported by relatives in Switzerland, came to Paris to plead for his release. She got nowhere, however, and escaped destitution only through the intervention of the chevalier Pawlet, an Irishman involved in educational projects in Paris, who arranged for her and her children to be supported by an orphanage for the sons of military officers. When at last he was freed, Pelleport joined his relatives in Stenay, then returned to Paris just in time to witness his former captors being lynched by the crowd on July 14. He tried to save de l'Osme, the major of the Bastille who had treated him and the other prisoners kindly, and barely escaped with his life. That exposure to street violence may have deterred Pelleport from throwing his lot in with the revolutionaries. As a radical pamphleteer who had been silenced by the state, he could have taken up a new career as a journalist or politician. Brissot and many others demonstrated that there were endless opportunities for an author with a sharp pen and a reputation as a martyr of despotism. But Pelleport disappeared from view after July 14. Apparently he retired to Stenay, leaving his children in the orphanage; and when he produced something for the press during the next few months, it was a bizarre, anonymous novel, which had no relevance to the great events of 1789.[14]

No direct relevance. But *Les Bohémiens* had an antihero, Jacques-Pierre Brissot, who appears in the first chapter as its main protagonist: "Bissot" (the "sot" suggesting stupidity), a hare-brained, flea-bitten philosopher. After being mocked throughout the text for his dogmatic absurdities, he reappears at the end as a bone-headed old-clothes dealer in London named "Bissoto de Guerreville" (a pun on Brissot's full name, Brissot de Warville). Having drafted the text during his long stay in the Bastille, Pelleport may have published it in 1790 in order to undercut Brissot's growing power as editor of *Le Patriote français* and a champion of the left. But there is no reason to suspect that Pelleport had any sympathies with the right. The novel had no overtly political message, and it condemned many of the injustices in pre-1789 France. Pelleport probably published it for the same reasons that move other authors—in order to see it in print and to make some money. But why did he harbor so much hostility to Brissot? They had been intimate friends. Their friendship came apart in the Bastille, however, and that experience, as Pelleport brooded on it during his long years in confinement, may help explain the circumstances and even some of the passion behind *Les Bohémiens*.

Pelleport and Brissot could hardly have been more different by temperament and background. Pelleport was a marquis, Brissot the thirteenth child of a pastry cook. Pelleport was dissolute, cynical, and witty; Brissot, serious, hard working, and humorless. While Pelleport served as an officer in India, Brissot labored as a law clerk. With the help of a small inheritance, he bought a cheap law degree from the University of Rheims (which sold its degrees after giving perfunctory examinations), but he abandoned the law in order to devote himself to writing and, he hoped, a career as a successor to Voltaire and d'Alembert. Although he eventually produced a shelf-full of tracts on subjects like the injustices of the criminal law system, he began by churning out hack pamphlets and living the life of Grub Street. He had to flee Paris in 1777 in order to escape a *lettre de cachet* that would have sent him to the Bastille for slandering a lady known for her respectable role in a salon. In 1778, he began to work as a journalist by correcting proof for the French edition of the *Courrier de l'Europe* put out in Boulogne-sur-Mer. There he met his future wife, Félicité, and her mother, Marie-Cathérine Dupont née Clery, the widow of a merchant—two persons who also would figure prominently in *Les Bohémiens*. When Brissot returned to Paris in 1779, Madame Dupont recommended him to a family friend, Edme Mentelle, a professor of geography at the Ecole militaire in Paris. Brissot became a regular member of Mentelle's literary circle, hoping to win recognition as an up-and-coming *philosophe*. Here it was that he crossed paths with Pelleport, a former student of Mentelle's who also was setting out to make his mark in the Republic of Letters. But while the trajectory of Brissot's career seemed at this time to point upward, Pelleport began to drift down through the literary ranks toward a makeshift existence as a hack and an adventurer. He left Paris for Switzerland, where he hoped to find employment in the Société typographique de Neuchâtel. But he managed only to land a job as a tutor in nearby Le Locle, and soon found himself overburdened with a family.[15]

Brissot sent Pelleport several letters during the second half of 1779. Under the mistaken impression that his friend had taken a job with the Société typographique, he proposed a whole series of books for it to print. Pelleport passed the proposals on to the publisher, which eventually produced most of Brissot's works before the French Revolution and maintained an extensive correspondence with him. Three of the first letters in Brissot's dossier in its archives are addressed to Pelleport and are written in a familiar manner that would have been unthinkable in the eighteenth century, except in exchanges between intimate friends. Brissot calls Pelleport "my dear friend," "my dear," "mio caro," and never uses the customary formal salutation, "your most humble and obedient servant." On August 31, 1779, he closed his letter as follows: "M. Mentelle and his wife are in excellent form and assure you of their friendship. Be persuaded that mine will last as long as my life. Adieu, I embrace you and am going to bed. Yours ever." In a later letter, undated but from 1779, he notes, "The beautiful neighbor is always charming. In our little get togethers, we often call up the memory of you." Brissot was referring to Félicité Dupont, who had left Boulogne in order to pursue her studies in the Mentelle household and soon would become his fiancée.[16]

Five years later, Brissot and Pelleport were occupying separate cells in the Bastille. The surviving evidence, though incomplete, shows how their careers converged and how the Bastille left its mark on lives lived in Grub Street. Brissot told his side of the story in a memoir, probably written in 1785, which reduced a complex set of circumstances to a simple conclusion: he was an innocent victim of despotism, and Pelleport was a dissolute libeler.[17] In justifying his own conduct, Brissot implied that he had only the slightest acquaintance with Pelleport before they met in 1783 and that he avoided the French expatriates in London, because their immorality repelled him. He found Pelleport particularly depraved: "Pelleport had plenty of wit, a bravura manner, an unbridled taste for pleasure, and a profound scorn for every kind of morality."[18] Brissot acknowledged that he had tried to help Pelleport, hoping to reunite him with the family he had abandoned in Switzerland. In the course of this charitable activity, Brissot had learned about Pelleport's speculations on libels, but he had refused to have anything to do with them—and therefore he was horrified when told by his interrogator in the Bastille that he had been arrested for complicity in the publication of *Le Diable dans un bénitier.*

Here Brissot was stretching the truth. Although he had not helped write the book, he had cooperated in its distribution. While in London, he had received a letter from his agent in Ostend, which acknowledged receipt of a shipment of *Diables* that Brissot had sent to him and that mentioned forwarding 125 copies to a bookseller in Brussels and six to a bookseller in Bourges.[19] Moreover, the police had confiscated a letter from Pelleport to a bookseller in Bar-le-Duc announcing a shipment of six *Diable*s along with several of Brissot's works,[20] and they had turned up more compromising correspondence between Brissot and his agent in Paris, a Parisian businessman named Larrivée. It showed that aside from the marketing of libels, Brissot's relations with Pelleport involved a murky "business connection."[21]

This information emerged from Brissot's interrogation in the Bastille. The police records of interrogations are dramatic documents, written in the form of a dialogue: questions and answers transcribed by a scribe, each page initialed by the prisoner as testimony to its accuracy. The questions show the police laying traps for their quarry; the answers document the attempts by the prisoners to avoid the traps and to hold back compromising information. Brissot stewed in his cell for several days without being informed of the reason for his imprisonment and without knowing that Pelleport had also been arrested. He was interrogated three times by Pierre Chénon, a veteran police officer—first on August 3, next on August 21 (this time for a full day, with a break at two o'clock for dinner), and then a follow-up session for a half-day on August 22. He seems to have held up quite well. When accused of collaborating on *Le Diable dans un bénitier,* he proved that the evidence against him had been fabricated.[22] Chénon then attempted to draw him into admitting some connection with eight other *libelles*:[23]

1. *La Naissance du Dauphin* (*The Birth of the Dauphin*)
2. *Les Passetemps d'Antoinette* (*Antoinette's Pastime*)
3. *Les Rois de France régénérés* (*The Kings of France Regenerated*)
4. *Les Amours du visir de Vergennes* (*The Love Affairs of Vizir Vergennes*)
5. *Les Petits Soupers de l'Hôtel de Bouillon* (*The Intimate Suppers of the Hôtel Bouillon*)
6. *Réflexions sur la Bastille* (*Reflections on the Bastille*)
7. *La Gazette noire* (*The Black Gazette*)

8. *Les Rois de France jugés au tribunal de la raison* (*The Kings of France Judged Before the Tribunal of Reason*)

Brissot denied having anything to do with them, but in defending himself during his first interrogation he let slip that Pelleport had been involved with some dubious publications and that his own involvement with Pelleport included some entangled financial affairs. Pelleport lived in a rooming house in Chelsea, and could barely support himself by giving private lessons in mathematics and French. Brissot said that he tried to help by finding him jobs copying manuscripts, translating English books, and contributing articles to the *Courrier de l'Europe*. But Pelleport kept coming back, asking for loans. Brissot gave him what little money he could spare. At one point, he bailed him out of debtor's prison, even though Brissot himself had been imprisoned earlier for debt. What pained Brissot most was the thought of Pelleport's wife and children (he said there were five of them), abandoned in Switzerland.

Brissot's responses made him appear generous and high-minded, but they also left an impression of two impoverished writers, struggling to keep their heads above water in the harsh environment of literary London. By the time he conducted the second interrogation, Chénon had accumulated a good deal of information about the economic circumstances of the affair. Letters confiscated from Larrivée and Brissot's brother showed that Pelleport's situation had become critical during the first months of 1784. Chénon informed Brissot that "Pelleport, pursued by his creditors in London and by merchants in France with whom he had been dealing, fell into a desperate situation and resolved to flee from London with an English widow named Alfraide." Moreover, after Brissot had left for France, Pelleport plotted with Brissot's enemy, Swinton, and his financial backer, Desforges d'Hurecourt, to produce a new French newspaper about British affairs. Pelleport would edit it, Swinton would help manage its launching, and Desforges would finance it by withdrawing the funds that he had invested in Brissot's Licée. Moreover, this conspiracy followed an attempt by Pelleport to pry funding for another speculation from Brissot's mother-in-law, Madame Dupont, in Boulogne-sur-Mer.

This last episode exposed a great deal about Pelleport's biography. According to evidence gathered by the police, his father died in late 1783, and he traveled to Paris (secretly, in order to avoid arrest) in the hope of collecting an inheritance. Acting as Brissot's friend and Parisian agent, Larrivée gave Pelleport a warm reception but then sent reports that he had run into trouble with his stepmother.[24] She had persuaded Pelleport père while he was dying to sell off an office that he owned for 70,000 livres, then transferred the money to the two children she had borne by him. She also employed various maneuvers to tie up the rest of the estate, managing to keep virtually everything out of the hands of the three sons her husband had had by his first wife. He had collaborated in this Balzacian plot, because he had quarreled with his first set of children—he had all of them imprisoned at one time or other by *lettre de cachet*—and lost contact with them after they left home for service in the army and adventures on the road. "Such, my friend, is the fate of certain mortals who have disgraced themselves in their youth," Larrivée concluded in one of his letters to Brissot.[25]

Unfortunately, Pelleport had counted on inheriting 20,000 livres and had spent it before he could collect it by speculating on champagne in Reims. One of his projects for striking it rich was a "foreign delicatessen"—or outlet for French luxury goods in London—which he planned to establish with Antoine Joseph de Serres de Latour, the editor of the *Courrier de l'Europe*.[26] Latour realized this speculation was a pipe dream in time to get out of it, but Pelleport had contracted about 15,000 livres worth of debts in Reims, and the crates of champagne were traveling to Boulogne-sur-Mer for export to England before he learned that he would inherit nothing. He showed up in Boulogne himself, penniless, sometime in early 1784. What was he to do? He could not even pay for his passage across the Channel. Somehow he persuaded Madame Dupont, Brissot's mother-in-law, who had continued her husband's business as a merchant, to lend him 150 livres for the rest of his journey and to store the champagne in her warehouses until he could dispose of it with a London retailer. The result was a financial fiasco, which ended in unpaid letters of exchange and a great deal of bad feeling. In June 1784, Brissot's brother, who was looking after his affairs in London, wrote to him in Paris, warning that Pelleport was a "liar" and an "impostor."[27]

This information may appear trivial but is worth mentioning, because it all turned up, thinly disguised as fiction, in *Les Bohémiens*. It also shows how interrogations in the Bastille could turn friends into enemies. Chénon probably dangled the evidence of Pelleport's duplicity in front of Brissot in order to provoke Brissot to denounce his former friend. For his part, Brissot was convinced that Pelleport had denounced him—a reasonable assumption in view of the fact that he had gone about his business undisturbed in Paris until the day after Pelleport's arrest.[28] The police often elicited denunciations by playing prisoners off each other through a technique known as "confrontation." When they captured two suspects, they commonly grilled them separately, then brought them together and read the transcripts of the interrogations to both of them. Because each prisoner had usually attempted to shift the blame onto the other, this device often triggered mutual accusations, which led to further arrests or a fuller understanding of the case. Whether Pelleport and Brissot turned on each other in this manner cannot be determined, owing to gaps in the archives.[29] But Brissot's papers contain a denunciation of Pelleport that he wrote in the Bastille in order to exculpate himself.

Entitled "Mémoire pour le sieur Brissot de Warville," it began with a sketch of Pelleport's character: "vigorous temperament," "a very agreeable wit," but: "He has a violent love for women and pleasure, which was his undoing."[30] Next, it outlined his checkered career in the army, as a drifter "reduced to expedients," and as a feckless husband and father in Switzerland. It provided damning details about Pelleport's libeling in London—his blackmail negotiations over *Les Passe-temps d'Antoinette*, his authorship of *Le Diable dans un bénitier*, and even his plans to produce an underground newspaper full of "spicy anecdotes," including an attack on the finance minister, Charles-Alexandre de Calonne. Brissot's wife Félicité considered Pelleport such a blackguard that she would not permit him to enter the house—and so earned his undying hatred (another theme that would turn up in *Les Bohémiens*). But, the memoir explained, Brissot continued to help him and even bailed him out of jail shortly before leaving for Paris. As soon as Brissot had left, Pelleport began plotting against him in other get-rich-quick schemes, including the speculation on the champagne, which turned into a swindle aimed at Latour. According to the last letter that Brissot received from London, Pelleport was about to run off to America with "a lady named Alfred." "Such is the monster who has just helped to get his benefactor arrested," the memoir concluded. Everything suggests that Pelleport felt just as angry. He must have realized that Brissot had provided evidence against him and must have resented it, for he remained shut up in the Bastille for more than four years, while Brissot was released after only four months.[31]

It is possible to form some idea of Pelleport's state of mind during his long imprisonment by consulting the few original papers from his dossier that have survived in the archives of the Bastille. He was granted permission to take occasional walks inside the prison yard in 1784 and to breathe the air from its towers once a week in 1788. He requested shipments of books, including Voltaire's *Le Siècle de Louis XIV*, a work on Prussian military tactics, and a treatise on the harpsichord. There is no complete record of what he read, but he wrote a synopsis of "the philosophical episodes" in Raynal's *Histoire philosophique de l'établissement et du commerce des Européens dans les deux Indes* (*Philosophical History of the Establishment and of the Trade of Europeans in the Two Indies*).[32] He also wrote letters, mainly to his wife. As already mentioned, she had tried but failed to win his release and had escaped destitution only through the charitable intervention of the chevalier Pawlet. While she continued to solicit for Pelleport, he petitioned the governor of the Bastille to permit her to visit him. The Bastille records show that they met three times in 1784, nine times in 1785, twice in 1787 and twice in 1788.[33] Permission for these one-hour meetings was withdrawn in 1786, evidently because Pelleport had misbehaved in some manner. Judging from a note to a friend named Lambert that his guards captured, he had attempted to escape: "I threw the rope down yesterday evening each time that you came, but apparently it did not reach the ground. I am counting on Pierre to leave the door open for me during the night. . . .Be patient, my dear Lambert, and wait for me. I want to be in London as badly as you do."[34] Whatever the reason for the cancellation of his wife's visits, Pelleport begged to have them continued at the end of 1786, citing the military record of his family ("which has served the state and our kings for six centuries") and his own misery ("three years of expiation and the most horrible pain").[35]

After the visits resumed, Pelleport's relations with his wife deteriorated. Somehow she had managed to persuade the authorities to allot her a meager pension of 25 livres a month from the budget of the Bastille, but she found it difficult to survive. "My situation is atrocious," she lamented in a letter to the Bastille's major, the chevalier de l'Osme, who treated Pelleport kindly and was his main intermediary in contacts with the outer world.[36] For his part, Pelleport complained in letters to the administrators of the Bastille that his wife refused to go to Versailles in order to lobby on his behalf. He suspected her of conspiring with his enemies to keep him in jail and perhaps of having become the mistress of her benefactor, the chevalier Pawlet:

> I have not yet reached a decision about what course to take, whether I will wait for an opportunity to demand justice for the abuse of authority by the sieur de Breteuil [Louis Charles Auguste le Tonnelier, baron de Breteuil, then in charge of the Bastille in his capacity as Minister of the King's Household] or whether I will put a swift end to my life. . . . All I ask is that I should not be torn violently from this dungeon cell, which probably will be my tomb. . . . I could never

have believed that M. le chevalier de Pawlet would make my dishonor and the loss of my liberty and my life the price that he charges for his bounty to my family. . . . A man's fate is certainly unhappy when, like a vile plaything of all that is close to him, he resembles a wooden top, which clever children spin around, now one way, now another, by beating it with a whip.[37]

Bastille prisoners often filled their letters with lamentations in the hope of softening their captors' resistance to pleas for their release, but there is no reason to doubt the despair expressed by Pelleport. As the weeks turned into months and the months into years, he had reason to believe that he never would be freed.

He filled much of the time with writing. From the beginning of his imprisonment, he was given a pen, ink, and paper.[38] The most important result of this liberal treatment was *Les Bohémiens*, but Pelleport also composed some poetry, which gave him an outlet for his feelings, as he explained in one of his letters: "The lot of Bastille prisoners is somewhat like that of unhappy Indians and miserable African slaves. . . . It is better to dance to the sound of your chains than to chew in vain on your tether."[39] The verse that survives in his dossier shows him venting his resentment in short, satirical *pièces fugitives* aimed at Bernard-René de Launay, the governor of the Bastille:

Avis au *Journal de Paris* sur un songe que j'ai eu

Laun.. vient à expirer! quoi! passant, tu frémis.
Ce n'est point une calomnie.
Pour son honneur, moi, je m'en réjouis.
C'est la meilleure action de sa vie.

Notice to the *Journal de Paris* about a dream I had

Laun.. just expired! What, passerby, you shudder?
It is not a calumny.
For my part, I rejoice at the honor he acquired.
It is the best act of his life.

Madrigal sur ce qu'on s'est plaint que l'auteur était méchant

Laun.. s'est plaint que j'ai l'esprit méchant.
D'un coeur si bon le reproche est touchant.[40]

Madrigal on the complaint that the author is wicked

Laun.. complained that I have a wicked turn of mind.
It is a touching reproach from one with such a good heart.

Pelleport scattered similar verse through his published writing. Most of it
had the same tone—biting, sardonic, disillusioned.[41]

A note of nihilism accompanied the mockery that Pelleport turned on
the world. The documentation that surrounds his imprisonment does not
provide access to his innermost reflections, but what little can be known
suggests that they were dark. He brooded over the denunciations that barred
his way to freedom while most others, like Brissot, were usually released after
a few months. He had scores to settle, not just against Brissot but against
nearly everyone whom he had known in London—especially Morande, "a
libeler and slanderer by profession."[42] "It would be a thousand times better for me to have fallen into the hands of the savages in Canada than in
those of the slanderers," he wrote to de l'Osme. "Better by far, Monsieur, to
perish from the blow of a tomahawk ["tomevack"] than to succumb to the
poisoned darts of the venomous insects who have reduced me to a state of
desiring death every time that I contemplate what remains of my existence
in the dark shadow of my tomb."[43] In his despair, Pelleport seems to have
abandoned all belief in higher principles. Such, at least, was the testimony of
another London libeler who was captured by the police in 1785, Jean-Claude
Fini, alias Hypolite Chamoran. Fini described Pelleport not only as the author of the worst of the libels produced in London but also as a "knave," a
"monster," and a "disciple of Diagoras [the atheistic philosopher from the
fifth century B.C.E.], who, when you ask him about the primary cause that
rules the universe, replies with an ironic smile and makes the sign of a zero,
which he calls his profession of faith."[44]

Whom to believe? How to sift through fragments from the Bastille in
order to piece together a picture of a life that shattered there? If indirect evidence be admitted, one can turn to a final source, the life and works of a man
who never testified about Pelleport but who shared the Bastille with him: the
marquis de Sade.

Sade's imprisonment in the Bastille, from February 29, 1784 to July 2,
1789, coincided almost exactly with Pelleport's: July 11, 1784 to October 3,
1788. Did those four years of cohabitation produce any intellectual exchange?
Impossible to say. The two men had a good deal in common. Both were mar-

quis from the old feudal nobility, both had been imprisoned at the request of their families for misbehavior in their youth, both wrote obscene novels—at the same time and within close range of each other. Their names appear in close proximity in the records of the Bastille.[45]

Daily life in the Bastille was certainly hard, but it is easily misunderstood owing to the myths that cloud the reputation of the place—the revolutionaries' nightmare of a house of horrors, on the one hand, and the revisionists' pastel-tinted picture of a one-star hotel, on the other. Modern notions of imprisonment do not correspond to eighteenth-century practices. The Bastille was a converted fortress, used for the confinement of special prisoners who were usually arrested by *lettre de cachet* and kept without trial for indefinite periods. For the small minority who remained confined for several years, like Pelleport and Sade, the psychological burden could be terrible, but they were not cut off from all contact with the outside world or even with each other. Prisoners did not share cells—nearly half of the forty-two cells in the fortress were empty throughout the 1780s—but sometimes by special permission they were allowed to mix with one another. The most privileged occasionally had dinner together. They played cards, chess, and even billiards for a while in 1788. They had ample opportunity to read and write, at least when the rules were relaxed during the late eighteenth century. They received plentiful supplies of books, paper, and writing instruments. Some even devised ways of exchanging notes.[46]

The Bastille had a fairly extensive library; and although it did not contain much fiction, the prisoners sometimes wrote their own. Did they have any knowledge of each other's literary activities? The surviving evidence does not provide an answer to that question. One can only affirm that imprisonment and the enforced leisure it produced weighed heavily on some of the prisoners, provoking them to reflect on their lives and to express their thoughts in writing. Despite its thick walls and general gloom, or perhaps because of them, the Bastille functioned as a greenhouse for producing literature. It was in the Bastille that Voltaire began *La Henriade*, that La Beaumelle completed his translation of Tacitus, and that Sade drafted *Les 120 Journées de Sodome* (*The 120 Days of Sodom*), *Aline et Valcour*, and the first version of *Justine*. While this strange neighbor was venting his passions through his pen, Pelleport drafted a work that expressed a similar gamut of emotions but with a sharper style and greater literary skill.

Such is my assessment. Others may find *Justine* far superior to *Les Bohé-*

miens. But Pelleport's book deserves at least to be known. Having described the circumstances of its production, I would therefore like to discuss the text.

The book opens as Bissot wakes up in a miserable bed in a garret in Reims. He has just bought his law degree, but that extravagance exhausted his savings, 300 livres, and he finds himself deeply in debt. What to do? The best solution he can hit upon is to become a philosopher instead of a lawyer—that is, to skip town before the bailiffs can clap him into debtors' prison. He justifies this resolution by delivering a "philosophical discourse"[47] to his brother, who serves as his sidekick and has been sleeping beside him. It is the first of many philosophical harangues scattered through the book, and it gives Pelleport an opportunity to parody Brissot's vulgar Rousseauism while slipping in some disparaging references to his origins as the son of a pastry cook in Chartres. In absurdly overblown language, Bissot deplores the inequalities of the social system, then veers off into a tirade against the tyranny of creditors based on his *Théorie des lois criminelles* (*Theory of Criminal Law*). As this and many other allusions make clear, Pelleport had a thorough knowledge of Brissot's early writings as well as of his background and family. The younger brother in the novel, Tifarès, corresponds to Pierre-Louis Brissot de Thivars, the younger brother of Brissot who was known as Thivars and who joined him in London in 1783 in order to provide assistance on various projects.[48] It was in that capacity that he had warned Brissot about Pelleport's duplicity in June 1784. Pelleport describes Tifarès as a skinny, superstitious simpleton, interested in little more than the next meal. When Bissot, continuing his oration, announces that they must leave Reims in order to return to nature and feed on roots and acorns, Tifarès protests that he would prefer to find a job as a kitchen hand. Finally, however, he agrees. He puts on six shirts—his way of transporting his entire wardrobe—and the two set off, Bissot-Brissot and Tifarès-Thivars, a modern version of Don Quixote and Sancho Panza.

Next scene: a primitive road in Champagne. Speaking in his own voice, the narrator-author declaims against the corvée and the exploitation of the peasants. He then deposits his heroes in a broken-down inn, where they spend their last pennies on a nasty meal—the occasion for another philosophic harangue, a parody of Brissot's *Recherches philosophiques sur le droit de la propriété* (*Philosophical Researches on the Right of Property*)—and continue, resigned to sleeping in a ditch. After night descends, a brigand suddenly emerges from the darkness, pointing a rifle. He turns out to be Mordanes (Morande, whose name was often spelled with an *s* at the end), the guard and chief poacher of a band of nomads, who are gathered around a fire, roasting the day's plunder. Instead of disemboweling the strangers, the "Bohemians" invite them to join the feast. While Tifarès instinctively goes to turn the spit, Bissot treats his hosts to the "reception speech"[49] that he had delivered at the Académie de Châlons-sur-Marne. The actual discourse, given at Châlons on December 15, 1780, concerned proposals for the reform of criminal law. Pelleport's parody of it mixes those ingredients with a declamation against despotism, religious intolerance, and assorted social evils, all served up in the pompous rhetoric of provincial academies. To address a troupe of brigands as noble savages—"wise forest-dwellers, illustrious savages"[50]—and then to change gears and treat them as straight-laced provincial academicians is to pile absurdity on absurdity, especially as the purpose of it all is to get a free meal. In the midst of his entangled oratory, Bissot glimpses an even happier outcome. If he can be admitted to the company like a neophyte in an academy, he, too, could live by plundering peasants. The same went for Tifarès, who offers his services in plucking chickens "according to the best *Encyclopédie* methods."[51] The Bohemians recognize the newcomers as men of their own kidney, and let them join the troupe.

At this point, Pelleport suspends the narrative in order to provide background information about the Bohemians. In describing them, he drops enough hints—references to publications, names obviously concocted as anagrams—for the reader to realize that the entire novel is a roman à clé, which will require continuous decoding. The guessing game begins as the president of the troupe, the abbé Séchant, introduces its main members to the newcomers. Séchant and his companion, the abbé Séché—their names evoke the aridity of their philosophy—are caricatured versions of two of the London libelers, the abbé de Séchamp and the baron de Saint-Flocel. According to a police report that was published in a selection of papers from the Bastille in 1790, Séchamp was a former chaplain of the prince of Zweibrücken who had fled to London after becoming implicated in a plot to embezzle funds from a merchant in Nantes. He took part in Pelleport's blackmail operation while attempting to launch a physiocratic-philanthropic review entitled *Journal des princes*, which was intended to undercut the somewhat similar periodical published by Brissot, *Correspondance universelle sur ce qui intéresse le bonheur de l'homme et de la société* (*Universal Correspondence About That Which Concerns the Happiness of Man and of Society*). Saint-Flocel joined him in this venture, having gained experience as a journalist on the *Journal de Bouillon*.[52] Brissot described Saint-Flocel in his memoirs as an "excessively dogmatic economist" and the police put him down in their files as an adventurer, who changed names and jobs in order to escape punishment for various swindles.[53] The third principal Bohemian was Lungiet, a burlesque counterpart of Simon Nicolas Henri Linguet, the famous journalist who had joined the colony of French expatriates after being released from the Bastille in 1782.[54] Pelleport could not have expected every reader to identify every character in the book, but he made it clear that the Bohemians wandering through Champagne were actually Frenchmen settled in London and that their main activity, robbing barnyards, corresponded to the slanderous journalism of the libelers.

Pelleport did not name the other members of the troupe, but he suggested that there were at least a dozen of them. The secret agents of the Paris police filed reports on everyone whom they could identify among the French refugees in London and came up with thirty-nine in all—an extraordinary rogues gallery of hack writers and confidence men.[55] Pelleport probably knew all of them. He certainly had plenty of colorful material on which to draw; but he did not attempt to portray the entire population of French writers in the Grub Streets of London, because he aimed a great deal of his satire at variations of French philosophy. He therefore divided the Bohemians into three philosophical sects: "the *Economico-Naturalistlico-Monotonic* sect"[56] led by Séché, "the *Despotico-Contradictorio-Paradoxico-Slanderists* sect"[57] led by Lungiet, and the "*Communico-Luxurico-Knavistic*"[58] sect led by Mordanes. The first represented physiocracy and the doctrine of natural law; the second, enlightened despotism tinged with reactionary social doctrines; the third, predatory self-interest. Taken with Bissot's utopian Rousseauism, the Bohemians covered a great deal of the ideological spectrum.

There also were camp followers. Pelleport named only two, a mother-daughter combination: Voragine and Félicité. Félicité Dupont was the "beautiful neighbor" from Mentelle's circle in Paris whom Brissot had mentioned in his early letters to Pelleport. They married in 1782 and settled in London, at 1 Brompton Road, near the offices of the *Courrier de l'Europe*, where Pelleport, a frequent contributor to the *Courrier*, visited them regularly, until Félicité barred him from the house. Félicité's mother, Marie-Catherine Dupont, was the merchant's widow from Boulogne-sur-mer who had become embroiled with Pelleport in the dispute over his unpaid bills of exchange and his speculation on the shipment of champagne from Reims, where he, like Bissot in his book, had run up enormous debts. She figures prominently in *Les Bohémiens* as the companion of Séchant and the sexual partner of anyone she could get, for Pelleport portrays her as a hideous, sex-starved hag. (Voragine appears to be an obscene anagram, which can be decoded in various ways, all of them nasty.)

Having introduced the principal Bohemians, the narrator steps out of the story and informs the reader that the troupe contains one last philosopher, the greatest of them all. He challenges the reader to guess this character's identity by deciphering the "hidden meanings"[59] of the description that follows. The philosopher belongs to no sect, subscribes to no religion, combines sensations without distortion in his common *sensorium*, bears his burdens without complaint, enjoys food and drink, and is a great lover. Who could that be? After a satirical tour of contemporary philosophy in which he debunks every variety of intellectual pretentiousness with a verve worthy of Voltaire, the narrator addresses the reader again: "O dear reader! you grow impatient, I am well aware: you cannot guess the hero whose faithful portrait I have limned above. But you—the quick-witted, frisky young village girl whom Love has so often prompted to lie with vigorous Colin? Then you, if you were the one reading this work, you would call out in delight: 'O! Our Colin! It's our donkey!'"[60]

The stylistic virtuosity in this section of the book typifies Pelleport's technique. He develops a story line that points the reader in one direction, then interrupts it with a digression that shifts the perspective, and returns to the action—or sometimes to a digression within the digression—in a way that calls everything into question. He employs a perverse Shandean method, teasing and playing with the reader, then administering shocks and surprises. The sardonic philosophizing, which runs through a dozen schools of thought, ends in a eulogy of the donkey who carries the baggage of the troupe. And to deliver the punch line, a second putative reader appears, a not-so-innocent village lass who doubles the shock value of the joke by lauding the donkey's sexual prowess—probably an allusion to the donkey of Joan of Arc in Voltaire's *La Pucelle* (*The Virgin*). From philosophy to bestiality, Pelleport turns the trick with a dexterity that outdoes his neighbor scribbling away in a nearby cell: the marquis de Sade.

The libertine undercurrent appears in the very first sentence of the book, where Bissot is described as awakening at the crack of dawn, when "prostitutes were just closing their eyes . . . ladies of quality or any claim to nobility had six hours' sleep left to go; female devotees roused by mournful church bells hurried to early mass."[61] A similar passage introduces the eulogy of the donkey at the beginning of Chapter 5, but here the narrator strikes another tone. He celebrates sex in a lyrical passage, speaking in his own voice without a trace of irony:

Ah yes, I recall the happy time when, lying in Julie's embrace on a curtainless bed, dawn's first rays drew me from the arms of slumber: a tenderly savored kiss brought my lover back to life: her heart opened to desire before her eyes opened to the light. I united with Julie; Julie's alabaster arms hugged me close; we saluted the principle of life through that union of celestial flame; we intoxicated ourselves with pleasure; and so we prepared for our working day.[62]

It is a scene from Grub Street. The poor author wakes up next to his mistress in a garret, and after making love, his thoughts turn to the tyranny of the rich, the powerful, and the bigoted:

O ye who poison with your sinister storytales the few brief moments we can consecrate to pleasure, believe me here: our prayer was more acceptable to the Being of Beings than the bad Latin you drone in his ears. Ye misers whose brazen hearts cover sordid avarice, you who fatten off the property of your fellow men, you who grow rich on finance through the poverty of nations, you whom tyranny stains with human blood, all you barbarous jailers who guard our doors and fall asleep at the keyholes—come watch Mordanes the philosopher get up in the morning, and may envy gnaw the withered remains of your fetid, putrefying hearts.[63]

The chapter then continues with the next adventure of Mordanes and the facetious praise of the donkey, but the passion of its opening paragraph provides a disconcerting overture to the burlesque passages that follow. The narrator himself has cut through the narrative with a *cri du coeur* that could have come from a cell in the Bastille, as if he were a prisoner railing against his jailors and giving full vent to his anger and his longing. The reader naturally asks: Who is the person addressing me in this strange manner, and where does he stand amid the philosophies he derides?

After his eulogy of the donkey, the narrator answers those questions by identifying himself. He does not give his name, but he provides enough information to explain his disenchantment with the dominant values of his time—and all his remarks fit the biography of Pelleport. He was born into a privileged social position, he says, but early experience taught him to despise it. Judging from some scornful remarks about wealthy bourgeois who buy their way into the nobility, he belongs to the ancient nobility of the sword.[64] At one point he hints at an abortive military career as "a penniless young gentleman."[65] At another, he describes his attempt to get an appointment through a family friend at court. The friend recommends him to a minister as "the marquis of ***: he is a true gentleman whose ancestors marched under the banner of my own in the first Crusade."[66] In the end, disgusted by these attempts to place himself in the world of patronage and prestige, he decides to become an adventurer:

> Only one ray of sunshine penetrated my breast—justice—and justice made liberty flower . . . and society's shackles dropped from my feet. I bade farewell to fortune, and began my existence. I decided: "I'll travel the earth; the fortifications of slavery shrink before me. Let the tyrant and his armies guard the frontiers of their kingdom: I throw down my weapons like the beaver before the hunter.[67]

Where did he find his inspiration? Jean-Jacques Rousseau:

> And you—virtuous citizen of despicable Geneva—you who dared hope to see equality reestablished on this earth, you who dared show men their tyrants' secrets: May you receive the incense I am about to burn on your altar. Guide my steps and my sentiments from the empyrean heavens.[68]

A paraphrase of Rousseau's declamation against property in the *Discours sur l'origine de l'inégalité* (*Discourse on the Origin of Inequality*) follows this confession of faith, but then is followed by more ribaldry and social satire. The narrator's Rousseauism turns out to be strangely Rabelaisian, miles apart from the gushy enthusiasm of Bissot. Bissot, however, like all the other philosophers, proclaims elevated principles and lives by plundering peasants. The narrator contrasts this hypocrisy unfavorably with the anti-philosophy of the donkey, "Nothing-ism," as he calls it, which consists of rejecting all systems of thought while satisfying one's appetite.[69] The pursuit of pleasure, unimpeded by social constraints, stands out amid all the pontificating as the only value worth pursuing. In that respect, despite their pretentiousness and hypocrisy, the Bohemians represent something positive. Their president, Séchant, describes them as "a band lacking neither appetite nor gaiety," when he introduces them to Bissot. They devote themselves to "Free-spirited, cordial liberty. . . . Liberty is what assembles us here from every corner of Europe: we are her priests, and her religion demands only that we refrain from interfering with each other."[70]

The Bohemians share an attitude rather than a philosophy. They take a stance toward the world that already looks like bohemianism.

Even as philosophers the Bohemians seem harmless—all except for one: Mordanes. He is the only member of the troupe who appears truly evil. He does all the plundering, while the others hurl platitudes at each other without inflicting damage. His principal employment, stealing animals from peasants' barnyards, serves as a metaphor for Morandes's métier: destroying the reputations of his victims by means of libels. And he enjoys inflicting pain for its own sake. The most revealing of his atrocities takes place when he bludgeons two copulating chickens to death. The narrator recounts this incident after a long, lyrical passage celebrating sex. Desire is the vital energy that courses through all nature, he proclaims, and free love is the noblest principle in the natural order: "come, enjoy yourselves, and do not cast the slightest shadow on the delights of other people."[71] As an illustration of this hedonistic Golden Rule, he celebrates the joyful lust of some chickens in a barnyard where Mordanes is prowling, and he invokes "the rooster crowing to his hens, choosing and caressing the most amorous one frankly, gaily, strongly, firmly, just as we would caress our girl-chicks if we were not hampered by an overabundance of good manners, virtue, and modesty—or perhaps a lack of something else."[72] But in the midst of the chickens' love-making, Mordanes, "Mordanes the barbarian," kills them with a brutal blow. He is giving Tifarès a lesson in the art of despoiling peasants. Overcome at first by pity, the basic sentiment of sociability according to Rousseau, Tifarès recoils in horror, then thinks better of it, and smashes the skulls of four ducks in a nearby pond. He has switched his allegiance from Bissot to Mordanes and learned to be a murderer.[73]

Mordanes's own expression of the universal sex drive is rape. He makes Félicité his target. As the Bohemians resume their march across Champagne, Bissot takes up with Félicité, just as Brissot had done, with Pelleport as a witness, in Paris. They pair off and copulate blissfully. A few days later, while Félicité sits alone contemplating her expected motherhood, Mordanes jumps her, wrestles her down, and is about to penetrate her, when she devises a trick. By suddenly shifting her posture, she makes him miss his target and sodomize her—her way of protecting Bissot's claim to paternity. It is also Pelleport's way of inflicting injury on his former friend: to ravish the wife is to humiliate the husband. Pelleport goes further: he implies that Félicité enjoyed herself, for Bissot is not much of a lover, he reveals, and the stud-like energy of the rapist releases a libidinal charge in her. She even gets satisfaction from her gymnastic ruse. The chapter sports a cynical slogan: "A mouse with only one hole is easy to take."[74]

The sexual current that runs through the narrative appears as a fundamental force of nature, which the narrator compares to electricity, friction, fire, and phlogiston.[75] Although neutral in itself, it is relentlessly phallocratic in its effects on society. While elaborating a discourse on natural law, Séché goes so far as to argue that men own women as a form of property that can be bought, sold, traded, rented, and inherited.[76] To be sure, this burlesque episode reads more like a satire against the subjugation of women than an argument in favor of it. The narrator constantly presents women as objects of male desire, yet he also attributes an aggressive sexual energy to them; for the same *élan vital* courses through all forms of life: women are for the taking, and they help themselves to men. While Félicité is being raped, her mother, the insatiable Voragine, overpowers Tifarès. She copulates with many of the other Bohemians, even, the narrator suggests, with the donkey. Séchant, who is incapable of satisfying her "uterine fury," dreams that she takes on an entire pack of Capuchins.[77]

The monks enter the narrative as if from some libidinal underworld. Ostensibly on a pilgrimage, they wander through the countryside in the same manner as the Bohemians, who come upon them in the middle of the night. At first the Bohemians take them to be satanic creatures celebrating a witches' sabbath, but soon realize that they are fellow spirits given to debauchery. The two troupes join forces and settle down for a feast around a fire. They guzzle and gorge themselves into a stupor, wake up, and start to copulate—in twos and threes, then heaps of bodies piled up and linked together in nearly all the combinations celebrated in the libertine literature of the eighteenth century, Sade included. The polymorphous perversion degenerates into a brawl. Fists fly, noses splatter, blood flows everywhere along with muck and fluids discharged from numerous orifices. The donkey leaps into the fray, braying and flailing about deliriously. It is a Dionysian donnybrook, worthy of the best punch-ups described by Rabelais and Cervantes.[78] As dawn appears, the rioters stop for breakfast. They enjoy another hearty meal together, then go their separate ways. A good time was had by all.

The orgy brings Volume 1 to a climax. Volume 2 takes the troupe through more adventures interrupted by more burlesque philosophic lectures, but most of it is devoted to a disguised autobiography of Pelleport. Pelleport had spliced a great deal of information about his life into the first volume, especially in a long digression about a fictitious monk, le révérend-père Rose-Croix, who steals a silver chalice from his convent in Cologne, wanders off to Rome, and then turns up in Geneva during the revolutionary upheaval of 1782. At this point his travels coincide with the itinerary that Pelleport probably followed: Geneva, Lausanne, Yverdon, Neuchâtel, Le Locle. Details about persons and events at each stop along the way suggest first-hand familiarity with the territory. By the time he reaches Le Locle, the monk's identity has merged with that of Pelleport, who remains unnamed but can be recognized by many references. He turns into a poet, the author of an antimonastic satire in verse, *Le Boulevard des Chartreux* (*The Boulevard of the Carthusians*)[79] and he becomes a tutor to the son of a local merchant, Jean Diedey.[80] The text includes an insider's account of life in the Diedey household along with well-informed descriptions of local customs, the watch-making industry, and the surrounding countryside. The monk then disappears from the narrative, but another digression, seven pages later, describes a journey to Pondichery in a ship commanded by a captain Astruc in 1774, which probably corresponds to Pelleport's experience as a young soldier in India. Anyone who reads *Les Bohémiens* while supplied with the main facts about Pelleport's life is likely to concur: an autobiography lies hidden in the text.

Pelleport constantly interrupts his narrative with digressions that contain fragments from the story of his own life. They can be identified and pieced together to form a second narrative, and in the last hundred pages of the book, the two stories intersect: Pelleport, in the person of an unnamed, wandering poet, joins the Bohemians as they are camping on the outskirts of his native city, Stenay. He recounts his adventures to them; and as they listen they reappear in his tale under new names and in a new setting—Grub Street, London. The intersection and imposition of the narratives creates a complex structure, but Pelleport spins the storylines together with a sure hand and a light touch: the last segment of the book carries the earlier bawdiness to a new extreme, as if to say that the human comedy is a farce, an off-color joke.[81]

The poet strays into the text while the Bohemians are setting up camp and preparing dinner. He has just been released from the Bastille and is about to join his brothers in Stenay but has paused to compose a song. Strumming a guitar, he sings a verse that, as he later explains, represents his true philosophy:

Voler de belle en belle,
A l'amour c'est se montrer fidèle;
Voler de belle en belle,
Aux Dieux c'est ressembler.[82]

To fly from fair to fair,
Is to keep faith with love,
To fly from fair to fair,
Is like the Gods above

Séchant recognizes a kindred spirit and calls out: An author! Taken by surprise, the poet panics. He wants to deny any connection with literature, because he fears the strangers may be a detachment of police. Not at all, they assure him: they, too, are authors; the donkey is loaded down with the treatises they are writing. They invite him to dinner, and while Tifarès turns the spit, the poet tells the story of his life, which he offers as an explanation of why he took such fright: "I do in some sense belong to the Republic of Letters; but nowadays this is a dangerous confession... As proof of which, I offer you my literary history."[83]

He was born in Stenay, he explains, as unfertile territory as any place in France for the flowering of literature. His deceased father, an old-fashioned military officer from the ancient feudal nobility, could hardly read or write. Neither of his two brothers got much of an education. His two sisters were packed off to convents. But his mother had a chambermaid from Paris who loved novels and read *Don Quixote* to him. It was his downfall. Soon he learned to read himself and memorized all the adventures of the man from La Mancha. After returning from the Seven Years War—notably the Battle of Minden, which Pelleport had described earlier in an elaborate digression about military tactics—his father was horrified to find a budding scholar in the family. But the boy had learned to ride, shoot, dance, and chase girls well enough to win over the old man, who agreed to let him have a tutor. They got along badly until the tutor abandoned all attempts to indoctrinate his charge with Christianity and they concentrated on Greek myths. Then, however, the boy's mother died, and he was sent off to boarding school. He became great friends with one of his teachers, an abbé who taught him the classics in a spirit of pure paganism and was eventually expelled from the staff for harboring suspicious sympathies for revolutionary Romans. (Jealous colleagues persuaded the school's idiotic governor that Brutus and Cassius were "rebels conspiring against the King in some Paris attic").[84] On his departure, the teacher gave the budding young poet copies of Ovid, Virgil, and Horace. This reference and many others—invocations to the gods, mock Homeric metaphors—testify to Pelleport's familiarity with the classics. His account of the poet's education also includes favorable references to science and mathematics, and it shows how the young man turned into a provincial *bel esprit*: he set himself up as an amateur astrologer, and used his predictions to make fun of the local notables, including his father's new wife, who had become his greatest enemy. She summoned a family gathering, which condemned the poet as a libertine and prevailed upon a local official to have him imprisoned by *lettre de cachet*. Tipped off by a girlfriend, he fled to Liège, where he did some hack writing for an almanac, and then to London, where he got a job on the *Courrier de l'Europe*.

By now, the poet was embarked on a literary career. He wrote articles for the *Courrier* on all sorts of subjects and got along well with its editor, Antoine Joseph de Serres de La Tour, though not its publisher, Samuel Swinton, owing to impertinent remarks that offended some subscribers. But he resigned from the journal, because his father died, and he traveled to Stenay in the expectation of collecting an inheritance. His stepmother dashed those hopes by manipulating the legal procedures. So the poet had to return, penniless and on foot, to London. He got as far as Boulogne-sur-Mer. Unable to pay his passage across the Channel, he found himself in a church after a midnight mass on Christmas Eve, December 24, 1783—and a miracle occurred.

Here the narrative takes a different turn. Between the poet's childhood in Stenay and his journalism in London, the well-informed reader could fill in the missing parts of Pelleport's biography by inserting episodes mentioned in other digressions: study at the Ecole militaire in Paris,[85] service with a regiment in India, and several years of married life in Switzerland. But Pelleport had not yet provided a full account of his experience in London—nothing beyond the caricatures of the French expatriates cast as Bohemians. In the last section of the book, he gave those writers new names and relocated them in London's garrets and cafés. He also shifted into a different key: the poet's tale, which had included some serious social criticism,[86] turned into an obscene farce organized around the notion of genital gigantism and the supposed craving of women for big penises.

Following the mass, the poet is accosted by a beggar, the only person left in the church, and he gives the poor wretch the last coin in his purse. It is an act of secular humanitarianism, not Christian charity, as the relentlessly irreligious text makes clear.[87] But it provokes a miracle. The beggar is transformed into the glorious Saint Labre, who rewards the poet by giving him a miraculous belt made out of knotted rope. He instructs the poet to hide the belt under his clothing, leaving an end that he can grasp through his watch fob. Whenever he needs aid, he should pull on the rope, moving from knot to knot according to the severity of the situation. His nose will grow three inches with each pull. As the saint himself discovered when he trod the earth as a poor, itinerant monk, women will find the big nose irresistible, and they will provide as much succor as needed—or more, depending on the number of knots pulled.

While Pelleport was spinning fantasies in the Bastille, the Catholics of Boulogne were celebrating Benoît Joseph Labre as their greatest native son, although he actually was born in the nearby town of Amettes in 1748. From his early childhood, he embraced the most austere form of Catholicism. By the time of his death in Rome on April 16, 1783, he had lived like a saint, mortifying his flesh in pilgrimages and performing miracles—136 certified cures, according to a hagiography published in Italian in 1783 and in French in 1784. Canonization did not come until 1881, but Labre's reputation for saintliness provided Pelleport with perfect material for a sacrilegious satire that would carry his hero across the Channel.[88]

The impieties begin in Boulogne itself and take Brissot's mother-in-law, Voragine in the first part of the book, as their main target. She reappears as Catau des Arches, a sex-starved widow of a merchant, who eagerly coughs up 240 livres to play with the poet's nose as soon as he pulls on Saint Labre's belt and dangles it in front of her. His purse replenished, he reduces his nose to its normal size by letting out knots from the belt, and sails for London, though not before collecting tribute from several other women, who provide occasions for some well-placed barbs about the hypocrisy and pretentiousness of provincial society.[89]

London, by contrast, appears as a teeming world of adventurers, mountebanks, philosophers, scientists, politicians, agitators, publishers, and journalists. Their names swirl by: Fox; Pitt the younger; Lord North; Paul-Henri Maty, editor of the *New Review*; David Williams, the radical deist; Joseph Priestley, the champion of Enlightenment and science; Jean-Paul Marat, then struggling to make a name for himself as a scientist; James Graham, the inventor of the electric fertility bed; and an assortment of extravagant characters, probably acquaintances of Pelleport disguised under unidentifiable names—a German charlatan named Muller; an English quack called Remben; a certain J.P.D.; Ashley, a balloonist; Katerfiette, a scientist; and Piélatin, a violinist. In the midst of them all, the poet encounters "a swarm of wretched starving Frenchmen"[90]—the colony of French refugees. They include Brissot, who now appears as "Bissoto de Guerreville," the son-in-law of the widow des Arches, who lives as a dealer in second-hand clothes—that is, as a hack writer who cobbles together works by other authors.[91] The poet mentions the journalists connected with the *Courrier de l'Europe* and some other scribblers, but he reserves most of his scorn for Morande, who resumes his treachery as "the liar Thonevet" (an allusion to Morande's full name, Théveneau de Morande).[92] Thonevet defames the poet, attempts to blackmail him, and denounces him to a secret agent of the Parisian police, exactly as in *Le Diable dans un bénitier*. But no intrigue, however nasty, can undo the poet, thanks to his marvelous nose.

Soon all London is talking about it, betting on it, celebrating it in prose, poetry, and scientific treatises. It provokes such a furious debate in Parliament that the government collapses and new elections are held. "As I love both liberty and Fox,"[93] the poet agrees to reserve his nose for the wives and daughters of candidates committed to the Whigs. While campaigning for Fox at Covent Garden, however, disaster strikes. A pickpocket slips his hand into the vital watch fob and disappears with the magic cord. The poet despairs. Reduced to the status of a writer with an ordinary nose, he returns to Boulogne in order to publish a book with the press that Swinton used for the edition of the *Courrier de l'Europe* marketed in France. That was the false move that cost Pelleport his liberty. In this case, the poet puts the blame for the catastrophe squarely on Thonevet. Out of sheer malice, Thonevet composes several libels, attributes them to the poet, and, with the help of widow des Arches, denounces him to the French authorities, who carry him off to the Bastille. Meanwhile, Bissoto has been trying to collect a new supply of rags in Paris. The police suspect him of collaborating on the libels; they thus lock him up as well—not in the Bastille, however, but in the nastier prison of Bicêtre, where he soon dies and therefore disappears from the narrative. After a long and miserable stay in the Bastille, the poet is finally released. While walking away, he hears a crier announcing an appeal from the archbishop for witnesses of Labre's miracles to testify to their authenticity so that Rome can initiate the process of canonization. As the most devoted follower of the saint, the poet decides to go to Rome himself. But first he must visit his brothers in Stenay. That is how he has come to cross paths with the Bohemians. He recommends a tavern to them, promising to join them for supper after he has had a reunion with his brothers. They pack up the donkey, continue on their way, and arrive at the tavern. The sun sets. Supper is cooking . . .

The novel ends there with a wonderfully open, inconclusive flourish. Before parting from the Bohemians, however, the poet offers a reflection that provides a conclusion of sorts to his story: "you see yourselves the misfortunes that my miserable attempt at literature has caused me, and how much I must loathe literature now. I vow nothing frightens me so much as hearing myself called 'author'! since at my back I always hear a band of alguazil police stationed at street corners and toll gates, so that the powerful may prevent the contraband importation of reason."[94]

Les Bohémiens is, among other things, a book about literature: literature understood broadly as a system of money, power, and prestige. Speaking through his narrator, Pelleport views the system from the perspective of Grub Street. He longs for a patron, so that he can strike it rich "without having to start up a lyceo-museum, or museo-lyceum, or academico-muzico-lyceum; and without having to write the kind of correspondence, newspaper, 'Mercury,' 'Courier,' 'Gazeteer,' gazette, placards, handbills, annals, bibliographic gazettes, summaries of the said newspapers or gazettes, etc., or other literary rackets that have now become so common."[95] But he has no patron, so he must fall back on all those practices so typical of Grub Street—and another one, too: the composition of libels. In one of his many asides to the reader, he asks: "Dear reader, have you ever been printed alive?[96] Have you ever felt so pressured by your baker and local tavern-keeper that you dragged your rundown shoes through the markets where literary rag-pickers traffic in the thoughts of human beings so poor they sell their dreams to support themselves?"[97]

He then turns on the reader and accuses him (not her, judging from the context) of living in luxury, thanks to dubious maneuvers within some business or bureaucracy, while the poor author starves. Very well, then, reader, he says: let me tell you what it is like to live as an author who lacks independent resources. You walk into the office of an important publisher, Charles-Joseph Panckoucke, clutching your portfolio. Would Monsieur be interested in some verse about a recently deceased great man or perhaps a novel in two volumes (that is, *Les Bohémiens*)? It won't sell, Panckoucke replies, and waves you to the door: he can't find time to talk with the likes of you; he has to catch up on his correspondence. So you drag your manuscripts to a publisher of the second rank, Nicholas-Augustin Delalain. His daughter greets you politely in the bookshop; but when she learns you are an author, not a customer, she turns you over to her mother, in order to spare papa from wasting his time. Maman won't even look at the poems: she has already rejected three dozen batches of verse this morning. And when you offer her your "philosophical novel" (again, *Les Bohémiens*), she falls into a fury and runs you out of the office.[98] The only remaining hope is a dealer at the very bottom of the trade, Edme-

Marie-Pierre Desauges, a specialist in hack works and forbidden literature who has already spent two terms in the Bastille. He finds your work excellent, just the thing that he can sell through his contacts in Holland. You return to your garret, overjoyed. Your landlord, baker, and wine supplier agree to extend more credit. You scribble away, adding last touches to your manuscript, until late at night. When at last you have collapsed in bed, there is a knock at the door. In comes a police inspector accompanied by the dread undercover agent Receveur, the antihero, along with Morande, of *Le Diable dans un bénitier*; out you go straight to the Bastille. While you rot in prison, Desauges, who has had your manuscripts copied after denouncing you to the police, prints your book and sells it through the underground. Your hunger verges on starvation; your health gives out; and when at last you are released, you have no choice but to turn yourself in to the poor house (Hôtel-Dieu) and die.[99] The picture is overdrawn, like one of Hogarth's caricatures that Pelleport probably saw in London, but every detail, including the names of the booksellers, corresponds to the realities of Grub Street, Paris.

In a similar digression, the narrator picks a quarrel with the reader. I know you are tired of digressions, he says. You want to get back to the narrative. You want action, but I won't give it to you, because you should learn something about what went into the book you are holding in your hands. You should acquire some knowledge of the literary marketplace. So here is another digression. Books have plenty of readers but not buyers. The ratio is roughly ten to one. One person may be willing to part with some change for a book, but ten or more borrow it or steal it and pass it around in ever-widening circles: from masters to lackeys, mistresses to chambermaids, parents to children, neighbors to neighbors, and booksellers to subscribers in reading clubs (*cabinets littéraires*)—all at the expense of the author. The situation is hopeless, unless the king were to deliver an edict that would transform the basic conditions of literature. For example, he could issue an *arrêt du conseil d'état* with a long preamble about the importance of authors and a series of articles, beginning with the following two:

1. No book may be loaned, except within families and then only as far in the collateral line as first cousins, subject to a penalty of 500 livres to be paid to the author.
2. No servants may pass around their masters' books, subject to a penalty of a year's wages or, failing that, physical punishment: they will be branded on the left ear with the letters P D L for prêteur de livres

(lender of books) and whipped in front of all the bookshops in the town.

Pending such a measure, the narrator-author (the two can be assumed to speak throughout the novel with the same voice) proposes a temporary solution. This very book, the one that you are now reading, must be sold only in a fine binding and at a high price, which is to be maintained for the benefit of its author. The publisher is therefore forbidden to sell it in sheets, boards, or paper coverings. The digression ends with a remark delivered directly at the reader, who is deemed to demand that the narrator-author get on with the story: "Your impatience is growing by leaps and bounds, but I had every right to take care of my own interests, before satisfying yours: every man for himself. No—I refuse to be a martyr to foolish impartiality, neglecting my own affairs. I admit I chat a bit about myself: but where do you find an author who forgets himself in his work?"[100]

In fact, of course, the author has inserted himself in the narrative throughout the book. The digressions reinforce that tendency by showing how the author's autobiography bears on the condition of literature in general—and how the reader is complicit in perpetuating that condition.

Did readers actually respond in the way called for by the text? Probably not, because the text had so few readers—next to none, judging by the number of copies that have survived and the lack of reviews and references in contemporary sources. The publication of *Les Bohémiens* was a nonevent situated at the heart of the most eventful period of French history. Even if a few copies made it into the hands of readers, they can hardly have provoked much of a reaction. The French in 1790 were creating a brave new world and doing so in deadly earnest. They had no reason to be interested in a satirical account of life in a republic of letters that no longer existed. Pelleport's novel was out of date before its publication. Pelleport himself was out of tune with his times. While his contemporaries threw themselves passionately into the Revolution, he stood apart and looked upon the world from a perspective that combined disenchantment with derision—or "nothing-ism." Yet he deployed a prodigious talent when he evoked the life of Grub Street under the Ancien Régime. Seen from the twenty-first century, his novel looks extraordinarily modern, and his Bohemians appear as the first full embodiment of bohemianism.

TRANSLATOR'S NOTE

As a translator, I have approached this novel from a literary perspective, coming first to the text. While Robert Darnton necessarily focuses on Pelleport's personal, literary, and political targets as "thinly disguised" people in a *roman a clé,* I have presented the Bohemians as fictional characters in the great tradition of the European comic novel, individuated through their voices and through the narrator's descriptions, within the freewheeling connections of their Bohemian existence.

My goal in the translation and annotation is to give a sense of the engaged and semi-complicit relationship Pelleport establishes with his reader through direct interrogative, indirect discourse, political in-jokes, cultural allusions, parodies, and literary pastiches. I have worked to convey the complex satiric field around Pelleport's former friends, his family, and the socioeconomic abuses of the Ancien Régime.

The narrator's intricate, even obsessional cross-referencing allows him to create a remarkably far-ranging shared contextual web with his longed-for reader, thanks to Pelleport's involvement in political intrigue, his philosophical awareness, and his familiarity with the classics. The associative pattern of these multiple references echoes the open-ended conversations characteristic of the novel.

Robert Darnton is responsible for the notes concerning Pelleport and the libellistes. I have annotated the other historical and contemporary references as well as classical and literary allusions. When Pelleport misquotes a Latin text, perhaps from memory, I have noted the misquotation and translated both versions. References to living people and historical personages, whether under their real or altered names, enable Pelleport to create the mesh of private-public information-sharing and withholding that appeals to his imagined reader, as it would have to readers of his libelles. Contemporary references include Rousseau, Voltaire, and Mirabeau in coded form, as well as named authors. Such puzzles are part of the enjoyment of reading political satire: the satisfaction of identifying more of them offers a sense of participation in the wicked fun of political gossip. At one point Pelleport's narrator, annoyed at the interruptions by a listener-reader protesting at digressions, replies that he intends his novel to "touch on everything"; my goal has been to appreciate as fully as we can the context, if not of "everything," then at least as much as possible of this imaginary world.

Beyond embodying the much-resented Brissot, his brother, the Dupont women, Linguet, and the archvillain Morande, the various characters in *The Bohemians* take substantially different forms as presented in the main structure by the narrator-marquis, from the characters in the linear autobiographical tale told by the Pilgrim-poet. For example, as Darnton has shown, Pelleport satirizes his former friend Brissot de Warville as both the ex-lawyer "Bissot" in the main narrative and the ragpicker "Bissoto de Guerreville" in the Pilgrim's tale. But the novel develops Bissot beyond his early presentation: foolish though he may be, his speech to the troupe's Carthusian hosts not only frames the troupe's Bohemian vagabondage but indicts the social breakdown that creates their sense of marginality and identifies it as a growing threat; literary ragpicker Bissoto de Guerreville is capable of no such argument. Brissot's wife, Félicité Dupont, is fictionalized both as Voragine's daughter Félicité in Champagne and as Bissoto's Quakerish wife Nancy in London. But although Nancy is mentioned as witnessing the Pilgrim's sexualized nose at a Quaker meeting, the Bohemienne Félicité's mock-naive narrative of her bed-trick and rape by the wicked Mordanes (in a document supposedly found in an archive by the novel's narrator) bears witness to the so-called historical veracity of the whole novel and its identification of the knavish Mordanes rather than Bissot as chief villain. Thanks to Félicité's documented voice, Mordanes as rapist becomes an eroticized menace, as the narrator shows him to be a teacher of murder: until he teaches Bissot's brother to enjoy killing innocent ducklings, Tifarès has been a largely sympathetic if credulous youth. On the other hand, within the tale the Pilgrim is telling to the Bohemians (including Tifarès), the treatment of Bissoto's brother is completely satirical. "Bissoto" in the Pilgrim's tale comes to a far more unsavory end than Bissot, whose attempts at intellectual discourse earn some interest, if not sympathy. As for Félicité's Bohemienne mother, the governessy stew-maker Voragine, her managerial skills make Bohemian vagabond life feasible; her interventions structure the chaotic interruptions of the philosophers that the narrator invites us to approve, though the "gags" she uses stifle free speech; her sexuality is more voluntary and less automatic than the Pilgrim's patroness Catau des Arches. In the Pilgrim's tale, on the other hand, as told to an audience including Voragine—identified as Mme Dupont, the wealthy widow Catau des Arches, Brissot's mother-in-law—serves no useful social function, and her sexuality is both mechanical and dependent on the money she has inherited. Pelleport's autobiographical Pilgrim-poet, on his way to testify to his lost sexual miracles, rejects any suggestion that he is an author and invites the Bohemians to join in his family reunion—ending the fiction in a very different situation from the novel's narrator. Robert Darnton's work has identified the origin of all these characters, and I hope in this translation to have given them fictional life.

Pelleport's imaginary "world elsewhere" creates a sense of the Bohemian vagabondage as specifically geographical and implicitly historical: from within the Bastille to countrysides devastated by military and economic pillage throughout history, and now socially disrupted as well. I have therefore annotated the geographical journeys he maps for the Bohemians through France, Belgium, Germany, Italy, Switzerland, and England. In doing so, he creates a spatial range of sites of economic and military devastation beyond the frustration of imprisonment, as well as honoring the peripatetic tradition of philosophers, the picaresque episode, and the Quixotic quest. The Bohemians and their friends travel through and refer to major battlegrounds as well as to cities that are religious, economic, and social centers. I have traced this geographic vagabondage from the miserable "Champagne" of Brissot's escape to the Pilgrim's hometown reunion in Stenay.

I have clarified linguistically and typographically the discourses and dialogues of the novel. The 1790 printed edition is not always clear, even by eighteenth-century standards, as to paragraphing and spelling, whether through carelessness on Pelleport's part or in the typesetting. Changes of speaker are not consistently marked, and sometimes uncertainly punctuated. Where I saw unintentional confusion, I have worked to offer a readable text. Yet in order to present the novel as a fiction that comes out of innumerable bookshop, Palais-Royal, Grub Street, coffeehouse, and salon conversations, my translation highlights its many dialogues among characters who appear out of nowhere (and may be unknown even to each other), multiple narrators, and anonymous readers. These offered particular challenges and pleasures. I have generally distinguished conversations among characters from direct exchanges between the narrator and his implied readers, of whom there are a number, by using quotation marks for the former and dashes for the latter. Sometimes a hitherto unidentified reader will address the narrator; elsewhere the narrator's aside may provoke a new reader to respond. I have sometimes identified speakers where Pelleport's intention was clear in context (for example, Bissot's speech on hospitality to the Bohemians' Carthusian hosts). In terms of spelling, the keywords "piety" and "pity"—orthographically close in French as in English—seem to be exchanged at important moments; I have noted this. I have generally retained rapid shifts in tense, as part of the Sternean discourse. I have occasionally translated names invented for burlesque comic effect within narratives, but annotated where I did so. I tracked religious references because whether arcane or historically documentable, their dubious veracity is part of the novel's play with verisimilitude. I translated where possible the wordplay and puns that engage the reader in this far-ranging representation of intellectual and social life at the centers and margins of the European prerevolutionary world. There are no omissions from the printed text; all ellipses are in the original.

Robert Darnton's foundational scholarship opened the intellectual and literary life of French libellistes and exiles to me, and provided the original notes with which to decode the relationship of this fiction to Pelleport's life and times. I am grateful to him not only for those notes but for his generous help as I added mine. I am of course responsible for the annotation as a whole.

Robert Folkenflik was the novel's first reader in English, as well as an appreciative and invaluable expert in-house companion in eighteenth-century literature and enthusiastic scholar of literary history. I also give heartfelt thanks for the intellectual examples and thoughtful advice from Julia Lupton and Robert G. Moeller, with whom I taught for three years a transformational Humanities Core Course at the University of California, Irvine, on "Laws and the Social Order." Jayne Lewis kindly read an early philosophical chapter; Cristiana Sogno helped with a Latin translation. I was glad to see that Patrick Castelijns and Mario Molegraaf had produced a modern Dutch translation, for the book deserves worldwide recognition. My thanks always go out to Core Course colleagues, including Gail Hart, Steven Mailloux, Ann van Sant, Ulrike Strasser, John H. Smith, Brook Thomas, Elizabeth M. Losh, Brook Haley, and Suzanne Bolding. Patricia O'Brien, Michelle Latiolais, David Folkenflik, and Jesse Baker offered constant encouragement during the time I was at work on this project. Jerry Singerman at the University of Pennsylvania Press welcomed and guided the publication, as did the helpful editors at the Press. The project was supported by a Hemingway Grant from the French Ministry of Foreign Affairs and the Cultural Service of the French Embassy in the United States, funding from Harvard University, and the International Center for Writing and Translation at the University of California, Irvine.

MAIN CHARACTERS

The Bohemians, "a dozen" male philosophers and several women Bohemiennes:

Bissot, a penniless ex-lawyer

Tifarès, his younger brother, a cook

Abbé Séchant, president and disciple of Abbé Séché, defends liberty as noninterference

Abbé Séché, leader of the *Economico-Naturalistlico-Monotonic* sect, argues for natural law and natural right

Lungiet, leader of the *Despotico-Contradictorio-Paradoxico-Slanderist* sect, nicknamed "Sérapion," argues for theocracy and serfdom

Mordanes, leader of the *Communico-Luxurico-Knavistic* sect, strategist and organizer of raids for sustenance and profit

Voragine, governess of the troupe and expert stew-maker

Félicité, Voragine's daughter

Donkey "Colin," who carries unpublished manuscripts, a devotee of "Nothing-ism"

"Reverend Father" Rose-Croix, a good fellow who travels as a Cordelier monk

The Capuchins, sixty mendicant Franciscans on a pilgrimage to Our Lady of Avioth: father superior, custode, cook, novices

The Carthusians, a proprietary order of monks at an abbey in Champagne: Dom Hachette the Procurator, Dom Coadjutor, Dom Prior

The Pilgrim, ex-author, with his family of origin in Stenay: officer father, mother, stepmother, brothers Louis Joseph and Claude Agapith

Catau des Arches—a widow in Boulogne, with her youngest daughter Mademoiselle des Arches; Miss Carabine, an English companion

Bissoto de Guerreville, her ragpicker son-in-law in London, with his wife Nancy and brother

The Bohemians

. . . . ! Cupido mihi pacis ! at ille
Qui me commorit, (melius non tangere, clamo)
Flebit, et insignis totâ cantabitur urbe.
   Horat. Lib. Ii, sat. 1.

---

*"I who am a lover of peace! But if anyone irritates me ('Better not touch me!' I cry), he shall weep for it, and his name shall be a byword all through town" (Horace, *Satires*, II. i. 44–46). Pelleport's punctuation.

CHAPTER ONE

The Legislator Bissot Renounces
Chicanery in Favor of Philosophy

THE SUN WAS about to rise from Amphitrite's bed, dawn was fleeting apace; prostitutes were just closing their eyes, and the bourgeois housewives of Reims squawking to rouse their servant-girls, since in Champagne nobody rings for them; ladies of quality or any claim to nobility had six hours' sleep left to go; female devotees roused by mournful church bells hurried to early mass: when fear of the bailiffs and the first ray of the morning star startled awake the lawyer Bissot[1] as he lay sleeping in a garret beside his brother Tifarès,[2] faithful companion of his lot and emulator of his philosophical works. After various futile attempts to drag the fortunate Tifarès from the arms of Morpheus, the lawyer pulled off his covers, sat his brother upright on his pallet, and exposed the miserable creature's emaciated body to the gaze of the sun.

At this hideous sight, blond Apollo thought he must be off track, and that his horses, instead of following the summer tropic, had carried him off to one of those caves used by ancient Egyptians to store ancestors' mummies. Himself annoyed at being awake so early in the morning, Apollo took a mischievous pleasure in sending rays to pierce the translucent fists that Tifarès, crouched on his backside as once in his mother's belly, was now cramming into the vacant orbits around his little eyes. So pure and ardent was Tifarès's love of sleep that it required this combination of divine and mortal efforts to awaken him; indeed only after one last embrace did Tifarès drag his black, withered leg from under a torn and dirty sheet; present that leg to the mouth of an oversized stocking; lend an ear; and listen at last—perhaps with some measure of enjoyment—to his illustrious brother's philosophical discourse, which you are about to read:

"O how wise are the natives of the Ganges, whose children are forced to follow their fathers' professions!" began Bissot.[3] "Would to God the companions of Clovis had adopted similar institutions: we would not have so many useless parasitical classes among us today![4] We would not see the hardworking laborer tanning rough leather in the noonday heat to protect the sweet, fresh skin of some voluptuous do-nothing prelate; no sailor would roam the seas so that an idle lubricious courtesan could wear India muslins; no hollow-cheeked soldier dying of hunger, barely clothed, his comrade-in-arms his only company and bedmate, while in a damask-curtained bed, a bored and fraudulent financier dozes on the breast of some young girl he has no idea what to do with. As for myself, instead of spending one hundred écus—the best money I ever saw in my life—on a squealing lawyer's silly hood,[5] I'd have been buying red-leg partridges to lard, bard, and bake in pie-crust, while you stoked the oven and carried the flour for your next batch of pastry. Soon we'd have expanded our business around the city of Chartres ten leagues and more; we'd be considered wholesale merchants; we could have taken our place among the Third Estate's most memorable aristocrats; and I wouldn't be awakened at the crack of dawn by the unwelcome fear of creditors descending on our wasted cadavers, after grabbing whatever écus we have left.

"O incompetent legislators—why don't you study my colleague Lungiet's *Theory of Civil Law*, or my own *Theory of Criminal Law*?[6] You would not allow creditors such limitless power over debtors if you had read these books; you would make decisions according to the principles of natural law and *lex talionis*, and show much better judgment. But you are at once feather-brained and iron-hearted.

"All the same, Tifarès, if we do not make an instant retreat to safeguard the life of the mind and philosophy, the only retreat we'll be making is to a dark and dismal prison. O Apollo, will that be the museum office you once promised me? . . . Instead, Tifarès, let us escape to the heart of the forest, where we can survive by eating acorns, roots, and wild fruits. May we forget societies established by the rich to injure the poor—may we spend our remaining years among wolves, howling at the misfortunes of Noah's posterity."[7]

At these last ominous words, all the hair or hairy substances on poor Tifarès's body rose up like bristles on an old boar at bay. Hands lifted in supplication to Bissot, one leg half-stuffed into his stocking, he sobbed: "Have you lost your courage completely, you whom nature formed to be an ornament to society? Are you such a coward as to deprive your contemporaries, not to mention the coming generations, of everything your rare talents promise? I might easily prove that forest sojourns, so humid, so unhealthy, attack man's generative powers; chilly forest springs enlarge the glands and stop the bowels; wild fruits are bitter and entirely indigestible. I could next concentrate on the terrible teeth of ravenous wolves, or elfin sprites who lead lost travelers into quagmires and over cliffs; but what point in such discourse to you, who are as sober as a Greek philosopher, and no more a believer in ghosts than the late Moses of materialist memory?[8]

"Yet though your own soul rises above suffering, has your heart no pity?" continued Tifarès. "Ah! pray listen to that virtue—or disposition—so natural to both men and animals and so much more valuable than moral treatises. See me now, mere skin and bones: do you feel less compassion than the wolf in La Fontaine?[9] It might not be so bad if I'd been eating my fill at wedding-feasts or my lord bishop's kitchen: but what's the daily diet of an attorney's clerk procurator with a Reims diploma? Nobody ever gained weight eating that. It might not be so bad if I were like the wild girl or the feral child of Hanover, then I could catch rabbits on the run[10] . . . But what am I thinking? The forests are full of game-keepers who herd all such game into poor people's fields, to fatten them up at their ease. Can't you see us both being hauled before the magistrates' marble bench? And then to the galleys, where some successor to M. Jourdain-Launey of Bastille memory would enjoy beating us until he lost his breath?* As for picking up nuts from under the trees—are we allowed by law even a single acorn? Have no doubt about this: if you keep your plan, pale Hunger, Death's eager messenger, will soon reduce me to barking desperation.

"Good Lord! Where to find a confessional? Who could give me my last sacraments, or grease me up with sacred oil? What—will I be deprived of holy water, and of the *requiescat in pace* of the faithful? What am I supposed to say when I reach Purgatory, if you please? Surely you don't imagine them welcoming my naked, unkempt, scrawny, ungreased, famished soul? Isn't it more likely that my soul will be chased head-over-heels, petrified, full of fears, down like a cannonball straight into Lucifer's cauldron?

*Father Jourdain began in the world as head of the galley stroke; then having married a bastard daughter of Argenson's secretary of state, he rose to Jailer of the Bastille, a high dignity that M. his son has now inherited.[11]

"Banish, banish all these depressing fantasies! Agreed: let us flee to distant climes. Point of honor: now that you are now a full-fledged diplomate of that worthy aggregation without which judges would be no juster than ordinary folk and would have to hand down verdicts according to law and common sense; now that you are a member of the brilliant order leading the Third Estate like a billygoat at the head of a herd, we can't return to lawyer Maître la Gripardière's study. You can find a place with some other provincial attorney, show him Parisian legal tricks, and dine off the shoulder of mutton served by the attorney's wife. As for me, I can become a sergeant's process-server and eat my stew at public expense; though should cruel fate refuse me this fond ambition, a pastry cook can find work anywhere in Christendom.

"O best of brothers, feel my tears, take pity on my body and soul; imitate the Gods, and listen to my prayers! Homer, that dean of poets and father of philosophers, compares our prayers to Jupiter's daughters who transmit a great manner of mortal vows. Yes, I already see you lend an ear to these winsome creatures! I shall now make haste; and in a few short hours we will bid an eternal farewell to the hillocks of Champagne."

With these words, Tifarès jumps out of bed, dresses himself in six layers so that he is wearing every shirt in his wardrobe, gives his elder brother a deep bow, and takes him to the Ceres city gate,[12] now wide open before them. Thus did Don Quixote, doubting which road to travel, leave the choice to faithful Rosinante;[13] thus does the imagination of so many serious authors follow the course of a brainless quill; thus may the cleverest ministers of state be guided by a coarse errand-boy ignoramus.

Following the lead of this excellent brother, lawyer Bissot now gains the road toward Rhetel-Mazarin, winding through the barren plains of flea-ridden Champagne: but before losing from view the Gothic towers of the Reims cathedral, he turns back to the barbarous city one last time and appeals to the Fates in the words of Isabella of Hungary: "*Sic fata volunt.*"[14]

CHAPTER TWO

The Two Brothers Wander
on the Plains of Champagne

AFTER THESE LATIN words to satisfy the rule established by great men from time immemorial in every time and place—never begin an enterprise without some sentence worthy of its importance and quotable at the head of the narrative—our two travelers plunged deep into the solitude of Pont-Favergé, along roads unfit for riders on horseback, passengers in carriages, or even simple pedestrians.[1]

Foreigners and city-dwellers looking at our kingdom through a post-chaise window always marvel with inexpressible admiration for its broad, extensive highways: the fine avenues to our filthy inns convince the rest of Europe that such excellent paths of communication cannot be found anywhere in the other seventeen major sections of this portion of the globe. But the itinerant philosopher who ventures between the desolate roads remains unimpressed by this elaborate apparatus, useful though it may be for transporting cannons and armies. Commodities transported on any path of this vast labyrinth may reach the rich man's door comfortably enough.[*] Nevertheless, the sweat and tears with which our wretched cultivators pay for these roads inspire them with such hatred of anything named "road" that they cannot bring themselves

---

[*] All this was true a few years ago; but thanks to the salutary institutions called (I know not why) provincial assemblies, the only practicable roads are those belonging to provincial metropolises. Two or three leagues away from any of these favored cities, the roads turn into quagmires.

to trim the mucky paths to their own miserable cottages.[2] After having ruined his own tools, livestock, and health to beautify the rich man's promenade, the laborer must burden them anew before reaching a road he himself has built: and on this easy-to-travel road he must watch a portion of his own cash tribute streaming from the capital to the frontiers. Nor can he hope to bring to his cottage door the least little capillary vessel of the noisy, fast-moving canals. Such were the reflections inspired in our two philosophers by the vile roads crisscrossing flea-ridden Champagne.

The sun had already accomplished more than half its journey when the two arrived at Pont-Favergé; they recognized dinnertime by a bunch of heather hanging by a fishhook on a wall (for in these cantons, one rarely sees either wooden signs or painting, which has not made much progress in Champagne). This hook was suspended on a hut that had neither cobblestone walls nor plank floors; a few old smoke-covered boards served to store the meager buckwheat that nourished its sober inhabitants, rather than as a kitchen ceiling. Five or six evil-looking pallets, likelier to kill off the sleepers than secure their repose, were scattered about the room. A few nasty chipped plates, a pot with an oaken lid, a big bread-bin, and a saltbox that must get filled with salt, willy-nilly, thanks to the wise laws of Philip the Salic: the peasant may do without bread if he so chooses, but must have enough money to purchase salt.[3] Such were the sumptuous furnishings of the tavern destined to welcome the greatest philosopher of France and his faithful admirer.

The owners of this impressive tavern, the best-furnished house in the village, were working in the fields. They had left in charge a deaf old woman paralyzed by apoplexy on the left side, and whose advanced age made her bald head oscillate like the pendulum of a turning spit. This woman seemed to be placed on earth specifically to encourage abstinence in any philosophers inclined toward rural solitude and retirement. She might have been seventy, or so one would judge by her face; since country curates keep no very exact ledgers of birth and death, as they know only holy writ and Palace hackwork, and are sworn enemies of other writing. This good mother reckoned her age according to the number of times she had eaten meat: except for their local fete, the richest inhabitants of the village lived on fava beans like Pythagoreans. Fortunately for our travelers, it was market eve in nearby Machaut and the week's eggs were already prepared, so a dozen eggs could be added to the salt soup that is these troglodytes' usual fare. Then a large glass of mediocre wine, a piece of black bread and some cheese: worthy products of a landscape consigned to the larks ever since the confounding of tongues, where livestock and humans alike are condemned to a state of eternal gloom by the pact between Noah and God![4] Yet our travelers paid twenty-four sous for this succulent repast: when food is scarce, even bad food costs dear.

The travelers felt satisfied with their dinner, however, and Bissot continued to praise the good villagers' abstemiousness as he swallowed his last stale crust. "Come all ye rich sybarites, effeminate denizens of our capitals," cried he, "come hither, and see at what price the poor pay for your luxury and enjoyments: take a taste, compare this salty soup to the holocausts served on the altars you call tables . . . Ah, may ye tremble! Some day these rude savages will tire of working solely to enrich you! They will gather together like your barbarian ancestors and swoop down on all the properties you claim to own by natural right. Like the harpies in the legend, they will pounce upon your tables and strongboxes—you will strive to repel them, but in vain.[5]

"This event will occur in an epoch of famine, an epoch of some war that erases your mercenary satellites from the book of the living. The property of others is sacred only for a property-owner: O governments! Admirable machines for the rich! How have you lasted so long? I am no longer surprised that M. de Serre de la Tour gets rich fabricating sugarplum *dragées de la Mecque*,[6] or that Mesmer should magnetize half the globe. We live in a century when every man who has enough money to rent a theater or trestle can be sure of pocketing the crowd's money. Priests, monks, soldiers, attorneys, lords great and little—you make common cause together: but watch out! The pulse quickens, the fever rises, the major blood vessels fill, the crisis may perhaps be coming soon. Someday, you may regret making the lymph rise to the head of the body politic."

While Bissot abandoned himself to such profound reasoning, the sun sank below the horizon; its sphere had become a mirage, and the dusk was fleeing the dawn, chased by deep shadows and separated only by a narrow arc. Timorous Tifarès could already see dark night in its mournful attire: its owl-drawn chariot with wheels made out of Purgatory souls bent into cycloids, giant bats with horseshoe-shaped noses flapping their wings to make it fly: two vampires mounted on werewolves were driving it, and three ogres riding white-tailed eagles were in the lead, crying "Whoo, whoo" in order to get daylight's chariot stowed away. Terror, a member of this mournful cortege, no sooner noticed timid Tifarès's shriveled-up heart than it made its home there, with all the alacrity shown by a bodyguard of the Marshals of France who, after three weeks of not dining at any gentleman's expense, now by the grace of our King and lords marshal stands guard in the house of some provincial against whom he has conceived a grudge.

Tifarès, Chartres-born unfortunate that he was, grabbed his brother's arm, held his breath, and began to walk like a barefoot beggar whose blistered feet pull back from the stubble where the reaper has not separated the wheat from the chaff. The gullies in the road were all that showed Bissot whether he was on the highway or the fields. As for Tifarès, the only road that mattered to him was the road to salvation; he said his prayers and kept his eyes tightly shut, a useless precaution that did not prevent his seeing all sorts of phantoms.

Both our travelers were exhausted, and could think of nothing better than spending the night lying down in a furrow. By now, Bissot had begun to notice the inconveniences of simple nature. "Savages," he privately acknowledged, "do not find the tablecloth laid beneath any hill where they are surprised by night; and what if their hunt prove unrewarding, or they are stuck in some sterile land where there be no fruit? . . . But never mind, one must support one's theory, and hunger and night chills cannot make me give it up." Thus to sustain his opinions will a minister of State who believes in his theory plunge the state into trouble and anarchy: in vain does he notice that social bonds grow weak, that parties are divisive: his arrogance makes him rather set all four corners of a province on fire, than suffer the disgrace of retraction; and he remains in his folly, until the moment when, driven by the fear of losing the position that he had desired so long to attain, he insensibly backs off.

I am not convinced Bissot would actually resist so consistently, however, because the philosophers of my acquaintance have at least this in common with preachers: the enormous disparity between their sermons and their conduct has given rise to a proverb followed by fools and dunces everywhere: "*practice counts more than theory.*" However intimidating and severe the advice of moralists may be, their actual behavior seems to me rather more accommodating.

Greatly to our wandering legislator Bissot's credit, the sound of a barking dog now rescued his philosophy, reinforced his principles, revived his courage, and bolstered his system with the hope of finding supper and some mean beds, which even if they were as wretched as the Pont-Favergé beds, would be better than acorns and stubble. But however much this barking may have put Bissot back on his philosophical high horse, it produced a totally different effect on Tifarès, whose stomach—empty as his brain—had rather inclined him to fear. He is ready to take flight as soon as the voice hits his ears. This dog's barks must rise from the depths of Erebus: Tifarès kneels to pray, convinced they must be the outcries of Lucifer's Cerberus, or at least Purgatory's porter. Only by threats to desert him can Bissot, newly hopeful thanks to this same barking voice, induce his brother to move in its direction: the voice seemed to arise from the bowels of the earth only because it was coming from a valley carpeted with fresh green grass, and watered by a stream whose murmur they soon began to hear.

Hardly had they gone fifty paces along this stream before the triple-throated mastiff began barking again in earnest; but now so near that Tifarès no longer took him for a ghostly dog, but rather a mad one. He therefore began to recite the late Saint Hubert's prayer,[7] which did not prevent the dog from cruelly threatening his skinny backside, and his six shirts were of little avail.

But what then, O flower of Chartrian pastry-makers? Then from a crook in the hill you felt the end of a shotgun pressing into your stomach, and heard a frightful voice call "Halt there! Who goes? S'death! Move, and I kill you."

O Tifarès! Fear gave you eloquence, and falling on knees callused like John the Evangelist's, you moaned in your mournful voice, "Lord have pity on us, and you, Sir thief, give us a moment to collect ourselves. We are not ripe for eternity. O grant the lives of two poor scholars whose love of philosophy and fear of bailiffs has driven them to these dreadful wastelands! Take our entire fortune—seven livres and ten sous—and may God show you the way to a tax collection! My brother is one of the most illustrious lawyers ever to get a Reims degree since the day they first started selling them, and he will serve you zealously and faithfully in any lawsuit you may have; do listen to our prayers, and kill us not."

"We'll see," replied the voice. "Follow in my footsteps; I'll soon find out how much veracity there is in your story."

Tifarès did not wait to be told twice, but followed the invisible rifleman, and soon perceived a number of people laughing and singing around a great fire. In the bright light of the fire, their guide came into view as an enormous giant.

They approached the troupe at last. "Here are two gentlemen who have done me the honor of taking me for a thief," said the redoubtable sentry; "they are lost, and as there is no village within three leagues, they must surely want to spend the night in good company."

"And to have a good supper," replied the president of the band, making room for Bissot and Tifarès to take their places around the fire. And so they came to learn that there is no situation in life, however distressing, even in the face of death, when one cannot hope to eat a good meal.

CHAPTER THREE

Supper Better Than Dinner

TIFARÈS WAS EMBOLDENED by this warm welcome to open his little eyes, which fear had sealed as hermetically as an Encyclopedist's purse or a devout woman's moneybox. His joy and his surprise were unbounded at the sight of two legs of lamb turning side by side on a long wooden spit, along with several partridges whose lives had been cut short by the fatal cord, and a goose whose flesh, bruised as the back of the late M. des Brugnières,[1] gave every indication of having ended its life with a beating. Fragrant corpuscles exhaled by the cadavers of these innocent creatures soon found their way to his larynx; Tifarès knelt by the fire, drawn by the magnetic virtue of the spit. Moving toward the burning coals, he cried out with bombast: "Allow me to add flammable air[2] to this fire, for thus may its intensity increase!"

From his manner and discourse, everyone present easily identified Tifarès as an apprentice philosopher; they would doubtless have begun to question him if his famous brother had not distracted their attention by coughing, spitting, and blowing his nose with the air of an orator who calls his audience to order. So Tifarès turned the spit and basted the roast, while Bissot became the center of the circle, and offered his reception speech in the following terms:[3]

"Gentlemen:

"If a love of philosophy and a dislike of business dealings are enough to earn membership among you, I flatter myself that I may claim this honor: I seek happiness and wisdom in rural solitude, and have abandoned legal chicanery and the attendant hope of making a brilliant fortune at the expense of the unfortunate. Nor was I mistaken in listening to the voice calling me into this desert. No, gentlemen: the proof is in my good fortune in meeting you and, even before formally taking up arms as a philosopher, finding adventures after my own heart; for I am convinced that you gentlemen must be illustrious exiles driven away from habitable places and led to pitch your camp in forest dell or hillside nook by the mistreatment of despotism, the disproportion between crimes and punishments, the hodgepodge of civil laws, the cruelty of the criminal code, the intolerance of the clergy, and the jealousy of accredited authors.

"Here, gentlemen, might I give a panegyric on your chosen state of liberty, its superiority to the life men lead in the richest, best-planned cities. How easily could I repeat everything so eloquently expressed by the celebrated Genevan, so endlessly repeated by countless hacks who write to earn their daily bread.[4] And how appropriate that would be, since I am not taking the seat of a member known to me, so I cannot open with a funeral oration. Ah! Would to the Gods I were filling the seat of some famous man, or at least someone who had cultivated a useful art! Instead of mere individual eulogy, I could expand my topic to praise science itself, and give you a summary suitable for publication, perhaps as a supplement to an article in the *Encyclopédie*. Or if only I had the slightest idea of your illustrious President's virtues and talents! How eagerly would I give you ten or twelve pages detailing what others might say in a few words! Rest assured, I am not a recondite speechmaker whose readers are obliged to think twice, or whose words signify everything and mean nothing, like Gospel expressions and church chimes. Give me a paltry apothegm, a senseless maxim, the slightest of texts, I can produce a volume. Nor am I a slave to my topic, fixated on dissecting it like a geometrician, no! not I, I fly bold and free: sometimes high as the attic, sometimes down to the cellar, with the hidden secrets and mysteries of science on each page I write—chemistry, physics, history, grammar, logic.

"So if I never mention your founder, gentlemen, that's because I have not yet the honor of his acquaintance; but this is no loss to him. Your society cannot be an ancient one, since I have never seen it mentioned in the thousands of newspapers and periodicals printed on the face of the earth. It is therefore only fair to allow our assembly's president several centuries of encomia. Indeed, why limit his praise to a few brief years? Is not the French Academy still busy—two centuries later—celebrating that cephalous Cardinal, that vision-blind minister of state, that talent-free litterateur, that hypocritical tyrant, that ignoramus of everything except the disastrous art of dominating a weak, lazy, and imbecilic prince?[5] Each variation inspires three fresh eulogies; indeed twenty or thirty centuries from now, if that most learned and useful of societies survives as long as a mendicant order, there will still be someone to eulogize the odious, incompetent Richelieu.

"O wise forest-dwellers, illustrious savages, I am loath to shower any monarch with praise in your presence. No monarch protects you; all are eager to persecute you; but sages like yourselves cannot be fooled by patronage suited to the ignorant and vile. No, gentlemen: may your institutional breast give rise to a burning enlightenment to melt like hot wax the despot's arrogant claims and the rich man's tyrannical demands! May this remind man of his primitive rights and natural nobility at last. May there arise from your bosom the vehement vociferators and profound politicians who someday shall head the order of the Third Estate,[6] like Israel's goats in the vanguard of the herd. And for myself, gentlemen, may I follow in your footsteps, eager to gather from you enlightenment to spread among your contemporaries and posterity, proud of the adoption I crave, honored to echo you: making no claim to originality, I will paraphrase whatever you tell the world. So I affirm upon entrance to your illustrious body, and these vows will I keep as scrupulously as any nun locked up behind twenty convent grills, guarding her chastity."

"Yes, yes," cried Tifarès, basting the roast with remarkable dexterity, "admit us to your pleasant company. Trust us, we are not bloodsucking parasites. Besides all his philosophical talents as a philosopher, my illustrious brother is a fine lawyer who could dispute any suits you have pending in court, whether seneschalsy, bailiff's, presidential, or parlement. I myself have been our bishop's scullion for the last fifteen months, so I have mastered the art of chicken-plucking; I bard, wash, rinse, lard heavy and light according to the best *Encyclopédie* methods; make chicken fricassee; and as for my pastry! . . . Are you aware, gentlemen, that our ancestor Bernier Bissotin was the inventor of Chartres pastries, so valued by great Henri IV during the civil war? His epitaph, transcribed by Master Desaccords in his miscellanies of the human mind, testifies to his talent, handed down in our family father to son unto your humble servant:[7]

> Here lies Potiphar Bissotaine,
> Who in his time did take great pain
> To make tarts and treats—indeed,
> The Lord forgive his least misdeed.

So, gentlemen, accept us right away, get busy and make my brother give up his wretched plans to live off acorns, beechnuts, and bitter fruit. Cold and indigestible foods are not suited to delicate stomachs. God's life! a lamb chop and a goose thigh mean more to me than four meals of the greatest Epictetus in Greece."[8]

The President must have replied to this speech, as you can imagine, since fine discourse deserves a reply: but by some misfortune I regret more than I can say, the memoirs I use as my source give only an extract from it: Félicité[9] limits herself to saying that as soon as he was admitted by general acclaim, Tifarès joined the troupe by spreading on the grass a tablecloth, napkins whose initials ran from A to Z, and plates of assorted manufacture. He then served a small cask of decent wine, de-spitted the meat to the assembly's admiration, and enjoyed his supper like any scullion who after falling from a bishop's kitchen to a low-level attorney's, has now eaten his dinner in a village of flearidden Champagne. Nor was Bissot far behind: he let himself go like any academician finding himself at a well-provided table, and glowing with the benefits of praise and good treatment. Supper was lively, with the meat course followed by seasonal fruit, for people who live at their neighbors' expense lack for nothing. And several rounds of wine later, the President of the assembly spoke to our philosophers the words you are about to read in the following chapter.

CHAPTER FOUR

Who Were These People Supping Under the Stars on the Plains of Champagne?

"ARE YOU NOT astonished, Sir," began the President, "to find a band lacking neither appetite nor gaiety at such a time and so deserted a place?[1] But I assure you: good health and good cheer are never found under the gilded ceiling of the farmer general, or in the courtesan's cabinet, or behind the merchant's counter. Free-spirited, cordial liberty camps out *sub jove*:[2] liberty possesses no property, forgets its clothes, spends the day shirtless, and would rather wear a beggar's rags or the dirty petticoat of a prostitute than a chevalier's cassock or prelate's surplice. Liberty is what assembles us here from every corner of Europe: we are her priests, and her religion demands only that we refrain from interfering with each other.

"You should now be introduced to the members of our college individually; I begin with the gentleman you see seated at my right hand."

At these words a pale figure with a bald head and half-sad, half-gay expression, obviously familiar with both women and wine, bowed deeply to indicate his approval of the eulogy that the President was about to offer him. (Thus may a fortieth Academician, still a novice in encomiastic commerce, first sniff the bundle of fragrant blossoms emerging from the sycophantic mouth of the permanent secretary, and gather them with seeming modesty.)

The President's eulogy began: "This gentleman is the great philosopher Séché,[3] head of the *Economico-Naturalistlico-Monotonic* sect, and famous author of *The Princes' Journal*."

Tifarès, nurtured at Chartres as he was in holy respect for philosophy, rose to his feet and opened his mouth when he heard this, but the terrible sentry gesticulated at him and his hoarse voice faded on his mulberry lips.

The President then continued his discourse, after the pause always necessary for a speaker to fix his gaze on a listener who burns to interrupt and can be forced into silence only by the orator's intimidating expression: "But perhaps you are not familiar with the *Economico-Naturalistlico-Monotonics*? This sect is the quintessence of the good ideas Reason crams into the heads of philosophers who spend their free time governing nations: a combination of the bread of liberty, the flour of natural law, potatoes, spergula, famine, grain markets, laws, paternity, population, and net product. All these drugs, artistically mixed together so they take turns rising to the top, then are blended *secundum artem*[4] to produce . . . a product . . . yes, in fact we have been compiling, extracting, reading, gathering for last twenty-two years, and we already have manuscripts. . . . Manuscripts that fill one of our donkey's baskets, and if the hour were not so late, I would show them to you; but for now, suffice it to say that we have finally discovered the three words, the magic refrain thanks to which we can establish the happiness of the human race, rule governments, and induce kings to moderate their powers of their own accord; we can make ministers render an accurate public account of their administration, and financiers give the money back; and prelates share their income fraternally with the poor; and ecclesiastics give up controversy in favor of morality; we can make judges award justice to their fellow citizens in public and free of charge; and lawyers speak only for those in the right; and turn soldiers into citizens. We make the officer modest; the bourgeois respectful and proud of the rights of man; the wife, a good housekeeper; the young girl less of a flirt. In short, these three little words alone . . ."

"But how about the little rod of Jacob?"[5] interrupted an ugly-looking drinker on the orator's left, who looked as if he never laughed except in malice.

For an instant the President gaped slack-jawed, like an awkward lackey who has bumped into a door. Yet he continued onward: "The gentleman who has just interrupted me is none other than the famous philosopher Lungiet, leader of the *Despotico-Contradictorio-Paradoxico-Slanderists* sect and the most eloquent Ciceronian to drink at our counter.[6] He was expelled from the bar by fraternity brothers who envied his fame and success. After wandering from one country to another, he threw himself into our arms and we admitted him to *our order*; we thus associate him with an enterprise in which, as you will soon find out, you yourself shall participate.

"Madame here is my governess, the mother of all philosophers, an angel of mercy, and the finest stew-maker in Christendom: her name is O.-B., and we call her *Voragine*.[7] Mademoiselle Félicité her daughter is a bit of a brunette, but fairly promising to be helpful to philosophy some day; her long nose, wide eyes, open mouth, and healthy white teeth form worthy instruments to perfect the great opus.

"As for the goodfellow you met on the road, that's brave Captain Mordanes,[8] valorous and fearless like the late Sacrogorgon;[9] limber, adroit, sharp-eyed, sharp of hearing, and leader of the *Communico-Luxurico-Knavistic*[10] philosophers. According to their sect, all material goods are common property—women, fathers, mothers, sisters, brothers, and above all, moneybags. The Captain is in charge of security and supervises our company's little army.

"I myself am the abbé Séchant; I am philosophical vicar to the abbé Séché, and accompany him throughout the world to propagate his doctrine."

Tifarès rose to his feet as soon as he was sure President Séchant had finished speaking, ignoring his brother's fears that he might commit some new naivety. Nimbly as a ballboy running in a tennis game, he took the floor and made an eloquent speech in honor of the vicar of Worms,[11] as a brilliant epilogue to the discourse of this memorable day. He was still talking by the time everyone else found a coverlet and the best available place by the fire; he followed their example; and Morpheus took excellent care of his beloved favorite.

CHAPTER FIVE

Reveille; The Troupe Marches Forward; Unremarkable Adventures

HOW MUCH IT costs to sleep in a fine bed! How many sacrifices it takes to buy those silk curtains, those gilded shutters to hide the morning star's faintest gleam from our eyes.—O liberty! You are the price we pay for accepting the treacherous refinements of the soft life, in exchange for destroying our finest faculties. Ah yes, I recall the happy time when, lying in Julie's embrace on a curtainless bed, dawn's first rays drew me from the arms of slumber: a tenderly savored kiss brought my lover back to life: her heart opened to desire before her eyes opened to the light. I united with Julie; Julie's alabaster arms hugged me close; we saluted the principle of life through that union of celestial flame; we intoxicated ourselves with pleasure; and so we prepared for our working day. O ye who poison with your sinister storytales the few brief moments we can consecrate to pleasure, believe me here: our prayer was more acceptable to the Being of Beings than the bad Latin you drone in his ears. Ye misers whose brazen hearts cover sordid avarice, you who fatten off the property of your fellow men, you who grow rich on finance through the poverty of nations, you whom tyranny stains with human blood, all you barbarous jailers who guard our doors and fall asleep at the keyholes—come watch Mordanes the philosopher get up in the morning, and may envy gnaw the withered remains of your fetid, putrefying hearts.[1]

Mordanes approached drowsy Tifarès, having appreciated his rare talents and destined him for an important role in the band, just as Dawn now parted on the horizon the wide curtain that prevents sleepy animals from seeing the light of day.

Meanwhile, dear reader,[2] you should surely be introduced to the shining star of the entire roster, about whom I think the abbé Séchant may have said little or nothing?—or just some passing word to which you were probably not paying attention, as you are unlikely to be the kind of attentive reader who weighs every syllable, seeks the hidden meanings of passages, and uses Aristotle to demonstrate the Trinity in the Gospel. But we can hardly overlook this member of the band, even though he was a member of no sect, and his main character trait was philosophical indifference. This member was endowed with plenty of ideas, but limited in his ability to combine them, so he did not credit creations of his own with attributes to be observed in nature's handiworks. Nor was he a plagiarist artist, who weakly or madly imagines a horse's head stuck onto a fishtail and bows down to worship the chimera.[3] One possible reason why his nonchalance protected him from such ludicrous error (though his *sensorium* was able to receive healthy sense-impressions) could have been that the natural vigor of his limbs had permanently affected his memory by imprinting the fibers of his brain too firmly. Perhaps this is also why he was never heard to make citations, or show the slightest mark of respect for Aristotle and other philosophical efforts at thinking, two thousand years ago, for the benefit of future generations. This member's physical health equaled his moral vigor; he showed no desire for fine cuisine, despite his excellent digestion, but chose the simplest foods. Bare ground for him was as good as a soft mattress, and he wallowed in grass, rolling around in it more than we might do on the fluffiest featherbeds. Ardent in love, he was as sure to rouse desires as to satisfy them; nature had given him loins befitting his organs' solidity and size; whenever he joined with a female whom desire had made submit to him, the fruits followed hard upon the flowers. In a word: the virtues of a Carmelite, the lungs of a preacher, the manner and coiffure of a prelate, and the dress of a lawyer. His religion? . . . that was . . . well, I don't know exactly how to answer, but I have it on good authority that he was neither Socinian, nor Manichaean, nor Adamist, nor Pre-Adamist, nor Maronite, nor Moravian, nor Quaker, nor Calvinist, nor Presbyterian, nor Catholic, nor Deist, nor Theist, nor Atheist, nor Jansenist, nor Molinist, nor Mohammedan, nor Pagan, nor Parsee, nor Hindu, nor Martinist, etc., etc. I once heard tell that he declared for "Nothing-ism," but I make no guarantee, as I have a principle of never stating other people's religion. Still, I must tell the truth as a historian, and I know the Jesuit Garasse[4] considered him a good-for-nothing atheist, while the late M. d'Alembert identified him as a Socinian, the Jesuits as a Jansenist, the Arnaulds as a Molinist, the ministers of Neuchâtel as a *non-eternitarian*. Also, he never ate pork, so I am sure they would have burned him in Lisbon; and M. Antoine-Louis Séguier, speaker of the king's law court, would have brought a major indictment against him in the assembly rooms, and prosecuted him as a philosopher or—worse yet—an economist. Nevertheless he belonged to no academy, and his bonnet was the only academic thing about him. But in this our world it is far more perilous to belong to no party than to belong to the wrong one, because in the latter case *manus omnium contra eum.*[5]

O dear reader! you grow impatient, I am well aware: you cannot guess the hero whose faithful portrait I have limned above. But you—the quick-witted, frisky young village girl whom Love has so often prompted to lie with vigorous Colin? Then you, if you were the one reading this work, you would call out in delight: "O! Our Colin! It's our donkey!"

—A donkey!

—Yes, sir! Yes, madame! Yes, mademoiselle! Yes indeed: the young four-year-old donkey who carried the troupe's baggage—and for whose grooming Tifarès was destiny's grand plan.

—Destiny!

As a philosopher, sir, you may laugh at destiny; but believe me, whatever you and your like may write to contest it, destiny does exist: a sequence of necessary events that follows inescapably from the collision and combination of things in this our world. Destiny keeps a huge book where events are written in a medium called "prediction ink," long before they happen. You and I can read only history past, but whenever the magus and astrologer approach the page to the flame of genius, the future appears clear before their eyes. Now, it was written in this book that one Bissot brother would become a great philosopher, and the other a donkey's groom; Captain Mordanes had exactly enough genius to read Tifarès's page; and thus by destiny's decree did Mordanes awaken Bissot's brother, put a curry comb into his hand, and lead him to the ass.

Have you ever had the joy of tasting the fruit of honest labor? Do you know how sweet it is to say to oneself: I earned this money with my own talent, my genius? the fruit of my own sleepless nights? How far this thought raises man above himself! Here is a thought that seats him, so to speak, by the side of his creator. I was born to wealth;[6] fortune destined me to profit from the public's serfdom; my task in life was to twist those bonds as tight as possible. Men scurried to maintain me in my indolence, and I watched proudly to see them do it. Only one ray of sunshine penetrated my breast—justice—and justice made liberty flower. Liberty: for the steadfast man, for the eagle in the heavens, and for the lion in the desert! Like that lion, the scent of slavery made me roar; and society's shackles dropped from my feet. I bade farewell to fortune, and began my existence.

O! how my self-respect—the source of every human virtue—doubled at the first gold coins I earned by honest labor! I decided: "I'll travel the earth; the fortifications of slavery shrink before me. Let the tyrant and his armies guard the frontiers of their kingdom: I throw down my weapons like the beaver before the hunter. I shall seek out free cities and tell their inhabitants: I bring you my arms, my industry, my health, my courage. I have seen the hairless neck of the collared dog,[7] and I have fled from sculptures that exalted its servile soul. And you—virtuous citizen of despicable Geneva—you who dared hope to see equality reestablished on this earth, you who dared show men their tyrants' secrets: May you receive the incense I am about to burn on your altar. Guide my steps and my sentiments from the empyrean heavens. You said: the first man who dared say 'This is mine,' and plant around his field the palisades which make poor men the slaves of five or six rich ones—that man should be buried together with the whole idea of property.[8] You said, but they pretended not to hear: property is the sinister jailer who turns the keys with which the powerful lock up their slaves at night; property unlocks these slaves before dawn, when the overseer's voice summons these wretched children of the earth to do the heaviest tasks; property is the bailiff who executes the sentence, *in sudore vultus tui vesceris pane, donec revertaris in terram de quâ sumptus es*;[9] property is the cherub guarding the gate to paradise."

However, Tifarès's earthbound soul may have been disinclined to such reflections, or perhaps his vanity made him think of work as a burden: so does serfdom degrade our species in its generative sources, and the atom in semen[10] become enslaved to an atom yet more powerful. No doubt this is also why as soon as our bourgeois become rich, they purchase one of the 4,750 offices conferring nobility, and renounce whatever profession has made their fortune. Why should Tifarès be more of a philosopher than a newly rich banker, or a farmer-general who makes his collections by bleeding his fellow citizens? Had fear of Mordanes replaced philosophy in his mind? I myself have no answer; I am not good at plumbing the depths of others' hearts and loins; for me, it's enough to tell you that Tifarès did a fairly intelligent job on the humble steed's toilette. Mordanes looked his approval, and taught him how to put the packload on his travel companion . . .

—Taught him how!

—Well, yes! Do you think packsaddling a jackass is uncomplicated?[11] Make an effort: You who are nurtured on Greek roots, but strangers to country work, just try it. . . . That's right, adjust the packload, keep turning it in every direction, manipulate it just like you do the truth: and then, try to understand its real meaning. See the mule-driver laugh at your awkwardness, despite your fine hat and breeches. You remind me of the emperor of China plowing a furrow.[12] You heartless geometrician—you who abandoned the goad you once used on the slow oxen that fed your family, and picked up in exchange the sterile pen of philosophy—go home to your natal village! Get to know your shepherd cousin, and your laborer uncle: cast your arrogance and egotism aside; try to drive the plow you should never have abandoned; and then if you give a sideways glance at the astonished onlookers, as your approval-hungry soul has taught your eyes to peek for applause, do you realize that their smile is one of mockery, as pointed in a village as in a lecture hall? You will be hissed and booed wherever you go in the country, as you were in town; your work miscarries everywhere, and all you collect will be catcalls.

On the other hand, Tifarès succeeded at once, and escaped lightly: our Bohemian beauties gave a few peals of laughter, and malicious Mordanes a smirk: "We'll see, the lad shows promise": the kind of encouragement given a penniless young gentleman new to military service by an old flag-bearer who was promoted thanks to flattery and tattling but, having nothing to fear from this new recruit, would rather see his place taken by a financier's son ready to open his fat purse to regimental rascals, and bend his knees before the colonel's shadow.[13]

While Tifarès accomplished his noble task, the wandering troupe arose and performed its ablutions in the clear, pure water of a stream. I have never quite figured out if they turned toward the East in the time-honored ritual of Western peoples, but I rather doubt it: the day promised fine, and the rising sun would have been in their eyes. However, I do happen to have in hand a scholarly dissertation on holy water that has long awaited publication in one of my works—and I believe, my dear reader, you will like me to make a bit of space for it here? I also have another dissertation on lustral water, three on the waters of the Nile, five on the waters of the Ganges, nineteen on eau-de-Luce water, twenty-seven on Carmelite-water[14]—all of which I plan to insert consecutively in the fifty-four volumes I hope, with the help of God and my fellow authors, to produce between now and next New Year's, provided we have in one of these years some issue relating to water, snow, ice, rain, floods, clouds, or even barometers, since the obvious relationship of all these things to the fluid element would allow me to digress a-propos, to which I can only trust no journalists, even the ones with no audience, will object. To what straits would authors be reduced, if they could not insert into their works whatever leftover material they have stored, just as contract builders re-use beams from the old house? The new house-owner is not about to strip plaster off the walls or take up the floorboards; readers generally act the same way, and scholars who excavate whited sepulchers are not being prudent; anyone who knew how a roof was constructed would never want to live under one. But for once, my dear reader, since that last sentence is as useful as my dissertation on holy water, I shall now return to my work: and if the good Lord inspired self-control like mine to bread-bakers, screw-ups, Benedictine scholars, and many who are neither Benedictines nor scholars, we would be let off with a scare.[15]

Having finished their religious or hygienic ablutions, the troupe started traveling once more. Captain Mordanes took the lead wearing his hat at an angle over one ear, double-barreled guns on his shoulder; a sword on his ban-dolier recognizable to every dragoon officer as Charleville manufacture; a too-short bright green coat beginning to fade into white; and gaiters that had oft been waxed to a shine: any constable would identify him as a deserter, but the troupe was impressed by his arrogant march-time cadence. Mordanes strut-ted, preened, and looked intrepid because others were cowardly; who dared pronounce judgment against this son of an Arnay-le-Duc attorney?[16] His dog ran back and forth in front like a plundering light hussar who gets wind of chicken and ham as a scout for marauders. The donkey followed quietly, sure of step and inattentive to the peacocking of the van. Just so do the fools we call "commonsensical" take the direct road to fortune undistracted by incidental knowledge, and prideful only because they are never distracted by detours.

Tifarès marched in the donkey's footsteps, encouraging him with words and strokes as noisily as any French carter; then came lawyer Bissot arguing to the bitter end with the other two philosophers, according to the immemorial practice of philosophers down from Anaxagoras[17] (of argumentative memory) and including Bissot himself. Séchant strolled with a damsel on each arm, now smiling at the one, now winking at the other, squeezing the mother's fingers, then tickling the daughter's palm. Thus will an old billy goat, once the beloved of the entire herd and broken more by pleasuring than old age, try in vain to get up on his shaky hind legs but yet take pleasure in reminiscence, while las-civious nanny goats respond to his flirtation, and a foul warm fluid moistens the old buck's tongue.

Two or three leagues go by quickly when one is dreaming, arguing, or making love.

—Have you never traveled on foot?

—Who, me?

—Not you, mademoiselle: you have destroyed nature's solid foundation for your body's frame by washing your delicate feet in bran-water, and stuffing them into tight slippers. Nor you, reverend father: you can't even reach the holy altar to sing Mass, what with your pregnant-looking tummy. No, I address my reader—my reader who, having neither responsibilities nor employment, nor commerce, cannot afford to fly post-chaise from one end of Europe to the other, seeing nothing but highways and station-masters' dunghills—my reader, who hates public coaches whose bumpy jolts upset one's brain, not to mention their passengers, assorted fools and bare-faced babblers from every corner of the kingdom: smelly monks whose odor is offensive; whores who circulate the pox from Lille to Perpignan, and Brest to Lyon; young officers who may grab a piece of such tasty morsels; newly-ennobled snobs whose fathers have bought one of the 4,750 positions exempting them from the taille[18]—and thanks to which boondoggle they deride the coachman, despise the horses, insult the women, and generally make so much of a racket that God could have spared himself the trouble of sending us the carriage bumps, the clickety-clacks of the post-boys, and the other hullabaloos common on the major highways.

"My God, sir! your sword has cut a hole in my lawn apron!"

"Oh sir, your sword is going right through my tibia!"

"If you please, sir, your sword could be hung from the leather straps holding up the waxed canvas carriage-curtains, as we have nothing to fear from highwaymen now that we have widened the roads, and positioned a regiment of soldiers at every league."

" Me take off my sword! No, by my honor; I haven't been wearing a sword for very long; my beloved sword, my only mark of nobility . . . s'death, master lawyer, if you breathe a single word . . ."

With my bilious humor, I can hardly bring myself to keep quiet in my corner and refrain from the satisfaction of slapping this parvenu's piebald face five or six times and breaking his worthless rapier in two—even though prudence reminds me that it is not my job to teach good manners to people who travel in the comfort of turgotine coaches.[19]

—But who *would* be able to bear that? Are you blind to the young officer who feels up the breasts of a young lady whose mother is taking her home from the convent, reaching right under her skirt? Or deaf to that monk who mumbles away in a whiny voice, with no respect for the meter, ridiculous psalms translated into wretched Latin, and calls all that verbiage his breviary? And what about that fat merchant on his way to the fair at Reims, whose nap sounds like the digestion of Polyphemus?[20]

"Hey, coachman, whoa! Stop a moment. Coachman: are you acquainted with Polyphemus?"

"No, sir: not on my passenger list; perhaps he is traveling on the ordinary coach, or even the old rattletrap."[21]

"Ha, ha! Open the door, open up and hurry up. Give my seat to whomever you wish! It is paid for. I will collect my luggage at the station. Phew! What a Noah's ark."

"Noah's ark, yourself, you mean; watch out for my sword, my sword. Him with his Noah's ark."

"He is surely a nonconformist? Or perhaps the marquis of V. . . . You see he did not even give me a glance."

"No, no, he is an abbé being sent to seminary."

"Heavens no? He is surely the madman who broke his chains two days ago, because he did not utter a single word, or laugh even when the officer here was telling tales to my daughter."

"He must be some geometrician or philosopher, with no more religion than Voltaire."[22]

At last the noble and the citizen, the officer and the monk, the mother, her daughter—everyone including the coachman, who fears losing his *tip,* chase me out like a band of abandoned children insulting the rear-guard of a wise and prudent general who makes his retreat before superior force.

Thank God I am quit of them! The coachman is swearing, the horses leaving, lo and behold I am alone: the wretched box can be seen in the distance, as it struggles to the top of a hill; the road unfurls before me like a great big ribbon; the air is pure, and I am soon environed by the pleasantest thoughts.

This is a moment when I enjoy every pleasure life can offer: the countryside has a thousand charms for me, I make plans to retire there. A little ready-built house, nicely decorated, whose neatness takes the place of magnificence; a neighborhood that easily affords all the society I need. The local lord is well-educated for a country noble, and has a natural wit that takes the place of acquired knowledge; he has collected good books, but not enough to fill whole rooms of the chateau; he never forgets he is human, though of ancient nobility; while his wife, a woman of quality, is neither insolent nor haughty.

Their older son, a youth of fifteen or sixteen who loves hunting and music, comes home from college and invites me, I am included in all his parties; and since his behavior is good and his morals pure, I never hesitate to join him. For a cleric, the parish priest is not particularly ignorant, and his office allows him to offer his neighbors courtesies that fill with humility those who must accept; this honest ecclesiastic is no bigot or drunkard, nor has anyone ever claimed he defiled his parishioners' beds. Admittedly we have never been introduced to the brother who fathered his niece, but many families scatter far and wide, and the girl is clearly well brought up. These excellent neighbors I occasionally invite into my home. I make punch for them: punch, the heart and the soul of society: when good people are seated around a full punchbowl . . . !

Yes, but my means are so limited . . .

Well, I'll go off to the capital, the place where talent is both welcomed and recompensed . . .

True. But what talents? . . .

Why, have I not a thousand talents? And surely I know twenty ignoramuses who left the depths of the provinces just like me, who arrived in Paris impecunious, and now possess thousands?[23] In finance, Messrs A B C D E . . . in the judiciary, Messrs F G H I . . . ; in the church, Messrs K L M N . . . ; in the civil service, Messrs O P Q R . . . ; in the army, Messrs S T U V X . . . : these are all nobodies who might have been able to write if they had ever learned to read, and they are all rolling in gold. I shall go to Court, I'll try to get acquainted with some duchess's maid or milliner; sidle up near a minister's lackey; chat up a cardinal's porter; ask the church bell-ringer which mass is frequented by people trying to look pious; find out from a discreet whore about hypocrites; ask the rich merchant for names of people who give long-term credit; but what if all that fails me!

Well, if all else fails, I will write. I will praise the French Academy, which praises anyone and everyone; I'll extol the Faculty, or the Royal Society of Medicine; I'll take sides in favor of Robert or Pilâtre; I'll get Blanchard to save me a place next to him in his char-volant balloon.[24] I will go applaud new theater plays and academic discourses; I'll start a newspaper; I'll establish a school, a museum, a philosophical school, an English garden—who knows? Philosophy is an infinite resource, don't you know? Just combining the simple ideas of ancient and modern philosophers, two at a time, three at a time, etc., one would sooner or later. . . . Moreover, the prince is the protector of talent: he hunts out talents, discovers them under poverty's thorny bramble, and wings them away to the very steps of his throne. I have read it a hundred times: if ever talent were to occur in a land that did not adopt this wise system, the whole world's praise would go to more deserving princes.

But lastly, I have to make my fortune because . . . relationships with women are a way of consuming one's money, and theirs if they have any. I am still in the flower of youth, and I can offer both my body and my soul, really a valuable combination, to any dowager who delights in the dual constitutive principles of human-faced creatures.

—Couldn't you win playing lottery?

—No; as ladies say, that's not a job for a country boy. A fig for games where you have to put up a stake in order to win! So let's get back to the court, that's the life for me.

"Ah, marquis! Enchanted to make your acquaintance! I so often raised a glass with your late father; I knew your departed stepmother quite well: what a woman, mistress of any situation!"

"Your grace; and how are you?"

"Very well! But yourself, what are you doing these days?"

"Alas, your grace, I am ruined."

"I understand, marquis: so you come to request a pension?"

"No, since I have done nothing to deserve a pension: but to ask for some useful employment in which to exercise for my own benefit and my fatherland's whatever talents I possess . . ."

"Excellent idea, but do get rid of the word 'fatherland,' the expression is completely out of style. Come along, I shall introduce you to the minister. I hope to be named ambassador in the immediate future, and I shall take you as my secretary. Do you know dead languages?"

"A little."

"Living languages?"

"Two or three, passably well."

"Public law?"

"A little."

"'A little, a little'—that's no way to answer when one is out to make one's fortune! One adopts a confident air, one answers every question 'Yes, my lord.' If a minister asks, 'Do you know Chinese?' you answer: 'Yes, Minister.' This is how one makes one's way; you must rid yourself of—I was about to say 'modesty,' but that word too is out of style, one hears it used only in the imperative mode. Follow me, and mind you show your merits right up front: a minister has no time to look for jewels at the bottom of the box, the merchant must take pains to display them . . .

"Monseigneur, may I introduce the marquis of ***: he is a true gentleman whose ancestors marched under the banner of my own in the first Crusade,[25] and we have been marrying their women since the reign of Philippe-Auguste. Then, too, the lad is a young man of merit: has his Latin like a professor; understands Greek; can speak German, Italian, and English like a native; knows as much public law as Grotius or Pufendorf;[26] in short, Monseigneur, if you approve, I shall employ him in my embassy."

"Certainly, Duke, enchanted to do anything to give you pleasure, except that my head clerk Cruchon expects to give you one of his wife's cousins, a young man of great merit, and I think you may as well take him on; as for the marquis, I will take charge of his fortune myself."

"My thanks, Monseigneur . . ."

"Wait until I do you a real favor to thank me, Duke, and give me the occasion very soon."

"O Monseigneur, for myself, I would be only too happy for any occasion to show myself the humblest servant of your servants . . ."

"Very well! In consideration for his Grace the ambassador here, you may depend on it: I undertake to make your fortune."

—And so, taking my promenade, that is how I made my fortune: straightforwardly, without having to start up a lyceo-museum, or museo-lyceum, or academico-muzico-lyceum;[27] and without having to write the kind of correspondence, newspaper, "Mercury," "Courier," "Gazeteer," gazette, placards, handbills, annals, bibliographic gazettes, summaries of the said newspapers or gazettes, etc., or other literary rackets that have now become so common.

—Surely the gentleman has entertained us about his own little self long enough? Would he kindly return to his heroes?

—On my honor, I had forgotten all about them. Wait a moment . . .

—What next?

—Let me see! I can't remember where I left them, any more than I know where I'm going to lead them, but mercy: if an author made a plan before writing his book, why would we need journalists to make extracts? Fortunately, I can find my place again.

—Devilish awkward! How are we to retrace our steps back through that labyrinth, what with the coaches, the Court, the minister, and Polyphemus?

—It's going to be fine. Nothing could be easier.

CHAPTER SIX

Cock-Crow

YOU MUST THANK me, gentle reader, for rescuing you from that damned coach at last—

—Whew! Whatever are you going to do . . . ?

—You are frightened? Calm down, never fear, I won't force you back right away; I'm not one of those writers who shake up your world until its natural warmth is extinct. Five or six hundred dozen quakes are plenty at one time; besides, if you are afraid of digressions, close my book. I write the same way I am treated by fortune: my style is weak, and my composition motley.

This comparison comes particularly apropos now while I am calling up remembrance of my multiscient troupe: no sooner did the upturned ear of my dear donkey strike the membranous processes of my optic nerve, than the animal spirits with which they are impregnated began to flow back to my brain; the moment these spirits collided in their retrograde path with the liquid globes inertly awaiting some movement in the tortuous sinuses of my lobes, the inside of my head turned into a sort of philosophical composite. Immediately my soul, asleep in a sinus near my nose, awoke with a start and clearly in the mirror of my mental . . . Hey! Help! Bonnet, Bonnet,* come rescue me, I'm getting tangled up in fibrous skeins! To cut matters short, to talk like a Christian, as if I cared about being understood, to talk to you the way people actually talk, I'll just say my motley composition reminded me of the donkey's mottled gray skin, and the donkey reminded me of my philosophers.

* Bonnet, author of a systematic treatise on the soul.[1]

Clear enough, let me hope? I could have spoken directly, but what credit do you get for using ordinary words to say a commonplace thought! Far better to tweak one's idea: an air of obscurity and profundity works wonders for a book. Anyway, I felt I now saw my philosophers advancing, gesticulating, and speaking to . . . well, to show off all their learning and eloquence. So goes the second reply in the catechism for sages:

D. Who created you and put you in the world?

R. Nobody.

D. Why did "nobody" create you and put you in the world?

R. To speak.

D. Why do you speak?

R. To show off my eloquence and win admiration.

D. Aha! Aha! Well done, bravo!

If I so wished, I could compose a chapter on this topic. A chapter, a book, a volume, an encyclopedia, a whole library if you argue for it; and if I did not hear the rooster crowing to his hens, choosing and caressing the most amorous one frankly, gaily, strongly, firmly, just as we would caress our girl-chicks if we were not hampered by an overabundance of good manners, virtue, and modesty—or perhaps a lack of something else.

Besides, this particular rooster might dispense with loud cock-a-doodle-doos about endless lovemaking. I have no fondness for men who flap their wings, get their hackles up, and climb to the top of their dunghill to sing about the favors they get from their ladies. But alas! on this score, dear Frenchmen, you are all cocks: this is the origin of the term Gallic. Whatever connection the Eternal Geometer may have made between your throats and your precious amulets, you all need to sing as soon as you have finished. Your numbers also include capons who sing all the time, though they never enjoy: as witness your falsetto poets crowing about the favors of *Iris, Phyllis,* and other lovelies ending in *-is.* Nor are those Parnassian eunuchs alone! Observe the swindler egret who dines off the scraps some capuchin pigeon has left behind: see him swell his chest, strut his wig-feathers, and exaggerate his achievements to his confidant like any tragic hero. Even a little abbé ruffles up his clerical bands to look as if he had just got lucky; may he be punished like the insolent rooster whose tale I am now about to tell.

From the village outskirts, Mordanes heard the telltale voice of the hens' husband: grabbing the arm of illustrious Tifarès, he called his dog, sent ahead the donkey and his acolytes, and set an ambush in a cranny of the nearest house.

"Curses be," said he to his companion, "on the churl who first invented chicken-gates."

"Chicken-gates?" asked Tifarès; "That is a word I never saw in the Dictionary of the Forty."[2]

"Me neither, as I don't know how to read. But since we say 'cat-door' for the hole in the wall where cats run in and out, we should be able to say 'chicken-gate" for the fence hole where chickens run away when they see hunters approach their dung-hill. We can always solve the problem by writing a footnote like Brissot de Warville: '*this word is a happy invention of the author.*'"

Tifarès was surprised to see the hens and roosters rush to the chicken-gate at first sight of the august donkey, no matter how far away they had been. He reflected with serious consideration on the foresight of volatile creatures that perceive Bohemians and their hawk approaching at a league's distance. After which, Master Sorbonnicker, just try to argue that animals have no faculty of judgment: they have more than you or I.

Observe this reasoning, I pray: *The peripatetic philosophers known to the general public as* BOHEMIANS *kill chickens whenever they can catch them.* Major premise, which comes either from tradition like so many other fine things, or from a series of experiments. Minor premise: *Here we have some Bohemians*; this minor premise presupposes the general type of a model Bohemian, so it contains the first and third mental operations. Consequently . . . consequently . . . you must agree our chickens lack only the last step, and articulate the conclusion accurately drawn from their premises. Take courage, finish the argument, Master Codex: let us agree that formal logic is not necessary for the discovery of truth, and your universals . . .

—Fie upon you, Sir! no one mentions such outdated philosophizing nowadays, any more than we discuss religion—it is now such bad form.

All the worse for your auguries: if no one bothers to make fun of your sacred chickens, you will soon lack bran to feed them. Apropos of which, I may now tell you the following story:

Once there was a man[3] from Normandy whom curiosity had driven to the banks of the Meuse; by the time he reached Cologne he was penniless, as he had not brought with him the gold he had spent on lawsuits in his native land. He accordingly took shelter with the Cordelier Franciscans under pretext of a pilgrimage to the tomb of the three wise kings who had been led to Jerusalem by a star more than one thousand seven hundred eighty-eight years ago,[4] and who decided to go to Germania on their way home, returning to Babylon via

Siberia and Kamchatka in an effort to trick the spies of Herod, of infanticide memory. However, since they had donated all their gold, silver, and myrtle to the carpenter Joseph and his wife Mary, they died of hunger and cold *in coloniâ romanâ,* where charity was practiced then as much as now. Their sad end made the three wise men feel sympathetic to the sufferings of poor travelers, so they always ask any good-natured-looking traveler what evil star could possibly have led him to the iniquitous Low Dutch. The Norman's fatherly air and straight short haircut appealed to Melchior, darkest and wisest of the three wise kings.

"Friend," whispered Melchior, "is anyone else besides you in this church?"

"No, holy majesty."

"Good, I will perform a miracle in that case: for nowadays it is inadvisable to have a lot of witnesses when one is doing a miracle—they just diminish the rate of success. These days a saint can count himself lucky if his best miracle gets him nothing worse than the pillory or the asylum. No one else here at all?"

"No, your holiness."

"In that case, take the silver chalice and run."

"*Bone Deus!*"

"Get out of here! Surely you don't want to die of hunger and cold like the three of us, you fool?"

"Aha! Aha! Well, you could be right about that . . ."

And the good Norman pocketed the chalice, left by the cloister door, found the robe of brother Eustache who was off splitting wood, disguised himself in that, walked through the corridor, noticed the custode father's[5] door was open, grabbed the convent seal, pocketed that too, and whisked out on the road to Jubilee; for he had heard the Saint's Gate was open. As soon as possible, he crossed the Meuse into the duchy of Juliers,[6] where he found Ben-Samson-Carra-David-Antoine-Tibe—son of a Frenchman who had emigrated for excellent reasons, grandson of a Jew who had abjured out of self-interest back when abjuration was a paying proposition, and great-grandson of a Muslim who had converted to Judaism out of a love for usury; this Antoine Tibe accepted the holy chalice, valued it at half its weight, and melted it down into ingots to make shoe buckles for his English shop. Thanks to the Israelite's ready money and an authorization stamped with the convent seal, the newly minted priest reached Rome without misadventure, stopping only for a visit to Notre Dame de Lorette.[7] But I nearly forgot to do him this justice: on Melchior's advice, he had touched the tabernacle key to the chalice and paten before pocketing them, so it would be very wrong to accuse him of stealing sacred vessels. Indeed, it is from his example that commissioners of his royal and imperial majesty derive their invariable practice of profaning sacred vessels and ornaments before their church-robbing, as wise Christians must always do in such a situation.

The first thing our reverend father did in Rome was to ask for an audience with His Holiness, but the Bishop of Rome was inconvenienced: he had sprained the levator muscles of his—fie upon you! What a nasty mind! Stop laughing and remember this is the head of the Church, who wears three crowns! In the levator muscles. . . . Mademoiselle, the pope was seventy years old! For young cardinals, let it pass, but a pope!—In the levator muscles of his index finger, which he had sprained giving holy benediction to a troupe of English gentlemen who traveled for want of employment, and requested the blessing out of curiosity.

Our reverend father, deprived by this accident of the honor of seeing His Holiness, managed only an interview with the housemistress-cardinal, to whom he sold an excellent preservative against crystallized fistulas. Next he sought a hospice; he naturally looked for a house of Cordeliers, but upon giving a paolo[8] to a beggar, the poor man's cicerone, he was told that these reverend fathers made a practice of stabbing any member of their order audacious enough to repent, or daring enough to ask forgiveness. So he wended his way toward the Dominicans; but upon seeing a man in a *sambenito*[9] come out the door of their monastery, he turned to the Benedictines; but he could not get the Benedictines to open their door because they were all, even the friars, busy making ancient *diplomas* for recent Italian princes. He was thus forced to resort to the Minims; and as he saw nothing at their door but a cask of oil, he ventured to enter. "*Minima malis, Minims from Malines, What can they be doing in Rome?*"[10] Ah, father Ange-Marie, you have no idea: you must ask to have the Latin explained by the learned Dom-Barthélemi of the Congregation of Saint-Vast.[11]

The Minims received the reverend father warmly, but gave him only oil to eat all day; next day they led him to the feet of the Grand Penitencer, who observed the old ritual of striking him on the shoulders with a rod while reciting the *Miserere* prayer, and made him swallow oil; the following day he rested, and they gave him more oil; the fourth day, the Minims showed him the door, wished him a good journey, and stopped giving him oil. The next day he noticed a girl pissing in a street corner, which aroused desires he satisfied claustrally under his robe; the day after that, he was found begging for alms by the Pope's sbirros, who instantly gathered a hundred of their finest men and enough courage to lead him to the Appian Way where, after getting his benediction and a tip of two paoli, they set him on a road going in the opposite direction from Hannibal's, and he proceeded without further mishap until arriving at the city of Geneva.

Back in those days, the inhabitants of Geneva were very polite to each other, identifying themselves by the titles of "magnificent" and "excellent," and calling their city "republic." Oh! what a pleasure to hear! The Genevans had drafted a perpetual treaty of offensive and defensive alliance with England, which was then waging war against France and America; the Genevans were planning diversionary action that would surely have embarrassed France.[12] Happily for us, Geneva then contained not one but three species of magnificent gentlemen, or we may say three varieties of the same species.[13] "Citizens" came first: those who had had the inestimable advantage of being born within the circumference of the republic and conferring with John Calvin in his time; this group claimed to be masters over the others, and the only ones to wage war, make peace, send ambassadors, strike coins, and exercise other rights of sovereignty, especially balancing . . .

—The scales of their shop counters?

—Ha! Not at all: the European balance of power. Next, the "Bourgeois" came second: those born in Leman, who were trying to convince Europe that France and England would surely need them to act as mediators sometime soon. "Natives" came last: those also born in Geneva but who had not bought the rights to bourgeois status, and never quite saw why their activities should be limited to measuring the passage of time spent by their august concitizens in such splendid activities.

The three magnificent species of clockmakers were divided under two flags: the first banner displaying an immense wig of argent on a sable field and in Hebrew letters the motto NEGATIVES; the other banner bearing a puce rodomont on a tawny field defending a wooden bridge and the device REPRESENTATIVES. The whole town had apparently forgotten all about the pope being the Antichrist; no one now discussed the "real presence"; voluminous Bibles and huge commentaries rotted away in bookstores, unread and unused except for single pages of odd volumes, used for the purpose of . . . Alas! What is to become of these last vestiges of religion? Either of the aforesaid two parties would have kissed the Pope's slipper, if his Holiness had sent a few troops against the other; indeed Bellona, mounting Clavière,[14] had already lifted her lips to the herdsman's horn for a call to tear up the city streets, assassinate an old woman, and produce exploits worthy to be some day sung by our own illustrious Bissot.

But let us not anticipate events that were to bring the magnificent gentlemen eternal glory forever, and content ourselves with explaining that their quarrel was about a legal code demanded by the Representatives but refused by the Negatives. The latter preferred to govern the former *ad libitum,* and M. de Vergennes, who was on their side, agreed with them.[15] The Representatives wanted positive laws, and claimed they need submit only to such laws. The clergy took the side of the Negatives, seeing the strength of their argument: "Christian scum, filthy kine," they preached from the pulpit of truth, "observe neighboring countries, examine their legal codes: Can't you see these codes are fit for nothing but for the small-room? Dare you say we have no laws? What of the Bible and Leviticus? Don't you realize those august books summarize Christian morality into three little words: *Pay your tithes?* Even if you passed more laws than all the earth's rulers put together, what point would there be to that, pray tell? Are such laws actually followed by people who have them? Come, oh imbeciles, and learn that laws constrain only the governed: governors use them for their sport. Pass laws or don't pass laws—either way, our magnificent Negatives will still be your masters, because they are richer than you."

In an effort to call this unruly city back to its senses, my friend Colonel Tissot wrote to the Dutch Republic for four corporals armed with whips and sticks. Also the barometer-maker Deluc[16] had hastened from England to offer himself as mediator, but as nobody would accept him unless he had paid up his bankruptcy, this claim meant his voyage was in vain.

While the city of Calvin was busy with all this negotiation and weaponry, down from the Alps came the Very Reverend Father Rose-Croix;[17] a Savoyard vicar who heard news both true and false had told him that the Capuchin renegade apostate Telichi,[18] the one who corrected the *Encyclopedia,* had announced the death of the immortal Jean-Jacques, who had ended his days far from his ridiculous fatherland. As he walked, our reverend father tossed flowers on the great man's tomb and wrote his TOMB OF JEAN-JACQUES, which he hoped to have printed in Geneva by Pellet,[19] who was less particular than he is today, having not yet been thrown into the Bastille.

Dear reader, have you ever been printed alive?[20] Have you ever felt so pressured by your baker and local tavern-keeper that you dragged your rundown shoes through the markets where literary rag-pickers traffic in the thoughts of human beings so poor they sell their dreams to support themselves?—No. You may have begun the world a tax collector's minion, poor as a church mouse and doing the work of a cellar rat; but your steady pilfering from drunken sots on the one hand, and taking crumbs from the poor who can hardly afford salt with your other hand, soon got you promoted to an office of your own. And now the world of letters knows your name: "Clerks, doormen, let him pass through!" You no longer fear a hunger strike, thanks to your happy youthful larcenies. You acquire a mistress, your mistress reads novels, you find on her dressing table this my true history, which you now have open to this very page, and your eyes alight on my question: a stroke of luck that now procures me the honor of explaining exactly how much money an unfortunate author earns by entertaining you.

"M. Panckoucke,[21] I have written some obituary verses on a great man."

"I pay hack writers a salary for that."

"Right here in my portfolio, I have a two-volume moral novel."[22]

"A work like that brings in too little money; besides, the scholars who are revising my *Encyclopedia* according to subject matter throw in trifles like that as part of the bargain."

"I have also brought . . ."

"God help you, my friend, today's a day for the *Courrier*; I can't give you a long audience. Go to the little bookshops and boutiques, where they can accommodate your miserable needs. Myself, I never even look at a work that doesn't weigh at least three quintals,[23] just as I buy butter only by the pound. Impossible for us to help the whole world."

Leaving the palace of the mercurial encyclopedist, the wretched man tells himself: "I made a mistake: he's just insolent because he is so rich. Suppose we try P***,[24] who publishes the *Almanac of the Muses*; couldn't he fit my verses somewhere into that? Then I might rise to the honor of small-format publication, and my name could be placed in the *Little Almanac of Great Men*."

The author makes his entrance in the next bookshop like a prospective purchaser; an affable expression broadens on everyone's face; young Fanchette runs up to him, and gives him as deep a curtsy as can be made to someone who has no coach at the door.

"What can we do for the gentleman? We have everything, all best quality: novels by Marmontel and bonnets from the mercer, I mean Mercier; different kinds of dramas: do you need a play, by any chance? A tragedy by Durozoy . . ."[25]

"I don't need them, Mademoiselle, I have come here to offer you a manuscript . . ."

"Oh Maman, the gentleman is an author; do come speak to him, or he will go and ambush Papa."

A woman of repellent mien now steps forward, while the little comedienne slips behind her mother to give a kiss to a glib-tongued buffoon who has just come into the shop,[26] thus cuckolding the poor author.

"What do you have there? Let's see your manuscript."

"Poetry, Madame."

"Poetry! All we ever see is poetry! Only this morning, I had to turn down three dozen verses brought in by the lackey of a lord who gives quatrains as tips, and poems for wages."

"But you see I have prose as well: a philosophical novel."

"You wretch, have you come here to bankrupt us? A philosophical novel! Get out at once, or I will hit you over the head with *The Incas.*"

The poor devil has barely escaped the wrath of Megaera. However, hunger is threatening him now. "Let's see," he muses, "what about D***?[27] He is venturesome, he has been in the Bastille not once but twice: he will be the person to whom I sell my forbidden book."

He now goes into D***'s shop and speaks with an air of mystery: "I come to you to open my portfolio," says he, "because I know the major avenues you have for trade. Take one look at this . . ."

The treacherous bookseller welcomes him, examining every fold of the briefcase: "Fine—very fine—excellent; I will be in touch; give me your address; this will sell quite nicely; I must have you write to publishers in Holland."

Feeling like a prince, the author goes home to his garret; his landlord, lurking in the hall, flatters himself that he will soon get paid; the wine-merchant brings a bottle of wine in expectation of the same; the baker weighs the bread rather more generously, though bread bought on credit tends to be the lightest and stalest in his bakery.

Two days later, D*** arrives—with Hope, that false and foolish virgin, riding his crooked shoulders—and as he enters, gives a smile to the assembled imbeciles: oh yes, he will bring people soon; he can't commit himself now. Nevertheless, our author keeps writing, polishing, working; midnight bells ring out, and he has hardly got between the white sheets procured for him thanks to D***'s visit when there comes a knock at his door. He opens the door: "On behalf of the King!" Enter a police officer, accompanying Henry and Receveur:[28] they force open his desk and chain him in irons . . .

There, he is sold to the police, his manuscripts are seized, and he is dragged to the Bastille; de Launay jumps with joy at the sight of this increase in the number of his unhappy victims. Bemoaning his misfortune, the writer curses his parents for never having made him learn a useful profession. Meanwhile D***, who has already had the manuscripts copied and printed, sells them clandestinely; and the starveling recovers his liberty only to walk around like the late Selius and die in a tooth-drawer's bed of the Hôtel-Dieu hospital.[29]

O honest soul, lured to put down your thoughts in writing by the hope of helping your fellow man; o reckless youth seduced by the deceiving smiles of vanity—behold the fate that awaits you. Ah! If there still be time, if your arms are not yet weak from habitual sloth, put your first scrawls into the fire. Pick up a spade or bend your back over a useful plow, return to the field, make yourself useful to the honest farmer; earn the suffrage of your peers, and learn the generosity to despise both the praise so economically dispensed by jealous men of letters to their writer colleagues and the pensions by which the swamp-owner buys the silence of the frogs.[30] What can you gain by writing? Pale hunger will hunt you down, and anxiously complaining creditors pursue; you will wither away your youth in fantasies of prosperity and feverish desires; the frosts of age will coagulate in your weary brain and whatever remains of your spirits. This is when the memory of the past eats away at you, the present overwhelms you, and attempts to envisage the future drive you to despair.

No sooner had the reverend father[31] set foot in Geneva, than children followed him around because of his robe, booksellers showed him the door at sight, and his landlord threw him out for not paying the bill. Rejected, dying of hunger, the reverend father was about to end his life in the river Rhône, when by chance he happened to meet a poetry-loving Representative. This was a person who took pride in himself as an amateur, and introduced himself as a patron of the arts.

A patron! Now that's a different kind of plague. A bookseller is nothing in comparison: the bookseller may insult and outrage you continually, but if one fine day the tricks of his fellow booksellers boost your reputation, the bookseller is immediately humanized, crawling and courting you. But a patron never becomes human.

First of all, the patron must read your works and submit them to his judgment, as these literary boobies are obsessed by a mania for judging, and this is their motive for protecting you.

"Such-and-such a line of verse does not please me; or this sentence is baroque; or the concept is commonplace: not new, and worst of all not striking; or the expression is not apt; or you are mistaken. Another writer I protect, A***, has demonstrated the contrary: come prepared to defend yourself, since he will certainly not allow you this opinion; he is a man of steady principles, and carries everything before him. Though perhaps, should you disagree with him, there may be no great harm in that, as a matter of fact. Literary arguments amuse me: I love to see two authors, fire in their eyes, attacking each other's broadside feathers, glossing away with vigor, their breasts heaving with a plethora of words, ready to spring. I applaud each peck of their beaks, for these tragicomic scenes stand out in a country where we have no cockfights. But nevertheless, you might change this one passage. Believe me, I am an expert as you know. The rest works fine; come and read your tragedy for the duchess, and you shall take supper with her ladies-in-waiting."

Once the reverend father had wrapped up his poems to suit his patron, they passed muster; as a result of this consideration he was given an old suit, his place was set at table, and his stanzas got printed. The patron sold them to his friends on behalf of the protégé: "Take one," he said, "poor devil, the verses aren't bad, now that I've corrected them; poor man, I felt sorry for him; in fact I wrote most of this stanza myself. Didn't have a pair of culottes to his name, and you could absolutely see his . . . Anyway, what's your own opinion?"

Nor is that all: patrons never forget the main chance, and insist on their protégés giving maximum profit: the Representative showed our man to a café, and insisted that he support the Representative Party. When the magnificent magistrate of the guard was informed, he summoned our man and insisted that he either speak in future for the Negatives, or leave the vast dominions of the illustrious republic within twenty-four hours.

"Twenty-four hours?" replied the Cordelier. "You are generous with your time, sir; twenty-four seconds will be plenty for me." And he reached the frontier a few minutes later.

To aid him in his flight, his generous patron gave him back all the copies of his work, without even a deduction for printing costs. These stanzas became the coin with which the reverend father reimbursed his hosts; and since Swiss tavern-keepers are no fonder of fine literature than French or German, the Cordelier preferred to be the guest of curates and castellans. He dined with the former and supped with the latter, like good minstrel Colin Muzet wandering in olden times from fortress to monastery, monastery to fortress.[32]

By following the edge of the lake, he arrived at last in Lausanne, and turning left, climbed up the Jura; after four or five hours on the road, he sighted the lake of Neuchâtel, and entered the little town of Yverdun. He made sure to deliver his stanzas to Colonel Roguin[33] and his wife, who had given poor Jean-Jacques asylum when the magnificent Bernese and Genevese exiled him from their lands. The Colonel paid splendidly for these stanzas about the countryside and cypresses adorning his old friend's tomb. The colonel's lady added several coins from her own purse, read through the stanzas, and ordered drinks for the enchanted Cordelier, who took his leave thanking heaven for the poetry that procured him money, the sight of a beautiful lady, and good wine. As a result of all this, he started to write again, and before he had reached Neuchâtel, he had already composed half his *Boulevard des Chartreux*.[34]

In Neuchâtel he found lodging at the Crown inn, still kept in those days by the lawyer Converd, who had not yet been made ambassador by the King of Prussia, but was already so distinguished an advocate and tavern-keeper that anyone could have predicted his advancement someday to the diplomatic corps. The Cordelier stayed at the Crown for a while, and might be there yet if gentlemen of the Venerable Class[35] had not informed the glorious Ministries that religion was under grave threat because lawyer Converd, showing no respect for Calvin, was sheltering a Cordelier. And so these religious magistrates decreed that he must depart Neuchâtel. As when in olden days Latona could not find a hospital or midwife for childbirth because Juno had made Mercury steal her purse, our poor reverend father was refused asylum by the earth. However, Le Locle proved a second Delos.[36]

You know full well, my dear reader, that pleasant valleys score the high peaks of the Jura in various directions; one particular valley, currently populated by thousands of rich clockmakers, was home forty years ago to a few dozen savage peasants living on oaten bread and cheese. This valley is called Le Locle; from the "Chaux-du-Milieu" to the beginning of the Erguel, which is to say about six leagues, it is now carpeted with handsome houses proclaiming the riches of the fortunate inhabitants, who send forth annually a hundred thousand watches. Kind hearts, the charms of natural wit, the pleasures of moderate luxury, the seeds of wise philosophy, religious toleration, and above all the love of humanity distinguish these lucky settlers from their neighbors: on the French side gross, ignorant, and miserable, but on the other side, toward the pleasant shores of Lake Neuchâtel, clever and of dubious religiosity. Moreover, Le Locle residents do not crowd house upon house; rather each has built at the center of his own little inheritance. Near enough to visit neighbors when they wish, far enough not to be inconvenienced by them, each family lives happily with its own. There we find the life and ways of the Golden Age: chaste, faithful, fertile wives; beautiful, healthy, loving, confident daughters; sweet pity[37] in both sexes, mother of all the virtues: in men's hearts, the sacred love of liberty, and a noble pride that conquers ministers of serfdom with a single glance.

Even in this prudent and fortunate company, however, the brilliant Jean Diedey[38] was a shining light: his love for the sciences, especially chemistry, went beyond the research prompted by vain and sterile curiosity; he penetrated the mysteries of optics, and his ateliers were full of wonderful telescopes; he had investigated gum shellac to learn the secret of fine varnish, and he made brasswork shine as brightly as Chinese colored porcelain. Nor did Diedey restrict his interests to the arts and sciences: he cultivated morality as well. A good father, he spared no expense for his children's education; a good husband, he let his wife direct and run his household. No man ever left Diedey's house without making libation to the Penates[39] with a glass of his good wine; no young girl crossed his threshold without an affectionate glance. Goodman Diedey, a priest of both Bacchus and Venus, served their altars more attentively and gaily than any local minister ever served the God Jehovah: his wife, content with being the mistress of the house indoors and out, never resented her husband's pleasures, and their fourteen-year-old daughter promised to become the image of her mother.

That honest citizen's home became a pleasant sanctuary for the reverend father; in this peaceful haven, he was entrusted with the son's tutorship; here too he finished his little poem *Le Boulevard des Chartreux*,[40] sketching with some accuracy the customs of various religious orders; but he omitted any mention of the sons of Saint Francis of Paola because of the memory of the oil with which he had been regaled by the Minims in Rome, and the unimportance and uselessness of that order, neither proprietary nor mendicant.

The reverend father's poetry was the talk of Diedey's neighborhood; one day the cure of Morteau was entertaining various Benedictines, a Cordelier, an Augustinian Recollect friar, and several Minims. The conversation happened to fall upon the poem that had just been born on this frontier. The Benedictine, belonging to an order always honored for its learning, smiled in silence; the Cordelier, celebrated for a love of gambling, dining, and women, laughed aloud; the Recollect, to whose humble garb the author had paid particular attention, eagerly doffed his cassock to defend his personal elegance; the Minims alone attacked the poem with all cannons blazing. Everyone was amazed at the end of the Franciscan Minim's diatribe, when he furiously exclaimed: "Not only that, he does not even mention one word about *us*."

I conclude from the Minim's example that Plato is a liar when he claims, "I would prefer no one to mention Plato, rather than call him a madman or a rogue." We all crave being talked about—this is what burned down the temple of Ephesus[41]—whether we are Minims or philosophers.

Meanwhile, all this time we were traveling off to Rome observing the priestly penitence, watching an amazing miracle, and helping to upset Calvin's city, our heroes have been sharp on the lookout, ready to pounce as soon as those chickens—foolish like our own foolish species—forgot that experience had taught them to distrust mankind, and thought only of eating food and making love: two needs that always conquer the best-founded fears. Driven by both needs, the rooster now reappears amidst his harem and prepares to make each of his Odalisques happy, regardless of all the arguments that have been published to inveigh against polygamy.

What a muddle has been made about polygamy by priests who have so long deceived the human race in Divinity's name, and by individual philosophers who deceive us today under their personal names! Master of his dunghill, the cock satisfies the burning desires of twenty feathered Messalinas;[42] nor does the bull in the field make any foolish promises about mounting a single cow; a stallion may rear on his powerful hocks before he decides whether to pick the brunette filly or the blonde, and abandons their plump haunches only to rush toward the gray mare. In spring the female partridge may share the task of hatching her brood with her timid cock, but in winter she returns to the community, and the following spring exercises her right to choose a new male partner. Constancy, that virtue of the impotent, is imagined by man alone. The appeal of a fresh young girl's moist eyes, parted lips, panting breath are supposed to be ignored, even if he might wish to profit from moments when his spouse, weak with pregnancy, thwarts his desires, and a wise and prudent Nature raises a mountain between them. Man must leave the fertile field fallow, and spread his sterile seed in a field where the grain has already turned yellow. And so the forsaken virgin must either fade like a neglected unplucked rose, or else submit her blooming charms to the sterile exertions of some miserable nun in the horror of a convent. Man, that proud being, himself incapable of creation, prefers to prevent nature's author, and deface nature's works. What! Must we either strangle dead the organs of fertility, or spread their seed on some monastery floor? Must we mistrust our own strengths because we are so much less fit for love than other creatures? Why should a pleasure-hungry female refuse us the ability to offer another woman the joys she once experienced, but which her degraded organs keep her from relishing now? Ah! Harvest-time is not the time to gather flowers.

O you who dare poison my young lover's soul with ludicrous depictions of the ghastly tortures of a chimerical hell at the very moment when I am falling into her arms, ready to break the rosy barrier that nature has once only, and so ineffectively, positioned to hinder my desires—May you become the target of some repulsive Capuchin's claustral furors! May you spend the rest of your days inconsolate, unable even to give young novices what you got from that father superior![43] But you whom love enchants—respect its pleasures forever: come, enjoy yourselves, and do not cast the slightest shadow on the delights of other people.[44] Observe how a sparrow caresses his companion: move not, lest you scare away fickle love in his flight. And watch the turtle-doves . . . Oh hold your breath! one puff, and their intoxication could turn to terror. Remember Tiresias! and as you cherish your own sexuality, do not interrupt the moment when lovebirds intermingle.[45]

Making no such reflections in this vein, Mordanes the barbarian expertly killed both cock and hen in the midst of their love-making; and although Tifarès shuddered and sighed to collect his greedy master's prey, his sentiment of pity[46] soon gave way to feelings of emulation. Tifarès's pity had been displaced by the same species of vanity that prompts the thief who tries to equal his captain; the bachelor who raves like a doctor; the friar of Saint-Côme who kills like a member of a medical faculty;[47] and the law clerk who steals like a prosecutor. In a single instant, his once-stupefied soul turned bloodthirsty. Innocent ducks were at play in a narrow ditch by the village; Tifarès now murdered four of these blameless victims, and the other ducks escaped only because they had immediately taken flight.

Delighted by the neophyte's debut, Mordanes immediately embraced Tifarès and foretold his brilliant future. "Someday," he added, "you will be worthy of your master; but first you must learn to run like the hare, as well as catch like the fox.

"The sun will soon be at tierce,[48] the peasants will come back from the fields to spend the noonday heat sheltered from its rays. Let us make haste to rejoin our companions: only there, Tifarès, where you will be praised in public, can you truly taste the first fruits of your triumph."

CHAPTER SEVEN

After Which, Try to Say
There Are No Ghosts . . .

HAVE YOU EVER been to Saint-Malo? I know nothing of the place, to tell the truth, and for once my ignorance proves my good faith; for you are not someone I would fib to, like travelers who lie with more impudence if they know their listeners have never been within a hundred leagues of the place in question. Ah well! Take me as I am: a man who has crossed the equator twice. If I had wished, I could have gone to hear the devil shrieking on the isle of Ceylon, as George Knox surely heard him during his long stay on that island; nor did anything in particular prevent me from going to Madagascar to see the sorcerers who counterfeit Saint Francis Xavier's miracles, or the original contract with the devil signed by the baron of Beniowski.[1] But in those days, all my curiosity was focused on botany and natural history, as you know; I would sooner have gone ten leagues to see two lemurs, than ten thousand to see Lucifer and his infernal court.

However, if you doubt the truth of everything I am about to tell you, just take yourself to Saint-Malo and get your own information about Captain Patrice Astruc,[2] own nephew to Chendard de la Girondais, who was carrying the bones of a Patagonian giant back from the Southern hemisphere when he was forced to toss them into the sea to appease a terrifying tempest, as is reported by dom Pernetty, defrocked Benedictine and Reverend Librarian to the King of Prussia. For your convenience in recognizing the aforesaid Captain Astruc, I will give you a geometro-zoographic description of him: this Captain Astruc is not a Patagonian himself, far from it, but a pygmy of the larger species: in 1774 he was four feet two lines 1'1" tall, measured with a surveyor's chain and using the newly standardized foot of the Royal Academy of Science.[3] The skin was ashen black; the hair was deficient, usually replaced by a wig or a velvet cap with gold embroidery; the opening of the eyes from one corner to the other, six lines long; the mouth, six inches; this mouth had once boasted twenty-two teeth, but only three were still to be seen: the left incisor on the upper jaw, the eyetooth on the same side, and the wisdom tooth in the corner of the lower jaw. Height of the head, between the base of the chin and the vertex, vulgarly known as the length of the face, was two inches eight lines; from the petrous apophysis of the right temple to the other bone of the same name, nine inches. Then if you draw a tangent through the top of the head, not counting his ears and nose, and reduce the perpendicular P-Q on this tangent by the lower extremity of the ethmoid bone across the capacity of the skull, you will have the smaller axis of the spheroid flattened by the poles enclosing the brain, cerebellum, and spinal cord of the said captain; and then, by an amazing conformity between theory and practice, you will find that the proportions of this smaller axis to the greater are :: 277:278. Let everything you have already taken *a priori*—the theory of the moon by dom Barthélémy, Benedictine of the Academy of Bordeaux, and d'Osembrai's squaring of the circle—be calculated into the anterior surface of the said captain's nose, and you will easily determine that this is a lemniscate curve of the fourth order resembling half a figure-eight intersected at its double squarable point, that its grid data are ydx-xdxr [aa-xx], and that each ear is a component of a logarithmic spiral whose pole is the auditory canal.[4]

Surely you now have an exact enough description of Captain Astruc for you to recognize him on sight. Do give him my compliments, and ask him to verify that I crossed the equator on his ship—and you might also inquire whether or not it is true that when he had landed in the bay of Pondichéry, his brother arrived from Saint-Malo expressly to inform him of a misfortune, two hours before being drowned in the bay. Perhaps you only half-believe the little captain; perhaps you are an inveterate pyrrhonist or out-and-out materialist, and then you will not believe him at all; perhaps you incline toward satire, and will laugh; but then he will show you his journal, and his brother's death certificate. What can you possibly reply?

Coincidence?

Ah! You are, perchance, a fatalist? Now then, unbeliever—read what happened to Mordanes and his companions in the deserts of Champagne. Read and believe: or rather, as a praiseworthy child of the Church, believe first and read afterward: no doubt the surest road to salvation.

But firstly let us keep in mind the words of the abbé des Fontaines[5] of sodomite memory: "narration must necessarily be simple, because whoever reports a fact must look and sound as if he had witnessed it. What kind of testimony could be given by a witness who seemed calculating, artificial, or brilliant? Wouldn't you think his testimony looked ridiculous? Does testimony look any less ridiculous if it is overemphatic, or loaded with figures of speech and eloquent ornaments? The rhetorician would be viewed as an impostor. Entertaining though it may be to sow handfuls of maxims and morals throughout a narrative, this contravenes the goal of the narrator: which is to make his story believable."

Very well! Let's put this into practice: lest evil temptation strike me again, let us copy the narrative of an ocular witness. But first, suppose we lighten our load. Into the fire with *Triumph of Tifarès*! that sounds too keen on describing ceremonies; the same goes for *The Troupe's Delight at the Theft of a Calf,* a portrayal of manners—into the fire, say I! *Philosophical discourse of Lungiet, which proves that as the Princes of Europe have freed their slaves against the rights of the people, the latter cannot legally object to the theft of their chickens by philosophers.* A pitiable dissertation: into the fire, the fire once more! *The Ghostly* ADVENTURE . . . Now that sounds like a good one: let's hear the witness.

—O the simplicity of his story! How naive! The twelve Apostles themselves were no simpler, one feels one is actually there, my hair is rising on my head; a cold sweat—dear heavens! . . . Someone just touched me; could that have been you?

—No, it wasn't. But very well! while my imagination takes a moment to recover, you shall copy out the following extract from Félicité's memoirs[6]:

"Just before sunset, we were walking along pell-mell, wondering which would be the best place to spend the night and cook our dinner in comfort, when we met two peasants coming toward us. They both stopped short and stared to see our donkey carrying a white baby calf with a red star on its forehead: 'Father,' said the younger to his companion, 'God and the Holy Virgin forgive me, here's our own white Godin: it's him, I know him as if I had made him with my own hands; methinks these gentlemen . . .' 'Keep quiet,' said the greybeard; 'there's more than one white calf in the world; our curate is not the only black coat in the diocese. Greetings to you, gentlemen: make haste! You still have three quarters of an hour to go before you reach the next village, but there at the sign of Saint Nicholas you will find a good inn, the best in all

France.'—'Father, by the late Saint John, as I am a Christian, it must be our calf.'—'Try to keep quiet, and never insult travelers carrying firearms.' The old man obviously recognized his own calf, but his own advanced age and Mordanes's terrifying appearance prompted him to dissemble. He may also have wished for his neighbors' advice before making any further claim, and must have thought it would be easy to catch up with us in the nearby village where he supposed we would spend the night.

"But the experienced Mordanes had overheard everything the boy said, and began planning for our safety once the sun sank below the horizon and we were out of the peasants' sight. We took the road on the left, toward woodland, determined to travel for at least four more hours. 'These peasants will rush home quickly,' Mordanes declared, 'and they will not waste time looking in the village for their missing calf. The whole community will be armed with pitchforks and cudgels to track us down; let us flee, since the fight will not be equal. Prudence is the better part of valor; we would be disemboweled by yokels, history would not say a single word about the fight.'

"Mordanes's speech made so much sense that no one claimed the satisfaction of rebuttal. The night was moonless, the stars were shining bright, like courtiers away from the brilliance of their prince; the light was enough for us to see fairly well, with no fear of being seen. We walked in silence. Bissot lent me his arm and stole a few kisses from me now and then. Lungiet walked ahead of us, leading my mother and caressing her as tenderly as anyone can do while on the move.

"After we had proceeded alongside the woodland for over two hours, Mordanes believed we had gone far enough from our calf's fatherland. He was about to decide on a place to strike camp when the donkey suddenly shied away and threw down Tifarès, who was holding his halter. Mordanes was instantly on the alert, knowing our donkey, and well aware that he was not a skittish animal; but he could see nothing. He did, however, hear some kind of murmur, so he chased the donkey forward in hopes of finding a spring or rivulet. The animal trembled as it moved ahead, resisting more than Balaam's ass when the Lord's angel appeared before her with a flaming sword and let loose her eloquent tongue.[7] Admittedly our donkey did not utter a word, but he testified to his fear so strongly that we were all frightened, even the bravest among us. Once he had entered the edge of the copse, no matter how hard Mordanes beat him, no matter how Tifarès pulled at his halter, the animal stood stock-still, bracing his legs so hard that it was impossible to make him go any farther.

"But then the halter broke, and how frightened were you, unfortunate Tifarès! You half-turned to your right, and what did you see then? A fire! only forty feet away, surrounded by a legion of squatting ghosts whose horrific mutterings were accompanied by the flutters of a black flag sprinkled with skulls and crossbones, waving in the breeze. You fell down on your knees, your long face grew an ell, your little round eyes opened wide, your mouth gaped, your stomach shriveled, your scrawny neck stretched. Indeed, Tifarès, coward that you are, how could you not be terrified, since the intrepid Mordanes himself was not free from fear? Mordanes's hair was standing so far on end that it lifted up his hat, and his dog had slunk between his legs.

"My mother fancied she might approach the Sabbath, and promised herself she would make Lucifer's acquaintance.[8] I am not so hardy as Voragine—so I hastily threw myself into Bissot's arms and grabbed him wherever I could, as one grabs hold of any branch when one is frightened. I could not be convinced to let go of the snake, that cunning beast, for quite some time: my whole fate depended on this moment. My actions therefore prevented my lover Bissot from making a full analysis of the adventure. Lungiet announced that we were seeing invalids cured by the blessed Pâris,[9] and assured us that this was a miracle, since miracles are always accomplished with numerous contortions and grimaces. Abbé Séché was completely puzzled; and as for Abbé Séchant, I could not really understand whatever he was saying.

"Meanwhile, our chieftain the brave Mordanes—he does love to be called that!—loaded both barrels of his gun and advanced as boldly as any poltroon trying to look intrepid well may do, ashamed of having revealed any weakness. He had taken only a few steps forward when he felt something grab his legs; his courage now failed him completely; and all our company's hearts froze to hear the tone of his cry: 'Who goes there?'

"'Alas, Sir Ghost! do not eat me,' moaned a faint, feeble voice barely recognizable as the terrified Tifarès, lying flat on the ground.

"'Poltroon of a dog! a plague upon you,' shouted the embarrassed fierabras Mordanes.[10] He now recovered, took a few steps closer to the astonishing creatures, and paused in contemplation: he was unable to make any sense at all of their incomprehensibly elongated heads, murmurs and ongoing wails.

"While Mordanes stood thus contemplating the enemy, Séchant harangued our horrified troupe like any ancient orator: 'Fear, dear friends, is the silliest and least reasonable of all the passions at play in the human body. Which nobody can deny—since fear both increases one's danger and eliminates one's ability to resolve the problem. How many armies have been cut into pieces after ill-advised flight when they would have experienced mere setbacks, or even won the victory, had they only confronted the enemy! I might easily offer you a thousand examples, taken from every age and nation. How many armies have we seen face each other at sunset, only to steal quietly away in the night, leaving both camps abandoned in the morning, to general amazement! *Panic* terrors, as such fears were called by wise antiquity because Pan, god of the forests, so enjoyed inspiring them. I myself refrain from either contesting or supporting this etymology. Nothing I say makes any difference, but if I dared, I would opine that the cause of our alarm is a troupe of Satyrs and Ægipans,[11] innocently diverting themselves with Nymphs. One might even notice a buck-like smell, nor need that smell surprise you, because since half the Ægipans' bodies resemble those warm-blooded creatures, their species naturally exudes the same odor as our nanny-goats' husbands. Whatever our conjectures, however, the main point for us now is verification: a decision dictated by both honor and prudence. Indeed, there is no point in our trying to escape, if these singular creatures should turn out to be gods, demi-gods, quarter-gods, or even one-eighth gods. Far better to appease them by our prayers.

"'But if these creatures be malicious spirits created by the evil principle for human torment, I have not forgotten how to perform exorcism! And I promise to banish them. Moreover, our captain is leading us forward, and it would be disgraceful of us to abandon him. What would posterity say of us? What would our contemporaries think of us? What would the *Courrier of Europe* and the *Gazette of Holland* say?[12] History shows us the severe punishments given legions who desert their commanders: in Europe, the Romans decimated them and threw one out of ten off the Tarpian Rock; the Gauls cut off their noses and ears and drowned them in a ditch; the Turks strangle them; the Dutch skin them alive. In Asia and Africa, they get impaled. The French shoot deserters, the Germans beat them senseless, the English flog them, the Spanish excommunicate them, the Russians send them to Siberia after giving them the knout: deserters are vilified by the historians of every nation. And so, by the enormity of our danger we learn the greatness of courage: O my friends! The die is cast: this little patch of woods is our Rubicon.[13] Séché, Bissot, stand beside me, we will form a battalion with Mordanes in the front line, while Lungiet and Tifarès bring up the rear, and our women stay with the baggage. Such has ever been the strategy of prudent generals: should the front line fall back, it could rally behind the second line, take a break, and return to the fray.'

"O the power of a fine harangue! Hardly had Séchant finished this speech than the least valiant felt their courage returning. Even Tifarès: timid Tifarès daringly took his place at Lungiet's left hand, while lean brunette Voragine was inspired to cry out: 'No! I refuse to stay back; my petticoats shall be your banners. Have I not sharp fingernails, and pointy teeth? O d'Eon![14] Illustrious Amazon, glory of our sex, thou who art seen sometimes as dragon, sometimes as diplomat, O inspire me! Allow me to invoke thee now. And you, my friends, banish shameful fear, and let us follow the hero who leads the fore like a ram at the head of the flock.'

"'As for me,' cried I, 'I shall stay with the donkey, 'but oh my mother! If you must succumb to be raped by a godless crew, never fear I will abandon you; no, I would surely hasten to share your burdens.'

"At this point, having listened in silence to their generals' harangues, our band all moved forward with a terrible shout; the echoing woods resounded and multiplied the fearsome noise. Encouraged by his soldiers' advance, Mordanes soon halved the distance between himself and the enemy army, and bellowed at the top of his most dreadful voice: 'Who goes there? Who goes there? Who goes there?'

"The shock of Mordanes's outcries interrupted the murmurs of the camp members, who were now disturbed and confused. Rising on their hind legs you might have seen thirty beasts whose reddish fur, upright ears, long tufty beards, and long white twisted tails made them look in the faint glow of the fire like some species of great ape.

"Mordanes's heart failed him. Séchant was convinced this must surely be Faun and his satyrs at play on the greensward, though he wondered at the flapping sound made by the flags in the breeze, because he had never read that satyrs used an oriflamme, and he racked his brain for an appropriate classical quotation. Meanwhile, the need to look brave brought Mordanes back to life, and he spoke these terrifying words: 'O ye who come to celebrate in the wilderness your ridiculous rituals—sorcerers, devils, genies, satyrs, thieves, or whoever you may be . . . Who are you? Stand and deliver! or I will fire into your group.'

"'Yes! We are about to fire upon you!' shrieked Voragine.

"The satyrs now began to writhe about most peculiarly, frightened by all these threats and by the sudden appearance of armed men in a copse where they had thought they could safely abandon themselves to their nocturnal rituals. Several lying down by the fire, whom we had not seen before, now got up and increased their number, and you would surely have thought they were rising from the earth's very womb."

—Fie upon you! This narrative is so cut and dried!... You tell it as if you were counting your rosary... Why are there no reflections? No comparisons?

—Too naked for you? Write it down this way: It all happened just as Ovid tells us when Cadmus, having killed the serpent Python, tossed his teeth into the sea in order to obey the oracle... (*Metamorphoseon, lib. I*)...[15]

—A plague on your citation! Author, devil, whichever you may be, it is finally time for you to give us information: who are these phantoms that have put such fear into your heroes?

—I *was* going to tell you, until you cut me short; I have a temperament like Cardenio's, I cannot abide interruptions. If some fool makes as if to interrupt me, my eyes begin to dart from side to side, my eyebrows furrow, my chin falls on my chest, I start thinking about Queen Madásima, the pen falls from my hands; and I need at least five or six chapters to get back on track.[16] Let's see—what shall I say in the next chapter? Physical science, now there's a fine field for digressions... Nothing actually keeps me from informing you all about the nature of movement and the causes for the refraction of light, as well as the weight of the atmosphere. I might prove this last property to you by the barometer, the clyster syringe, Heron's fountain, and the aerostatics of Montgolfier.[17] In this work—where I intend to touch on everything—I have not yet discussed Blanchard's aeromaritime voyage,[18] let alone inflammable gas, and gas would naturally push me to digress brilliantly on chemistry. Our second-rank ladies of fashion could follow me perfectly, as they are always musing on gas and mephitic air. So nothing prevents me from teaching you about the production of gas by the use of vitriolic acid and iron filings; or how the gas that reaches all the fibers of your entrails therefore causes the nutrition and development of all your bodily parts. Nor would anything keep me from explaining how Nature's author, with one puff of light and elastic air into the uterus, slowly expands this once-flaccid and shriveled hydrostate, animating the embryo that has barely begun to swim in seminal fluid and quickly becomes an absurd balloon, ricocheting across the surface of another balloon that itself pirouettes in equilibrium on its own axis, as a spinning top revolves around another balloon: in conclusion, inflammable gas is the universal principle; everything is balloon in this our world.—Howsoever, I think it is better to explain Newton's theory to you first, and teach you how much his mechanical physics owes to Galileo and his disciple Torricelli... Although before anything else, you must read the two volumes in quarto by the barometrist Deluc,[19] citizen of Geneva, Reader to Her Majesty Charlotte of Mecklenburg Strelitz, queen of England, wife of the most gracious king George III and mother to . . .

—Ha! The madman! O the damned author!

—Eh? You think I jump from pillar to post? Very well then: to prove I can concentrate, from now on I will not desert an author until I have exhausted him. I will show you in detail all thirty-seven volumes of Deluc's letters to Queen Charlotte; then you'll understand what an ignoramus M. de Buffon is, and how the Bible, Moses, and the Flood are . . .[20] Ay ay ay! He is strangling me . . . aargh, he has cut my breath off.

CHAPTER EIGHT

The Denouement

Ha! You threw my book into the fire? No problem, I swear, no problem—I had ten thousand copies printed. Burning my book! O the horror of it! Going to the Bastille would make my reputation. Ah well, since you spoil me like a favorite child, I will pick up the thread of my narrative, and unwind it to the core. I should probably start with the reply made to Mordanes by the beings whose entire lives depended on one flexor movement of his index finger.

"Do not shoot, whoever you may be," they cried, "beware! Your salvation depends on it—you would be *ipso facto* excommunicated! We are all priests, or at least unworthy Capuchin friars, making a pilgrimage to Our Lady of Avioth[1] to accomplish a long-ago vow sworn by a father superior who felt an urge to become Cardinal. We have come on our voyage barefoot, camping out under the stars; early tomorrow morning we are supposed to say Mass in a village two leagues from here, so we are reciting the offices, and our young brothers sleep by the fire as we wait to do Matins. So be sure not to harm us if you are Christians, but give us some money in honor of the blessed Saint Francis and come warm yourselves at our fire."

"We are most willing to do so," Mordanes replied. "We too are on a pilgrimage to Our Lady of Luxembourg, to accomplish a vow we made in great danger . . . We must admit that you did nearly frighten us, but nevertheless we are happy to join you, and share with you whatever scanty provisions we take along on pilgrimage. Tifarès, go find the donkey. We shall all sit down and feast with these goodly Church fathers."

Tifarès now calls out, running back toward the donkey: "It is Capuchins, mademoiselle, Capuchins."

"So they are not really ghosts? Are they raping my mother?"

"Not at the moment," says Tifarès, pulling forward the donkey, which preferred to come closer rather than be left behind on his own.

The donkey was quickly unloaded, and soon became friendly with the Capuchins. A rivulet invited him to quench his thirst, the abundant and tender grass appealed to him; after a good long wallow, he began on his supper, while Tifarès and the Capuchin cook rekindled the fire to prepare supper for their masters.

CHAPTER NINE

Nocturnal Adventures That Deserve to See the Light of Day, and Worthy of an Academician's Pen

IF I EVER some day write an epic poem—or somehow find my imagination fertile enough to write a novel without borrowing episodes from my colleagues right and left—then I promise to let my heroes sleep in peace from sunset to dawn every night. Wouldn't you say daytime allows plenty of time for cut-and-thrust swordplay? At the rate of one arm and leg per minute, which is easy for a goodfellow after a night's sleep, the daylight hours are surely sufficient to obtruncate an army of fifty thousand men, even at the winter solstice. Whenever inclined to spread worldwide death and destruction, I awaken my Achilles before daybreak and send him out in the killing fields with no break until nine o'clock; at nine, he pauses for tea with nicely buttered toast, as the "Annalist of the Eighteenth Century" elegantly informs us is the English custom;[1] then after tea has been drunk and the newspapers read, the fighting continues until three o'clock. The following two hours are plenty for an active man's dinner and digestion; then from five o'clock to dusk, enough time remains for him to chop off heads and immortalize himself if the weather is fine. Do admire the brilliant flourishes of my imagination: rather than restrict my hero to a single deadly weapon like a dread medical doctor, I vary the genre of my hero's exploits, and do not fear to reveal them in the light of day.

My delicacy is a disadvantage in one respect, because nocturnal surprises are so useful for an author. But everybody knows there is something annoying about them, though I can't say why; they seem more characteristic for a highwayman than a war hero. Surely anyone who invents his own heroes should make decent people of them. Aren't there enough rapscallions, fools, traitors, calumniators, and cowards in the world without stuffing them into our books? On the other hand, if a military surprise is absolutely necessary, our modern generals make it easy to arrange for high noon; the verisimilitude of your surprise is then all the greater. Basically, the whole surprise genre is a simple one. I can give you an army in retreat with two strokes of my pen. Listen closely:

The two armies that must decide the fate of both Brutiens and Galles[2] were now but a league apart, the sun had traveled a quarter of its career, and fierce Mars, thirsty for bloodshed, had just stripped off the godly armor forged for him by the cuckold Vulcan, who works night and day in a Sicilian cave for his heavenly wife's lovers and bastards. Brandishing his lance and a barbed spear like the ones used by Africans, the god of war tapped his foot and foamed at the mouth, impatient for the moment when he would be awash in human blood. Just so, impeded by the tight virgin charms of a young nun, will a hearty Cordelier gasp, sweat, squirm, and shudder with rage. Sometimes he may use his hand to guide his lance, then again use the strength in his loins to push it; the bed trembles under these vigorous blows; the only thing that can calm the lubricious ardor of the intrepid Franciscan is blood flowing from the broken hymen and merging with a torrent of semen; and he bathes in this mixture several times, withdrawing only to feel anew the burning desire to plunge back in. Meanwhile Apollo, never any too fond of Mars, has taken wicked pleasure at sunburning his warlike colleague in order to increase his ardor, while in Jupiter's closet Fate has donned her spectacles, eager to read the names of mortals whose competition to kill or maim each other would be contributing to Olympian entertainment later in the day.

Having already exploded a landmine under Sloth and set traps for Stupidity, Surprise is quite touched by seeing the God of War nearly dead of devastating thirst. She has always been on close terms with him, a topic for occasional gossip on Olympus. She approaches him on tiptoe, covers him with her gray cloak, and addresses him in more or less the following terms: "O Mars, thou who art aflame with thirst for blood, whose steely teeth crush the brittle bones of earth's rash children—no! I cannot suffer thee to die victim to cruel hunger, as if thou were some Gascon poet. Pick up your divine tunic, wipe from your brow the drippy sweat, and soon you will discover that Surprise and Mystery, her husband, are entirely capable of depopulating this planet on their own, without the help of any god. I will have your bloodbath ready in just a moment."

Having spoken, she flies to the camp of the Brutiens.[3] Now the Brutien king had long made his brother kings tremble at his surpassing knowledge and valor: proficient in the art of destruction, Jupiter often entrusted him with his thunderbolt, and the Cyclops themselves had taught him to use lightning. Laughter and warfare had made this king the dean of princes and generals. All princes schemed for his support, and fixed their eyes upon his as if to ask anxious permission to declare war, while the daring young Khan of the Hermains[4] bowed before his genius, and feared to risk his nascent fortune against the old warrior's talents. The Brutien king calmly watched them quarrel, and intervened only to take a share of the booty. So may a lion whose senses have been cooled and impetuous ardor slowed by age allow strong young mastiffs to chase animals in his forest; he makes an appearance only after they find their quarry, to take the biggest share. The camp of this old lion of the North[5] was on a hillside, and the right flank was shielded by a wood; the left flank, by deep marshy swamps; countless brass cannons were loaded to project fire and cannonballs, so that the center was protected by a cross-fire. In this position did the old king wait for Chance, the blind man presiding over godly and human councils, to proffer him some favorable opportunity. In his camp ruled order and silence; the Brutien soldiers, having little to eat and little to wear, grown gray in army service, awaited their general's orders with the same confidence as the tripods of Olympus, which although endowed with movement and intelligence, stir only at Jupiter's command.

The commander of the army of the Galles,[6] Borcas, was unfamiliar with this prize-winning practice of warfare; nor did he show any sign of the sort of innate genius and impetuous ardor that lead to victory and conquest. Brought up in a frivolous, brilliant court, Borcas had been wafted to the head of the army as if by miracle, thanks to his prince's friendship and the sultanas' favor. His soldiers, hostile to discipline, acted as if they had joined the army to find independence and pleasure. Borcas's generals had brought all the luxuries of the capital in their train. Every one of them distrusted the leader they served, so each gave whatever orders he wished, hoping to find that his subalterns were pawns or accomplices interested in covering errors and insubordinations of their own. Disorder ruled in the camp of the Galles, and wild mirth could be heard around the altar of that fickle God: by day, prostitutes danced to the sound of the fifes and drums; by night, the unfortunate creatures gave the soldiers dreadful diseases that soon kept them from being in any condition to fight. A spirit of vertigo presided over Borcas's councils of war, and his tents, though open to every variety of pleasure, were closed only to discipline.

On the contrary, prudence alone ruled in the tent of old Pederastos[7]: eagle-eyed, ears alert, measured in action. The Brutien king maintained spies in his enemy's army, paying them well so that the information they gave him would be accurate. These spies had free access to him at any hour, and found his purse and his ear equally available. Surprise now takes the form of their most capable member, and slips unexpectedly into the tent, addressing William's son in the following words:[8]

"O Pederastos, has old age frozen the courage that has made you the terror of the neighborhood for so long? What can you possibly wait for, under these cowardly ramparts? Can you not see what weak and despicable enemies oppose you today? Such unworthy offspring of the heroes you defeated in your youth! Twenty years of peace have softened the Galles' delicate limbs and befuddled their courage. They care only for their preposterous toilettes, so the only qualifications they demand in their soldiers are the virtues of a valet, while their officers' talents are limited to judging a buckle or spotting the stain on a waistcoat. No longer are they that formidable nation trained for battle by fifteen centuries of bloody wars, and led by brave and honorable veterans. Noblemen who once led in combat now languish on their estates—or are given only subaltern employment,[9] unknown, obscure, and despised, while tax officials' sons purchase the serious responsibilities of warfare. National honor will never grow deep roots in their ungrateful soil. Stop taking unnecessary precautions! Present yourself to the fray, and your enemies will scatter like dust before a puff of the North Wind."

This speech warms the cockles of the once-brilliant fire in Pederastos's heart; he chooses the best men in his army and entrusts them to his brother.[10] The prince his brother is at the stage in life when men no longer seek to gain, but have not begun to lose anything, and his soldiers have confidence in him. He is the adoration of his army and nightmare of the enemy: prudence precedes him, probing with a stick the ground on which he will walk, while activity follows fast on his heels.

"Leave immediately," orders this prince's master, "not a moment to lose; the Galles our enemies do not expect you, they are abandoning themselves to senseless delight. Bloody their pleasures, and may they drink their own blood with the wine that so intoxicates them."

The prince departs the minute Pederastos has spoken. He turns past the wood where the right wing of their army was installed; this had been the outpost of scouts who had been harassing the enemy's flank for so long that they aroused only disdainful nonchalance. The Sun was just approaching the middle of its daily course; its winded horses begged a moment's rest, and the sun drew them to a halt, taking a moment to observe the Brutien prince's exploits. Surprise guides the Brutien prince to the left flank of the enemy troops; the Galles mistake him for those scouts infecting the woodlands, and they do not bother to take up arms. In any case, Borcas had no idea what was happening on the left side of his camp, as he was at table with his generals, who cared more about courting him than minding their brigades. Mars gives the signal, and a firestorm consumes the tents of the Galles' left flank, while Pederastos, coordinating his troops' movements with his brother's, brought his cavalry forward against the center. The rest of his army now follows; and thus he profits from his own expertise in the art of strategy he has developed: his soldiers form bold menacing rows as they emerge single file from undercover.

The Galles, attacked both in the center and on their flank, dare not confront their enemies; they abandon their tents, baggage, and cannons, which the Brutien prince soon turns against them. Borcas barely escapes, regretting the remains of his banquet, and the army of the Galles—once so brilliant and gay—now scatters and melts like snowflakes in the sunny rays of Mars.

Now look at that—that's a surprise! Here at noon, who would expect anything of the sort? How different from all those nocturnal surprises no one has ever actually witnessed! How I hurried toward the denouement! How I avoided digressions! How laconic I was! Who could have prevented me, for example, from describing the arms, the uniforms, the horses of both armies? Or telling you the genealogy of the leaders? Or other details that do not escape a clear-sighted historian by daylight, but at night are never seen by anyone at all? Indeed I myself have no fondness for nocturnal affairs, and if not for the veracity of my history, which compels me to portray people exactly as they are and narrate events as they happened, I would never have torn aside the dark veil that once concealed so many surprising actions from profane mortal eyes.

Capuchins, Bohemians, philosophers—everybody soon gets acquainted. Mordanes, who never saved for tomorrow because he collected his dues every day, acted as generously as any open-hearted prince giving rich courtiers the property of the poor. Watch him spread out his fat and plentiful provisions; the friars dance attendance, while one lights the fire, another draws clear, silvery water from the neighboring stream, and a third skins the calf. Tifarès and the Capuchin cook cut the calf up into cutlets, some to be fried in the pan, others grilled on the coals; they toss its head, mug, and feet into the stockpot; a spit turned by the alms collector and fastened to the back of the stockpot holds in a row the ducks, the hen, and her rooster. Just so at a bourgeois wedding, do the bride and groom vie with the guests in their eagerness to supply the feast. At last they all sit down to table, and the Capuchins have a second supper, with the best appetite in the world. Mendicants are like philosophers in this: their appetite is intermittent, re-born in hope of satisfaction. Everyone eats joyfully; the Father Superior orders up a barrel of sacristy wine, which they drain dry with every expectation that Providence will provide wine for her rituals. Soon a jug of whisky replaces the tapped cask; the ladies sing, the mendicants chant the chorus—without bleating, for priests can sing in more than one key, and their rumination in debauchery bears no resemblance to their pious mutterings.

Meanwhile conversation becomes livelier. Lungiet has actually laughed several times, the laughter that is born of gaiety, almost entirely free from malice. The ladies, whose knees were being felt up by various young preachers, grew aroused by succulent foods and strong wine; they swooned as they swallowed, while more than one novice's undergarments were already damp.

According to Félicité, the first to publish this instructive history, everything was going fine until that point—and surely would have turned out fine if Love, on his usual nocturnal run, had not happened to pass by, abandoning two young lovers who had just been married that morning.[11] At this late hour, Love was going to see an opera girl sell her first night to a young provincial who mistook her for a goddess. Cupid was in no hurry, as he was sure to find stupidity, satiety, and avarice in the beauty's chamber: bad company even for Love. The odor of food, the aroma of wine rose to the winged traveler's godly nostril. Straight away, he raised his head to peek above his blindfold, cheater that he is, just like dear Sally playing blind-man's bluff with me.[12]

At the center of the troupe, Love noticed a merry plump woman he knew quite well: that vigorous semi-fresh, if semi-faded, peasant woman who spends her life cruising the convents of Venus and the monasteries of monks. With her soft, uncovered bosom, half-closed eyes, and lips open to receive a voluptuous tongue; her half hidden charms, somewhat the worse for wear; and her intimidating lip, a double organ that permits her to satisfy two lovers at once and offer shelter to anyone who does not fear the enemy at his gate—this peasant woman was in fact the impure goddess Luxuria, now appearing to Love's view. It is Luxuria who invented the instruments our nuns use to console themselves for their foolish vows; she alone guides the skillful hand of our young ladies' fresh little chambermaids; she it is who forged the Pinto cannula and the golden spoon of the marquis de Villette;[13] she is the one who takes under her skirts the frequent offerings of schoolboys, and inspires that naughty habit which even Venus has such difficulty making them renounce in future years. Shameless Luxuria is her name, and she is related to Love.[14] She was now enlivening the feast, so that the donkey puckered up, roused by her sharp spurs; he seemed in the dim firelight to be mounted on five legs.

Love now swoops down upon this cousin's breast. Forgetting every delicate lesson his mother taught him, he prefers this profligate creature to the modest, sensitive nymph burning with impatience upon her bed of roses. So it happens—I must blush to admit—I do sometimes neglect my own tender, adorable darling, I occasionally climb Rosalie's or Durancy's stairs to pass the time at their tables with Laboureau and other whores' companions, waiting for champagne and lubricity to pique my senses, which have been rather dulled by sexual enjoyment. God though he may be, Love sits at table with both beggars and Luxuria: he takes the fiercest desires to heart, and is impatient for the moment when he can satisfy them.

Meanwhile, daylight was delaying that happy moment. Love is not particularly modest by nature, but at this moment he feared proud Psyche, whose jealous eye scans the horizon far and wide. He therefore resolves that the pleasures he promises himself must be shrouded in shadows. Sleep, following as always close behind, divines his thought and draws nigh. Love now commands Sleep to close the friar cook's eyes, and make everyone else in the troupe start to feel their eyelids grow heavy.

Obedient Sleep flutters his wings, which are composed of leaves the publishers have been unable to rescue from the bite of time spent in booksellers' attics. The heavy dust no sooner settles into the travelers' eyes than the old Capuchins start to snore as if at a sermon; the young ones yawn and stretch their arms; and each feels his way to a place he can sleep. Love promptly tosses Luxuria down on the ground. The universe silently, attentively watches them embrace; the earth quivers under their urgent strokes; an igneous fluid penetrates deeply between the impure goddess's thighs; she responds by moistening Love, who feels a mixture of attraction and repulsion for the pleasurable panting and broken breathing our ignorant doctors call hysterical vapors. Nor did the little love-god obstruct his lover's movements, since his wings held him suspended. He had experienced intense pleasure twenty times when a damp cloud arose from Luxuria's thighs, touched his fluttering wings, and drew him down motionless into her arms at last, his head to one side.

Afterward Love hovers nearby for a moment; taking advantage of this, the insatiable goddess staggers to her feet and banishes Sleep from several members of the company.

Lying near the father superior, Séché and Voragine were the first to feel the goddess's goads; Séché's flabby breast offered her spurs no resistance, but after an instant he fell back into cowardly sleep. Not so Voragine. For some time now, Mordanes had been maintaining a semi-secret connection with her; as soon as her frail companion began to snore she began creeping on all fours toward the spot where she had last seen him. Meanwhile, urged on by identical desires, the vigorous Mordanes was crawling toward Voragine; but each was so terrified by the noises made by the other, that they crossed paths without pause or recognition.

Luxuria could not but smile at the error of her favorites. She first rewarded them by leading voracious Voragine to innocent Tifarès: Voragine touches him, recognizes him, and places his hand into a vast field where it has free rein; her own busy hands happily intensify the miasmas of Luxuria; soon she has made Tifarès ready to lose himself in that immensity, and their tanned hides and pointy bones interlock, rub away at each other, and burst into flame. So it is that if in a bitter frost the withered boughs of two elderly chestnuts are shaken by impetuous winds, the flame breaks open the woody capsules, the sparks explode; and the lost traveler trembles at the sight of the sheltering forest on fire. Just so did Voragine and Tifarès spread their phosphoric sparks. Attracted by the phenomenon, brother Gabriel—who had not been entirely unaware of Tifarès's steady stares and little round eyes—approaches the electric hearth and after a moment, realizes what is going on under his very nose. Filled with jealous envy, he leaps on Tifarès's back and robs him of the precious jewel he had been saving for the pastrychefs and pastrymaids of Chartres.

Forgive me, reader, for fixing your eyes on this lewd trio; let us rather turn our gaze toward some pleasanter object. O divine Mordanes, what have you meanwhile been up to? Did your flame die or blow away as smoke because your quest was fruitless? No doubt a possibility, had not Luxuria come to the rescue, and led your vagabond hand to the aperture of the father superior's cowl: your confusion was fostered by his bushy white beard—the glory of the order—since with the passage of years the good man's gaping mouth was entirely bare of teeth. Mordanes mistakes the sacred beard for the slippery fleece of his lady companion, spreads open the cape, and obliterates the epiglottis of the venerable father superior.

Dignified, venerable old man! What a surprise for you, shocked awake by this profane violation! You try to cry for help, but alas! The enormous morion[15] left your jaw no liberty to do anything beyond a light shiver every time your enemy took a break; you believe yourself free; vain error, the outrageous ram withdraws only to attack. His bawdy is piqued and his ardor increased by a few scanty roots, remains of your former dentition. Finally a pale liquid torrent, propelled as if by a fire-engine, penetrates your sacred larynx: you try to pronounce *excommunicatur,* your voice dies on your lips, and your only recourse is to grab at the vacillating reservoir of this polluting pool. Then Mordanes—somewhat calmed by his ejaculation—gives you a few moments' respite, and you say to him in a fatherly tone: "Alas! my son, midnight has come and gone, but how do you expect me to sing the holy mass tomorrow?" Mordanes, surprised to hear this babble issuing from his dear Voragine's organ, was tempted to declare a miracle; but he had had so much to drink that he put it down to Capuchin monkeyshines, turned over, and went back to sleep.

Love had performed wonders while Lady Luxuria was enjoying these quid pro quos: he aimed his arrow straight into young Félicité's heart, and waved his torch over Bissot, whose noble destiny he foresaw. Sleeping at the feet of the Bohemienne girl, the philosopher felt his strength and faculties increase: he approaches, and a lascivious kiss becomes the signal for amorous struggle. His hand, almost unresisted, pushes aside her kerchief, and gets as far as the little rosebuds which had turned hard and organic on their ebony breasts, stiffening under his amorous tickling fingers, a sure sign of defeat to come. Seizing this precious instant, Bissot dives into his charmer's embrace. At first a slight obstacle opposes his burning desires; his flame redoubles as he tries to get past it; aroused by her trivial discomforts, Félicité tries to find a solution, and ends by seconding his efforts; they outdo each other in pressing on, the hymen breaks, and now the two of them form but one body. Love! Love! You yourself guided the philosopher and placed a few sharp pebbles under his lover's dusky behind, thus offering her from the start a habit acquired only through long experience by so many others. Félicité is now no longer a maid; a wandering egg traverses the Fallopian tubes, and Voragine becomes a baby philosopher's grandmother.

Satisfied, Love seems to have forgotten his own wings; even Luxuria seems exhausted by the work of this celebrated night, and they all flatter themselves that they can spend the rest of the night in peace; but such is the fate of unfortunate mortals, that no sooner is a god weary of tormenting them, than five or six more divinities, resenting his repose, awaken him and rob him of this one relaxing moment.

Jealousy—for all Olympus came to the Champagne foothills that night—Jealousy, say I, seeking Love everywhere, deserting him never, had the misfortune to find him here in the middle of the shorn, bearded, Capuchinized horde. Instantly her imagination starts to work, exaggerating the pleasures available to sixty Capuchins and a dozen Bohemians. The goddess unites them two by two, three by three, four by four—in a circle, in a battalion square, in a corner, in a phalanx—in a word, she combines them more ways than Kalio composes in his tactics of troops in their battle orders.[16]

Nor does Jealousy omit the gray donkey and greasy kitchen-boy in her calculations. "Voragine is just as ardent as Pasiphaë," she muses, "and accustomed as she is to Mordanes, she needs no labyrinth to submit her vast scraggy charms to the donkey.[17] But if only I had been here from the beginning! Capuchins have all the fun; these friars take on a whole squadron of houris while I, wretched goddess that I am, wander among the tombstones; I am the one who gets bitten by the snakes of the cruel Eumenides; I follow hot on Love's trail, but the ingrate no sooner catches sight of me than he takes wing and runs away: indeed, my efforts to keep him seem just to scare him away!

"Ah well," she adds to quarrelsome Zizanie, who is carrying her torch and dagger,[18] "at least I shall have my revenge. Just take a look at Love and Luxuria, drunk on pleasure and the smoke from their holocausts. Should all the other gods have victims galore, while you and I are the only divinities men neglect? Never, as the gods be my witness! I swear it by Juno's moustache!" For once Jealousy gets started, she swears like a carter stuck in the mud. At first she is sweetly timorous; she resorts to weeping; then she has a fit of the sulks; she becomes insufferable; and finally she abandons herself to furies whose consequences are impossible to predict.

Jealousy thus examines each heart with close attention, and judges abbé Séchant the most likely to welcome her appropriately. She had already alerted the good priest to Voragine's and Mordanes's intrigues, and even made him mention them to Séché, who for some weeks now had been perusing natural law in hope of finding reasons why Mordanes might be persuaded to respect Voragine as his exclusive property. An open attack on the dread Mordanes would have been dangerous, and perhaps ineffective, but writing a book seemed easier, and Séché settled on this method. He did in fact publish soon afterward a little volume called *Counts-Monopole*,[19] recently translated into English and printed by F. Becket, bookseller and descendant of the famous Archbishop of Canterbury.[20]

Séché demonstrated in Part One of his work, using the law of *primo occupanti*, how a man can acquire possession of a woman; then, using the laws entitled *On Property Conservation*, he proved that the man cannot lose the woman unless he expressly renounces her, whether contractually like those who rent, lease, or sell their wives and mistresses, or else through an *intervivos* gift, or thirdly by testamentary bequest. Next he demonstrated that the custom of civilized nations is for this kind of movable not to be seized except in exchange for money or merchandise; that throughout history, entrepreneurs have always amassed a certain quantity and rented them, as we see is the practice with sedan chairs, cabs, vinaigrette two-wheelers, etc., and marked them with their crests and liveries; whence the necessity for police inspectors, bishops' mitres, dispensations for prohibited degrees, obligatory payments to the pope for marrying one's cousin, etc., etc. . . . That all governments associate with these entrepreneurs through special privileges; that great noblemen have not disdained participation in such profitable trafficking either underhandedly or openly, and that the traffic can be practiced without derogation, witness the cases of the maréchal de Richelieu and M. de Bertin;[21] and this business is so well established that not one of a hundred thousand maidenheads is lost without money changing hands. Thus Séché concluded that maidenhead is real property, and that he who owns one cannot be deprived of it without violating *property ownership*, the first branch of natural law. Part One has fifty printed pages, including a preface and preliminary discourse.

Séché then shows in Part Two that consensual rapine or seduction is contrary to personal safety, meaning the persons of the proprietors: because it is only too common for professional seducers, endowed with the talent to *enthrall* women, to communicate various noxious qualities to them, which are then transmitted to the real owner of a woman's person, which is contrary to natural right, because in these moments a woman no longer possesses herself unless she be with her husband or habitual lover, since *ab assuetis non fit passio.*[22] Part Two is about sixty pages long, including a twenty-five-page title.

Séché shows in Part Three that liberty of action is also infringed by such behavior, since nature has made this carriage a one-seater, and the natural proprietor may wish to use it when the usurper is occupying it, and then the owner has either to wait or to mount from behind like a cardinal's lackeys, which may interfere with the liberty of his actions; from which it is easy to conclude that consensual rapine by seduction is contrary to these three branches of natural law: personal safety, liberty, and property. For all these reasons, the philosopher Mordanes should take pains to avoid it, and renounce his unlawful drinks from Voragine's *krater.* Q.E.D.[23]

Our above extract may offer some idea, however inadequate, of philosopher Séché's fine work: we have had to summarize it from an English translation, as the original has been lost. I can tell you in confidence that His

Imperial and Royal Majesty is strongly suspected to be the occasional cause of this disappearance. According to reliable sources, when His Majesty heard that our philosopher was going to publish in London a book entitled *Observations on the Reforms of the Emperor, etc.*,[24] he feared the effect on his subjects of such a brilliant treatise about monastic property, and so he instructed his ambassador to have the publication suppressed. The minister decided there was no prompter, more economical way than stealing it from the author; he unfortunately gave this responsibility to an illiterate Prussian officer who mistook another manuscript for that one, so what he actually sent to Vienna was *Counts-Monopole*, which an Englishman who had been given it to read was hastily translating. I am informed that the Emperor presented the original manuscript as a gift to the King of Prussia, for inclusion in the records of the Academy of Berlin, but that one of the Queen his wife's ladies-in-waiting happened to find and burn it, as containing dangerous heretical principles. I have therefore been obliged to content myself with the translation, which people say is about as faithful as a rich dotard's wife. This is how so many good books are lost: by both the wickedness of the great global powers, and the faithlessness of translators.

Meanwhile, as soon as Jealousy was well established in Séchant's heart, she sent him one of the delusive dreams the gods send humans whom they choose to mock. The almoner's eyes saw a vision of the sere Voragine on her hands and knees, while Mordanes and a string of Capuchins were making forceful, if futile, attempts to calm her uterine fury. Ten of the strongest friars were taking turns in relays.

"Enough, enough," squealed good Séchant, "stop now, oh insatiable Voragine! Or if a whole battalion is required to satisfy your desires, why not let the troops march under the flag of the worthiest philosopher of all?"

Jealousy then flew to repeat these words in a deafening voice in Séché's ear: this philosopher rolls over, and thinking to grab Voragine, places his hand on the beard of the venerable father superior. Since the monk's beard was still wet from Mordanes's outrages, the filthy fluid's odor easily convinces Séché of Voragine's infidelity. He instantly decides to punish the faithless woman, and in an entirely pardonable mistake seizes the friar's beard, flattens it over his eyes, and begins plucking out the hairs one at a time. Unable to bear it, the father superior kicks out ferociously. His sandal tip rams hard at poor Séchant's bony aquiline nose; Séchant, still infuriated by his hallucination, now attacks both the Capuchin and Séché. Unfortunately Séchant lands his patella directly in the stomach of divine Mordanes, who has been sleeping soundly and thinking about nothing at all. Mordanes awakes with a start and descends on the combatants; the melee increases, the combative echoes resound. Plucking away, the depilator Séché has by now devastated half the reverend beard, and the father superior shouts that he is being attacked and raped by devils. The custode friar tries to move towards his father superior's voice, but trips over Tifarès and falls flat on the ground, his nose coming to rest in a spot Voragine had left uncovered so as to cool it down: thus if a foolish gourmand river-rat who sees a half-open oyster buries his mug in it, hoping for food, the oyster-shells snap shut, and the gallant is caught. Exactly so did the flabbergasted custodian get trapped between the inflamed walls of bawdy Voragine.

But now the Bohemienne's piercing screams bear witness to her surprise; the Capuchins awaken, trip on each other, and begin attacking each other as best they can. Discord Zizanie's joy is at its height, while Jealousy rushes to hide the naked bodies, out of fear lest any indiscreet, vagabond hand might be enjoying pleasure. Finally Saint Vincent, the patron saint of Saragossa, who enjoys the task of spreading vain terror on earth since the departure of Pan,[25] grabs one of the donkey's ears and shouts right into it with such a terrifying voice that the donkey, deathly afraid, jumps right into the middle of the throng, crushing a foot here and fingers there, until he lies at last pell-mell among the reverend fathers.

Indeed my book would have ended with everyone lying dead like a tragedy by divine Shakespeare[26] had not Dawn, by great good fortune, opened the gates of the morning sun. Scarcely does Discord catch sight of its first feeble rays than she flies away to attend to two brothers' awakening elsewhere; Jealousy rushes to hurry the work of a locksmith from whom she has ordered a dozen padlocks; the god of Love, fearing the Sun god's wicked tongue, does not tarry to be shown lying on the breast of the goddess Luxuria, who goes peaceably back to sleep in the knickers of the youngest Capuchin. Saint Vincent can plainly tell there is nothing more for him to do here, so he flies off to drink his chocolate with Saint Ignatius, and peace amongst the flock takes the place of those wicked divinities. Thus will waves agitated by fierce heat in a brass vessel subside once their components are no longer moved by the flames.

As soon as Lungiet sees calm reestablished, he assembles the entire band with a meaningful glance and a beckoning wave, and gives a splendid impromptu address: "These events are nothing new," he cried in his shrill voice; "the very same thing happened in the inn where Don Quixote and Sancho, after having concocted the Balm of Fierabras, were beaten by an enchanted

Moor introduced by the incontinence of Maritornes.[27] Moreover, the same disorder also occurred once at an hostelry in Le Mans, where a troupe of provincial actors were staying, when the host had intercourse with a she-goat that was giving suck to puppies, instead of his wife; no surprise, then, that Capuchins—who are also bearded—should cause similar distress during the night. Be that as it may, it is customary for some sane and wise individual to intervene and reconcile the combatants; this role is scarcely appropriate for a lawyer, but I herewith accept this responsibility anyway, by inviting you all to breakfast on the remains of last night's supper."

Lungiet's harangue suited the taste of the entire assembly, and they all set about eating with the best appetite in the world, a thousand reciprocal compliments, and an equal number of glasses of wine to season them. The good friars could not bear the thought of the separation soon to come. "Our Lady of Avioth is just as important as Our Lady of Liesse," said they.[28] Come with us to Grandpré, where you will visit the ancient chateau of the counts of Joyeuse, and we shall all have dinner in the Premonstratensian kitchen."[29]

Mordanes refused to change his route; they all parted at last, not without shedding a few tears. Wicked people have claimed, but I never believe, that in the general melee the father custodian lost five or six gold louis, which Mordanes had happened to find in the good father's sleeve.[30] They also say that finding these coins was what made Mordanes keep his plan, and take a sharp left turn: but I exhort you, my dear reader, to imitate my Pyrrhonism,[31] and keep in mind that what is probable is not always true.

CHAPTER TEN

The Terrible Effects of Causes

"What a country! What a landscape! Miserable inhabitants!" So spoke the illustrious Séché to the band on the rutted tracks leading to the abbey of Mont-Dieu:[1] "Look at this unfortunate hamlet: scrawny, starving livestock; filthy, sickening, exhausted peasant women, real remedies for love;[2] flies eating away at the thin carcasses of man and beast alike. But then! a half-starved priest and greedy tax-gatherers swoop down on whatever meager sustenance these unfortunate villagers have left." Séché's speech seemed so eminently unanswerable to his colleagues that for once, none of them tried to refute it.

But the Demon of Diatribe—the darkest, noisiest, weariest in all Hell, the quarrelsome child of Controversy—was so annoyed by the general agreement prevailing among our voyagers, to philosophy's disgrace, that he whispered a question in Félicité's ear: "*What is the cause of all these problems?*"

Little Félicité repeats these words aloud like a parrot taught to say *dominus vobiscum*:[3] scarcely has she pronounced the fateful phrase than the philosophical elements grow excited and combine: dark black vapors rise from every limb of our thinkers' bodies toward their brains, their animal spirits crowd into the base of their tongues, and they all begin shouting their answers at the same time:

Lungiet: "It's all because of Liberty!"

Séché: "It's because of the Violation of Natural Right!"

Bissot: "It's the lack of *Lex Talionis*!"

Mordanes: "It's the Maréchaussée police!"[4]

Séchant stood there with his mouth agape, since he always agreed with the current orator and it was hard for him—not to have so many different opinions at once, nothing in the world is commoner—but to repeat so many different catchphrases at once. So the worthy priest assumed the posture of a devotee ready to receive her Maker, opening her mouth as wide as the holy sepulcher of Jerusalem and apparently trying to bring it into proportion with the greatness of the One about to enter it.

Meanwhile Voragine, still full of last night's events, clung to Tifarès's arm and pinched his withered cheeks to no avail. Dehydration glued his yellow parchment so flat onto the bones of his face that a crucial incision would have needed no second cut of the scalpel to reveal all the apophyses, epiphyses, holes, and cavities in the twenty-one bones of his head.[5]

Félicité was following with some difficulty, since the presence of the reverend fathers had restricted her morning toilette to a manual *lavabo*;[6] the poor girl's vessel was filled with the essence-of-philosopher Bissot had poured into it, and the part that had spread over her lips had combined with the dust raised by the winds to form globulous and uncomfortable corpuscles that now stuck to various stray little hairs and scraped away at her.

—Where was that?

—Where? You are too curious; I told this anecdote only *ad usum*[7] for our young ladies leaving the convent, where they have been permitted to wash nothing but their hands: entering society, and ignorant of what happens to a young girl leaving the convent, they expose and betray themselves if they do not take precautions. So it is only right to teach them that mothers are sometimes curious, and laundresses indiscreet . . . Moreover, Englishwomen, who are the most philosophical and shrewd women in our world of woe, never neglect this: a neatly positioned handkerchief is the best protection against evidence that would be difficult to deny—unless, of course, they want a divorce, in which case they save all the evidence they can get to present before my lord the Archbishop of Canterbury, so as to get rid of an annoying and inconvenient husband.[8]

That worthy successor of the martyr Becket, wishing to rule only on incontestable proof, always summons chambermaids and laundresses:[9] "Susannah, do you swear on the Holy Bible and the damnation of your soul that you will tell the truth?"

"Yes, my Lord, God help me."

"Susannah, have you seen *Some Stains On Your Masters' Linen*?"

"Yes, milord, yes."

"And what kind of stains?"

"*Futuum*, milord."

"*Futuum*! How well you know Latin, Susannah."[10]

As for you, curious little lady, since you know neither Latin nor English, you must guess what that means, and believe what I tell you. A quick hand-kerchief at the time, a glass of water afterwards, and problem solved: you leave Susannah with no opportunity to speak Latin.

Meanwhile Félicité, hampered by that inconvenient friction, was not pay-ing much attention to the frightful hullabaloo caused by the magic word . . .

—Which magic word?

—Truly, you are my favorite kind of reader! My dear Piélatin, you are obviously a member of no Academy, not even the one at Châlons.[11] If you wish to continue your music and have any care for your tympanic membranes, the word you must never pronounce aloud before philosophers is the word "cause." "Cause" is the word sorcerers always use to summon the denizens of disputation for the philosophers' Sabbath. Have you ever seen a learned apothecary expose gold precipitate dissolved in *aqua regia* to a source of heat?[12] The heated matter makes a thunderous noise striking the sides of the vessel, and the amazed spectators expect the chemist to throw a lightning bolt. In a philosopher's ear, the word "cause" is similarly powerful and far quicker-acting: it sets off a process of caustic fermentation on scholarly topics. Then the air is repeatedly struck by blows from the philosophers' tongues, resounding in all directions, and the many oracles spewed forth by their foaming mouths are more than the reverberations can transmit.

Anyone acquainted with smart people knows that each sect has two or three favorite catchwords that support their entire body of knowledge: such a word can saddle any steed, the wonder-working nostrum of Academies. Moderates have only one such word; next come the two-word people; then the magical Trinitarians.[13] However complex a thesis may be, its skein can be unraveled and rolled up onto their balls of yarn. Such formulas are the bed of Busiris.[14] If the truth is too big, crack! These gentlemen clip its head and feet for you: if too short, they winch it on the capstan for you and turn away, turn away, until the truth is stretched.

A neighbor of mine goes around every day in a cloak decorated with a bit of fabric cut like the cap of Momus[15] and lined with the pelt of a cat: this man is a scholar, a theologian; he is even said to have been a Jesuit, in the days when there were Jesuits.[16]

"Doctor, doctor, I've got a scruple; can't you make it calm down?"

"Ah certainly, my son; faith . . ."

Faith is his rod of Jacob:[17] if I have that, I no longer have doubts. Such a brilliant man! What a doctor, what a man! Look at the way he reasoned in the consultation where he prescribed an emetic to that poor mother of a family, may she rest in peace; she died within an hour after the consultation.

"Doctor, can you give me a diagnosis?"

"Certainly, I know everything, I can explain everything with phlogistic. The cause of your malady is phlogiston. Phlogistic science provides diagnostics, prognostics, etc.; moreover, phlogistic also predominates in medical cures and natural crises; I'll give you a prescription."[18]

"Enough! I am feeling well, and not tempted to try any of your emetic or phlogistic—since you make all the endings rhyme with -ic."

Our encyclopedic and economist philosophers, worthy successors to those know-it-alls with their Latin endings in –us, have inherited both their skill at complicating their subject matter and their mania for explaining everything with catchphrases. For one philosopher, it's all about movement: for another, natural right; a third resorts to despotism.

Suppose you ask, "Janetta, why did you let the ragout burn, when you knew perfectly well there would be company for dinner . . . ?"

"Alas! Monsieur, I don't know why."

"You don't *know*?" Then follows the charivari: "It must be because of despotism."

"Oh no, sir! it's because of phlogistic."

"Ignorant woman! It's the gas . . ."

If you want more of these divergent and fiery opinions . . . just listen to the latest news from the echoes of louse-ridden Champagne.

Champagne is a countryside that, on its own, produces no scholars, and more cranes and bustards than philosophers. You could easily go fifteen or twenty leagues without meeting a man who can read, or a curate who understands his own missal. The words *Calvin, Luther, Jansenius* have never been pronounced in this fair land. No one pronounces the word "void" except when levying taxes; nor "plenitude" except when girls have heartburn and nine-month hydropsies after the troops have left. These Champagne echoes lack the linguistic articulateness that distinguishes Parisian echoes, and they were all terribly hoarse after our travelers passed through.

Perhaps indeed these echoes would have lost their voices forever if Voragine had not known from long experience that scholars are incapable of taking turns to speak, refraining from interruption, and understanding others in the group. As a woman of prudence and true amatrice of philosophy,[19] therefore, Voragine always carried a number of gags, attached to her belt on a sort of key-ring. As soon as she noticed that the subject matter had become important enough to merit full discussion, she made the orators draw for the short straw, and gagged the candidates whom fate had not favored. On this occasion, destiny decided to favor Lungiet; and as soon as Voragine had duly gagged Séché and Bissot, the illustrious lawyer began a discourse that richly deserves a chapter of its own.

CHAPTER ELEVEN

Uncivil Dissertations

"I SPEAK," BEGAN Lungiet,[1] "on behalf of that unfortunate portion of humankind which lives in abstinence and nudity, and against the rich and great who dine well and dress magnificently. My clients' existence, their daily life, their happiness—I am the only person who cares about them; I alone am predestined to defend them. Now for the second time in my life I have hesitated, and felt I might lose heart. Had people been attacking only my life and liberty, I would not have hesitated a moment; but my envious enemies have attacked my reputation and my honor. And so I paused to think. Why all this? said I to myself—They accuse me as the apostle of slavery, simply because I declaim against liberty? I am seen as the panegyrist of priests, simply because I senselessly sing their praises? I am to be called an enemy of bread, which I devour, simply because I call Ceres's gifts indigestible and monotonous? These and other equally iniquitous injustices tempted me to abandon my clients' causes. Yet when I look about me, I see no one else inclined to defend the cause of the indigent oppressed by Liberty; therefore will I devote myself to it like a modern Curtius, and close forever this chasm of iniquities.[2] I now speak on behalf of the villagers who call for serfdom, and against the rich who have forced them into acquiring liberty."

Voragine had happened to notice that Séché was making such efforts and grimaces to interrupt Lungiet's fine exordium that he had dislodged his gag; so she tightened its ribbons, taking advantage of a moment when the speaker was spitting and blowing his nose. After a quick glance to check Brissot's embouchure she gave a signal, and the orator then picked up the thread of his discourse:

"The liberty afflicting Europe today is not such a longstanding evil as some might think. It was not until the middle of the twelfth century that the three Garlande brothers and the monk Suger, ministers to Louis the Fat, begin introducing liberty into the kingdom.[3] Before this fateful moment, men vegetated peacefully in sweet serfdom; but ever since, the unlucky Gauls have been constantly afflicted by all kinds of misery and sorrow. Just as when an espalier, previously forced by kindly pegs and salutary wires to produce appetizing sweet fruits for its master or the gods' altar, sprouts sterile branches and fails to produce edible fruit if it is released from its bonds, similarly populations dragged away from their chains are no longer useful to anybody. The people are a spoiled child who needs the whip and the rod. The short-sighted benevolence of those families for whom God has created the human race would have degraded our species entirely if there had not yet remained a few trees sparkling with salutary constraint. And yes! our mother Holy Church has maintained them in proper dependency, filled with tender love for her children. The monks of Saint-Claude still keep serfs; Poland and Russia are teeming with serfs; and God has preserved serfs in almost every country of ancient Asia.[4] So it is that this foresighted Being nourished in Babylonian captivity on the banks of the Euphrates those Jews who were destined to rebuild the temple, and that M. de Saint-Germain keeps some light-horse, a number of armed guards and a few rabbits, for fear that their race should not become extinct.[5] Someday no doubt they will multiply, and the population of rabbit-warrens will rival the barracks of the red musketeers.* Someday, no doubt, serfdom will ascend once more—tardily, slowly—her peaceable throne, and plunge human beings back into the pleasures of tranquil insouciance.

"How sweet was serfdom, how beautiful in her cradle! Clovis—that gentle philosopher, a Christian so filled with love for his fellow-man, given by two saints the grace on high, the heavenly child who received for his baptism a vial of Provence oil, and for warfare a standard of Lyons silk—that great man, as I was saying, crossed the Rhine at the head of an elegant, light-hearted court.[7] Soon he had routed the Gauls and Romans, and forced them to share the happy yoke he imposed on his own family. Liberty, pushed back beyond the Loire, took asylum there for but a moment; soon afterward, shunning both

* Oh! M. de Brienne has settled that perfectly! He has given the officers of the French Guard the position of delivering *lettres de cachet*, as we have seen, and extirpated the Reds root and branch for fear that they might object to any such indulgence. A great man, this M. de Brienne; if Leo X had treated the Cordeliers the same way, Martin Luther would not have made so much of a stir in the world.[6]

Germans and Burgundians, Gaul achieved the honor of becoming enslaved to the Franks. Romans, Goths, Burgundians alike ran before the yoke; for our wise ancestors never kept their slaves shut up indoors like the Romans, assigning each a specific task, whether easy or difficult; no! as Solomon teaches, enclosure is unhealthy, and man's breath unhealthy to his fellow on both physical and moral levels.[8] Rivaling the Jewish king in wisdom, our conquerors gave each slave a private dwelling where serf, female, and offspring could live pellmell: the serfdom of these good folk consisted merely in choosing which of their fruits and flocks they would offer their master; also hides and woven cloth; while the vassal could keep whatever was rejected by their lords. Thus did the happy Gallic people spend two fortunate centuries under Clovis's grandchildren, drowsing in nonchalance on his throne. This auspicious epoch was the silver age, all things considered: and it was followed by the veritable golden age.

"In this golden age Pepin, father of Charles the Great (whom you all call Charlemagne) established universal monarchy, with the support of priests and his noble knights. By setting him above the French, Saint Peter gave him the Gauls as his property, which is proven by the letters of both that sainted Swiss guard of paradise and also his successor Steven, not to mention the profound writings of M. Gin, who is a former member of M. de Maupeou's parlement.[9] Charles enjoyed his colossal power by traveling back and forth from the Pyrenees to the source of the Danube. Then it was that poor Louis the Debonair, whipped by priests, insulted by his children, and robbed by his successors, bequeathed to descendants as feckless as himself the task of making the vast estates he had inherited from his father into fiefdoms for local lords.[10]—This race of saints and heroes presided over the finest, happiest, golden age of monarchy. A wonderful time! A real carnival for the poor! Do let us pause a moment to cast our eyes on this fortunate epoch.

"There I see peaceable slaves drinking, eating, embracing their companions without fear of bailiffs, clerks, subdelegates, intendants. Ever eager to save them meaningless effort, the lord of the manor hastens to spare his men the effort of their first bridal night. What dogsbody work, what hackwork that ceremony is, as we all know. Well then! A villein thought a maidenhead as rare a bird in those days, as it is a *rara avis* for a Parisian or Londoner today.[11] And the nuisance! What an effort for the lord, who often had to marry off more than two hundred vassals in a single year. Was it not simply fair to keep him fat, strong, and healthy? Nor did his conscientious purveyors neglect this concern. How freely and liberally they behaved in those honest olden days! You would see his purveyors go into the serf's hut every week, unhook his hanging hams, clear away his chitterlings, collect his eggs, pluck his pullets, slaughter his calves and sheep, and herd whatever fat cattle looked unsuitable for field-work into the citadel, modern Geryons that they were.[12] Since no one could decently expect Milord's head steward to carry such heavy loads on his own fine shoulders, he would take the best four-year-old horse in the serf's stable and lead it straight into the courtyard of the baronial chateau. Can anyone find fault with such an equitable operation? Are not legislative and executive powers self-evidently co-proprietary? Clearly so, since my lord baron made the laws in his council together with his almoner and bailiff, and then had them executed by his servants with no possibility of appeal, as is still done today by the majority of European princes; milord united the two powers and was therefore both the owner of men and co-proprietor in their property.

"In those days luxury was no more familiar than idleness. A dwelling built of a few pickets stuck together by their pointy tops, rather like our col-liers' huts, would have but a single opening to let in the odd gleam. Cur-rents of smoke and familial exhalations would counter fresh air and light; if the weather was not sunny, the chimney could always be blocked with a few boards. Every day was spent in the fields breathing fresh air; should anyone neglect his agriculture, the communal mentor's censor came armed with a whip as long as his arm, forced the serf to lie face down and bare the parts of his body usually hidden by tattered rags, and thrashed a few hundred blows on the scrawny muscles of his behind. Here is the simplest operating procedure, the most expeditious, the surest in right. Moses—whose mildness no one can reasonably doubt—does not Moses himself say: 'qui percusserit servum suum vel ancillam virgâ, et mortui fuerint in minibus ejus, . . . reus erit, sin autem uno die supervixerit non subjacebit poenæ: quia pecunia illius est,' Exodus 21:20. '*And if a man smite his servant, or his maid, with a rod, and he die under his hand; he shall be surely punished. Notwithstanding, if he continue a day or two, he shall not be punished: for he is his money.*'[13] Flagellations are thus well and truly part of divine right.

"And now consider the days and weeks serving for the corvée: imagine them all rushing to the castle! One to drag stones, one to pick-axe the road, one to pull the baroness, one to carry young mademoiselle to church, one to hold milord's stirrup, one to lead the pony for young master.

"I said earlier that serfs never went to war, and that their masters fought on their behalf—but let us agree to forget I said any such thing: I must admit I misspoke. I was quoting from memory and without reference books; but now

I see, in Visigothic law, these noteworthy words: 'whenever the Roman and the Barbarian are called for campaigns, they are obliged to bring to camp with them, well armed, one-tenth of their serfs.'[14] Even more to the point, I also find in the charters of Louis the Fat that he made serfs perform trials by combat in closed field, notably monks and churches, such as the fathers of the abbey St.-Maur-des-Fossés and the cathedral in Chartres.[15] However, you can understand why I never knew these old ordinances, which are no longer publicly cited. Nor do these ordinances prevent a person from desiring enslavement or begging noblemen to accept him among their flocks, so as to be somebody's possession rather than homeless. And observe how attentively the lords cared for the serf in return! Whenever Milord felt the least little tickle, his serfs took a beating. Supposing a marquis of Halberds refused to give precedence to a count of Hatchets, the latter could immediately arm his serfs and rush to his neighbor's vassals to seize their horses, cattle, and donkeys; massacre any vassal who resisted; kidnap those who didn't; rape young women and kill the old; burn the golden wheat; graze in the pastures, and trample on fields ready for hay-making.[16] Then it would be the baron's turn next year: some fine night, he and his vassals would arrive on horseback, descend on the villeinage, cut down the green wheat and leave nothing outside the dungeon keep but famine, present and future.[17] Thanks to the general misery, a period of peace would ensue; but then the Duke of Disgust-heart commands his vassals to fight for his lord the king, who seeks redress: the baron in turn arms and rallies one-tenth of his remaining serfs under his banner, to take his rank under the suzerain's flag. In the meantime, while our lords are wearing themselves out, their lands are occupied by the "Great Companies" of *filii belial guerratores variorum* who make love to the women and girls, and live as they please off the combatants' lands.[18] Now consider: would all these people have slaughtered each other, torn each other's guts out, mutilated each other in this way, had their masters seemed not to care for them? Obviously not! So for this reason, milord the baron never showed himself to be ungrateful. His serfs were his fortune, and he always had up his sleeve some clever sorcerer available to provide the Balm of Fierabras.[19] And this is why the population was much more numerous, and commerce far more flourishing, than in our own iniquitous days.

"Moreover, remember that the children of serfs dead in battle were never abandoned as orphans; no, Milord brought them up so that they might serve him in the future; then too, if by any chance some sharp prick prompted one of Lord Bandeville's villeins to get with child a female serf belonging to Lady Doucon, the lord and his neighbor lady could then split the offspring just like animals, as you can see according to the charter given to Guines-la-Putain, which explicitly and formally says: *si villaneus Domini nostri urbis erectionum, facit filios aut filias servæ, aut servis dominæ dulci conis, partiantur sicus catulos.*[20]

"After the faithful picture I have painted of those happy and pleasure-filled centuries, you would weep to see me sketch our own unfortunate times. Shall I portray poor devils who, for the price of a day of backbreaking work, cannot earn the cost of the coarsest food? Or those obliged by their superior to gamble in some game of chance where—as in other lotteries—they will surely be the losers? Or worse yet, laborers who lose any recompense for an entire year's work thanks to hailstorms, drought, or frost? Who are forced onto the open highway to compete with their own livestock for nibbles of the parched and unwholesome grass beside the road? Should I portray old men begging at a hospital door? Or old women uglier and viler than the janitresses these villagers call their wives? Yet such are the results of liberty—liberty, which we hear praised with such effrontery! I shall not pause for legalistic objections from my learned friend Séché, whom I see foaming at the mouth and ready for rebuttal, but only conclude: may it please princes, kings, and other sovereigns of this world to send my poor clients into the presence of the rich, so that they can be taken into the sweet status of slavery! While as for lawyer Séché's clients, may they be constrained and shackled, so that everything goes for the best in this world of woe. And all this to happen despite whatever objection has been made or may be made in the future; and then all will be well."

I have no idea whether Lungiet was actually going to stop here, since so many good points remained to make on this topic, but in any case, poor Séché, having wriggled his jaw up and down all through the oration, finally broke through his gag. His words crowded out in frenzy, and their sheer volume reduced Lungiet to silence. Thus when internal air compressed by its own weight within the earth's entrails is suddenly heated by the central fire, a flow of heterogeneous matter rushes toward the volcano's mouth. At first these matters press against each other and thrust horribly against the walls of the giant vase: the earth trembles; the terrified inhabitants await the fatal eruption in dismal silence; then the flaming materials open a passageway, at the expense of the mountain's lips; then the fiery lava runs like a flood, it burns, it overturns, and . . .

Voragine nimbly picked up the gag that had been holding back Séché's flow of words; she now muzzled Lungiet in his turn; the illustrious audience made ready to hear the scholarly rebuttal of Séché.

"O Lungiet!" Séché began. "Can you possibly believe your argument, embellished as it is with sophisms, capable of confusing our principles? Do you imagine you have proven that serfs—in the days of slavery—were happier than our free peasants today? No, not at all, far from it, my learned friend. Even if you had been able prove such an untenable proposition experimentally, what would your experiments be worth against my three principles, or my natural right? What argument could you advance against a geometric demonstration, or against the eternal truths I displayed atop my *Journal des Princes*?[21] As I now demonstrate yet once again *ab ovo*,[22] serfdom is manifestly contrary to liberty of action, to personal security and to property; and you may throw my *Journal* into the fire if I cannot prove all these propositions."

"Take that!" cried Séchant; "well spoken! Such a man! The king of philosophers! O my friend! My dear master, I promise you an acrostic in your praise, an acrostic where . . ."[23]

Even as the interrupter Séchant was pronouncing those last words, Voragine slipped behind him, adroitly inserted the fatal device, and . . . lo! See my man Séchant with a gag in his mouth.

—Serves the back-stabbing idiot toady right for interrupting! Pray, sir, continue with your harangue.

—Ah! How good it would be for our own bluestocking provincial hostesses to hang gags on their mantelpieces to make a firescreen! Egad, my love! Why not introduce this custom at Squealhaven, my own chateau?[24] Voragine is so right: whenever the politicians of our neighborhood quarrel over the course of a riverbed or the dismissal of some politician; when your cousin the representative is debating the existence of God with our almoner Friar Nicodemus, or when Count Fiasco has some dispute over a hind's fumets with the Chevalier of Thrust-corner—I shall just gag everyone in company! Then perhaps it might be easier for me to get the general gist of their conversation. What say you, my love?

– As you please, sweet baron; you will set an instant example, no doubt! since you, dear heart, are the model of elegance for our entire province, not to mention for the court and the town.

Meanwhile, Séché could taste victory on his lips: he was already aligning his words and phrases, bringing his hypotheses to the fore, ranking in battle order the heavy brigade of his theses, and relegating to the rear his conclusions, some of which were crippled and had to stay with the baggage, as they could not keep pace. But for the moment, all these machinations were in vain. The travelers were now approaching the cross of Mont-Dieu, and the silent atmosphere surrounding the charterhouse had no sooner *ambienced* our philosophers than an urge to drink replaced their desire to speak; and although the hour was not late, they all agreed when Voragine proposed that they make a stop at the abbey.

Voragine therefore unmuzzled the sufferers, and the donkey, delighted by the hope of good lodging, began to intone his usual hymn. Within the abbey, mares made answer in their high-pitched voices, while my friend Dom Hachette the Procurator, scenting a faint Capuchin after-smell, barricaded himself in his cell and sent out the Coadjutor who called "Attack! Attack!" in his big bass voice.[25] They were then led into the abbey by a friar, and Tifarès unsaddled the donkey, who noticed an open stable and jumped inside, like a true Bohemian ass. The hay-box was open, and I leave you to determine what a feast he had.

But alas! so uncertain are human affairs, so close does ill-luck tread on the heels of happiness, that this world below is plainly the home of neither man nor beast. Dom Prior's valet, sly and mean as any page, sighted the donkey taking his fill; so this rascally valet, whether by envy or natural malice, slipped behind the innocent animal and slammed the hatch-door of the hay-box down on the scruff of his neck. Poor donkey was trapped like a rat, and despaired even of being able to swallow a last morsel before dying—thinking no more about salvation than any greedy, drunken old functionary, choking after dinner from surfeit and apoplexy, considers revising his will in favor of relatives he has kept at a distance all his life.

So it would have been all over with the donkey, and heaven only knows what would have happened to his soul if Love, ever watchful over the destiny of jack-asses, had not pricked Bissot and Félicité to take shelter in the same stable where the donkey lay in his agony. You can guess their emotion at the fate of the steed; lovers always are tender-hearted, especially girls, as we know from the example of young Mademoiselle Pérette, who interrupts her lover if even a flea might get squashed. But alas! despite all their efforts, Bissot and Félicité's arms were not powerful enough to release the poor beast, and they had to call for strong-armed Mordanes to come rescue the donkey.

No sooner was the donkey freed than he wiggled his ears in testimonial to his gratitude, and stole another mouthful. The lovers, disturbed in their intended pleasure, vowed to make it up to each other as soon as they possibly could. Mordanes suspected something was up, and since donkey-like he could never see an opening without poking his head or his hand into it, he swore— even while poking hay into a little sack he carried on the offchance—that he would not let newcomer Bissot enjoy an exclusive right for long: that this young girl would soon offer him the same pleasures as her mother had done. Hearing his oath, Love grieved that he could not immediately gratify his dear Mordanes, but vowed to do whatever Destiny might allow without much trouble, and meanwhile went to take his usual place between Bissot and his sweetheart, who had returned to the troupe.

CHAPTER TWELVE

Parallel of Mendicant and Proprietary Monks

"WELL, COOK, DID you give the Capuchin fathers their supper?"

"Capuchins, Dom Procurator? No Capuchins came here today."

"Liar! I could smell them: go ask Dom Coadjutor."

"You are mistaken: they are a mere itinerant camp, traveling with a donkey."

"With a donkey! That proves they must be Capuchins. Good God, they have women with them! Stubborn idiot—can't you see they are Capuchins who have run off with girls?"

Dom Hachette said no more, because he was contradicted no longer.[1] My friend had such well-developed nostrils and so strong a hatred of mendicant orders that no one could have made him deny his sense of smell unless four evangelists had appeared in person to swear these travelers were not Capuchins; and even then he would not have believed these authors of eternal truth without confronting them to make sure they were not contradicting one another. Even then, he would have had to submit his reason to his faith. On any other subject, Dom Procurator was less skeptical.

You, Sir, you whom I have already let in on the secret, you know whence came the Capuchinal odor that led this venerable priest into error. What astonishes you is to see a respected Carthusian so prejudiced against monks that he can smell them a quarter-league away, as confidently as the lead dog of the pack gets the scent of an old boar in his cover. I was surprised by this just like you, and I said so to my friend one morning while he was showing me, in his gallery, a portrait of Saint Francis that he had painted himself. "Indeed," I told him, "I am amazed to see you choose this particular subject, you who cannot conceal your hatred for the children of Saint Francis."

"A neat turn of phrase," replied Dom Hachette with a smile. "You consider my aversion for mendicant priests a scandal, and you wish to discover its cause. I will not deny you this satisfaction, but you must listen to me closely, and judge my reasons with care.

"Worldly people like yourself, who look at things casually, use the term 'monks' to include all religious orders: despite what the proverb tells us, if a man's appearance and clothing differ from yours, you make him out as solitary, and solitary is the meaning of the word 'monk.'* But if we need a definition to cover under one common name everyone who has adopted a rule, let us use the term *religious*. A 'religious' is a man who, besides taking the three vows of poverty, chastity, and obedience, lives under a specific rule, under a particular regime that distinguishes him from worldly people. This rule reminds every religious that he must not follow the worldlings' dissolute customs, but try to lead them back toward virtue by example and prayer. The difference among these 'religious' would therefore be unimportant, if they all took the formula of their vows in exactly the same way. In general, 'chastity' is something they all understand better than they observe; 'obedience' is something they may argue about as to extent and degree; but 'poverty' is a word to which they attach completely different ideas. The major division of religious orders into 'proprietary' and 'mendicant' comes from this last difference of opinions.

"Proprietary religious can be divided into two classes: on one hand, a class of monks properly so-called like ourselves, the Trappist fathers, etc.; and on the other hand, a class of religious living together who also take the vow of poverty, but have a different understanding of that vow—mendicants whether gray, black, shod or barefoot.

"Proprietary orders locate religious poverty within the individual members: that is the main point of the contract drawn up between the religious and his house; the house is obliged to give the regular religious everything he needs in life as defined by the rule, on condition that he renounces every kind of property. He is poor, because he possesses nothing himself: his habit does not belong to him; he may wear it, but not sell it. The religious house must provide all his needs so long as he fulfills the clauses of his engagement: to fast, pray, work with his hands: in a word, to contribute to the community's welfare. The main obligation of the community is to spare him the slightest con-

* From *monos,* which means solitary.

cern unrelated to his condition, and particularly to ensure that he will never be dependent on worldly society or any worldly personage, even in illness or old age. By ceasing to work for the state, he no longer expects its protection. In this sense, the community is sovereign over the individuals who compose it. The religious members have no relationship at all with the civil magistracy: the community, and not the individual, has a relationship to the state. The religious house guarantees the state its members' conduct; it is responsible for their existence, it hugs them to its bosom, and it protects worldly people from the disturbances that would arise within their families if a religious were ever to rejoin them. In return, the state guarantees the community permanent possession of its property, preserves its existence as a group, protects its members, and lastly secures the community liberty of action within the boundary traced by law.

"Members of such a proprietary order are never a burden on the public, for they have a privileged mortgage on the wealth of the house: before a religious member could lose this privilege, the community's possessions must be annihilated, or be taken away by the state. The first case is impossible in the present situation, because communities are legally considered as minors; if the second instance were ever to arise, the state would be placed in the stead and position of the religious house, and could not refuse to provide for us.

"The utility of our proprietary orders is a subject I need hardly debate: during my thirty years' affiliation, I have lived too comfortably to satirize them, and absorbed too much of their spirit to eulogize them. But the interest of religion, the dignity of the clergy, and eternal justice make me think very differently about mendicant orders.

"These parvenu orders have transferred the idea of poverty from the individual to the order itself. It is the order itself, no longer the individual, that renounces property! As a result of this conceptual reversal, the body has no longer any obligation to nourish its members—rather, its members are committed to nourishing the body. Thence follows the necessity for roaming the world, bowing to the caprices, the weaknesses, even the disorders of worldly people. Worldly people can set whatever price they wish on their donations: humiliatingly, they often mete out their alms in proportion to the hunger they chance to observe on the alms collector's face. That is the cause of the contempt for the mendicant in France—a contempt spreading to the proprietary monk: from the monk to lay clergy; from lay brother to bishop; from bishop to his archbishop; and finally to the God they preach. The mendicant and his religious house have no guarantee in their contract; the state cannot negotiate with a vagabond body of no fixed abode that may shake the dust from its sandals and disappear at any moment.

"Society regards the mendicant order as a boulder poised to trigger a crushing landslide, and its members as a hungry pack of wolves that could go mad at any moment. Mendicants have provided ready-made armies to popes driven by ambition. If one regiment were to be favored over another, civil war would break out; and the most aggressive, fearsome regiments came from mendicants' cells. Since the number of religious mendicants has so increased, and cannot be supported by alms alone, they have decided to live off their industry, and traffic in holy objects. We have seen mendicants, official bull in hand, chase proper pastors from their chairs and tribunals; their complaisant confessionals attract the flocks of other priests, and the expiations they give always profit their order. Meanwhile, wandering among the laity, mendicants have encountered frequent opportunities for debauchery; they have eaten and drunk not *from* whatever was offered, but *everything* offered them. Women, weak and fond and generally more open to outward appearances and the surprise of novelty than men, inundate mendicants with respect—and even, if we believe worldly gossip, with caresses. How could any man resist, exposed to such strong temptations? Even alone in his cell, does a hermit never hear the voice of the flesh? As for monks who go out among sinners, I have no very high idea of their morals.

"Now you may well object that the mendicant must have a preservative in his repellent appearance, his personal uncleanliness, his stench that nauseates me even at a distance, unlike even the rankest of beasts? But the odor is a preservative against *what*? Not against the desire of the person emitting it. Whereas women's curiosity—! But let us rise above that notion.

"Mendicants' slovenly appearance offers yet another reason for me to hate them, both as orders and as individuals. If we premise the necessity for the church's splendor, prelates' luxuries, and the imposing exterior that religion must present if she is to impose on men, must we not admit that the degradation of her ministers reflects badly on her? Hearken to rude village women: they threaten their children with Capuchins as if they were wild animals: 'Keep quiet, or I'll give you to the Capuchin! Be careful.' On the other hand, the man of the house bellows: 'Woman, I'll thank you to keep those hooligans out of my house! Don't you go inviting those nasty monks to come near me.' Men are influenced by opinion alone; general contempt adds an insurmountable obstacle.

"Finally, the act of joining a mendicant order which can possess nothing means that one renounces work with one's hands, one disobeys God's own precept, and one vows to live at the expense of others. The Capuchin has to eat, like any Benedictine or Carthusian; thus he too should work.

"Some who try to justify mendicant orders argue that they do work, and more usefully than ourselves. 'What does a Carthusian in his cell produce?' they inquire. 'Brooms, chaplets, worthless objects, superfluous prayers? In days of yore, they made copies of manuscripts, and until recently vast compilations, but today Benedictines do not seem to make themselves particularly useful. Contrariwise, the Capuchin is ever ready and willing: we see him run to the aid of a sick curate; we see a Capuchin on the scaffold standing by the criminal; we find him on the battlefield in the heat of the melee, exhorting the nearly-dead; it is the Capuchin who braves the fury of the waves, makes his voice heard in the tempests, and enters the fishing-huts of savages with such intrepidity. If mendicant monks had property, would they abandon it to brave such hazards? Are your proprietary monks likely to leave their idle life in exchange for that mendicant life, so active, so unsettled?'

"Far from intending to downplay the glory of the Gospel's hero, I am happy to repeat the praises made of him by mendicants; nor will I argue about which requires more courage: the uniformity of a cloistered life, or the variety of what is perhaps an agreeable life. However, I will point out that by actual count, Capuchin almoners and missionaries tend to be secular rather than regular. Secular stipends are real property, and a Capuchin almoner has broken his vow. Similarly, missionary orders do not follow Saint Francis's rule, and we would be as ill-advised to glorify Saint Francis for missionary achievements as to accuse him of the horrors committed by some of his children who take shelter under his wings.

"It remains for us to examine the utility of the help town and country clergy may get from cloistered communities. Supposing that half the 104,000 parishes of France each employ a mendicant during one week a year: this hypothesis will reduce the available number of Capuchins to one thousand, because if there are fifty-two thousand parishes employing this help, and each parish uses it for one-fifty-second of a year, then it is as if there were fifty-two times fewer Capuchins employed in the year. Let us suppose that instead of Capuchins, one were to have in these various dioceses a thousand itinerant vicars at a stipend of five hundred livres each, but paid by the church of France as a whole. I ask you now to compare the five-hundred-thousand-pound cost of this establishment with the money now paid out by the kingdom for the upkeep of these mendicants, their chapter-houses, their churches, etc. Local curates would also gain the cash amount they are presently paying their current mendicant assistants, as well as the oblations and offerings snatched away from the parish by those religious orders: their only costs would be food and lodging for the ambulant of the proprietary order, during whatever period they needed him.

"Let us conclude this lengthy discourse. I daresay I have proven to you that mendicant orders are dangerous for the state; useless and even harmful to religion; a threat to bishops; and a cruel enemy to all other clergy. This inner conviction is the cause of my hatred for these orders, and my lack of respect for their individual members."

Having listened to this discourse attentively, I must admit I had not a word to say in reply, and was entirely convinced. I transcribed it at the earliest possible moment; and I am not sorry to have rediscovered it now, so not everything in my wonderful book will be trivial. Not all my readers may be equally interested, especially those who enjoy the exploits of Mordanes and share his appetite for Félicité's brunette charms. But I must beg such readers to remember that their minds should not always be filled with enjoyment; although if I happen to have any reader who honestly tells me he is ever-ready for the joys of love, then I'll promise him to talk to him only about that, as my part of the bargain.

At any rate, let us return to our heroes, and discover what they have been doing since the donkey's unfortunate misadventure.

Our long-eared animal had long ago forgotten his whole hatch-door disaster. His philosophy—which I consider a reasonable one—was to eradicate every trace of pain from his memory, and actively preserve reminiscence of even his most minor pleasures. In his mind he would re-masticate his favorite thistles, or pounce once more upon the cruppers of she-asses whose passions had corresponded most warmly with his own. Occasionally he reviewed the she-asses on parade, so as to concentrate countless pleasures into as short a time as possible. Donkey Stoics criticized him for this: they spoke a hundred fine reasons to praise suffering; yet the donkey never listened with even half an ear. One hears tell that if a lascivious auditress happened to be in church, the donkey did not even wait to hear the end of the sermon before demonstrating that the attractive power of pleasure is stronger than the power of words. Indeed we are told that he was often ogled by the infuriated Stoics, a few of whom might well have imitated him if vanity, their inseparable companion, had been their only witness.

CHAPTER THIRTEEN

Various Projects Highly Important
to the Public Weal

YOU GROW IMPATIENT, dear reader: you seem annoyed to see the heavy curtain of rational discourse lowered onto the stage. If I took your word for it, my actors would have no interval to catch their breaths. I am thrilled to hear the stamping of your feet and your neighbors' canes interrupt the orchestra, while provincials in the audience call: "*Begin! Begin!*" Hearing that word in thirty different dialects assures me that I can find readers in every geographic parallel of our kingdom—I only wish I could say buyers! But in the past few years, a perfidious practice was introduced into France by which the latter number only perhaps one-tenth of the former. Many, many bachelors, when it comes to reading, now possess no books of their own. These gentlemen live off the common expense, or rather off the purse of unfortunate authors. A single copy is enough for an entire city. Sometimes the valet of a local lord discovers an unbound last-season stitched paperback in the waiting room of our generous small-town librarians: what then? The scoundrel pockets it silently; his master reads it on a rainy day; milady weighs it contemptuously; the daughter of the house reads it secretly with her chambermaid; a bored neighbor borrows it; and so you have the honor of being read, judged, covered with muck in a hundred chateaus and a hundred shops by a million spectators, only one of whom has paid at the door.

This revolting injustice horrifies the "Annalist of the Eighteenth Century," who has written a fine Memorandum on the topic.[1] I hardly know why the government has paid it so little attention—a fatal misfortune, as we may agree if we whisper low, very low; and before mentioning anyone in power:

—Jasmine tea, sir?

—First, look out the window to get rid of any spies flying around; excellent; now, shut the door. Between ourselves, now that no one can overhear us: The powerful at court have forgotten the maxim of Charles V. This prince did great honor to men of letters. One of his courtiers (as spiteful as our own, and more daring) saw fit to reproach him on this score. But the king replied: 'Authors and scholars cannot be valued too highly, for this kingdom will continue in its prosperity so long as it pays honor to wisdom; but when wisdom is cast aside, the kingdom will fall.'[2] Wisdom has been "cast aside" for some little time now; a dreadful conspiracy has been formed against her; it is time to set things right. It is in the interest of all men of letters:

Our entire body shall declare
In my favor everywhere!

Alas! authors' declarations are sadly unproductive when it comes to money. But a decree from the Council . . . why not? Is that so difficult?—Here in my portfolio I happen to have a draft by an economist; I happened to rescue it from the fireplace of a State minister, who had condemned it sight unseen. The prologue is worthy of the premier mandarin in China:

"Decree of the King's Council of State, with a ruling on book-lending within the kingdom.

"The King having in his Council been apprised of memoranda by various authors, booksellers, and peddlers in both Paris and the provinces, on the new and abusive practice introduced, to their detriment and manifest loss, of book-lending and, worse yet, pamphlet-lending: circulating a single copy not only between brothers and sisters, cousins male and female within the forbidden degrees of relationship, but also through an entire town; the King having also been informed that in their criminal cupidity certain booksellers have opened so-called lending libraries, where private citizens may procure for a nominal annual fee the fruit of said authors' travails; His Majesty, holding that letters constitute an essential part of a kingdom's glory and are useful to its mores by sweetening tempers and civilizing citizens, hereby sees fit to extend his royal protection to authors. His sense of justice drew him to take this step: Writers and others involved in the circulation of knowledge, systems, projects, remarks, histories, stories, fables, theatrical plays, etc., etc.: possessing like all our other subjects the right to live, and be rewarded for their work, the abuses of book-lending would cause inestimable harm to the said authors, booksellers, and peddlers. Authors would no longer earn as good a price for their manuscripts, so that many among them might contract debts, and be carried off to prison, where some could die from hunger or cold; while an even greater number would abandon Parnassus and resume practicing mechanical professions, to the great scandal of literary amateurs. Moreover, the King considers that in view of the modest funds being allocated for the recompense of their labors and the virtual impossibility of pensioning every encyclopedic academician and economist, some of these writers and others from different sects or no sects at all are reduced to earning a living off their writing. Therefore, it is in the interests of commerce to increase the sale and conservation of books, and a matter of equity that no one should be entertained—or bored, for that matter—at an author's expense, without paying him some sort of compensation. Wishing to provide for this, the King in his Council with the approval of the Keeper of the Seals, has ordained and here ordains the following:

"Article One. No individual of any rank or condition may in future lend or borrow books except within his own family, and this privilege will extend in direct line only to the third generation, and collaterally only to the first cousin once removed, known also as a Breton cousin or cousin-germain; the penalty is a fine of five hundred livres, payable to the author of said book.

"Article Two. His Majesty forbids all lackeys, waiting-women, coachmen, kitchen-maids, scullions, chefs, and cooks to lend each other the books of their respective masters, and even more strongly does he proscribe their carrying these books without asking permission from one house to the next: and this, under pain of a year's wages. And anyone who cannot pay this fine, should be branded on the left ear with the letters "L.O.B.," Lender Of Books; and then whipped at the doorstep of every bookseller in town.

"Article Three. His Majesty nevertheless permits his subjects to petition the Permanent Secretary of his Academy for a dispensation to buy and to read aloud books in private rooms, although not to carry these books away with them; the said Permanent Secretary will issue this permit in the form of a bull for a given number of years, or for life.

"Article Four. The Permanent Secretary shall be authorized to sell this bull at the same prices as a Crusade Bull,[3] and to excommunicate from literature any person who does not make such a purchase once in a lifetime; without such excommunications affecting those made by bishops and curates within the kingdom.

"Articles Five and Six . . . up to 100,000, as the Minister may wish; His Majesty ordains that the present decree be registered in every literary Academy and society within the kingdom, and posted where necessary. Done in the Council of State, in His Majesty's presence, at . . ."

While awaiting the government's issuance of this decree or one like it, I have devised a way to end the swindle. My solution is to have this book bound in calfskin, with gilt edges, and forbid my bookseller to sell stitched brochure copies; and thus, on my own authority, plenary power, and positive science, I forbid the aforesaid *** to sell my work in loose pages, in boards, or stitched in marble paper or even sewn in blue, on pain of being denounced to posterity and my contemporaries as a pirate and thief: all this, for the very first work I produce.[4] Ha! Ha! . . .

Your impatience is growing by leaps and bounds, but I had every right to take care of my own interests, before satisfying yours: every man for himself. No—I refuse to be a martyr to foolish impartiality, neglecting my own affairs. I admit I chat a bit about myself: but where do you find an author who forgets himself in his work? Mine is the contemporary style. Nor have I yet told you about my family affairs, or my genealogy; I have not kept the conversation exclusively trained on my own wit; until now, my egotism has kept within reasonable bounds, so you must admit you have no cause for complaint.

The species of my heroes is the real cause of your impatience. If I were describing the lives of the saints, digressions would not shock you, and Dom Coadjutor himself feels exactly the same. The little troupe's baggage train, its atmosphere of liberty, its women's glances, the whole thing makes the Dom just as impatient as you are.

"I must go see for myself," he says, "they are sure to be hiding something. Our bursar Dom Procurator has a sensitive nose, and he does not make mistakes. We see so many Capuchins abandon their frocks and go a-wandering with young girls."

Dom Coadjutor was a man of great common sense: his modest and simple appearance had kept him from being marked as one of the Order's geniuses, but he had the natural wit that always amazes society people whenever they identify it in peasants. He had no dislike for the fair sex; his assignment as supervisor to the smithy did not prevent him from glancing over at the blacksmiths' wives and daughters, but that was as far as he went. I cast no doubt on the purity of his intentions: eyes may be libertine while the rest of the body remains chaste.

Saint Bruno's habit offers none of the sumptuary glories with which

Heaven gratifies its worldlings.[5] But the Carthusian habit is not a tattered Carmelite undergarment, either—on the contrary! Some medical doctors have even claimed that the mini-pricks of the hair-cloth, the knots in the discipline. . . .

Oh the calumny, master doctor, pure calumny! Admittedly, Carthusians are not blindfolded to sights that arouse the devil in the flesh, but what an uncharitable spirit rules in the world today! Free-thinkers are such spoilers: they dispose of souls the way doctors kill off bodies.

"Good evening, gentlemen, good evening to you, ladies," said Dom Coadjutor.

"Your servants, reverend father."

"O reverend father, we ladies are your humble servants, too."

"All this 'reverend father' talk!" thought Dom Coadjutor to himself: "Dom Procurator was right! Maybe there really is at least one Capuchin disguised among the troupe! 'Reverend father!' Nobody would ever call a Carthusian 'reverend father.' It makes every sense. Who would abandon the title of *dom, dominus,* meaning 'my lord,' for the common title of 'father,' used for beggars? Fie, fie, the disgrace: every Honorable should get honored.—Now, gentlemen, whither do you travel in this fashion?"

"We make pilgrimage to Our Lady of Luxembourg," replied Séchant in honeyed tones. "We would not wish to pass so close by your cloister, without asking its blessed inhabitants for their benediction and hospitality. We have vowed never to take shelter under a profane roof, and we have observed this vow all week long. We spent last night praying with reverend Capuchin fathers who are traveling to Our Lady of Avioth."

Dom Coadjutor had to smile at the way these last words connected to his old friend's sense of smell: here then was a solution to the problem he was trying to decipher.

How pleasurable it feels to solve a problem—so flattering to one's self-love—nature has done so well by us! We would never take on pain if there were no attractive pleasure to gain. You, madame: would you ever expose yourself to the predictable pains of childbirth if you were not blinded by love's delights? Scholars are much the same: they are willing to pore over a problem in a sunless room for seven days, for the pleasant glory of solving it on the eighth. Once their calculations are complete, they can sit on scholarly tribunals, cross-examine each other and hand down their verdict. Their sentence is a warrant of immortality. Occasionally the public appeals the verdict, with cries of "*Hoc est cur palles?*"[6] But too late, too late; my man is already in possession. If the tribunal of self-love has a score of one to ten, possession is nine points of the law.

One is always pleasanter to other people, when satisfied with oneself. Dom Coadjutor had scarcely felt the first pin-pricks of delight at discovering the cause of his colleague's error than his face became more serene and open. "Surely, gentlemen, you'll take a few bottles of wine with your crust of bread?" The monk rang a bell and ordered four bottles of Sillery, delicious nectar that it is, and well-suited to revive the guests' eloquence.[7]

The sight of these Sillery bottles and a glance at Félicité's eyes set Bissot's blood on fire; his animal spirits began circulating rapidly; the spectators perceived his overwhelming desire to speak, and listened impatiently for whatever might come out of his mouth. Thus will an entire assembly hold its breath in suspense at the contortions of a pious old Quakeress, when her cranial cavities are stuffed with the spirit of God.

CHAPTER FOURTEEN

On Hospitality

"Nowhere on earth has Hospitality taken refuge for the last three hundred years," began Bissot, "except in cloisters—the only lodging this goddess still can find.[1]   Your own order, sir, yes indeed: your Benedictine scholars alone still preserve the faintest notion of Hospitality, first among the ancient Roman virtues. All Europe is filled with tourists and cabarets. The only way to travel across it is to go purse in hand, or else sleep under the stars. As for our scientists and philosophers, they are making no effort to resuscitate this communicative virtue; scientific and philosophical interests are more likely to be aroused by a butterfly wing, a flower's stamen and pistil, than by the human heart.

"As you must admit, gentlemen, virtues have become quite rare among us moderns, and whatever vestiges we have are dying out.   Today, man is completely deluded about the true object of whatever virtues remain to him. He has actually tried to root out gentle, affectionate feelings of sensibility from his heart, training himself instead to focus on distant goals that are the product of his own imagination. He donates alms, but no longer helps the poor; he wages war, but not necessarily for his fatherland; he makes peace, but no longer out of love for his fellows. This is why it is now humiliating to receive charity; the practice of the military profession disgraces the soldier; and peace has become just another virgin timidly trying to escape war and discord by fleeing across the borders from one country to the next.

"Man has more of a taste for travel now than ever in history, we all allow, and yet travelers on the road have never met with so many mortifying obstacles. At the gates of every city, he is stopped by soldiers and searched by customs officers, as if the prince suspected his subjects of theft the minute they lose sight of their hometown's clock-towers. Out in the countryside, the traveler is narrowly inspected by local police, trying to identify his facial features with the description of a known thief—and woe unto him, if they find any resemblance between his face and the man they seek! Woe unto him, if he has forgotten to buy a passport before leaving! Either way, he is dragged into a dungeon cell, and there is nobody to bail him out.

"Even if the traveler escapes these humiliations, however, he will not escape the sharp claws of the greedy innkeeper. Welcomed to the House of Avarice in direct proportion to the elegance of his baggage train, he is greeted by bowing and scraping until he has crossed the threshold. The sly innkeeper beams at the hope of fleecing him at leisure; his wife, if at all pretty, sparkles her eyes like a gilt-painted sign; maidservants rush round him, and bear him away to his chamber in triumph. Meanwhile they prepare him a dinner of tough meat, hastily cooked; they cut and sophisticate the wine so that it tastes drinkable but is noxious, and only makes him thirst for more. They make up his bed, and if he is careless, he may well find himself sleeping between sheets rumpled by another guest's body. Worst of all: if overheated by his road trip, hot with treacherous drink, excited by pepper and spices imported from the Orient as snares for his virtue, if he falls for the tricks of the scheming sirens treacherously spreading dirty sheets on his hard bed, then he may expect only the bitterest consequences. What now flows in his veins will be a sickness contracted from itinerant monks and soldiers, grafted onto the corruption of lawyers, stuck onto the fruit of the bachelor seducer's intemperance—. O unfortunate man! Quit the pleasure of that embrace! A thousand men before you have savored it, and they have all left within that receptacle a few germs of the dreadful evils sent back from America to Europe; or perhaps, home from China, some imprudent traveler has strewn on his path the hideous fruits of a promenade along the river Canton. Be wary of the proverb *piano è sano;* this is the least sanitary thing in the whole world.[2] Get into your nocturnal nest quickly, and get into it alone.

"In any case, whether or not your bedtime is surrounded by these delights and attentions, the only courtisan in attendance for your wake-up call in the morning will be avarice. Can you hear your hostess's shrewish voice? The fatal quarter-hour is nigh: you must pay a bill ten times the value of your foul meal and hateful lodging. The girls' faces have completely altered: look at their expression as they examine your six-sous coin. Anyone might think they suspect you of passing counterfeit money! Nor are you yet done with them all; whether you traveled on foot or on horseback, the stableboy is nagging for a tip.

"Not so was the voyager treated in ancestral days: hardly had he set foot under a portico than slaves rushed to wash his feet and perfume his beard; his host immolated a calf, the lady of the house and her daughters spread a good bed for him themselves; he established friendships with both father and son. Then for generations to come, the children of this sociable family would expect the voyager's children to arrive; they remembered his name; and if they ever traveled to his homeland, were sure to find safe asylum and warm welcome.

"Now when exactly did we abandon this wise and admirable custom? at the very moment when we need it most urgently. Today the Bordeaux merchant on the road no longer finds a pied-a-terre in the home of his Nantes counterpart; the count of Grand-Pré now lodges the Marquis of Rhetel's horses and servants at his local inn; the archbishop of Reims does not so much as exchange a simple blessing when the bishop of Soissons is traveling nearby.³

"In conclusion, religious houses are now the only places where hospitality is practiced. But wait—does it matter that in this case the motive for hospitality is love of the Christian God? Should we not be drawing distinctions between—?"

"Take another glass, sir," interrupted Dom Coadjutor. "You preach one of the finest sermons I ever heard in my life; anyone would swear you were a Capuchin, and that this was not your first Lent sermon."

"You are mistaken, my dear Dom, it is an academic discourse, excellent, super-excellent," rejoined the abbé Séchant, shaking his head gently to and fro on its atlas vertebra.

"I would have sworn it was a sermon."

"Our neighbor the Baron of Stone was just telling us the other day that philosophers nowadays do nothing but preach or plead in court," cried Séché, "and this is why they are hated by both preaching friars and lawyers."

"And why they persecute them," Lungiet put in.

"Professional jealousy," added Mordanes.

If the two women added not a single word, it was because they had gone to bed as soon as the harangue began, while Tifarès was off getting acquainted with the scullions, and discussing their art in a corner of the kitchen hearth.

After a moment of general silence, the white monk inquired: "What is your own profession, then, gentlemen, may I ask?"

"Philosophers of various sects," replied Lungiet, "wandering the world for its enlightenment. If you would like to hear us, I have written a fine panegyric of the clergy that could pay our share . . ."

"As for me," interrupted Séché the ever-interrupter, "I have geometrically proven the only reason Jesus Christ came on earth, which was to teach natural law."

"I was taught he came to save us," the good monk meekly replied.

"Exactly the same thing," Séché answered, "so if you are curious about . . ."

"Not curious myself; but I will mention it to Dom Prior, who may be happy to listen. We have here in the cloister a philosopher to teach our novices the art of disputation, and perhaps you can have a joust with him. My own job is to take care of the smithy and wine cave."

"Now there's true philosophy!" remarked Mordanes.

As it was ten o'clock, they now separated: the travelers to bed down in the men's quarter, and Dom Coadjutor to his room and his reflections on the workings of chance, which had collected so many philosophers at a Carthusian abbey in the depths of Champagne.

CHAPTER FIFTEEN

Morning Matins at the Charterhouse

THE CHARTERHOUSE BELLS had already tintinnabulated more than once, and every little altar had been honored by a sacrificial victim. Time for breakfast: fresh rolls, cylinders of butter, and half-bottles of wine awakened the appetites of the peace-loving hermits in various quarters of the house. Crossing the courtyard to his own rooms, Dom Prior met the Coadjutor who approached him with a half-modest, half-cavalier air, well-polished boots, a whip in one hand, and his robe hiked gallantly up on the other side. Getting ready for any journey, a monk puts on his hat, struts, looks in the mirror, and practices his formal manners; does he want to look laughable in society's eyes by presenting himself as an awkward soldier of the Cross? No—he is not such a fool. Watch any Minim, simple Franciscan though he may be, walk down the street. Ahem! He lifts his hem gracefully, draping the cloth at an angle to reveal silk knee-breeches, brilliantly white stockings, and diamond buckles, with a watch-chain as long as the one any attorney's clerk sews to his breeches. See how he carries his head, and his benedictory greeting. Aha! father, father! But Margot may still turn up her nose at your patron saint, poor Francis of Paola, even if she admires your dashing figure.

The Coadjutor had a twinkle in his eyes. Noticing this, his colonel wished him a very good morning in a way that hinted: "Come on, make me laugh too, friend Coadjutor! I'm ready for a laugh: what's going on? An adventure with a girl?" For when a monk is laughing, there's a girl either in his sight or in his heart.

"The funniest traveling camp in the world! Two passable women, a frisky donkey, and men who preach away like sermonizers in Lent. Dom Hachette thought they must be Capuchins, and they do smell rather like; I thought them Bohemians; but they call themselves philosophers. One of them would like to pronounce a panegyric to the clergy in your presence . . ."

"Delighted to hear it," replied the Prior. "And I'll convoke our monks in the small chapter-house, because today is our day of recreation. This spectacle may offer some diversion, since solitude has been affecting their minds of late."

"No fear! We have at present the lowest level of insanity on record in this cloister; we count at most five interned madmen out of the thirty, and the new arrival makes only six."

"Agreed," replied the Prior. "First dinner, and then the sermon." And he continued his promenade.

The Coadjutor transmitted the order, and Lungiet prepared himself to appear before this venerable audience.

In the meantime, while the Prior's message was being transmitted to Dom Vicar in the cloister, Dom Jean, a friend of mine who happened to be in Dom Vicar's cell at the time, heard it too. Dom Jean rushed to share the news with his colleague Dom Xavier: "A contingent from the Academy is lodging right here in the cloister, and assembling after dinner in the little chapter-house to read their work to the community! These are the premier philosophers of Europe."

"Fine news," said Dom Xavier, "I will plaster their faces and model them in wax, to add to my bust and medallion collections."

Dom Xavier's comment was heard by Dom Michel, who immediately dropped the reed he was cutting for an embouchure and ran to tell the news to Dom Vincent, who was stringing the beads of a chaplet.

Thus did Rumor in cowl and scapular ring out from cell to cell: news of the arrival of the philosophical apostles rushed throughout the cloister within fifteen minutes. Never had the sons of Saint Bruno observed silence so poorly. They all chattered together on the way to the refectory:

"What d'you know about all these philosophers? Surely from the French Academy."

"Not at all! a detachment of the Academy of Sciences."

"Must be from the Academy of Letters, here to examine our charters."

"But I tell you they are from the *museum* in the rue Dauphine."

"They have a donkey," remarked the older monks.

"And women," said the younger monks.

This scandalous rumor made the walls resound in shock: every monk felt too impatient to eat; they all ran out of the refectory and crowded into the little chapter-house. Dom Prior took his seat; each monk settled down in a stall.

Finally, the philosophical quartet made its appearance. Bissot took the lead, followed by Lungiet the Sérapion, marching between Séchant and Séché.[1] With a solemn air Lungiet mounted the tribune, waited for everyone to gaze attentively at him in silence, and began to speak in the following terms.

CHAPTER SIXTEEN

Panegyric of the Clergy

"I HAVE NOT taken this chair to instruct you about the utility of the clergy to which you belong—for who would dream of attacking the existence of the clergy?[1] which is as necessary as the worship it supports. The slanderous topics of attack on the clergy are: its riches, its mores, its love for the government, and its open-mindedness. And on these scores will I undertake to justify it.

"I shall demonstrate that within the church, all the excesses for which her ministers may be justly accused are individual divagations; the overwhelming majority of the clergy are pure, as loyal to its morality as to its dogma, and vigilant over sweet politics and pure religion. First, I prove that a separation of powers between politics and religion is not essential to Christianity; then that such a distinction was born of royal decadence, and adopted by the clergy as a safeguard rather than a principle of justice. Therefore nothing prevents the clergy from wielding both temporal and spiritual power: not only may the priest become a magistrate, but also there is no impediment to his ascending the throne. In conclusion, the only remedy for mankind's ills is either for the king to take holy orders, or for us to crown a priest. The only revolution capable of eliminating the obstacles to the reestablishment of true principles lies here: thus we reunite on a single tree trunk two branches which ought never have been divided in the first place, and lead mankind into the delightful, pleasant grove promised him by religion, but so oft denied him by passion.*

---

* The Mullahs of Persia maintain that royalty must never be separated from the sacerdocy; that as the sole source of civil law is the Koran, knowledge and interpretation of law should be

"What is the Clergy? What is this body whose members spend their whole lives trying to bring man closer to Divinity? We must go back to origins, and investigate the sources of our holy religion to discover the truth about who or what the clergy must have been before the existence of priests in this world. Not in the writings of the Gospel, not in the Church Fathers, but in other respected texts written by the Holy Spirit with a plume from an angel's wing, may we discover its Type or venerable model. Indeed, the clergy in Rome have always sensed as much: they have always taken the tribe of Levi for their model, and built their organization along the lines of its theocratic government: high priest, pontiff, levites correspond to pope, cardinal, bishops, priests. The deserts of Palestine offer prototypes for even the lowliest monks.[3]

"Examine the world's first clergy, led by Aaron: we will see it wield a single power: the executive power to carry out God's laws. This body never arrogated to itself a distinct legislative power. God gave his laws on Mount Sinai; Aaron put these laws into practice in the field; Moses marched at the head of their armies while his brother dispensed justice.

"The ungrateful populace, weary of theocracy, begged for a ruler: 'Give us a king to lead our armies.' But the sort of king they were asking for was a simple captain; the high priest was the supreme interpreter of law. Samuel supports Achish against King Saul. In Ezra's time, who but a priest could re-establish the code of statutes? And was not Caiaphas the judge at the first trial of Jesus of Nazareth?[4] Let us conclude, then, that secular and religious powers were combined under ancient law. Or rather that there existed only one single power: and this power belonged to priests. Didn't the author of our own religion say he came not to destroy the law, but to perfect it? Therefore, whatever he did not change in the Law must clearly stay the same.

"Some people do object, claiming to find a basis for two separate powers in Jesus's saying 'Render therefore unto Caesar the things which are Caesar's; and unto God the things that are God's.'[5] But their interpretation is labored and inadmissible. Jesus had been asked a different question: whether tribute must be paid to a foreign ruler, not a question about the power or body of the priesthood. Moreover, when Caiaphas rendered judgment, he did not do so in Caesar's name: and Jesus never considered Caiaphas an usurper, so far as we can tell. Similarly, after Jesus's death, the apostles dispensed justice to

limited to priests; that the nation is legitimately governed only by imams ever since the time of Mahomet, who was both its king and its pontiff; and that secular authority is the true usurpation. Chardin (Chapter 16, vol. 3).[2]

Christians, and considered it a crime for Christians to appear before secular judges. If Phi*** and his wife make a false declaration about their property, Peter acts as both judge and executor, so to speak.[6] Is that not the formal act of a high court? To be sure, we do not see that bishops handed down laws or sat in judgment for the Empire under Constantine and his successors, but there is a simple explanation: the bishops were not strong enough; they could not divest the moneylenders; and yet they allowed themselves to censure the emperors' edicts as best they could. One bishop tore down an edict of Diocletian's, and no bishop showed respect for the emperor whom we call Julian the Apostate, and whom our common enemies the Encyclopedists have named the PHILOSOPHER.[7]

"When we examine the principal powers of the West, we see that these governments were all founded by the clergy. Were not the clergy's fear of the Arian heresy and alarm at a possible threat to their temporal power the reasons why their puissant body promoted Clovis's ambitions, making a vial of holy oil come down to consecrate Clovis, and a thousand and one virgins spin a flag to rally his soldiers?[8] Who but a Pope could have had the power to make Saint Peter write the letter giving Charlemagne his imperial crown?[9] Didn't Charles the Bald hold his kingdom thanks to the bishops? And so the bishops specifically advised him in a body at Aix-la-Chapelle: 'Receive this kingdom by the authority of God, and govern it according to His divine will: and so we advise you, exhort you, and command you.'[10]

"But now is the time to raise our gaze to more shining hours. When Hugh Capet instigated the deposition of Arnulph, archbishop of Reims, by the Council of Bâle, for felonious crimes, Pope John XV disapproved of his enterprise and instead proclaimed: 'I will send a legate to release Arnulph from prison and depose archbishop Gerbert.' Shortly afterward, when Emperor Lothair was excommunicated, Charles the Bald and his brother, who had been awaiting this moment with some impatience, instantly invaded their half-brother's lands; and thus did temporal power pass from the bishops to the pope.[11]

"Ancient and respectable practice, then, was the basis on which popes founded their custom of dispensing crowns however they saw fit. Innocent III was merely following this practice when he released King John's subjects from their oath of fealty and received from the king suzerainty over England.[12] This is the indefeasible right of ministers of religion. Soon, indeed, their right will be revived with more power than ever, rather like our Breton nobility, who have been so mistreated by fortune.

"No member of any ecclesiastical order doubts, in his heart, the eternal sovereignty of the church in both temporal and spiritual questions. The day must come when the church takes back these usurped rights: such a moment is prefigured as celestial Babylon in the ancients' writings, while in the moderns it appears as the Last Judgment and the valley of Josaphat. This is indeed the only true natural law . . ."[13]

"*Contra quod argumentabor et contendo,*" interrupted Séché in his usual fashion: rising on his tiptoes, spreading his hands, stretching his neck, shaking his head, and flashing his eyes.[14]

"Do let him finish!"

"Why must you always interrupt?"

"Wait for your turn to speak."

Everyone intervened in vain trying to settle the dispute; orator Lungiet would not have picked up the thread of his oration for an hour or more if Dom Xavier, a young man of remarkable ingenuity, had not turned one end of his cowl into a cork with which to plug Séché the challenger's wide-open mouth.

Lungiet then resumed point two of his speech: "However, while supreme power, like unto a fire smoldering in the coals, resides ultimately in the hands of bishops, judicial power incontestably is and always has been in the hands of monks. For time immemorial, monasteries have detained dethroned kings and held the tribunals that judged them: indeed at Saint-Denis, in chancellor Suger's time . . ."

But now, just as Lungiet pronounced these words, came a loud knock at the door; suddenly the door was flung open; and a voice that alternated between tenor and bass filled the room to distract the audience's attention.

The voice of the donkey! Sociable animal that he was, the donkey hated solitude: finding the church portal ajar and nothing to entertain him in the sanctuary, he had proceeded with resolute step up to the little chapter door. Recognizing Lungiet's familiar voice as it penetrated his long ear canals and reached the sinus of his brain, he brayed in donkey lingo: "Gentlemen, let me in! I am so bored! A hermit's life is not for me."

The donkey wanted company, needless to say, since he had heard repeated in the fields the old maxim about one's own company being bad company, and had also read Seneca's letter on the dangers of solitude.[15] I can hardly blame him for craving company, and I was extremely distressed to learn about the ungracious welcome given our communicative ass:

"Where can that Tifarès be?"

"Why can't he make his donkeys keep to their duties?"

"What do you think Mordanes is up to?"

Truth to tell, I have been wondering the same thing all through Lungiet's discourse. Perhaps you too are wondering about Mordanes? Do you suspect him of paying a little visit to the cells or sacristies, perchance? For a long time I must admit I was of your persuasion; but since I never afterward heard of any thefts from the main house, I then suspected he must have had business elsewhere. I consulted others; I asked endless questions; finally, by pure chance, I discovered in a London Lyceum a bundle of papers that contained a fragment which is, as I believe, transcribed in the hand of one Claudinette.[16] I seized upon this fragment, deciphered it with great care, and then perused what you are about to read in the next chapter: note well that the speaker is Félicité.

CHAPTER SEVENTEEN

A Mouse with Only One Hole Is Easy to Take

"MAMAN'S EYES HAD never looked so odd: she was staring at Tifarès the whole time I was trimming the edge of my green skirt with a white ribbon.[1] Her eyes were brimming with water, her breath was almost panting. 'Maman,' I asked, 'do you need some fresh air? Would you like me to open a window?'

"'No,' she replied, 'I am going to take a walk; this gentleman will offer me his arm. Finish your skirt.'

"I was longing to go out with them, but I thought . . . I don't know quite what ideas could have entered my mind; I rose to my feet, went to the window, and watched them go up into a little woods. I was deeply lost in wonderment: 'But what if Maman should be taken by a wolf?' when I felt myself grabbed from behind. It was none other than Mordanes, who had come up from the corner of the poultry-yard where he was catching hens as soon as he saw Maman step outdoors.

"'Oh stop that, sir! Why frighten me so? I thought you were the wolf.'

"But as the proverb says, never cry wolf . . . Alas! I felt too soon how true this was.[2]

"'Your mama is not quite ready to return,' Mordanes said, seating me on his lap; 'and our philosophers are busy with the monks. This is too good an opportunity for me not to take it—one I have desired for so long.' He then insisted on kissing me. His hands were so strong, hard, like iron; I did my best to defend myself, but in vain.

"All I could say was: 'Hurry up, get it over with.' But his tongue soon stopped my mouth. My body was bent over his left arm, and his mouth was glued to mine, and his right hand . . . I feel ashamed whenever I think of it. He had gone straight to a spot so sensitive, so delicate! Books must never mention this part of the body at all, for Bissot's hand has never quite located it. I would rather have felt no pleasure, but I was not in control, and I decided it made little difference: I could not cry for help. And I would have been lucky if Mordanes had stopped at that point. The bed was right nearby: he picked me up like a child and put me down in the middle.

"'Leave off, I am going to yell, I will tell Maman!' I crossed my legs—but alas! not for long. He soon pried them open, and made me feel that philosophers are not the strongest of men. His stomach on mine was like a rock, like the mountain pressing down on the Titans.

"But I knew I might already be pregnant—and I realized I would not want there to be any doubts about the father of my child. This notion gave me courage, and love gave me the inspiration for a trick that pleasure would surely condemn. Just when brawny Mordanes was trying his hardest, a slight imperceptible movement of mine shifted his target out of range. His lance missed its mark, and only bruised me. But he began huffing and puffing in a terrifying way; leaning on one hand, he helped himself with the other. He was getting closer to his target; and the closer he came, the more strength I needed to resist him. He soon discovered my ruse, and squeezed me down on the bed between his wrists, allowing me to move in only one direction, up and down. I almost gave in—but with one last effort I lifted myself yet another inch higher: he was pushing hard, but I knew that if I allowed him his mistake I could remain faithful. I soon felt myself penetrated in a place very different from the one I had been saving for my sweetheart. I—who always disliked even a cannula lubricated with sweet butter!—You be the judge of what I suffered. Every buffalo blow hurt me, though in a way it was also pleasurable; at last a soothing balm announced relief, and I congratulated myself on my fidelity.

"Afterward I found he had left me covered with blood; I rushed to make the bed presentable, while he went back to his chickens. Maman returned almost at the same time. She seemed so flushed, her bonnet seemed so awry, and Tifarès seemed so undone, that I thought perhaps she had resorted to my very same trick! But she paid no attention to my disarray; I avoided looking at her also, and I thought she was glad of it. She must have known perfectly well that one morning when I awakened next to her in bed, I had pretended to ignore the noise Mordanes was making in her arms. Séché and Tifarès might not be anything much; but Mordanes really was a big deal."

CHAPTER EIGHTEEN

How Lungiet Was Interrupted by a Miracle

IT IS SO painful for a historian to begin his tale convinced no one will believe him, that if I thought belief had quite vanished from the face of this earth, I would leave this page blank. But there are still good souls left in the world: our problem is not total incredulity, but rather the rarity of miracles, which we have lost the habit of believing in. Yet miracles happen every day. Such a pity the skeptics from the Academy of Sciences were not present at this miracle; what a shock it would have given them!

Lo! At this very moment when the donkey intruder had been chased out of the chapter, and monks, shavelings, philosophers, and orator Linguet were ready to listen and to speak, respectively, the statue of Saint Bruno in a nearby niche moved to cover its eyes with its hand, which had always been stretched forth in the posture of a Saint giving benediction.

Dom de Scy was the first to notice the Saint's change of posture: "Miracle!" he cried, pointing to the statue. The entire assembly commented in surprise. But while everyone present agreed on the miracle as fact, they all began to debate among themselves as to means and cause.

"Saint Bruno must have been annoyed to see a layman in his chair!" said the first.

"The speech must have offended him," others replied.

"Oh no! It would have been his ears that he covered, in that case."

"Maybe the donkey's entrance caused a pollution—"

"You think this is the first ass who ever walked into a chapter house?"

Would you like to know the true cause of Saint Bruno's prudish gesture?

A cause no Carthusian could guess, at least not without divine revelation? Dear reader, the cause was Mordanes's terrible assault on the lovely Félicité, taking place at that moment. The same instant that offered her hope of deliverance gave the astonished Saint Bruno evidence of depraved tastes; until then he had watched in silence, but no sooner had he seen with his own saintly and lynx-like eyes the workings of the ejaculatory mechanism than he cried: "Oh! that's it—you are a . . ." And in modesty, Saint Bruno covered his eyes. No one except, perhaps, a graduate of Reims or Saint-Omer would have acted differently;[1] I can hardly blame Saint Bruno. A miracle of modesty is an excellent thing.

And honestly, I don't understand why this miracle should be so difficult to believe: if I were to claim that Saint Ignatius of Loyola or Saint Francis Xavier had hidden their eyes for such a trifle, I might expect people to distrust it. But Saint Bruno! In any case, what is the problem about miracles? Why can't things that happened a thousand years ago happen again today? Does not Horace himself inform us that the god Priapus's statue moved in a certain way because of Lydia and Canidia's incantations?—Why shouldn't Saint Bruno be as good as any pagan god?[2] Now tell the truth: if we fed five thousand people on five loaves and three fishes nowadays, wouldn't you believe they could take afternoon tea later on, with no risk of indigestion? At the Feast of Corpus Christi in 1768 or '69, what happened when we saw a paralytic cured?[3] All Paris saw it—but because the paralytic was a Jansenist, our lord archbishop determined that he had never been paralyzed in the first place. Though as I recall perfectly well, the learned doctor Abbé Chessimont of the Sorbonne assured me it was as much of a miracle as ever miracle was. The seed was good, but the ground was not prepared; so nobody believed. In another two days, no one even mentioned it. Surely you know the blessed Saint Labre, a native of Boulogne, the professed mendicant?[4] Saint Labre went to Rome and died in the odor of sanctity not long ago there; but if he had come to Paris instead, the constables of the porridge bowl would have forced him to beat hemp all day in the Saint-Denis workhouse; and if he had tried to take fifteen minutes off to pray, preach, or perform one percent of the miracles witnessed in Italy, some irreligious turnkey, doubtless imbued with philosophical literature, would have beaten him with a thousand strokes of the bullwhip.

Yet you complain that miracles are rare! Blame the government: why don't they establish prizes for miracle workers? On Saint Louis Day, shouldn't they be awarding laurels to saints, rather than to worthless scribblers of panegyric praise and frigid verse?[5] Why not have first prize for a saint who makes a tax collector impartial; second prize for a saint who converts a prelate's tastes to study and humility; honorable mention for a saint who makes a High Court lawyer concise; second honorable mention for a saint who discovers a continent, sober, scholarly monk? But the age we live in cares for nothing but trifles.

Dom Prior knelt piously at the feet of the statue: "O great Saint Bruno!" he prayed, "forgive us if we have had the misfortune to offend you! We are all sinners, I well know: but which one of us in particular has offended? Whoever it is, I will banish him forever from your presence."

Every listener perked up his ears, but to no effect. Not a single word did Bruno utter; but then, who can expect an oracle and a miracle to happen on the very same day!

Dom Prior immediately dismissed the assembly and ordered the philosophers to vacate the monastery. And thus Lungiet's peroration on natural right, as well as the brilliant points Séché would surely have made in rebuttal, are lost to us.

CHAPTER NINETEEN

Which Will Not Be Long

HAVING DEPARTED SO late in the day from the Mont-Dieu monastery, our philosophers could get no farther than the village of Stone, where thanks to the Capuchins' silverware they procured the best this poor village could offer. They supped frugally, they drank bad wine, and they had to make room for each other in a hayloft overnight. I am unable to discover exactly what happened that night, but everyone was out of temper. Mordanes most of all: he kept hideously cursing miracles in general, as he had hoped to line his pockets a lot better before leaving the hostel. The troupe's free-thinkers claimed this particular miracle of Saint Bruno had been simple sleight-of-hand. The women were yawning with boredom at hearing these cliché arguments pro and con miracles during dinner. Tifarès recited the litanies of Saint Bruno, his squinty eyes wide open for once. Voragine desired the company's charms, while Félicité smiled as she recalled how she had tricked Mordanes.

At last, everyone fell asleep. Bright and early the next morning, they awoke and breakfasted at Beaumont-le Vicomte, a place-name whose "m" of the first word has been switched by the god of concord with the "c" of the third word, as we readers are informed in an excellent book on the divagations of the human mind.[1] After breakfast, they traveled next to Stenay, a little town called Satanilcum by the ancient monks because the inhabitants all worshiped Jupiter and detested monks—for those were the days before Jupiter had quite given way to the Heavenly Father.[2]

CHAPTER TWENTY

A Pilgrim's Narrative

THE SUN HAD almost reached the height of its career, and the heat was un-
bearable; the poor scalawag donkey made little progress, loaded with provisions and manuscripts, panting, his tongue out: he would take twenty paces,
tail between his legs, and then lie down and wait, as if to tell his master in
donkey dialect: "Whoa right here under this beech."

At that moment, emerging from the woods, our travelers found themselves
in a beautiful meadow watered by the serpentine Meuse. Above the stream, trees
on the hill formed an amphitheater inviting the weary travelers to repose before
the evening cool, and enjoy the delightful hay-time spectacle as far as the eye can
see: a meadow between low hills, a town, two dozen villages, and golden fields of
grain bordered on the horizon by the vast and majestic Ardennes Forest.

Mordanes leads his troupe to dine and take their ease in the meadow;
everyone lies down on the grass in the health-giving shade, except for himself
and the worthy Tifarès. The indefatigable Mordanes has gone to collect dry
branches from the woods, while his pupil unsaddles their faithful donkey, prepares the food, puts the meat on a spit, fills the stewpot, and places the water
barrel to cool in the stream.

But now their moment of silence was pleasantly broken by the voice of
a young traveler dressed as a pilgrim. Accompanying himself on a guitar, he
sang the following verses:

O vain fidelity,
Tra la la la, tra la la la,

Why faithful should we be?
'Tis but our vanity *(3 times)*.
For Love detests both lock and chain,
Tra la la la, tra la la la.
Fidelity we try in vain,
Love flies away and won't remain.

*

To fly from fair to fair,
Is to keep faith with love,
To fly from fair to fair,
Is like the Gods above (3 times).
In chapels everywhere,
In hearts with zeal aflame,
In chapels everywhere,
Adored be their name.

As soon as he had sung each verse, the young traveler wrote it down; he seemed lost in thought, the very picture of a poet suffering the agony of improvisation. After the fifth verse Séchant, familiar with the labors of intellectual childbirth, cried: "Gadzooks! Here is a most amoral author!"

"Author!" cried the young man, lifting his head, immediately putting his guitar into its shoulder strap, and leaping to his feet like a terrified man: "Did you say author? O heavens . . ."

"Yes, yes," warbled Séchant in admiring tones, "and you are not the only one: we gentlemen are authors too! Do not hesitate to admit your profession, come join us, and let us all dine together."

"Forgive me, sirs, I thought . . . but are you actually authors? You're sure you're not setting a trap for me? You may be a squadron of secret police, sent to . . ."

"Not at all, sir," replied Séché, "your suspicions are an insult to us. Just look at this basket, which is entirely filled with manuscripts."

"Since that is so," returned the pilgrim, "let me take advantage of your good company, and I shall sing you my newly composed romance while your dinner is prepared."

"We heard your song just now, sir, and to tell the truth, we considered it of dubious morality; were your words in jest?"

"Forgive me! I am no preacher or rhetorician; I am singing the simple truth. I did once set to music a folio volume summarizing my theories of ethics and behavior—and illustrated with engravings—but alas!" The pilgrim could not keep himself from weeping a few tears.

"Alas good sir!" intervened Sérapion: "might you be an unfortunate victim of persecution, forbidden to sing or write? Excommunicated from the ranks of musicians? Speak, tell your misfortunes to your fellow unfortunates."

"Oh, mine is a long story, and you gentlemen might be bored . . ."

"We could never be bored by a handsome cavalier like yourself, sir, believe me," cried Fanchette.[1]

"You will offer us the extremest pleasure," added Voragine, whose beady wet gaze had already scanned the pilgrim up and down a thousand times.

Their invitations were seconded by Mordanes, who arrived carrying a load of mostly dry wood and a few green twigs; Tifarès turned the spit; and the pilgrim began his story.

History of the Pilgrim

"Ladies and gentlemen: You all saw my distress at being called an author just now. Let me now admit to it, I do not blush for it; I do in some sense belong to the Republic of Letters; but nowadays this is a dangerous confession . . ."

"Certainly," interrupted Séché the continual interrupter, "and besides . . ."

"Beware the gags if you interrupt so soon! Why can't you listen quietly and let other people talk?"

"We can only hope the gentleman is willing to continue."

". . . A dangerous admission nowadays: not only to be an author but to admit it! As proof of which, I offer you my literary history.

"I was born in the little town you see before you now—the least likely soil in Europe to produce a man of letters. Thirty years ago none of the inhabitants could read so much as the missal; even today our court clerk is the only one who can write, and it's often hard for him to read his own handwriting, except in a lucky guess. If we believe the ancient documents preserved in our bell tower and deciphered by scholars including Mabillon, a native of the last village you went through, our town was founded by a colony of Trojans who settled in the forest of Ardennes, although sent by Dido to populate England after their city was taken; this origin seems likely, since our inhabitants have never learned Greek.[2] But everyone knows how our town flourished under king Dagobert: the palace on the site of the little chapel down below, for all to see, the drowning pool where he drowned his dogs if they got bilious.[3] The father Benedictines of Moulon, whose twin bell towers soar above the trees to your left, have proven these facts in numerous volumes known and respected by academics, based on title deeds recognized as authentic by the Council of Donzy, as I have been often reminded by the Abbé Creston, one of our anti-quarians and the best teacher of nightingales in the neighborhood.[4]

"Truth to tell, gentlemen, I do not get all this from family tradition. You may as well know that my ancestors did not inhabit this province; I was born here thanks only to what my late father used to call the luck of the garrison. Yet though my family cannot be called aboriginal, we certainly deserved to be. My grandfather achieved high military rank although he could not sign his name, and my father was the most anti-intellectual officer to bear arms since the creation of armigerous nobility.

"As a youth, my father had played the violin like the late Saint Cecilia; at dinner he could drink ten bottles of Sillery without showing it; he had been taught to ride horseback, shoot, and hunt superbly; his dancing master was Marcel, and he could play an accompaniment for Mademoiselle le Maure; but I find no record of penmanship lessons. Between ourselves, but let this go no further, my father may have been unable to write more than the nine letters of his name;[5] I vow I never saw him pick up a book; and since he never answered the letters I wrote respectfully asking for money, I cannot swear he read them.

"When my father remarried late in life, his second wife made up for this by having a lot of documents written which he signed unread;[6] you can thus imagine my humiliation at being called an "author." If my own mother had not been the soul of virtue, I would think I must have been a bastard, since my other ancestors were no more learned than my father and grandfather; and I must say my brothers both inherited the family illiteracy.

"My brother Louis Joseph, the elder, was born with such an aversion to letters that as a boy he burned the psalm books our servant girls carried to fan themselves in church. When he noticed a few verses inscribed on the fire screens captured by uncle Colonel Bisanus in the last Austrian war, his insur-mountable dislike of Cadmus's art inspired him to throw them into the fire;[7] in this way he reduced our town's entire stock of poetry to ashes within fifteen minutes. He was sent to school, as was the degenerate custom even in those times, but school made him so violently splenetic that he swallowed a bellyful of ink in an attempt to commit suicide. Thus he forgot how to read by the age of twenty; he developed instead a passion for drawing. He had heard the words *musa, dominus, pater* repeated so often enough that he carved their ideas into his brain: when asked in public to give a first-declension noun, he drew a table; for second declension, our Lord with the long white beard; and for third declension, a Capuchin monk.[8] It was in an effort to give my brother some notion of world geography that my friend the great geographer du Manteau invented maps without place names, although we still had to cut the inner labels off the scrolls for Louis Joseph.[9] If you talk to him about the King's wisdom and goodness, he draws you a picture of the d'Argent family, or perhaps the expulsion of the wretched Breteuil . . .[10] If you ask him, "What are the letters of the alphabet?" he answers: "Nasty little signs that engravers put on their plates after they print the best proofs." We managed to teach him to play church hymns and Christmas carols on his bass viol; his fingering and bowing were passable; but he broke the violincello into bits after his old music-master Gault had died and we suggested he learn to read music. I may therefore assure you that Louis Joseph is as ignorant as any priest of the Ardennes.

"Claude Agapith, the youngest brother, had less of the family loathing for learning, but in his youth I told him that he had natural wit and genius, and he feared that he would lose his originality if he studied the thoughts of other people. In fact if his garrison had not transferred him to Strasbourg, far away from his mistress in Grenoble, he would never even have learned to spell. I counseled him to read Roman history; he opened the book, but was scared off by Romulus's she-wolf; I advised the history of France, but the book fell from his hands as soon as he discovered that French history was built on material torn from the ruins of immoral edifices erected by superstitious and ignorant monks in honor of imaginary saints. I recommended modern history, but he unfortunately opened to an article on our recent wars, and closed the book under the pretext that this was all he ever heard about at the inn from the veteran officers of his regiment. An ex-Jesuit uncle of ours suggested devotional literature might appeal to his tender heart, but all Claude Agapith wanted to see were the portrait of the Virgin; the portrait of Mary Magdalen; and a book demonstrating '*the un-eternity of the Universe*' and the necessary existence of God. My neighbor the baron de Pouilli,[11] who knows *ex professo* about all European religions, happened to be Calvinist that year and lent him a Bible; but Claude Agapith got stuck in the opening verses on chaos, and decided the words '*God's breath moving upon the face of the deep*'[12] would produce more hot air for flying balloons than you could get by making smoke out of straw, or inflammable gas out of vitriolic acid and iron filings. One day I offered Claude Agapith a fashionable English novel to read—but he said he didn't 'enjoy dreary portrayals of bourgeois manners'; I lent him *Cyrus*—but he tired of the preciosity;[13] then twenty more novels—which he claimed were like village wedding parties, where one's only interest was the bride; finally I dedicated my first almanac to him and sent a gilt-edged copy bound in red morocco—but the cruelty! he sent back the volume with a message saying why bother to count the days, when they are all alike?

"When I struggle against Claude Agapith's peculiar mania for learning nothing, he just replies: 'The world is swarming with plagiarists, we hear; and you are trying to get me to become another bad copy?'

"'A *daub*, you should call it—that is the term of art,' adds Louis Joseph, drawing away the whole time.

"My two sisters are all there is left to describe; but since they have been in a convent since the age of seven, and have never had lovers, I have no idea whether they can do any writing at all.

"You see me an exotic plant, gentlemen; my ill-fated taste for letters has led my family to consider me an unfortunate phenomenon, which occurred *inde mali labes* as follows.[14] If memory serves, this evil inclination first came to me in the year of grace 1759, when my father was inquiring into my frame of mind before leaving for the Hanover front. 'Send to my neighbor LeClerc for a crate of his best wine,' he ordered, 'and beg him to lend me something from his pocketbook' (for there was no money in the house). He was brought the wine and a pocket-sized book, the Verdun catechism.[15] While he opened a bottle, my mother, crossing herself, read aloud from the book: '*Who created you and brought you into the world?*' This put me right to sleep. My father instantly slipped a half-glass of Champagne between my lips and ordered the boot-and-saddle trumpet call to be played in my ear by a regimental trumpeter whom he had brought along for recruitment purposes. I sprang awake at this martial music, and my father went off to war happily convinced that his son was no degenerate. Now how can anyone believe in young people's horoscopes? Major effects are so often produced by minor causes.

"Unfortunately for me, my father had brought my mother a Parisian chambermaid who was a habitual novel-reader; amidst the feminine attire in her trunk this maid had hidden as contraband both *Don Quixote* and La Fontaine's fables. She first recited a few fables; next she began reading them aloud; then behind locked doors she told me the story of the Knight of La Mancha; finally she taught me to read his story myself, and I soon knew the entire thing by heart.[16]

"When my father returned home, having lost his mules, horses, and equipment in the marvelous municipality of Minden,[17] he pronounced me a spoiled child, a little beggar who would grow up to be a great big good-for-nothing. But since I had also learned to fence, to dance a little, to ride quite well, and to hitch up our servant-girls' petticoats in the right way, I soon made my peace with him.[18] I had made myself a roundel out of a tin plate, and a lance out of a spit used for skewering little birds. One day I grabbed the village barber's metal basin, and when the good fellow cried: 'Return my basin at once, little mischief!' I shouted back, 'Rustic bumpkin! Know that this is the armor of Mambrino! Take the field and prepare to defend yourself!'[19] And I skewered him in the side and drew blood with no concern for his advanced age.

"Hearing these exploits, my father paid for the basin and realized that the military and literary were not incompatible; and when a cousin of mine who had been to the theater three times informed him that Alexander, Caesar, and various other ancient generals were neither ignorant nor stupid, he made up his mind to tolerate a tutor. That foolish little preceptor first tried for some reason to talk catechism to me. To me—who loathed the catechism as much as Louis-Joseph hated writing! I took my tutor for Tristan the enchanter, and only stopped beating him when he decided to tell me the myths about Phaedra. Abracadabra![20] He and I became best friends forever.

"But then alas! I lost my beloved mother, the dearest anyone ever had. My father sent poor Abracadabra off to the barefoot Carmelites of Luxembourg, where he took the habit. As for me, I was sent to a famous school, the Académie d'Amiens, where I studied Humanities under the learned Abbé Porcellus, the cleverest, least pious professor in the world.[21]

"The Abbé Porcellus knew ancient Rome as familiarly as the rue Saint-Jacques; his mind ran constantly on Numa, Brutus, and Horace.[22] One day while celebrating Mass, he bethought himself Neptune's priest, and offered libation instead of the communion wine. Another day instead of inviting the Lord to lead us with the '*Dominus vobiscum, age age,*' he shouted: 'Lead me that white virgin calf so I may sacrifice to Neptune.' When the late Christophe de Beaumont, archbishop of Paris, duke of Saint-Cloud and peer of France, himself a devotee of the *Short Method of Prayer* or a short passage from *Day of a Christian* rather than the complete Latinity, discovered that the Abbé Porcellus never said his breviary and was in odor of paganism, he denounced him under a *suspendatur a sacris*.[23]

"In those three words Abbé Porcellus found five solecisms and nine barbarisms, and he wrote to prove as much to the universe. The learned doctors, furious, wanted him burned at the stake; but milord archbishop replied that bonfires were reserved for parlements and Jansenists. The Abbé was a simple pagan, so he was not bonfire material.[24] The pedants were amazed that the archbishop refused to burn my professor, but they did not lose heart over so little; they went to the governor of my school, a stubborn and despotic old soldier, to accuse Abbé Porcellus of praising Brutus and Cassius in a Latin oration. The doctors tried their hardest to explain to the governor the sentiments of Brutus and Cassius, who the old soldier thought were rebels conspiring against the King in some Paris attic. The governor immediately informed the lieutenant-general of police, and my poor professor was thrown out, along with every Latin book in the house. This good old man left me his Ovid, Virgil, and Horace in parting, and I think of my old master whenever I re-read them; I occasionally go to pour honey and wine on his tombstone, a sacrifice that cannot displease his ghost.

"Meanwhile, as losing dear Abbé Porcellus had made me detest the military, my father sent me to study philosophy with the Mouson Capuchins; I did logic under the famous and celebrated A. P. Jack-ass, whose reputation had spread as far as the slopes of Sedan, the gates of Verdun, and the banks of the Meuse.

"I was just about to begin studying theology, when I was by some misfortune introduced to Brother Leopold, mathematician in ordinary to the Stenay Minims; I immediately abandoned myself to the exact sciences, and I would have made real progress if chance had not cruelly deprived me of this master also.

"One day as the commandant of the town was out drinking with his friends, good Brother Leopold went around collecting alms; these gentlemen grabbed hold of him and made him drink too much wine; a jokester profited from the friar's drunkenness, attached a leash to a most delicate part of his body, and paraded him stark naked around the public square. The ensuing scandal made my illustrious professor abandon Stenay forever.

"I maintained my vocation nonetheless, and taught myself enough astrology to understand the Almanac of Liège, tell people's fortunes, and give advice.[25] For example, I told a young girl she would die an old maid, because she was ugly, annoying, and bitter; I foretold the physician Gillet would kill himself if he took his own medicine; I predicted that our curate would die of boredom if he re-read his own homilies; and I said to our commandant that some day he would get drunker than usual, and crack his head open. People from a league away came to consult me. I told ladies when it was time to trim their nails—not one would have so much as washed her fingertips, if I had not announced it was time for the sign of Aquarius. I kept an old Grenadier captain, a cousin on my mother's side, limping for over a month because I forgot to tell him to cut the corns off his foot when the moon was on the wane.

"However, gentlemen, all talents give rise to envy, a tribute they must pay to public ignorance. One fine day at a secular assembly convoked by our ladies of rank, I was asked to read aloud an article from the necrology you call the *Gazette de France*; I agreed without hesitation, and acquitted myself so fluently that I had as many enviers as auditors. An old marquis eyed me askance. A sallow lady stared at me with haggard pea-green eyes from under her black eyebrows. My cousin Mimi smirked at me. Worst of all, I noticed Louis-Joseph sketching a prison cell in the fireplace cinders with the tip of his cane. I left the assembly feeling gloomy and distressed at this last inauspicious sign, because Louis-Joseph is my sacred chicken.[26]

"A second, and this time catastrophic, experience soon confirmed these depressing presentiments: someone sent my father ninety-nine legal counts of indictment against me. Here are the principal counts: A Jesuit in disguise, confessor of the nuns whose convent you can see from here, swore she had heard Louise of the Sacred Heart say someone in the parlor had told her I was a Jansenist. Our curate supported the Jesuit's testimony, commenting that he would never have believed me so impious as that, but had long suspected me of atheism and Manicheanism because I slept through his sermons. To this they added the letters of an old crone who had been in love with me complaining she had found me in default; attributing such defect to physical vice on my part rather than ugliness on hers, she advised me to get myself circumcised. A local wit easily discovered the hidden meaning of her letters, and showed this was a brilliant way to get me to become a Jew, or a Mohammedan, or perhaps a Turk. Other letters accused me of Molinism, Nothing-ism, and deism. Finally came two fat notebooks, one calculating the tables of the moon and the other filled with differential equations, reason enough to suspect me of practicing magic, like Marshal Fabert of sorcerer memory.[27] Worse yet, I had even predicted that my stepmother was going to die in a fit of rage. I now spare you the rest of the accusations, and move on to the trial.

"As soon as my father received this terrifying memorandum, my stepmother ran panting to give it to a man who is now secretary to a Verdun farmer-general, but was then passing his time in the public square leading Minims around on a leash, you-know-where the leash was attached: this secretary extended, embroidered, and padded the memorandum as thoroughly as if he were writing an official report. Armed with this weighty weapon, my father sought out his brigadier cousin: the most hunchbacked, mean-spirited little brigadier in the King's army, but the only sharp-witted cousin he had among the multitudes in our fair city.

"This hunchback did not trouble my father to wait while he read the in-folio. 'Hand it over,' cried he; 'rather than read one page of this pile of papers, I would sign off on the imprisonment of your sons, your daughters, my daughter, my son-in-law, and all my friends and relations.'

"Despite this last remark, the hunchback brigadier and my father agreed to convoke a family council: but since none of my other relatives wanted to attend their council of war, they collected a bunch of scoundrels from the highway, like the wedding in the Bible.[28] The hunchback cousin was planning a second marriage to the daughter of a blind, one-armed, one-legged old invalid officer named Cinq-Ton,[29] whom he appointed to be the learned assembly's president. Another judge was a heavy, stupid distant cousin on my father's side, stupid, so very stupid that he could not be convinced two and two make four, despite the efforts of sixteen mathematics professors for ten long years. Also present were the laziest court clerk in France, a good fellow whose exquisite wife was a cousin in the twelfth degree to the grandmother of my stepmother; the dimmest sergeant-at-arms in the royal household; and another friend of my father's, an ass who drank all day and played the violin, but whose name escapes me now. All seven archons sat at the hunchback brigadier's table, tossed the documents under the table to make room for more bottles, and began to drink away steadily until ten o'clock at night; they had started before breakfast so as not to miss the appointment. When they were completely intoxicated, the secretary handed them a family-council decision that he had already written, and everybody signed without reading it.

"Unluckily for me, the Minister was another illiterate, so he did not read the *lettre de cachet* that he sent to the city commandant for my arrest; and since they noticed my brother Louis-Joseph drawing figures in the ashes with his cane, and traveling as usual with a small woman and a little dog, they generously included him in the epistle of incarceration. But the very same book-learning that had attracted this thunderstorm over my head, now helped me escape it. The Commandant was just as unable to read as the Minister, so he sent his lackey to carry the missive to the schoolmaster, who was supposed to summarize its contents to him. However, I happened to be advising the schoolmaster's daughter as to the best moment to pluck her eyebrows and wash her hands; she gave me timely warning, and poor Louis-Joseph and I fled to Liège.

"There my reputation for astrological science prompted Mathieu Lans-berg's successor Lauterberg to hire me for the coming year as a prophet. There too I came to know the reverend Rosicrucian Father, an ex-Franciscan just back from Rome, where he had been secretary to the cardinal-governess, youngest and most lovable of the sacred College. The Rosicrucian Father was at this time translating the works of Dr. Williams.[30] I predicted a very dry spring, we had constant rain, and the Rhine flooded a suburb of Cologne; the problem was that I did not write my predictions after the event. But this infuriated M. Lauterberg, and he fired me without even paying my skimpy wages as a prophet.

"Hearing that the Prince of Orange sought an astrologer for the Queen of England, I managed to travel to London as best I could; I arrived to find the barometrist M. Deluc already appointed. But one day while hunting for a rich lord in need of a hired prophet—not easy to find, given the hard times for prophets these days—I passed by the Haymarket Coffee House and saw in the street a funeral; many of the followers were obviously French. The de-ceased, they informed me, was an old man named Gouix, brother to my lord Gouix; this Gouix had died of indigestion, and his position on the *Courrier de l'Europe* was now vacant.[31]

"I immediately went and offered myself to M. de Serre de la Tour, who engaged me to write in correct prose the articles '*Dragées de la Mecque*,' 'Co-lombo Elixir,' 'Packet-boat from Brighton to Dieppe,' 'Milord Saint's Hotel in Calais,' 'Refutation by Thomas Evans of Bastille Memoirs, including its epigraph *My design is to reason and not to declaim*.'[32] I had made my fortune at last, or so I believed, and I saw myself in possession of a post that would last my lifetime, or at least the lifetime of the newspaper.

"But Fortune had not yet finished persecuting me. A lady subscriber wrote us a letter complaining about trifles by Madame de Sillery and others supposedly infecting children's education; that a German Jew named Mon-sieur Camp used a dancing bear to demonstrate the existence of God to his pupils; and that M. Berquin's style sounded like the marquis de Mascarille in the guise of a shepherd.[33] For whatever reason, God now gave the breath of life to one marquis du Crest, a person previously unknown to me, who thought these last words of our lady correspondent had been aimed personally at him; he protested that this was an intentional insult on my part to him, despite his rank as marquis and as author. His complaints soon reached the ears of Samuel Swinton, Esq., a man who never allowed his paper to offend the least little marquis of Europe: and I nearly lost my job.

"At this juncture, however, my father happened to die.[34] As I thought it essential to look after the succession in person, I paid my compliments to my friend M. de Serre de la Tour and brought my literary existence to an end.

"You have seen enough already to understand whether or not I am right to fear to be taken for an author! But you do not know even half the ways a life in letters has harmed me. Nothing you have heard compares with the rest of my story for persecutions and amazing miracles, which all really happened to me."

"Delighted as we certainly are by the tale of your career as a philosopher," Mordanes now told the pilgrim, "earnestly hoping as we are to hear the rest of your adventures, we must postpone the pleasure of your kind offer until after dinner. How painful it must be for you to remember these hardships, and wine will give you more comfort than a hundred pages of Seneca."

The pilgrim followed the Bohemian's advice; but all during dinner, he had to answer the inquisitive Séché's many questions about the little town of his birth: composition of the land, freedom of trade, rate of taxation, population, local customs, and happiness of the poor.

"Our soil is scanty," replied the former man of letters, "and not naturally too fertile. It produces some wheat, wine, and wood, but not much, partly because it is exhausted and partly because the people who cultivate it have no means to make it productive. Since we have no industry, and our people must get whatever ready money they need by selling part of their wheat and straw to the nearby garrison, they possess only a few thin, weak, hungry beasts, and can barely pay the inconsiderate taxes imposed by the Condé family, to which our land belongs. Once we were not acquainted with luxury, everything cost little, and our ancestors could pick up enough wood in the forest to maintain a hearth that kept the family warm in winter. Now all that has changed. The Prince brought and won an unfair lawsuit against us: on our most valuable lands, which he had no right to grab, beside the mill where ancient tyrannical feudal right obliges us to grind our wheat, he has now dug a canal and built a forge. The forge in turn raises the price of our wood.

"We have no compulsory militia, true, but since we also have no industry, necessity forces our young men to earn a living by either joining the army or becoming servants. Since our daughters lack for husbands, they let themselves be seduced by officers and soldiers, go to Rheims and Paris to give birth, and almost never come back home. The handsome river before you is navigable, but we operate nary a single boat because our farmers are so afraid of contraband. In town, we count five or six miserable second-hand dealers for every merchant. We are poor, all things considered, and we live poorly.

"To flourish, we would need only capital and intelligence: we are well positioned to become a communication center between Verdun and Sedan, Lorraine and Champagne. We might establish a warehouse for wines of the Bar region, and magazines for the local Ardennes ironwork; manufacturing pins and needles would be a great success here, and so would lace-making; printers and bookshops would circulate money as a commonplace occurrence, and along with that affluence increase love of country, and love of virtue.

"But as things are now, I cannot see the point of shutting up within badly-built city walls four thousand individuals who should be spread out equally on the face of the earth. When, as today, the armed nations of Europe have all agreed to respect the peasant and avoid waging barbarous wars, the pestilential and debasing aggregations we call small towns serve no purpose. Workers in towns and villages must often walk a league before reaching the field they are obliged to cultivate; their weary beasts have another league to plod before getting back to the stables, and sometimes yet another before their pastureland.

"These various causes of poverty do not keep our morals high, or prevent the rise of luxury. The low cost of commodities makes residence in our neighborhood attractive to people of independent means—Germans, Englishmen, aging valets whose masters have pensioned them off, retired army officers, agents for German princes. All such people come here to live here in noble style—that is, to drink, eat, sleep, play, and be idle. Since they cannot spend their whole income on food, they adopt Parisian fashions and build miniature palaces. The bourgeois townspeople imitate them; so the draper must sell his cloth dear, and the judge raise the price of his verdict; the attorney has to steal a bit extra; more people engage in smuggling contraband. Humble people who do not control their daily wage grow more unfortunate, eat and dress poorly; and while the lady wives of the procurator and the provost may wear silk, their nephews and cousins are begging door to door. Meanwhile good company assembles in the gambling rooms, where our friends' hopeless extravagance is a target for ridicule by the garrison officers—for you know, as soon as a man acquires a brightly colored silk decoration for his coat sleeve, he forgets he too is a Frenchman, or even human. Thus do mastiffs chained up in the bull ring bite and slash at their comrades, once they enter the lists. An officer looks in disdain at the bourgeois, as he calls him; what he wants is the wife of the bourgeois, his daughter, his table, his purse, and most frequently all at once."

"Take it easy," cried Mordanes, "*de milito nihil nisi bonus*": words he had heard from a trial attorney for whom he had clerked in his youth.[35]

"I know as well as you do, sir," replied the traveler, not to be intimidated by the Bohemian's swashbuckling, "that it may seem dangerous to speak one's thoughts so freely. But you started me off: and once the stream reaches the mill, the wheel turns devilish fast. I love the military well, but truth better: take me as I am, I am a man who has spoken truth to power on more than one occasion. I am well aware that there are officers and soldiers who are both French and human, but unfortunately for both France and humanity, these are relatively few in number. The ignorance in which our troops are kept about their most sacred duties should make our leaders tremble. What limits can possibly restrain a band of unprincipled, poorly paid, ill-nourished, unappreciated individuals? The army is a corporation of men who would do better to cultivate their own patrimony than frighten the peaceful citizen. When regular armies were first established, our kings employed priests to guide the men, but now *nec pueri credunt nisi qui nondum aere lavantur.*[36]

"Can you conceive it politic, sir, to decommission the people and entrust the kingdom's defense to a bunch of imbecile mercenaries? One more day like Malplaquet, and our state will become defenseless.[37] Our once-brave nation—martial from ten centuries of fighting—will be gone, never to return. No, any barbarian who wins a single battle will be able to make our kingdom bow under the yoke. There, sir, you see the result of the hateful petty politics that now divide the king's interests from the nation's, ruining the ancient nobility that once united head to body, and obliging it to release its arm and hand over its sword."

"Bravo! Bravo!" Bissot and Séché competed with each other to applaud. "The gentleman speaks like a true philosopher. We'd agree with him completely if not for the honor and respect we owe brave Mordanes."

"All well and good," replied Sérapion, "but the gentleman has not explained how feudal government . . ."

"Not the point, the question is liberty and bread for the poor . . ."

"Quiet! Enough!" shrieked Voragine. "You mind-numbing philosophers have rehearsed this stuff a hundred times! For God's sake stop your endless homilies and dreary debates or, i'faith, beware my gag. This man has his story to finish, and it is only right to listen."

Voragine's combination of curiosity and threats finally led to peace and quiet. Just so did Neptune show his annoyance when King Aeolus's offspring, in an attempt to please jealous Juno, were raising merry hell above his head: ruler of the deep, irked at their airs and commotion in his watery realm, he burst out of the waves accompanied by countless Triton cornets, one elderly

Triton and Ino nursing the infant Melicertus at her droopy breasts. The winds, astounded and aghast at the apparition of Jupiter's admiral with his fearsome oaths and pitchfork, fled a-whistling through their fingers and got tossed, sots that they were, back into the bastille of damp-bearded Aeolus.[38]

Meanwhile Tifarès offered wine glasses to everyone and Félicité followed with the brandy bottle, serving gracefully as Ganymede or Hebe ever poured nectar on Olympus, whilst the company leaned on their elbows, craned their necks, and listened to the stranger resume his narrative, which we shall relate in the following chapter.

CHAPTER TWENTY-ONE

Continuation of the Pilgrim's Narrative

"ANOTHER MOTIVE I had for returning to Paris upon the sad news of my recent loss, beside my concerns about inheriting the succession, was to ensure the appropriate masses, vespers, paternosters, Ave Marias, and other minor prayers to get my father's soul out of purgatory, should it happen not to have gone straight to Paradise.[1] The preceding on the explicit condition that the aforesaid masses, vespers, and other prayers of lesser value would be applicable to the soul of my grandmother; and should her soul be unavailable, to the nearest-related soul in direct line on my father's side, taking precedence over an equal degree of relationship on the mother's side, present in purgatory during the *ite missa est* of the last of these masses, with no purgatorian being able to take or claim any portion of it unless in the absence of the dead previously mentioned; all this to be properly stipulated and explained so as to prevent any proceedings, outcries, clamors, or lawsuits for costs and expenses among the aforesaid souls. For the payment of which masses, vespers, and prayers of lesser value, I would assign the first deniers found after breaking the seal on the door of my said father's house, up to the value of 366 masses (given the bissextile year), 52 vespers, and other money for ten great masses, prayers, verses, and various minor offerings.[2]

"However, good sirs, my aforesaid father's second marriage having left a daughter with a gift for taking things, my inheritance was despoiled, as was eloquently explained to me by Antoine l'Arrivant, bourgeois of Paris.[3] In order not to fail in my filial duties, I found myself obliged to empty my purse into the hands of the reverend Capuchin fathers and return to London on foot;

and so I certainly would have traveled, like some nameless Jew from days of yore or perhaps Neptune's horses—making no comparison—if I had only known the secret of walking on water.[4]

"Having thus got myself as far as Boulogne on Christmas Eve in our year of grace 1783, my finances reduced to the minimum, I became deeply and painfully aware of how hard it is to cross the English Channel. In this extremity, I thought my best option would be pious attendance at every mass sung in church by our most reverend Capuchin fathers. Since heaven had graced these good fathers with the ability to live without work or expense, I felt they might easily fund my return trip back to England.

"And so there I was, gentlemen, at a beautiful ceremony held by the Boulogne Capuchins to celebrate midnight mass: novices dressed as angels and saints singing Christmas carols; Father Anne-Marie as the Holy Virgin, with an honest village cuckold marvelous in the role of Saint Joseph. An infant who had been miraculously found at the convent door the preceding night, was now laid in a crèche. Around the infant: a fat Roman Catholic Irishman, living in Boulogne for easy access to wine and the holy mass, enacted the bull's part to perfection; a philosophy professor played the ass to general satisfaction. After making my ceremonial devotions, I retreated to pray in an alcove; the congregation and Capuchins went off for Christmas feast; and I found that the only other person in the church was an ancient beggar who was praying with the best grace in the world.

"But here, gentlemen—now this is the most ticklish part of my narrative, and if you are worldly sorts whose faith would not have sufficed to move even a little hill in the olden days when mountains moved around like baby goats, then you may think me an impostor . . ."

"Pray continue, sir, we are Catholic, apostolic, and Roman, thank God," cried Tifarès; "and you can tell us nothing as miraculous as what just happened to us only twenty-four hours ago! Although I must also say how glad I am to find you a good Christian, since the first part of your story made me think you might be some sort of agnostic geometrician, or heretic, or deist, or atheist, or other kind of modern miscreant so common nowadays. The gentlemen here before you are Lungiet, who has been crucified and seen miracles in his time; Séchant, who is a godly priest; Séché, who was once a man of the cloth . . ."

"Shut up, you damn idiot," said Mordanes, observing poor Tifarès's religious perplexities; "did anyone ask you to make our profession of faith? Continue, good sir: we shall believe every word coming out of your mouth as if it were gospel."

"And that would be an excellent decision on your part! Mine is no obscure out-of-the-way miracle, but has been witnessed by thousands still alive; if martyrdom were still fashionable, no doubt thousands of men would volunteer to be martyred this very day to prove my miracle true.

"Once the congregation had disappeared and we were alone in the church, the mendicant approached and begged for alms in a humble, soft, pitiful voice. I had only one écu left to me but the old fellow looked so pale, so defeated, and claimed to have gone for such a long time without eating—or so he said—that I gave him that last little coin. But then what did I see before me! No longer that repulsive leathery, red-eyed, rheumy old graybeard dressed in patchwork rags and tatters. No, gentlemen, I now beheld a figure shining in glory, his shorn scalp encircled by a crown of beautiful red hair; his perfumed beard was swathed in a pink taffeta nosebag; he was clothed in a silver-cloth levite robe fastened with a sash of fresh roses as is worn on Corpus Christi feast day, and covered by a long ermine-lined cloak; his feet, rubbed down with almond paste, could be seen peeking out of red-and-white slippers laced in the fashion of ancient times.

"'Never fear, dear brother,' said this figure, in a voice gentle and harmonious as any opera-girl; 'I am content with your good heart, although I read therein that you are giving alms out of human rather than Christian charity. Surely evil in the Lord's eyes; but that evil does not release me from the obligations of gratitude. I know your predicament, and have come to help you. Take this bit of rope I used to gird up my loins while still I inhabited this mortal coil; the cord will serve you well. In the days when I used to solicit alms, I made a practice of begging from women, of whatever rank. I noticed that women making donations were always staring at the recipient's nose, so I asked the Holy Ghost, with whom I am on excellent terms, for the grace of growing my nose in proportion to my needs. And the same pigeon that had borne the Holy Ampulla immediately appeared before me, holding in its beak the sacred rope from which your cord is taken; and this rope was made, I have since discovered, from the hair of the goat Amalthea.[5] After that moment, instead of turning me down, women rushed up to me. Here is how you must use it: Put one end into your watch-fob pocket, and then—according to how long you want your nose to grow—insert a knot between your trousers and your body. For each additional knot, your nose will grow another three inches; when you remove the rope, your nose returns to its natural condition. I am the blessed Labre.[6] Go forth and prosper.'

"With these words, the Saint turned to a four-legged winged capuchin attached to a pew by a golden chain, and pawing impetuously at the ground.[7] I hurried to help the blessed Saint Labre onto the stirrup of this impetuous animal, which had wings shaped like a capuche on its back. With a quick blessing to me, the Saint gave the heavenly steed free rein. The hypo-Capuche spread its monkey wings in flight, dipped down to genuflect five or six times at the Holy Sacrament, rose to pierce the canopy overhead, and vanished from my sight.

"No sooner had the holy duo disappeared from mortal view behind a solid wall than I knelt for another act of thanksgiving and put my rope to the test. Weak mortals that we are, who get more joy from seeing than believing! To my complete astonishment my nose, my ordinary nose, suddenly grew all the way down to my knees.

"Oh madame, alas!" cried the pilgrim, seeing Voragine's eyes gaze steadily at his nose. "Oh why must I recollect a pleasure now lost to me, now that my poor nose is no longer under divine protection? Why can't I give it you as big, fat, and red as in those happy moments? I then believed that I would remain forever in a permanent ecstatic state of contemplation at the tip of my nose, like the monks of Mount Tabor: O the redness of it! How radiant! What celestial light surrounded it—and soon *ter spumam effixam, et rotantia vidimus astra.*[8] You must not imagine my nose hanging down to my mouth in a way that would block my breathing, or that it was nasty with warts and other excrescences: this nose looked more like a sugar loaf, or perhaps a doctor's bonnet without the toque on top. A faint noise from somewhere in the church made me anxious about jealous observers, so I stuffed the rope back into its watch-fob pocket, and my nose resumed its natural shape. I had the impression, however, that it had more of a propensity to shrink than to grow, an observation subsequently confirmed by experience.

"On my way back to my inn, I thanked the generous beggar with every step I took. Next morning, I began my inquiries: which among our local ladies had a reputation for liking big noses?

"'Indeed, every one of the ladies,' replied my hostess; "all are more or less fascinated by the captivating things; do admit, a man with a substantial nose is always attractive. And in particular, we have the widow des Arches, a famous enthusiast.[9] But whyever should that matter, sir, to you? The size of your own nose, I fear, is not likely to attract our lady experts. You needn't have come so far for so little! Ha! Ha! Ha!'

"'Whoa!' I replied. 'I would not exchange my nose—such as it is—for any other.' And I asked to be shown the way to the house of the widow des Arches.

"There I found a heavyset woman with a leaden complexion, a knife-sharp nose, and fine dark eyes buried in their orbits by the passage of years, though still alert. I could see half her tousled hair was pure white, but I stuck in two knots to introduce myself properly, and her eyes became warmly curious. A third knot, and she invited me to dine. Nor, as you may well believe, did I demur.

"During the whole meal, both mother Catau des Arches and her daughter focused almost exclusively on my nose, which they were ogling through their lorgnettes. A wretchedly homely Englishwoman stared so hard with her squinty little eyes that if not for my amulet, my nose would have shrunk right back into my head. 'What about that nose!' hissed a hunchbacked, bandy-legged nephew to his cousin. Meanwhile in the antechamber, my wonderful nose was the only topic of the servant girls' conversation.

"After dinner I was kept for tea; after tea, for supper; but as this was the night of the annual Boulogne-sur-Mer grand ball, the daughter, the bandy-legged hunchback nephew, and the Englishwoman were all obliged to attend the ball, to their great regret, and leave me for a pleasant tête-à-tête with mother Catau.

"The minute we were alone, I put in two more knots; this time the good widow could take no more, and her eyes revealed her overwhelming desire to touch my nose. However, I had sworn that she would get nowhere near it without proof positive of her intentions. All her simpering added up to zero: in vain she assured me that she had been analyzing sentiments for over thirty years. I had sworn no one would analyze my nose for under ten gold louis, and I would not have broken my vow for all the old sinner-ladies in Boulogne-sur-Mer. Nevertheless, I consider myself a well-brought-up young man, and I try to give the ladies what they like.

"'Madame,' said I in the tenderest tone imaginable, considering that I was addressing an elderly widow, 'precious moments are fleeting. I'm about to leave for London, and in too much hurry to take one turn of the screw at a time. I notice that looking at my nose gives you pleasure; you would be welcome to touch it, except I swore by my baptism in the waters of Saint Gregory's well—holy as the river Styx—that anyone who wanted to lay a hand on it would have to give ten new gold louis, full weight or overscale, for glorious Saint Labre. Indeed it was he who gave me this enchanting and miraculous gift: I am the ever-wandering keeper of the flame. No one has touched it, I vow: you shall be the first.'

"Mother Catau responded to my speech like a woman who had made a fundamental analysis of the situation. My speech was in a very different style from those sugar-sweet Celadons who make a poor woman's mouth water, give her a taste, and leave her hungry for more.[10] 'Anyone except me would probably bargain harder,' she replied, 'but I am going to lock the door so we can come to a clear agreement on the details.'

"While she was locking us in, I stuck in two more knots; my nose now looked like an enormous telescope.

"The affectionate widow then picked up the thread of her discourse: 'Dear traveler, what lucky star has led you to our shores? I had thought my departed husband enjoyed one of the finest noses of Europe; but alas! what an error, how deeply I was wrong.'

"'Not to handle, madame,' I declared, seeing her reach out to grab me; 'my nose is ticklish, and devilishly . . .'

"'Ah cruel one! Would you have me pine away? O ghost of my husband, here at last is a moment when you may see, balanced on a nose that would have done you honor, the generous half-moon lunettes that gave you such delight. So different from that little pug-nosed geographer who can't deal with anything bigger than a monocle lunette, or that feeble harpsichordist with a waggly nose like flotsam adrift o'er the sea. O ghost of my husband! We honor you when we show lords of this world that your nose was the equal of one Heaven-sent! I promise I will give blessed Saint Labre ten louis to see these half-moon spectacles—belonging to you of course—spend a few brief hours upon this most marvelous nose.'

"'Go gently, madame, hold your horses, please; the blessed Labre would prefer a single reality over all the promises on earth.'

"The widow counted out ten louis for me; and as an honest broker, I promptly delivered my merchandise.

"Just as when, at the end of Lent, a priest familiar with the sacred ritual does not uncover the long-hidden crucifix to the congregation all at once, so I uncovered bit by bit the antique demi-lunes that had once belonged to old man de l'Arche. A piece of black muslin covered a bit of dirty damask, under which a scrap of flannel underlay a linen lining. I came next to the sacred rims. O miracle! I saw them, and my nose did not entirely shrink away. A bony old dried-up frame, covered with yellow wrinkled parchment and surrounded by graying boar hide, assaulted the eyes of anyone rash enough to risk the enterprise.

"'Courage,' cried the widow, 'courage, young man: first appearances are not enough, what matters is to keep it up; two steps forward are the only excuse for one step back. Since my husband's death, my lunettes have been worn by only twenty curiosity-seekers. Look how I wrap them in rabbit-skin to warm their pineal glands—the best rabbit-skin, the loveliest gray color; courage, my boy.'

"Rattling the guineas and spurred on by their delightful clink, I turned away my mouth, closed my eyes, and hurled myself into the yoke I had to bear:

Ah! miser
Quantâ laboras in caribde.[11]

I managed to get to the point where the half-moon rims—worn away by hard use—broke right where their circumferences touched the nose, and I had to resort to the whole rope: to the honor of blessed Saint Labre, I almost filled the vast and echoing cavern. If I had listened to goodwife Catau, I would have stayed with her ancient spectacles forever, she thought they suited me so well; but at last, to my great relief, the clock struck the end of the evening. My nose shrank back into itself so quickly, that I would have thought I would never see its tip again if not for the power of the blessed saint; or rather if I had not been moved to perform an additional miracle before getting into my own bed, to show the innkeeper's servant what a fool her mistress had been.

"Meanwhile the goddess Fame had put her trumpet to her lips, and the traveler with the marvelous nose was the only topic of conversation at the grand ball.

"'How happy that woman must be!' remarked the noblewomen among themselves. 'That Catau des Arches! I must say commoners have all the luck; why should a wine-merchant's wife, a fishwife really, possess the finest nose in town! Such a disgrace for the nobility!'

"'Oh cousin, dear cousin!' the des Arches girl was greeted by all the young bourgeoise girls mingling with the blood of the gods, as fortune decrees during dinner parties and balls. 'Do tell us the miracles of the gigantic nose: Have you actually seen it? Did you touch it? Have you . . .'

"An old blind man, the local Saint Julian,[12] called out while he fiddled the minuet: 'Keep your nose to the side of the street so I don't get hit in the stomach with it—which happened to me just yesterday, banging into a plowshaft somebody left right in the middle of the road.'

"The next morning, I awoke to find a card inviting me to come back and spend the day as before. When I left the inn, I could observe a few chamber-maids and kitchen-maids who had been sent by their respective mistresses to inspect my nose; but as the weather was bitter cold, I stuck my nose into the cuff of my sleeve through the hole I use for my horse's bridle, so that not one of them could boast even a glimpse of it.

"After dinner, an elderly lady was announced, accompanied by two charm-ingly pretty young girls. When I heard the girls murmuring: 'Why, it's nothing but an ordinary nose . . . !' I slipped out two knots; they stopped short in mid-sentence. When I slipped out a third knot, their aunt, a well-informed Spanish lady, whispered between her teeth: 'From Bayonne to Cadiz, that nose has no equal: not the noses of Monsignor Saint Christopher, or even Monsignor the Grand Inquisitor.'

"A young noblewoman approached me next, a true provincial beauty of Lower Brittany, alert and well-developed: loose hair crowned by a wreath of artificial roses like a priestess of Flora; a taffeta gown with a train that dragged majestically in the dirt; and an air of languid superiority toward the assembled bourgeoisie. Her rank and condition were obvious from her aristocratic way of seating herself in an armchair, with an aristocratically dismissive nod of the head; and I pushed two knots for the honor of her ancestors. Moreover, since I never embourgeoisify myself if I have any other options, I sat down beside her, and we began to chat about noses and half-moon spectacles as if we had been doing so all our lives.

"Afterward we played two or three light-hearted games of whist, at a penny for three points; we argued with our partners according to the noble custom of good company in small whist-playing towns; we took half an hour to divide three sous among ourselves evenly. The company rose from the card tables for supper; but then after supper I had to don the half-moon spectacles once again. My vitreous humor was starting to evaporate, my orbs beginning to deflate—it takes a miracle to wear spectacles for so long at a time.

"I was therefore delighted to learn that the packet boat of one Captain Cornu was under sail. Mother des Arches, who possessed both the inconve-nient responsibility for a sixteen- or seventeen-year-old daughter, and a dim-witted son-in-law who sold second-hand frippery in London, now engaged me to take this her fourth daughter to London and unload her on the son-in-law.[13] I was also responsible for taking home the ugly Englishwoman with the face of a screeching feline.

"See me now, bound for the quai: first came a rogue pushing a wheelbarrow loaded with the boxes and baskets of my female travelers, who followed on foot; then a bear, a monkey and dancing dogs headed for London to perform while the opera was on vacation; lastly the widow and I, bringing up the rear. Mother des Arches carried a long white handkerchief in her hand like an old-fashioned tragic heroine, while I dragged her in my wake like the triumphal victor of a ruined city. After the various maneuvers necessary to take on board women, a bear, a monkey, a dozen or so scullions dressed as hussars, I don't know how many boxes, and two turkeys destined for the stupid son-in-law's Christmas dinner, Captain Cornu set his mizzen-sail, and we sailed slowly past the new jetty that now expands the port of Boulogne.

"Meanwhile back on shore, Madame Catau, leaning despondently on her confidante's arm and draped in black, her handkerchief to her eyes, hurled insults at the wind as she followed our ship's progress. Myself a grateful traveler, perched in back on the poop's taffrail, all my knots paid out, responded to her illustrious grief by waving my nose frantically. Finally my nose had to be retracted, since Captain Cornu pointed out that it risked getting caught between the rudder and the stern post; and I proceeded to retreat with as much dignity as the rising ocean swell allowed. Yet there were moments when I glanced back toward shore: I really felt widow Catau ought have followed the rules and flung herself into the sea. This was partly because of the appropriateness of the location, but also because drowning herself would have increased the fame of the miracle of blessed Labre; and also because we have examples galore of women throwing themselves into the sea over less of a loss.

"Perhaps, ladies and gentlemen, you will judge me indiscreet and criticize all my revelations about Boulogne ladies' taste for fine noses; but after due consideration, you must agree that the honor of the Saint requires it, beyond my own annoyance that widow des Arches somehow neglected to drown herself; Time's scythe has by now toppled her into her grave. This sad news I got from my friend Samuel Swinton, Esquire, along with the epitaph he commissioned from the poet he bankrolls, the illustrious Courrier-Cuirassé.[14] May we now shed a tear for the good widow! Here is her epitaph as it appears on the monument erected to her in Boulogne, right under a portrait of her lunettes, painted from nature:

Beneath this tomb a lady lies
Was neither mean nor small,
To play troll-madam in her hole
Requir'd a cannonball.[15]

"For Madame Catau's half-moon spectacles had often served the generous Scotsman who had erected this monument; and thus may a person fulfill his duties to her shade and glorify the blessed saint at the same time.

"The sea was wide, the waves rough, Captain Cornu's packet-boat rolled around like the devil, the bear was growling, the dogs were howling, the ambassadors of the King of Sardinia played their pipes and beat their drums, the old Englishwoman slept, our sailors toasted cheese in our cabin fireplace, the little des Arches girl became seasick, and I felt seasick to keep her company; miracles were very far from my mind.

"Toward midnight, we came to the port of Dowers—or as you call it, Dover. An English sloop approached and kindly offered to take us onshore for *a guinea per package;* our spirit of economy was stronger than our seasickness, so we suffered another three hours and agreed on *a guinea per person.* We finally disembarked and went to the York Hotel; the proprietor my good friend Mr. Payne is not yet rich like Mariet, but much more polite.[16] After recovering from the hustle and bustle, I noticed that the chambermaid was fairly attractive, so I brought out three knots from my bundle.

"'*Good God,*' cried she in English! '*What a nose!*'

"And so long as she serves in a hostelry, she will surely remember the traveler with the enormous nose.

"After the weary nuisance of getting back our trunks and parcels from the grasping clerks—a process that, as in every well-policed nation of Europe, began with being ransacked and ended with ransoms and tips—we set forth in a three-seated coach, headed for that cursed capital which once worshipped the Pope and now burns him every year: human nature does not age gracefully.

"As we traveled the road, Miss Carabine was trying dreadfully to grab my nose, but besides her homeliness and ill-temper, and my general indifference to ugly women with no money, I wanted sleep more than I wanted a miracle. We stopped at Canterbury for tea. The hostess was a pretty girl; I have a natural weakness for hotel maids, so I produced a semi-miracle for her.

"By six o'clock, we reached Shooters' Hill, where I saw a 'gentleman'—as we call such people—approaching at a quick trot, and looking mighty like a highwayman; I instantly put down the window, turned to my sacred rope, and took out three or four feet of my venerable nose. The gentleman galloped off, mistaking my nose for a blunderbuss, and we reached London with no further incident. I unloaded my females as quickly as possible: Miss Carabine at the Highgate coach, Mademoiselle des Arches at her stupid brother-in-law's, while I escaped to my little house where I found my own little Irish sweetheart. Two knots were enough to show her that travel, as they say, makes the man.

"Two or three days later, I read in the *Morning Halloo*: 'The day before yesterday, at eight o'clock in the morning, arrived in town the famous traveler with the expandable nose: he will begin his exhibitions Monday, the fourth of this month, at a location still to be announced. Our city ladies wish this to take place in the Vauxhall Rotunda, for their convenience; but the nobility much prefer Mr. Gallini's magnificent room, which he offers gratis as a gesture of his gratitude to the noblemen and gentlefolk who honor him with their patronage.'[17] This last, you see, was a knavish trick by Mr. Gallini, who wanted me to pay an exorbitant rent to perform exhibitions in his wretched space. But I decided not to perform in public: only in private whether at ladies' toilettes, or after dinner when they withdraw together and drink champagne.

"In clubs, in Parliament, and in the Council of State, my marvelous nose was the only topic of conversation.[18] Lord March offered to bet against all comers that my nose would not last three weeks in London. Mr. Fox, in a most eloquent discourse, compared it to the royal prerogative, which in the beginning seems unremarkable and moderate but then grows by hidden or secret means so that it threatens to surpass all other powers. Lord North made a thousand witticisms about my nose, of which two were passable. The rest of the party sifted through the pros and cons of the orators' speeches, but came up with nothing new. They did, however, point out that the Minister could find no way to pay off the public debt, except in the cause of the continued increase of my nose. At this point, several questions were put to Mr. Pitt, who replied that 'public ministers of the Crown were not obliged to reply to members of the House,' and proposed a new tax without further ado. Colonel N. seconded this strongly, declaring that my nose was a mere elephant's trunk, gift of the Nabob; that I had no doubt brought it back from the Indies; while the important thing was to discover whether I had an import license from the Company, and confiscate it if not: the aforesaid confiscation to be made by virtue of the Company's privilege.[19] Tempers grew heated, the session became stormy, and the King was obliged to dissolve Parliament immediately.

"I can't tell you how many fine statements were made in the House of Lords on the self-same subject: the Chancellor drew important consequences in support of monarchical despotism, whereas Lord Stormont pronounced this a sign of divine wrath against the present Minister, who should be dismissed from office and shown back to his place as soon as possible. The quick-witted peers assented in uniform as usual: '*mutum ac turpe pecus*.'[20]

"But while Parliament reflected on my nose and the King broke up Parliament, rival journalists were busily competing against each other.

"In his new Review, Dr. Maty argued that there was no need to put all London in an uproar, since my big nose was not worth a second glance: 'A novelty like this—a French importation—corrupts our national taste,' he exclaimed with his usual heat.[21] 'Leaf through the great, grand models of antiquity—all quite ordinary noses. Homer tells us everything a person ought to know, and he never dreams of mentioning a hero's nose unless it's hacked off with a handsaw. We find not a single line, no not a hemistich, on Achilles' nose, or Priam's—we would not even know the human organism so much as had a nose. Ulysses describes Polyphemus's eye, Scylla's claws, the Laestrygones's appetite, and Charybdis's insatiability; nary a word about their noses. Then note wise Virgil: is there a word in Virgil about the nose of pious Aeneas, or the furious fighter . . . ? Leaf through the learned polyglot Bible of Dr. *** or the Hexapla of Origen, or the translations of Jerome; decipher the fragments of Sanchoniathon or Berosius, or the Parian marbles; excavate the ruins of Palmyra and Herculaneum; plumb the Egyptian pyramids, decode the obelisks: you will find nothing but ordinary noses.[22] Who gave a thought to noses in divine Shakespeare's time, literature's finest hour? King Lear, monster Caliban, the Moor of Venice who made the two-backed beast—all have ordinary noses. To sum up, is not the only nose-praising poet to celebrate his hero's nose Voltaire, a man without taste, wit, or genius![23] An ass, gentlemen! Indeed, a decent respect for antiquity forbids the introduction of any such portion of the human body in the writings of our refined, judicious authors:

Nec deus intersit nisi dignus vindice nodus'.[24]

Thus wrote the learned Mr. Maty in his newspaper of February 4, 1784.

"Other writers, less fanatical admirers of the ancients, were quick to argue in refutation: 'The reason ancient writers never describe noses for us may be that their own noses were not big enough to mention. However, Roman ladies set great store by massive noses. Consider the medal collections that you preserve so carefully. Examine Caesar's nose: the volume of it! Then look at

Brutus, and Lepidus! Mark Antony's nose was a little flat, but broad; Germanicus's not deficient; Tiberius's large and long; Caligula's bulbous; Nero's big as a cucumber. And what about the Antonines' noses? Or Hadrian's? Or Julian, whom fools call apostate, and wise men a philosopher? Gordian's nose also deserves your attention. The first to be dishonored by his nose was Licinius; after that, the decline of the Roman empire continued down to Augustulus, who was a total Pug.'[25]

"Nor were these periodicalists the only writers to debate my nose: Dr. Pieslay listed my nose among the causes for the corruption of Christianity.[26] Dr. Williams, who was publicly preaching deism at this time, found my nose a source for winning arguments against Providence.[27] An escapee from Provence[28] who had published the posthumous writings of a man buried alive and authored a calumnious little libel on the late King's ministers of state used my nose to help himself maintain the dignity of a name difficult to bear, he said, in the wake of his respected father. This Provençal portrayed my nose as a mark of nobility or order of chivalry; he dared say that my nose would be a fitting '*pal*' for His Majesty;[29] and added that if France did not come to the rescue, I would undoubtedly use my nose to pierce the Netherland dikes, a project that had been proven entirely feasible by a much-celebrated, little-known geographer. The Physicists of the Royal Society proposed to show how and why my nose proved a corollary of the general law of attraction. On the other hand, M. Marat argued that my nose was an effect of the electricity in my pineal glands.[30] A German named Muller claimed to discover the secret of perpetual motion in my nose; my friend Dr. Remben asserted in print that he had already extracted twenty-two babies from it, and intended to try for twenty-four. And finally Catau des Arches's eldest daughter, wife to the rag-picker Bissoto de Guerreville, had now become a Quaker: she chose my nose as the text for her first address to the shakers' meeting, to complain that my nostrils were concealing the inner light within them.[31]

"I was soon inundated with letters from every corner of London and Westminster: a young heiress wrote describing her particulars and proposing marriage, while a rich widow promised me an *inter vivos* donation in exchange for a private quarter-hour interview. The merchant J.P.D., a usurer in Great St. Helens Street,[32] offered me one hundred louis at five percent for my nose, if I could add collateral securities such as diamonds or pure gold and silver articles, double in weight to coinage. He then offered to include a sonnet of his own composition, an epigram against any person I might select, and a packet of gloves bearing the legend:

White gloves of kidskin
One dozen within.

"Rag-picker Bissoto now proposed that I allow an engraving to be made of myself with my nose in all its splendor, to appear in the gallery of Famous Living Men whom he happened to be immortalizing at that particular moment. A villain named Thonevet threatened to invent an old-fashioned libel about me unless I gave him either a tithe of my income or the exclusive right to produce my nose for patrons of his boutique.[33] An abbé who was a business manager for opera girls offered me on behalf of two high-flyers one hundred louis and permanent free admission in exchange for my secret, with which they planned to revive the old wobblers who cluster like honeybees in the dressing rooms where actresses metamorphose into goddesses.

"Every mountebank announced my appearance on his program.[34] Ashley, who had cheated London with his hot-air balloons that never took off the ground, printed posters advertising onstage 'Mr. Naso,' the famed traveler, would have the honor of playing his trumpet in a duet with Mr. Rossignol's true-to-life imitation of every bird in the universe. Dr. Katerfiette promised to show that his black cat's tail, when seen through his solar microscope, was twenty times larger than my big nose, as he had already demonstrated in private audience to the king and the royal family, who had been so delighted by his exhibition that they had come back the next day unannounced and had been unable to find seats because of the crowd, which he himself, Col. Katerfiette, had found particularly distressing because of the personal introduction that his friend the King of Prussia had given him. Dr. Graham lectured *ad hoc* on the inestimable value of noses like mine for both propagation and ladies' welfare, next to the electric bed upon which sterile women get with child in the Hymen Saloon at his Temple of Health. Dr. Graham claimed that the only reason I could do everything I pleased with my nose was because I had done as he, Dr. Graham, advised both ladies and gentlemen to do: washing it regularly in cold water, eating a vegetarian diet, and sleeping in the open air. A London dentist announced in the newspapers that my nose was a simple fungous polyp, which he had just extracted, stuffed, and would show for a shilling. Dr. N*** offered me money in advance for posters, announcements, and exhibitions, provided that we share the profits fifty-fifty, as was his arrangement with his authors.

"While these London authors and charlatans—almost the same thing—were making their pronunciamentos on a phenomenon about whose causes they knew nothing, I spent my time peaceably with M. de S*** de la T*** making Perigord goose-liver sausages, which we washed down with first-rate Burgundy.³⁵ I offered in return to show my nasal experiments before his lady wife, but she begged me to do no such thing, since the only nose she cared about was her husband's.

"I attributed her indifference to big noses to the trimness of her little mouth and feet, since I note that women with sweet, neat body parts never like gigantic things; the curious women are the ones like the thin, dried-up Bissoto woman, Mrs. M*** with the bulging eyes, and Mistress J***, whose mouths all gape as if they were astride a hobbyhorse in the Invalides.

"My friends pleaded with me to take immediate advantage of my good fortune: the great violinist Piélatin offered to bring his best musicians and play the orchestra at my performances; the brilliant, elegant, obliging, amiable clavecinist Desforges offered to perform a sonata of his composition with his usual spirit and grace.³⁶ I was just on the point of agreeing—my laissez-faire attitude has always been my greatest flaw—when I had a visit from Mr. N***. Mr. N*** came incognito to offer me two thousand guineas on behalf of the Whigs, if I restricted the use of my nose exclusively to wives and daughters whose husbands and fathers voted for Mr. Fox; reserving the right, after the election, to show it to whomever I wished.

"I was easily seduced, as I love both liberty and Fox: and all the prettiest women belonged to his party. The Queen, then active in Lord N***'s cabal, sent her reader-in-ordinary M. Deluc to offer me her copy of *Letters to a German Princess*³⁷ if I agreed to support the Court party; while if not, to threaten me with drowning in Lady Harbord's maw.³⁸ You be the judge whether I, I who had seen the spectacles of old widow des Arches and her rich gray rabbit-skin with all its surrounding and abutting circumstances and dependencies, could be intimidated by an English gullet. True to the cause, I took my place under the flags of the beautiful duchess and the Prince of Wales.³⁹

"Upon learning that I had great expectations of imminent fortune, a swarm of wretched starving Frenchmen, shoeless on the streets of London and a disgrace to our nation, came to flatter me in the dual hopes of scrounging some shred of it, and scuttling me out of envy. The liar Thonevet swore under oath to an inattentive secretary of State not only that I was being paid by France to measure with my nose the caliber of every cannon in England, but also that I was own cousin, in the sixtieth degree, to the very Lamothe⁴⁰ he had ordered hanged in the recent war. Turning to the other side, Thonevet also told the wood-carrier of the French ambassador's cousin that I had freely made fun of his master in the public newspapers; and he wrote to the principal informant of a clerk to the inspector of police in Paris, directing him to be sure to tell the office boy who polishes the desk of the secretary of the police chief that I had stolen my nose from a merchant traveling back from the promontory of Cape Nez.[41] Finally, he composed and attributed to me a stale and seamy libel against the stable boys of a man in high office, and this with the express intention of ruining me.[42]

"The patron-poet Labou***[43] came to alert me to these underhand maneuvers, which I found laughable. We drank some bottles of Porto or d'Oporto together, he promised me an ode in praise of my nose, and he began an epigram the morning after. Fortunately, however, he got intoxicated by the first verse and fell asleep at the second. Awakened with a start by the jealous Thonevet, Labou*** told him I was the lover of a duchess who had given me a casket filled with gold. This made Thonevet so sick at heart that a fever threatened him with the just fate he so richly deserved. But then in the end, a twist of Fate transformed my property into a combination of milkmaid Perrette's jug and the curate's cart.[44]

"One Saturday, May 12, I went to Covent Garden to start my operations on behalf of Mr. Fox, and I was just about to push in a few knots into my watch-fob pocket when a pickpocket, believing I was concealing my watchchain, adroitly stole away my miraculous rope. Judge of my astonishment, my despair; I felt annihilated, I was frantic; I advertised for my rope, I promised rewards—but all in vain.

"I crept back to my modest home—I will not say crestfallen since I no longer had a crest to speak of, but ashamed and irritated. My little housekeeper consoled me thus: 'You still have plenty left,' she said, 'enough for any gallant.' But she spoke in the tone of voice used by inconsolable friends attempting to comfort a friend more desperate than themselves.

"Now who should appear at this moment but the widow des Arches coming to London to force me, willy-nilly, to wear her ancient spectacles, as she had been unable to find anyone else's nose capable of reaching both sides of her demi-lunes at once. You can well understand that in my miserable condition, I had to refuse to see her. In vain she sent to me by Scaramouche, the brother of her ragpicking son-in-law Bissoto, husband of her elder daughter Pernelle.[45] I confined myself to the house as best I could. At last, however, harassed by her persecutions and eager to publish the posthumous works of my late friend the v. Rev. Rose-Croix, I made an arrangement with Sam *** Esq. to use one of his printing presses in Boulogne.

"Back I traveled across the Channel, under the delusion that there I might escape the widow's pursuit. But vain hope, alas! Hell hath no fury like a woman whose spectacles are scorned. Joining forces with this furious widow, the calumniator Thonevet took it into his head to write several more of those atrocious libels and attribute them to me. He and the widow wrote to the Minister, with the following result: in the city center of Boulogne I was kidnapped at high noon and taken to the Bastille. Since the ragpicker Bissoto was then in Paris hunting for rags to patch up some slashed doublets intended for the American savages, they suspected him of peddling my supposed libels and sent him to Bicêtre, where he died soon after of a withered brain.

"As for myself, I stayed in the Bastille a very long time indeed, for it is the hardest thing in the world to disprove the calumnies of shameless scoundrels who brazenly accuse you of crimes that have never actually been committed by anyone. In the Bastille, I did not let a day go by without praying to the miraculous Labre and mourning my miraculous nose, but to no purpose. The governor, who is naturally an extremely compassionate soul, consoled me thus: 'What good would such a nose be to you in here, anyway? We would never have allowed you to keep it; that's not our practice: you might have pierced your cell walls with it, or bribed your keeper.'

"One fine day the Minister finally made up his mind that I was unjustly accused of writing libels nobody had ever seen, and I was thrown out of the Bastille. As I was walking down the Rue Saint-Antoine, I heard a crier announcing a mandate from Monsignor the Archbishop, ordering everyone with any knowledge of the miracles of the blessed Labre to come to his officiality to testify, because the canonization was under way in Rome.[46] I decided that simple gratitude obliged me to travel to Rome myself: and turning in the other direction, I followed the boulevard out through the Porte Saint-Martin and then took the road back home here. I plan to spend a week or two with my brothers and then continue on my voyage.

"Such are the miraculous events I have to relate, ladies and gentlemen: you see yourselves the misfortunes that my miserable attempt at literature has caused me, and how much I must loathe literature now. I vow nothing frightens me so much as hearing myself called 'author'! since at my back I always hear a band of alguazil police stationed at street corners and toll gates, so that the powerful may prevent the contraband importation of reason.

"But the sun is setting, and we scarcely have time to get into town. Follow me, and I will show you to an honest tavern in the suburb where you may find a warm welcome, decent beds, good wine, and an attractive hostess."

The Bohemians and Bohemiennes now arose and took to the road with the Pilgrim, telling him as they walked how delighted they had been to hear his story; Tifarès and Mordanes saddled and loaded the donkey and followed their trail. Soon after sunset, they all reached the gates of Stenay and the inn of honest Radet, the finest innkeeper of all Europe.[47] And then after making the Pilgrim promise to join them for supper, the Bohemians granted him the liberty to go embrace his brothers while their supper was being prepared.

THE END.

NOTES

INTRODUCTION

1. The 1762 edition of the *Dictionnaire de l'Académie française* gives the following definition: "BOHÈME, ou BOHÉMIEN, BOHÉMIENNE. They are also called Egyptians. These words have not been placed here in order to characterize the people of that part of Germany called Bohemia, but only to designate a variety of vagabonds who drift from place to place, telling fortunes and filching things with great dexterity. 'A troupe of Bohemians.' Speaking familiarly, one says of a household where there are no rules or order, 'It's a bohemian house.'" Of the many studies of nineteenth-century bohemianism, see especially Jerrold Seigel, *Bohemian Paris: Culture, Politics, and the Boundaries of Bourgeois Life, 1830–1930* (New York, 1986) and Cesar Graña, *Bohemian vs. Bourgeois: French Society and the French Man of Letters in the Nineteenth Century* (New York, 1964).

2. In one of the earliest references to literary bohemians, *Le Chroniqueur désoeuvré, ou l'espion du boulevard du Temple* (London, 1783), vol. II, 22, caustically described a boulevard theater, Les Variétés amusantes, as "that den of bohemians."

3. Antoine de Rivarol, *Le petit almanach de nos grands hommes* (n.p., 1788).

4. I have tried to develop this argument and to provide statistics about French writers during the eighteenth century in "The Facts of Literary Life in Eighteenth-Century France," in Keith Baker, ed., *The Political Culture of the Old Regime* (Oxford, 1987), 261–91.

5. Louis Sébastien Mercier, *Tableau de Paris*, reprint edited by Jean-Claude Bonnet (Paris, 1994)—see especially the chapters entitled "Auteurs," "Des demi-auteurs, quarts d'auteur, enfin métis, quarterons, etc.," "Auteurs nés à Paris," "Apologie des gens de lettres," "Trente écrivains en France, pas davantage," "Les cent hommes de lettres de l'*Encyclopédie*," "La littérature du Faubourg Saint-Germain, et celle du faubourg Saint-Honoré," "Misère des auteurs," "Le Musée de Paris," and "Les grands comédiens contre les petits."

6. See Aleksandr Stroev, *Les aventuriers des Lumières* (Paris, 1997).

7. See Pat Rogers, *Grub Street: Studies in a Subculture* (London, 1972); John Brewer, *Party Ideology and Popular Politics at the Accession of George III* (Cambridge, 1976); Han-

nah Barker, *Newspapers, Politics, and Public Opinion in Late Eighteenth-Century England* (Oxford, 1998); and Arthur H. Cash, *John Wilkes: The Scandalous Father of Civil Liberty* (New Haven, 2006).

8. The richest source of information about the French expatriates in London is the archives of the French Ministry of Foreign Affairs at the Quai d'Orsay: Correspondance politique: Angleterre, especially mss 540–50. The following account is also based on the interrogations of Jacques-Pierre Brissot in the Bastille, which reveal a great deal about Pelleport's activities: Archives Nationales, Fonds Brissot, 446 AP 2. The most important printed sources include the anonymous and tendentious but very revealing libel by Anne Gédéon de Lafitte, marquis de Pelleport, *Le Diable dans un bénitier et la métamorphose du Gazetier cuirassé en mouche . . .* (London, 1784); the police reports published by Pierre-Louis Manuel, *La Police de Paris dévoilée* (Paris, 1790), 2 vols.; Manuel's edited and paraphrased versions of papers from the Bastille, *La Bastille dévoilée, ou recueil de pièces authentiques pour servir à son histoire* (Paris, 1789–90), 9 "livraisons" or volumes, depending on how they are bound; and the superb collection of documents published with extensive commentaries by Gunnar and Mavis von Proschwitz, *Beaumarchais et le Courier de l'Europe* (Oxford, 1990), 2 vols. The most important secondary work on Charles Théveneau de Morande is still the thin and inaccurate biography by Paul Robiquet, *Théveneau de Morande: Etude sur le XVIIIe siècle* (Paris, 1882). The other London libelers are discussed in Simon Burrows, *Blackmail, Scandal, and Revolution: London's French libellistes, 1758–92* (Manchester, 2006), which takes issue with my earlier studies of the subject collected in *The Literary Underground of the Old Regime* (Cambridge, Mass., 1982). In addition to the above sources, the following essay draws on other material concerning Brissot: *J.-P. Brissot: Mémoires* (Paris, 1910), 2 vols., Claude Perroud, ed.; *J.-P. Brissot: Correspondance et papiers* (Paris, 1912), Claude Perroud, ed.; and Robert Darnton, *J.-P. Brissot: His Career and Correspondence 1779–1787* (Oxford, 2001), which can be consulted online at the website of the Voltaire Foundation: www.voltaire.ox.ac.uk/.

9. *La Bastille dévoilée*, III, 66; *La Police de Paris dévoilée*, II, 235–36.

10. Paul Lacroix, "Les Bohémiens," *Bulletin du bibliophile* (Paris, 1851), 408–9. Lacroix said that the book was printed by Charles-Joseph Panckoucke, who then destroyed most of the copies after discovering that he was slandered in it. A printer named Lavillette produced the title pages that appeared on the surviving copies, according to Lacroix's account, which unfortunately does not mention any sources.

11. The address suggests the publishing house of Charles-Joseph Panckoucke, also in the rue des Poitevins, at the Hôtel de Thou. According to the *Almanach de la librairie* (Paris, 1781), Panckoucke was the only bookseller located in that short street. Pelleport used false addresses as a form of satire in his other works, and he satirized Panckoucke's pretentiousness and overbearing treatment of authors in Les Bohémiens (1790), I, 112–13. As mentioned above in n. 10, Paul Lacroix believed Panckoucke originally printed *Les Bohémiens*, then attempted to destroy the entire edition. There is no information relating to the hôtel Bouthillier or *Les Bohémiens* in Suzanne Tucoo-Chala, *Charles-Joseph Panckoucke et la librairie française 1736–1798* (Pau and Paris, 1977).

12. It is conceivable that Pelleport wrote the book in 1789, but that seems unlikely, because it is a long and complex text and Pelleport apparently spent much of that year traveling between Stenay and Paris, trying to put his affairs in order. He was released from the Bastille on October 3, 1788. The only allusion in the book that can be dated is a reference in vol. I, p. 113 to Antoine Rivarol's *Le Petit Almanach de nos grands hommes*, which was published in 1788. A reference in vol. I, p. 98 implies that the narrative takes place in 1788. A footnote in vol. II, p. 22 refers to the principal minister Loménie de Brienne, who was dismissed on August 24, 1788, as if he had recently fallen from power. A few vague allusions to the Third Estate—for example, vol. I, p. 11—suggest that Pelleport may have been aware of Louis XVI's decision on August 8, 1788, to call the Estates General. But Pelleport mocked the governor of the Bastille, Bernard-René, marquis de Launay, as if he still occupied his position (vol. I, p. 9). *Les Bohémiens* contains many descriptions of monasteries, seigneurial dues, royal taxes, and the social order as if the Old Regime were still firmly in place. Nothing in it suggests a society about to erupt in a revolution or any of the revolutionary changes that occurred after 1788. The copies of *Les Bohémiens* that I have been able to locate are in the Bibliothèque municipale de Rouen, the Bibliothèque du Château d'Oron, Switzerland, the Library of Congress, the Boston Public Library, the Taylorean Library of Oxford University, the Bayerische Staatsbibliothek of Munich, and the National Library of Sweden in Stockholm.

13. *La Police de Paris dévoilée*, II, 235–36.

14. *La Bastille dévoilée*, II, 66–75. This account was obviously touched up for dramatic effect in some places, but there is no reason to doubt that it provides accurate information from Pelleport's dossier in the Bastille, which has disappeared since then. It agrees with a similar description of Pelleport's early life by Brissot, which includes some additional details about Pelleport's married life in Le Locle (Brissot said he had two children; *La Bastille dévoilée* said he had four) and his activities in London: Brissot, *Mémoires*, I, 303, 346, 318–21, 395–96; and II, 8. Pelleport seems to have been born in Stenay in 1756 and to have died in Paris around 1810. The most revealing information about his career after 1789 comes from a report by the Préfecture de Police dated November 10, 1802, Archives Nationales, F7.3831, and published in Alphonse Aulard, ed., *Paris sous le Consulat: Recueil de documents pour l'histoire de l'esprit public à Paris* (Paris, 1903–1909), III, 386: "The prefect of police had one Aimé-Gédéon Lafite de Pelleport [*sic*] arrested for having made remarks against the government. Pelleport is forty-six years old. He served in the (Indian Ocean) islands; he was sent to the Bastille under the accusation of having produced libels against the Queen. Later he was employed as a cavalry captain but without having been attached to any corps. It appears that he served as a spy under the Ancien Régime and later during the Revolution. He agrees that he had emigrated, boasts about his nobility, and does not deny the remarks attributed to him. He does not carry any papers that are in order. In fact, he does not seem to have a solid source of support." Pelleport probably acted as a secret agent for the French foreign ministry during the summer of 1793, according to a short essay, "Lafitte de Pelleport," signed S. Churchill in *L'Intermédiaire des chercheurs et curieux* (30 October 1904), vol. 50, columns 634–37. Pelleport also appears as a witty soldier-poet in the army of

the prince de Condé at Steinstadt in the summer of 1795 in *Journal d'un fourrier de l'armée de Condé: Jacques de Thiboult du Puisact, député de l'Orne*, ed. Gérard de Contades (Paris, 1882), 63, 65, and 69. In a note on page 63, Contades claims that Pelleport left the army in November 1795 in order to join a sister in Philadelphia, a doubtful claim that is not born out in the brief notice on Pelleport in *Biographie universelle (Michaud) ancienne et moderne* (Paris, 1843–1865), XXXII, 398, which has him die in Paris, probably in 1810.

15. In addition to the sources cited above, n. 4, see Eloise Ellery, *Brissot de Warville: A Study in the History of the French Revolution* (New York, 1915), which is still the best biography.

16. Darnton, *J.-P. Brissot*, 63–72. Brissot also indicated his close friendship with Pelleport and his worry about the dangers connected with Pelleport's literary activities in letters that he wrote to the Société typographique de Neuchâtel from London on October 7, November 11, and November 29, 1783: ibid., 279–85.

17. See Claude Perroud, ed., *J.-P. Brissot. Mémoires (1754–1793)* (Paris, 1910), I, 302–97 and II, 1–27. As Perroud points out in his introduction, pp. xxv–xxvi, it seems likely that Brissot wrote most of this text in the summer of 1785, when he was defending himself against Desforges d'Hurecourt, the financial backer of his London "Licée," who had sued him for misappropriation of the funds. The first editor of the memoirs, François de Montrol, incorporated this and other material in an edition that he passed off as an autobiography written in 1793 while Brissot was a prisoner in the Abbaye awaiting trial before the Revolutionary Tribunal. In fact, only a small part of Brissot's memoirs was composed in such dramatic circumstances, and Perroud did not weed out everything that Montrol had added from extraneous sources.

18. Brissot, *Mémoires*, I, 319.

19. Vingtain to Brissot, April 3, 1784, in Brissot, *Correspondance et papiers*, 467. See also François Dupont to Brissot, May 14, 1783, ibid., 54. Bruzard de Mauvelain, a close friend of Brissot's who lived from shady dealings in the underground book trade in Troyes, sent two letters to the Société typographique de Neuchâtel (STN) about Brissot's *embastillement*, which he attributed to the compromising connection with Pelleport: "Il a eu un tort de se lier avec un imprudent, et un plus grand encore—celui de se mettre sous la coupe du ministère de France." Bruzard de Mauvelain to STN, August 20, 1784, in Darnton, *J.-P. Brissot*, 349. Mauvelain probably had inside information from Brissot about the production of libels in London, because he asked the STN to supply him with several of the most extreme works, including "6 *Passe-Temps d'Antoinette* avec figures." Mauvelain to STN, February 15, 1784, Bibliothèque publique et universitaire de Neuchâtel, Papers of the STN, ms. 1179.

20. Interrogation of Brissot in the Bastille, August 21, 1784, in Brissot papers, Archives Nationales, 446 AP2, no foliation.

21. Ibid.

22. Morande had sent the police a statement by a London printer certifying that he had received proofs of *Le Diable dans un bénitier* corrected by Brissot and delivered by Brissot's brother, Pierre-Louis Brissot de Thivars, who was serving as his assistant in the Licée

de Londres. Brissot observed that *Le Diable* had been printed before his brother joined him in London, and Chénon seems to have accepted that argument.

23. The titles are quoted as they appear in the manuscript of the interrogation. Different versions of them can be found scattered through the correspondence of the comte de Vergennes, who as foreign minister supervised the attempts of the police to root out the libel industry in London: see footnote 8. Most of these books were never published. Their titles were probably invented by the libelers in order to extract blackmail. Pelleport certainly wrote one of the eight, *Les Petits Soupers et les nuits de l'Hôtel Bouill-n* ("à Bouillon," 1784), and he probably wrote another, *La Gazette noire par un homme qui n'est pas blanc* ("Imprimé à cent lieues de la Bastille, à trois cent lieues des Présides, à cinq cent lieues des Cordons, à mille lieues de la Sibérie," 1784).

24. Twenty of Larrivée's letters to Brissot are in Brissot's papers in the Archives Nationales, 446 AP 1. Writing to Brissot, who was then in London, on November 8, 1783, Larrivée reported that Pelleport and his brothers had recently arrived in Paris, hoping to collect as much as 20,000 livres apiece from their father's estate. Although he would later change his mind, his first impression of Pelleport was favorable: "He is a most amiable man, who seems to have a beautiful soul. . . . He seems to me to be very attached to you."

25. Larrivée to Brissot, December 15, 1783, ibid. In this letter, Larrivée referred to "the difficulties raised by the guardians of the children by the second wife, who have creamed off nearly everything in favor of the latter, given the absence of the children by the first wife and their father's disgust with them."

26. Larrivée mentioned this project in his letter to Brissot of November 16, 1783, and Chénon described it in the interrogation of August 21, 1784.

27. Those were the terms used in a furious letter to Brissot from his brother dated June 11, 1784, according to Chénon's description of the affair in the interrogation of August 22, 1784.

28. *Mémoires*, II, 8.

29. Full records of interrogations and confrontations for this period are missing from the papers of the Bastille. In one scrap that survived, dated July 20, 1784, an official of the prison noted: "Officer Chénon had a session with Pelleport and carried off his [illegible word]. Then he had a session on the same day with Brissot d'Warville." Bibliothèque de l'Arsenal, Bastille Papers, ms. 12517. Confrontations are mentioned fairly often in records from earlier periods, as if they were a standard procedure. In one of the rare dossiers from the 1780s, Pelleport disputed some testimony about his activity as a libeler that had been made by another prisoner, Hypolite de Chamoran, in 1785: "I demand once again that he be heard and confronted with me." Undated letter, probably to the governor of the Bastille, Bastille papers, ms. 12454.

30. The memoir is a nine-page document, unsigned but written in Brissot's hand: Archives nationales, 446 AP/2, dossier 6. It noted that after leaving the army, Pelleport set off for Switzerland "without money and without hope." He did all sorts of odd jobs, it claimed, "going so far as to hire himself out to farm the land." Eventually he found a position as a tutor in Lausanne, where he developed a liaison with the woman who had

been a chambermaid to Mme Du Peyrou in Neuchâtel. "And as most Swiss women read *L'Héloïse* and have a romantic turn of mind, she thought she had found a St. Preux. But she insisted on marriage." M. Du Peyrou, "one of the most philosophical and obliging men in existence," opposed the marriage but finally agreed to countenance it and got Pelleport his tutoring position in Le Locle, where he lived with his wife and two or three children for a year before deserting them.

31. After the storming of the Bastille, Pierre Manuel, a radical member of the Paris Commune, sifted through its papers and published excerpts from them in two anthologies of documents, *La Bastille dévoilée, ou recueil de pièces authentiques pour servir à son histoire* (Paris, 1789) and *La Police de Paris dévoilée* (Paris, 1790). Both contain information about the London libelers. In the latter, vol. II, 28, Manuel wrote a biographical sketch of Pelleport, comparing him with Brissot: "Brissot de Warville, whose only fault is the same as that of the severe Cato, namely the passion for virtue . . . should not be put in the same category as the marquis de Pelleport, who, though endowed with wit and strong sentiments, only loved women and pleasure." That testimony should not be taken at face value, however, because Manuel was a close friend and political ally of Brissot's. Instead of printing Brissot's police file along with the others in *La Bastille dévoilée*, he turned it over to Brissot and invited him to write his own account of his imprisonment. Brissot obliged with an article that disavowed any connection with the libelers: "The true cause of my detention was the zeal with which at all times and in all my writings, I defended the principles that are triumphant today": *La Bastille dévoilée*, III, 78. See also Brissot, *Mémoires*, II, 23. Pelleport received very different treatment. In summarizing the case against him in *La Bastille dévoilée*, Manuel made him out to be the chief of all the *libellistes* in London: "The various interrogations that he underwent could serve as a catalogue of all the pamphlets that appeared during the last six years. He was suspected of having composed all of them": *La Bastille dévoilée*, III, 66. *La Police dévoilée* went further. It reproduced a police report that described Pelleport as an immoral adventurer and concluded, "This La Fitte de Pelleport is the author of the *Petits Soupers de l'Hôtel de Bouillon*, of the *Amusements d'Antoinette* [evidently a reference to *Les Passetemps d'Antoinette*, a libel that may never have been published], of the *Diable dans un bénitier*—in short, of all the horrors in this genre": *La Police de Paris dévoilée*, II, 236.

32. Undated note by Pelleport among various letters and messages that he asked the administrators of the Bastille to transmit and that they confiscated instead: Bibliothèque de l'Arsenal, Bastille papers, ms. 12454.

33. Records of these visits and other details regarding Pelleport's confinement appear in the administrative correspondence of the Bastille's officers: Bastille papers, ms. 12517.

34. Undated note, Bastille papers, ms. 12454.

35. Pelleport to the baron de Breteuil, December 16, 1786, in Bastille papers, ms. 12454.

36. Mme Pelleport to de l'Osme, April 1 [probably 1788]: Bastille papers, ms. 12454. One of de l'Osme's relatives had served with Pelleport's brothers in the army, and de l'Osme treated Pelleport in a friendly manner. Pelleport remained grateful to him and tried unsuc-

cessfully to save him from lynching after the storming of the Bastille: *La Bastille dévoilée*, III, 69–70.

37. Pelleport to François de Rivière de Puget, lieutenant du roi in the Bastille, November 22, 1787, Bastille papers, ms. 12454. In a previous letter to de Puget, undated and in the same dossier, Pelleport wrote that despite his reproaches to his wife, he still felt "a great deal of friendship for her."

38. In an undated note to the Bastille's governor, the marquis de Launay, de Losne recommended granting the following request from Pelleport: "I request, Monsieur, that you permit the sieur de Pelleport to write, that you give him books, a pen, ink, and paper." A note at the bottom, dated July 11, 1784, indicated that such permission had been given: "Done as requested." Bastille papers, ms. 12517.

39. Undated note by Pelleport to an unidentified person, Bastille papers, ms. 12454.

40. Undated verse by Pelleport on a scrap of paper under the heading "Mes adieux à Pluton," Bastille papers, ms. 12454.

41. Pelleport published a thirty-one-page, satirical poem, *Le Boulevard des Chartreux, poème chrétien* ("à Grenoble, de l'Imprimerie de la Grande Chartreuse," 1779). It contains a great many attacks on monasticism written from a worldly perspective, and it celebrates the good things in secular life, especially women and liberty (21): "Liberté, *libertas*, vive la liberté / Plus de cagoterie et point d'austerité" (Liberty, *libertas*, long live liberty/ No bigotry and no austerity"). Although the poem is anonymous, Pelleport clearly identified himself as its author in two autobiographical passages in *Les Bohémiens*, I, 124 and 129. He also cites it in the preface to his translation of a tract by David Williams, *Lettres sur la liberté politique, adressées à un membre de la Chambre des Communes d'Angleterre, sur son élection au nombre des membres d'une association de Comté; traduites de l'anglais en français par le R. P. de Roze-Croix, ex-Cordelier* ("seconde édition, imprimées à Liège aux dépens de la Société, 1783–89"). In the preface he describes himself (the translator) as "the Reverend Father de Roze-Croix, author of the *Boulevard des Chartreux* and of many other short works in verse." The only copy of *Le Boulevard des Chartreux* that I have been able to locate is in the Bibliothèque municipale de Grenoble, section d'études et d'information: 0.8254 Dauphinois.

42. Pelleport to de Launay, undated letter, Bastille papers, ms. 12454.

43. Pelleport to de l'Osme, November 16, 1784, Bastille papers, ms. 12454.

44. Jean-Claude Fini (known as Hypolite Chamoran or Chamarand) to de Launay, undated letter (probably mid-1786), Bastille papers, ms. 12454. Chamoran was detained in the Bastille from November 27, 1785 until July 31, 1786. He and his supposed wife, Marie-Barbara Mackai, seem to have been involved with Pelleport in the production of libels and the blackmailing operations in London; but he denied everything and denounced Pelleport vehemently during his stay in the Bastille. He is mentioned briefly in *La Bastille dévoilée*, III, 101 and in a letter from Morande to the foreign minister, Armand-Marc, comte de Montmorin, April 28, 1788 in von Proschwitz, *Beaumarchais et le Courier de l'Europe*, II, 1013.

45. For example, in notes about special requests and permissions granted to prisoners, a clerk recorded that de Sade's wife had sent him a waistcoat and a candle on November 13,

1784, and that Pelleport's wife had visited him on November 19, 1784: Bastille papers, ms. 12517, folios 79 and 82. Two recent books in the vast literature on de Sade contain detailed accounts of his life in the Bastille: Laurence L. Bongie, *Sade: A Biographical Essay* (Chicago, 1998) and Francine du Plessix Gray, *At Home with the Marquis de Sade: A Life* (New York, 1998). On Sade's writing in the Bastille, see especially, Jean-Jacques Pauvert, *Sade Vivant* (Paris, 1989).

46. See Monique Cottret, *La Bastille à prendre: Histoire et mythe de la forteresse royale* (Paris, 1986), 31–33 and 129; Claude Quétel, *De Par le Roy: Essai sur les lettres de cachet* (Toulouse, 1981), 48–49; and Joseph Delort, *Histoire de la détention des philosophes et des gens de lettres à la Bastille et à Vincennes* (Paris, 1829; reprint Geneva, 1967), 3 vols.

47. *Les Bohémiens*, I, 3.

48. Darnton, *J.-P. Brissot*, 257.

49. *Les Bohémiens*, I, 33.

50. *Les Bohémiens*, I, 38.

51. *Les Bohémiens*, I, 41.

52. *La Police de Paris dévoilée*, II, 244–47. On Saint-Flocel and the *Journal des Princes*, see Jean Sgard, ed., *Dictionnaire des journalistes* (Oxford, 1999), II, 899.

53. *Mémoires*, I, 329 and *La Police de Paris dévoilée*, II, 246–47.

54. See Darline Gay Levy, *The Ideas and Careers of Simon-Nicolas-Henri Linguet: A Study in Eighteenth-Century French Politics* (Champaign, 1980) and Daniel Baruch, *Simon Nicolas Linguet ou l'Irrécupérable* (Paris, 1991).

55. *La Police de Paris dévoilée*, II, 231–69.

56. *Les Bohémiens*, I, 47.

57. *Les Bohémiens*, I, 50.

58. *Les Bohémiens*, I, 51.

59. *Les Bohémiens*, I, 56.

60. *Les Bohémiens*, I, 60. In a later aside to the reader, the narrator, who can be identified with the author, seems to subscribe to the donkey's hedonism: II, 63–65.

61. *Les Bohémiens*, I, 1.

62. *Les Bohémiens*, I, 53.

63. *Les Bohémiens*, I, 54–55.

64. *Les Bohémiens*, I, 65. See also the similar remarks in vol. I, 75 and 181.

65. *Les Bohémiens*, I, 68.

66. *Les Bohémiens*, I, 87. An earlier passage in this scene, page 85, evokes Pelleport's father and his dead mother. As mentioned above, Pelleport attempted to get favorable treatment in the Bastille by citing his family's six centuries of military service under French kings.

67. *Les Bohémiens*, I, 63.

68. *Les Bohémiens*, I, 64.

69. *Les Bohémiens*, I, 59. "Nothing-ism" ("Riénisme") suggests the "zéro" mentioned above that Hypolite Chamoran claimed was Pelleport's "profession of faith."

70. *Les Bohémiens*, I, 45–46.

71. *Les Bohémiens*, I, 135.

72. *Les Bohémiens*, I, 93. See also the similar remarks on I, 132.

73. *Les Bohémiens*, I, 136. See also I, 127 on "sweet pity, mother of all the virtues."

74. *Les Bohémiens*, II, 113. The rape scene is recounted with false naiveté by Félicité in a journal that the narrator claims he discovered in the "London Lyceum"—a reference to the philosophic club that Brissot attempted to create in London after the model of the Parisian Musée of Mamès-Claude Pahin de la Blancherie: II, 112. In an earlier episode, the narrator presents Félicité as eager to be raped: I, 158.

75. Pelleport had studied science and mathematics, and apparently taught both while he was employed as a tutor in Le Locle and London. *Les Bohémiens* includes a long digression about science, inspired in part by contemporary balloon flights and experiments with electricity, which concludes that "inflammable gas is the universal principle": I, 164. Metaphors about phlogiston or inflammable air permeate Pelleport's descriptions of sexual activity. Thus the references to "igneous fluid," I, 192; "phosphoric sparks," and "electric hearth," I, 195; "flame," I, 199; and "fierce heat," I, 214.

76. *Les Bohémiens*, I, 203–9.

77. *Les Bohémiens*, I, 210.

78. Pelleport invokes *Don Quixote* at the end of the description of the brawl: *Les Bohémiens*, I, 214.

79. *Le Boulevard des Chartreux, poème chrétien*: see n. 41.

80. The only information I have been able to uncover about Jean Diedey is a letter that he wrote from Le Locle to the Société typographique de Neuchâtel dated July 29, 1778: Bibliothèque publique et universitaire de Neuchâtel, papers of the Société typographique, ms 1142, fo. 93. It merely concerns a payment of a bill of exchange.

81. While maintaining an elevated tone and using classical rhetoric, often in a mock-heroic manner, Pelleport sometimes jolts the reader by interrupting his narrative with veiled obscenities or dirty jokes, such as a gross witticism in vol. II, 128.

82. *Les Bohémiens*, II, 131.

83. *Les Bohémiens*, II, 135.

84. *Les Bohémiens*, II, 152.

85. An example of the autobiographical allusions that Pelleport scattered through the text is a passing reference to Edme Mentelle, the professor of geography at the Ecole militaire who had befriended him and Brissot, as "Manteau" in *Les Bohémiens*, II, 141.

86. See the long declamation against the injustices of the social order in vol. II, 167–77, notably the poet's condemnation of the "ancient tyrannical feudal right," 168.

87. *Les Bohémiens*, II, 185.

88. The biography of Labre written shortly after his death by his confessor, Giuseppe Loreto Marconi, *Ragguaglio della vita del servo di Dio, Benedetto Labre Francese* (Rome, 1783), was translated into French a year later by Père Elie Hard under the title *Vie de Benoît-Joseph Labre, mort à Rome en odeur de sainteté* (Paris, 1784). See the article on Labre in the *New Catholic Encyclopedia* (New York, 2003), IX, 267.

89. Catau des Arches may be a play on Catherine Dupont. The text heaps scorn on

Madame Dupont, stressing her hideous body and frustrated sex life. It claims that she devoured twenty miserable lovers while maintaining a facade of bourgeois respectability in Boulogne. Evidently Pelleport held her responsible, with Morande, for his imprisonment. In vol. II, 231, the poet refers to collaboration between Madame Dupont (Catau des Arches) and Morande (Thonevet) in the plot that led to his arrest in Boulogne.

90. *Les Bohémiens*, II, 227.

91. Brissot republished essays by others in a ten-volume anthology entitled *Bibliothèque philosophique du législateur, du politique, du jurisconsulte* (Neuchâtel, 1782–1785). In his account of his voyage to London, the poet says he accompanied the youngest of Madame des Arches's four daughters and deposited her in the London residence of "a boneheaded son-in-law, an old-clothes merchant" (II, 202), whom he later mocks as the "old-clothes merchant Bissoto de Guerreville" (II, 219). Madame Dupont did indeed have four daughters; the youngest, Nancy, joined the Brissots in London in 1783. She may well have made the trip in the company of Pelleport, who is mentioned along with her in the correspondence between Brissot and members of the Dupont family. See the three letters from Nancy's brother François Dupont to Brissot, April 22, 1783; May 7, 1783; and May 14, 1783 in Brissot, *Correspondance et papiers*, 52–55. See also Brissot, *Mémoires*, II, 302 and 338.

92. *Les Bohémiens*, II, 227.

93. *Les Bohémiens*, II, 226.

94. *Les Bohémiens*, II, 234.

95. *Les Bohémiens*, I, 88–89. Among other things, these references evoke Brissot's Lycée de Londres and his journalistic *Correspondance universelle sur ce qui intéresse le bonheur de l'homme et de la société* as well as his *Bibliothèque philosophique du législateur, du politique, du jurisconsulte*. While settling accounts with Brissot, Pelleport presented him as a typical hack writer struggling to survive in the difficult conditions of Grub Street.

96. The following description of a poor writer trying to sell his manuscripts—in fact, the text of *Les Bohémiens* and various poems—to Parisian publishers provides the most vivid account of author-publisher relations available anywhere in the literature of eighteenth-century France. Although obviously tendentious, it is highly realistic and describes actual *libraires (éditeur*, the modern term for publisher, had not yet come into general use) at three levels of the trade, from the wealthiest to the most marginal. At the same time, it expresses an imagined relationship between the author and his reader. Pelleport pictures his reader as a nouveau riche who began as a miserable tax collector (*"rat de cave"*) at the bottom of the tax-gathering administration (*ferme générale)* and rose to wealth through cheating and peculation. By casting the reader in this role, he picks a fight with him; he will continue to provoke, quarrel, and make up with an imaginary reader throughout the novel.

97. *Les Bohémiens*, I, 111.

98. This scene, recounted in vol. I, p. 113, takes place in the bookshop of the publisher of the *Almanach des muses*, who at that time was Nicolas-Augustin Delalain. But the text identifies him as "P . . ."; so I may have failed to pick up the allusion intended by Pelleport.

99. *Les Bohémiens*, I, 111–18. This long passage, brimming with concrete details, demonstrates a thorough familiarity with life among the hack writers of Paris, but it also conforms to a genre, the dangers of life as a *littérateur*, which was a favorite theme of well-known writers such as Voltaire and Linguet.

100. *Les Bohémiens*, II, 76.

CHAPTER 1. THE LEGISLATOR BISSOT RENOUNCES CHICANERY IN FAVOR OF PHILOSOPHY

1. Jacques-Pierre Brissot de Warville (1754–1793), the future leader of the Girondins during the French Revolution. After clerking with an attorney and taking a law degree at the University of Reims in the winter of 1781–1782, he abandoned the law in order to pursue a career as a man of letters, aligning himself with the *philosophes*.

2. Pierre-Louis Brissot de Thivars, the younger brother of Brissot de Warville, joined the Brissot household in London in 1783 and worked as his older brother's assistant.

3. Brissot submitted several philosophic discourses to the prize essay contests sponsored by provincial academies, hoping to win recognition as a *philosophe,* just as Rousseau had done in 1749. After awarding him a prize in 1789, the Académie de Châlons-sur-Marne elected him as one of its corresponding members. In the following parody of academic oratory, Pelleport caricatures Brissot as a vulgar Rousseauist. He contrasts Brissot's pretentious, overblown philosophizing with his miserable condition as a hack writer, and he also mocks Brissot's origins as the son of a master caterer and pastry cook in Chartres. Writing as a member of the ancient nobility, Pelleport makes sport of the Brissot brothers' poverty and low birth throughout the novel. From time to time, however, he drops this satiric tone and criticizes the injustices and inequalities of the Ancien Régime from a perspective that is more radically Rousseauistic than Brissot's.

4. Clovis (c. 466–511) ruled the Frankish kingdom and parts of Gaul; he is considered the founder of France.

5. The University of Reims actually sold its law degrees after staging farcical oral examinations. Brissot paid 600 livres for his degree, not 300, as Pelleport indicates (one écu equaled three livres at this time). But Pelleport was very well informed about Brissot's past and accurately represented Brissot's decision to abandon law for a literary career.

6. Allusion to *Théorie des lois civiles* (1767) by Simon-Nicolas-Henri Linguet (1736–1794) and to Brissot's own *Théorie des lois criminelles* (1780). Linguet, at this time a member of the bar, presented a defense of absolute monarchy in this work. His historical and journalistic writing countered the thinking of *philosophes* such as Montesquieu and liberal or constitutionalist monarchists. By the late 1780s, he was in favor with the court.

7. In parodying the theme of noble savagery and the need to return to nature, Pelleport again makes fun of Brissot's Rousseauism. Brissot's early treatise, *Recherches philosophiques sur le droit de la propriété* (*Philosophical inquiries into the right of property,* published in 1781 but probably written in 1774) shows the influence of Rousseau's *Discours sur l'origine et les*

fondements de l'inégalité parmi les hommes, the *Discourse on the Origin of Inequality* (1754). References to Rousseau's writings can be found everywhere in Brissot's works, which Pelleport clearly knew intimately.

8. Moses Mendelssohn (1729–1786) was a German Jewish philosopher who is considered the founder of the Jewish Enlightenment or Haskalah; his work argued for the compatibility of metaphysics, including a belief in the immortality of the soul, with rational analysis.

9. In the fable "The Wolf and the Lamb," by Jean de La Fontaine (1625–1691), the wolf takes no pity on the lamb because, he argues, lambs feel no compassion for him (*Fables,* I, 10).

10. The sixteen-year-old "wild girl" of Issaux, in the Pyrenees, was found in 1719; she may be one of two persons mentioned by Rousseau in his *Discourse on the Origin of Inequality*. The feral child of Hanover, Peter of Hanover, found 1724 in the German town of Hamelin, was an instant celebrity.

11. The marquis de Launay, governor of the Bastille, who is mocked here for his plebeian origins. De Launay was to be killed in 1789 during the attack on the Bastille witnessed by Pelleport; this may be of interest in dating the passage as prerevolutionary.

12. The "Porte Cérès" was a Roman memorial arch in Reims, dedicated to Ceres from the time of the Antonines and later incorporated into a gateway in the city wall; it was destroyed in 1798. Ceres is the Roman goddess of agriculture; the gate opens to the fields of Champagne.

13. The knightly hero of *Don Quixote*, by Miguel de Cervantes Saavedra (1547–1616), "calmed down and continued on his chosen way, which in reality was none other than the way his horse chose to follow, for he believed that in this consisted the essence of adventure" (tr. John Rutherford; New York: Penguin, 2003, I, ii, 30).

14. Isabella Kazimira Jagiello (1519–1559), widowed queen mother of Hungary, is said to have carved the initials SFV ("Sic fata volunt," this is the will of fate) into the bark of an oak tree while traveling in exile.

CHAPTER 2. THE TWO BROTHERS WANDER ON THE PLAINS OF CHAMPAGNE

1. Now Pontfaverger-Moronvilliers, in the Champagne-Ardennes. Pelleport maps out a detailed geographical trajectory as a component of his fiction, arguably to make the satire seem more probable.

2. An allusion to the *corvée* (forced labor) on the construction of roads, one of the most hated forms of taxation under the Ancien Régime. In this chapter, which contrasts with the satirical tone of the previous chapter, Pelleport shows himself to be an outspoken critic of the injustices in French society before the Revolution.

3. The salt tax (*gabelle*) required French subjects to purchase certain amounts of salt, at ruinous prices, from a monopoly controlled by the state.

4. Upon seeing the city and tower of Babel built by the children of men, the Lord decides to "confound their language, that they may not understand one another's speech" (*KJV* Genesis 11:7).

5. Winged harpies were sent by Zeus to snatch food away from the table of the seer Phineas, son of Poseidon, before he could eat it. Aeneas describes invasion by the Harpies: "Along the curving coast we build our couches. / We feast on those rich meats. But suddenly, / shaking out their wings with a great clanging, / the Harpies, horrible, swoop from the hilltops; / and plundering our banquet with the filthy touch of their talons, they foul everything." (*The Aeneid of Virgil*, tr. Allen Mandelbaum, III, 294–99 [New York: Bantam, 1961]).

6. Antoine Joseph de Serres de La Tour was the editor of the French journal published in London, the *Courrier de l'Europe*. An avid gardener and gourmet, he concocted *dragées de la Mecque* (Mecca) and sold them with great success to the London public. Franz Anton Mesmer and his medical practice, known as animal magnetism or mesmerism, was a vogue in Paris in the mid-1780s.

7. Perhaps Saint Hubert (c. 626–727), who on Good Friday in the forest saw a cross appear between a stag's antlers.

CHAPTER 3. SUPPER BETTER THAN DINNER

1. A police officer who often arrested authors and carried them off to the Bastille.

2. The theory of the existence of phlogiston, a flammable substance that combined with air to cause fire, was already outdated by the work of Antoine-Laurent de Lavoisier (1743–1794).

3. The following harangue is a parody of Brissot's reception speech at the nearby Académie of Châlons-sur-Marne on December 15, 1780, after he was elected as one of its corresponding members.

4. Here Pelleport alludes to the attraction of Rousseau for hack writers, known as "les Rousseau du ruisseau" (Rousseaus of the gutter).

5. Armand-Jean du Plessis, cardinal and duke de Richelieu (1585–1643), was known for policies fostering absolute monarchy at home and a stronger foreign policy for France abroad. He dominated Louis XIII (1601–1643) both during the regency of queen Marie de Medicis, and afterward when Louis took power. Richelieu was Louis's first minister, the first protector of the Académie française, and the first theologian to write in the French language.

6. Pelleport alludes here to the movement to promote the power of the Third Estate (a category that included all Frenchmen who were not members of the clergy or nobility) during the campaign for the elections to the Estates General, which were to meet on May 1, 1789, according to a decision by Louis XVI announced on August 8, 1788. Pelleport was released from the Bastille on October 3, 1788. He spent the following months in Stenay, trying to put his affairs in order. Although he may have added some finishing touches to *Les*

Bohémiens during that period, it seems likely that he composed the main text in the Bastille. It describes an Ancien Régime that is still firmly in place, and it never refers to any event that occurred after the end of 1788.

7. "Master Desaccords" is a reference to *Les Bigarrures du Seigneur des Accords* (1582) by Étienne Tabourot, sometimes known as "Tabourot des Accords" (1547–1590). Tabourot's miscellanies contained poetry as well as Rabelaisian tales.

8. Epictetus (55–135) was a Greek Stoic philosopher who taught that human judgment should not be affected by external objects such as food.

9. Speaking through the voice of an anonymous narrator, Pelleport pretends to base his novel on memoirs written by Félicité Dupont, who married Brissot on September 17, 1782. Pelleport was a frequent guest in the apartment that Brissot rented at 1 Brompton Row in London, but Félicité took such an aversion to him that she refused to admit him to her household by the end of 1783.

CHAPTER 4. WHO WERE THESE PEOPLE SUPPING UNDER THE STARS ON THE PLAINS OF CHAMPAGNE?

1. As the text later makes clear, this orator is Séchant, the "president" of the band of Bohemians. Séchant is a thinly disguised version of the abbé de Séchamp, who had been a chaplain to the prince of Zweibrücken after fleeing from Nantes, where he was suspected of involvement in a theft and murder. Séchamp then emigrated to London, became a prominent member of the French expatriate colony, and collaborated with Pelleport's blackmailing operations. In the following passages of speechifying, a parody of oratory in the Académie française, Séchant invokes the ethos of the Bohemians—devotion to liberty and the pursuit of pleasure on the margins of society—and introduces the leaders of their three main "sects." Each leader, like Brissot, is a hack writer with philosophic pretensions. The philosophers argue and interrupt each other in endless dogmatic debates that give Pelleport an occasion to pour scorn on the principal intellectual trends of his time.

2. In the open air.

3. The Bohemian Séché corresponds to Saint-Flocel, an obscure journalist who worked for the *Gazette des gazettes* (otherwise known as the *Journal de Bouillon)* and then sought refuge with Séchamp among the French expatriates in London. In 1783, he and Séchamp began to produce a new French periodical in London, *Journal des princes ou examen des journaux et autres écrits périodiques relativement au progrès du despotisme,* but they abandoned it after three issues. Saint-Flocel was a fanatic partisan of physiocracy, the economic theory that favored free trade, especially in cereals. The name Séché means "dried-out"—president Séchant's name would be "drying"—as in Dry and Drier, or Walter Scott's Dryasdust. The last segment of the French nonsense-term "économico-naturellico-monotonique" sect suggests the reduction of everything to natural law.

4. "Secundum artem": according to the rules of art or skill. The text has "secondam" [*sic*].

5. Jacob's "rod": Lungiet is making a sexual allusion to Genesis, possibly to prompt intercourse. In Genesis, Jacob plants his poplar and chestnut rods in drinking troughs: "And it came to pass, whensoever the stronger cattle did conceive, that Jacob laid the rods before the eyes of the cattle in the gutters, that they might conceive among the rods" (*KJV*, 30:37–41).

6. Simon-Nicolas-Henri Linguet (1736–1794) produced his enormously popular, long-running *Annales politiques, civiles, et littéraires du dix-huitième siècle* (1777–1792) from London during 1783–1784. His *Mémoires sur la Bastille* (1783), which recounted his imprisonment from September 1780 to May 1782, probably did more than any other work to popularize the mythology that identified the Bastille with despotism. After his release from the Bastille, Linguet settled in London but moved with his *Annales* to Brussels in 1784. He was notorious for advancing paradoxical arguments and for favoring the unrestrained power of the monarchy as a means to relieve the suffering of the poor. He had been expelled from the bar by having his name stricken from the tableau or register. The last segment of the French nonsense-term "despotico-contradictorio-paradoxico-clabaudeuristes" suggests yelping animals or vicious gossips.

7. Marie-Catherine Dupont, née Cléry, Brissot's mother-in-law, was the widow of a merchant in Boulogne-sur-Mer, where Brissot got to know her and her daughter Félicité while he was working on the Boulogne edition of the *Courrier de l'Europe*. Pelleport attempted to tap Madame Dupont's wealth for a speculation on imports of champagne for the luxury trade in London. This project turned into a disaster (hence the allusions to the pitiless creditors in Reims at the beginning of *Les Bohémiens),* and it led to a quarrel with Madame Dupont, whom Pelleport pilloried throughout the novel. Voragine's nickname initials "O.-B." are, as pronounced in French, a pun for English "obey."

8. Charles Théveneau or Thevenot de Morande (1741–1805), author of *Le Gazetier cuirassé* (1771) and the most notorious of the French libelers in London. Pelleport had attacked him as a secret agent of the French police in *Le Diable dans un bénitier* (1784), and Morande retaliated by helping to engineer Pelleport's arrest in Boulogne-sur-Mer, which led to his imprisonment in the Bastille.

9. Sacrogorgon is a blustering swaggerer in Voltaire's mock-heroic *La Pucelle d'Orléans* (1762), rather than truly brave.

10. Predatory self-interest. The last part of the nonsense term "communico-luxurico-friponistes" identifies these philosophers as *fripons* or rogues; it may also suggest "fripier," a term for old-clothes dealer or rag-picker that Pelleport uses for hack writers.

11. Probably an allusion to Séchamp's past as chaplain to the prince of Zweibrücken, whose territory and titles extended to Worms.

CHAPTER 5. REVEILLE; THE TROUPE MARCHES FORWARD;
UNREMARKABLE ADVENTURES

1. In Rousseau's widely read novel *Julie, ou la nouvelle Héloïse* (1761), Julie is the hero-ine famous for her pure yet eroticized intercourse with her tutor Saint-Preux; this name would link the fervor of Pelleport's narrative voice with Saint-Preux's passionate description and protest of the obstacles to their union set by her father's conventional beliefs.

2. The interpellative aside to the reader, the first of many scattered throughout the book, suggests the influence of Laurence Sterne (1713–1768), whose novels were popular in France at this time. While teasing the reader and enticing him or her to enter into a guessing game, Pelleport delivers another satire of contemporary religious and philosophic thought. Although the passage begins with a straightforward invocation of Lockean epistemology, it ends with a cynical and obscene conclusion typical of Pelleport's brand of libertinism.

3. This is a garbled allusion to Horace, *Ars Poetica* 1–5: "Humano capiti cervicem pictor equinam iungere si velit . . ." ("If a painter chose to join a human head to the neck of a horse, and to spread feathers of many a hue over limbs picked up now here now there, so that what at the top is a lovely woman ends below in a black and ugly fish, could you, my friends, if favoured with a private view, refrain from laughing?" (tr. H. Rushton Fairclough, *Satires* [Cambridge, Mass.: Harvard University Press, 1926/1966]).

4. François Garasse, *Rabelais réformé par les ministres* (1619). In the barrage of allusions that follow, Pelleport refers to d'Alembert's article on Geneva in the *Encyclopédie*, which treated the Genevan clergy as Socinians (heretics who denied the doctrine of the Trinity and the divinity of Christ); to the Jansenist-Jesuit controversies (the Jansenists, whose leading theologian was Antoine Arnauld, accused the Jesuits of favoring a laxist morality by embracing the philosophy of the Spanish Jesuit, Luis Molina); to polemics about the eternity of the punishment of the damned in hell (triggered by the sermons of Ferdinand Olivier Petitpierre, this controversy caused great agitation among the clergy in the principality of Neuchâtel and Vallangin at the time Pelleport settled there); and to the persecution of the *philosophes* by the Parlement de Paris, led by Antoine Louis Séguier, the public prosecutor, whose denunciations (*réquisitoires*) made him a conspicuous enemy of the Enlightenment.

5. The hand of all will be against him, "Hic erit ferus homo manus eius contra omnes et manus omnium contra eum." (Genesis 16:12)

6. This is the first extensive autobiographical passage in the novel. After an oblique reference to his birth in a family from the ancient nobility, Pelleport alludes to his life as an adventurer on the road and invokes Rousseau as the source of his inspiration. At this point, his tone changes. He advocates an authentic egalitarianism derived from Rousseau's *Discours sur l'origine et les fondements de l'inégalité parmi les hommes* in contrast to the vulgar Rousseauism and the other philosophies that he had satirized earlier. He also embarks on a series of digressions and digressions within digressions, which recall the technique used by Sterne in *The Life and Opinions of Tristram Shandy, Gentleman.* Rabelais and Henri-Joseph

Dulaurens, author of *Le Compère Mathieu ou les Bigarrures de l'esprit humain* (1766), seem to be Pelleport's other principal sources of inspiration.

7. In La Fontaine's fable "The Wolf and the Dog," the wolf is tempted by the easy life of the tame dog, but rejects it in horror when he sees how the dog's collar has scraped bare his neck (*Fables*, I, 5). "So ran Sir Wolf, and runneth yet" (tr. Elizur Wright, 1841).

8. Jean-Jacques Rousseau (1712–1778). "The first man who, having enclosed a piece of ground, thought to say 'This is mine,' and found people simple enough to believe him, was the real founder of civil society" (*Discourse on the Origin and Foundation of Inequality among Men*). Rousseau became an exile from Geneva and gave up his citizenship after the burning of his book *Emile* (1762).

9. Genesis 3:19: "In the sweat of thy face shalt thou eat bread, till thou return unto the ground."

10. Semence: seed or semen; the word is used in this second sense by both Diderot and Sade.

11. Bât: packload or packsaddle, often made of wood and presumably awkward, hence the proverb "personne ne sait mieux que l'âne où le bât le blesse," the ass knows best where the burden pinches most.

12. The tradition of the emperor of China plowing a furrow and throwing five seeds into it every springtime to show his people his and their relationship to nature was familiar to Pelleport's contemporaries; J. Hector St. John de Crèvecoeur cites it in *Letters from an American Farmer* (1782): "The father thus ploughing with his child, and to feed his family, is inferior only to the emperor of China ploughing as an example to his kingdom."

13. Probably an allusion to some quarrel that led to Pelleport's expulsion from a regiment in which he had enlisted as a poor *sous-lieutenant* from an old military family. According to his dossier with the police, Pelleport had been expelled from two regiments and imprisoned by *lettre de cachet* four or five times at the request of his family "for atrocities against honor."

14. Lustral water for purificatory rites. Eau-de-luce was a popular compound named for the French apothecary Luce, used among other purposes as smelling salts (and in India to cure snake bite); it contained spirits of wine, sal ammoniac, soap, and oil of amber. Carmelite water, eau des Carmes or Melissa water: a tonic sold near a Paris Carmelite church, variously used as a sedative or an elixir of youth, and sometimes associated with sperm; it contained flowering balm, lemon rind, cinnamon, cloves, nutmeg, coriander seed, dried angelica root, and alcohol spirits.

15. The "fear" of bread-bakers not accomplishing their task may refer to a scarcity of bread due to grain shortages; the "great fear" (Grande Peur) of summer 1789 developed over time. Screw-up: Courgébelin may be a compound word; courge or gourd can be used colloquially to mean fool (with the accent as a transition); belin is a regional word in Southern France for penis.

16. Morande was the son of an attorney in Arnay-le-Duc, as related here. He reputedly deserted from a regiment in which he had served as a young man, then took up life in the gambling dens and bawdy houses of Paris, spent two years in prison, and after his release

sought his fortune in London as a pimp, libeler, and blackmailer. Charleville, capital of the principality of Arches and a center of trade in Champagne, was known for its manufacture of metal goods.

17. Anaxagoras (c. 500–428 B.C.E.) based his philosophical method on inquiry; his controversial theories suggested that the cosmos had originally been a mixture of "everything-in-everything" and that the motion of mind or "nous" had caused the cosmos as we know it. He was prosecuted for impiety and obliged to leave Athens.

18. Pelleport often referred disparagingly to rich bourgeois who bought their way into the nobility by purchasing ennobling offices, known as *savonnettes à villain.* As a marquis from the ancient *noblesse d'épée,* he expressed nothing but scorn for the arriviste *noblesse de robe,* yet he also subscribed to the Rousseauistic principle of the natural equality of men. The burlesque dialogue, set in a stagecoach, bears witness to the experience of a man who had spent much of his life on the road, both in coaches and on foot.

19. Anne Robert Jacques Turgot, baron de Laune (1727–1781), was a foremost French economist who believed in human progress and, as controller-general of France, attempted reform. He replaced "diligence" coaches with more comfortable ones known as "turgotines."

20. In Homer's *Odyssey,* the giant Polyphemus digests his cannibalistic meal and unwatered wine coarsely, and to Odysseus' or Ulysses' disgust (Book IX).

21. *Guimbarde*: a rattletrap coach.

22. François-Marie Arouet de Voltaire (1694–1778) was known for his critiques of the Catholic Church, for example in his *Dictionnaire philosophique* (1764), copies of which were publicly burned.

23. Here Pelleport takes up the common theme of the provincial youth who seeks his fortune in Paris. But it develops an autobiographical twist when he (as the narrator, speaking in the first person) describes himself as a young marquis seeking patronage in Versailles.

24. These balloonists were the talk of the town in the 1780s. Jean-François Pilâtre de Rozier (1754–1785), for whom the hot-air Rozier balloon is named, is credited with the first recorded manned balloon flight in 1783; he and a companion died crossing to England in 1785. Also in 1783, Marie-Noel Robert (1761–1828) ascended in the "aerostatic globe" he and his brother had helped Jacques Charles design. Jean Pierre Blanchard (1753–1809) invented a "char volant" ("flying vessel") with wing-like oars; in 1784, he was attacked by an armed man insisting on a place in his balloon. Later that year, Blanchard's American patron John Jeffries won a place for himself in the first Channel crossing only after invading Blanchard's camp in Dover by force.

25. When Pelleport solicited favorable treatment in the Bastille, he described himself as coming from a family that had served French kings for six centuries.

26. Hugo de Groot or Grotius (1583–1645) wrote *On the Law of War and Peace* (1625) relating natural law to international law and "just" war. Samuel Pufendorf (1632–1694) developed Grotius's concept of natural law and a theory of the state as formed by the association of individuals.

27. Literary societies known as *musées* and *lycées* were popular in Paris in the 1780s; they attracted large numbers of unknown writers who could not penetrate the grander salons and academies. Brissot attempted to found a "licée" with a journal attached to it in London, taking the Parisian "Musée" of Mammès-Claude Pahin de La Blancherie as his model.

Chapter 6. Cock-Crow

1. Pelleport's note refers to Charles Bonnet (1720–1793) and his *Essai analytique sur les facultés de l'âme* (1760). Bonnet was a Genevan preformationist whose work related memory and reflection, the workings of the mind as soul, to the physical optic pathways of the brain.

2. The dictionary of the French language established by the forty members of the Académie française.

3. It is difficult to recognize all the allusions in this long digression about a wandering monk, who is later identified by one of Pelleport's pseudonyms, the Reverend Father Rose-Croix. Some allusions may refer to fugitive thieves among the French expatriates—possibly dom Louis, a defrocked monk who stole some gold medals from the Abbaye de Saint Denis and fled to London, where he turned out works against the church and crown in France. But from the point at which the monk enters Geneva, his life story runs parallel to that of Pelleport, and the autobiographical current in the novel surfaces again.

4. Another indication that Pelleport composed his text or added the last touches to it in 1788. Cologne cathedral is built around a shrine believed to contain relics of the Three Magi; these relics, which had been transported from Constantinople to Milan, were then given to the archbishop of Cologne by the Holy Roman Emperor Frederick Barbarossa in 1164; the shrine is a site of pilgrimage.

5. "Custode" is a title given by the Cordeliers to the head of their order.

6. The county and then duchy of Juliers in the Holy Roman Empire; now Jülich, Germany.

7. This eighteenth-century oratory on a hill near Arras, raised in 1712, was destroyed in 1794.

8. A silver coin used in the Papal States and named for Pope Paul III (1468–1549).

9. A tunic worn by penitents condemned by the Inquisition.

10. *Minima malis*: the expression is *minima de malis,* choose the lesser evil. Minims are an order founded by St. Francis of Paola in 1435, based originally on the order founded by St. Francis of Assisi; they are devoted particularly to the virtue of humility, and abstain from eating meat, eggs, milk products, and fish. Malines, or Mechlin, is a city in Belgium.

11. Possibly dom Nicolas-Michel Barthélemy, an erudite Benedictine of the Congregation of Saint-Vanne.

12. The American Revolution of 1776–1783.

13. Pelleport describes the three social groups involved in the fierce struggles for power

in Geneva during the second half of the eighteenth century. The oligarchic elite of citizens known as the party of *Négatifs* dominated the republic's civic life through the *Petit Conseil* and *Conseil des Deux-Cents* to the exclusion of the bourgeois party of *Représentants* in the more democratic *Conseil général*. The *Représentants* appealed for support to the *Natifs*, artisans who had no civic rights, and they invoked the democratic theory of Rousseau, a fellow Genevan, who defended them in his *Lettres écrites de la montagne* (1764). In April 1782, the leaders of the *Représentants* seized power in a mini-revolution, only to be expelled in July by the intervention of an army composed of troops from France, Savoy, and Bern. Several of the *Représentant* leaders, including Etienne Clavière, sought refuge in Neuchâtel. There they met Brissot, who had traveled to Neuchâtel via Geneva in order to arrange for the publication of his works with the Société typographique. At the behest of Clavière, Brissot defended their cause in a strongly Rousseauistic pamphlet, *Le Philadelphien à Genève* (1783). Pelleport alludes to these events in the following two chapters. He got to know the Genevan crisis first hand, probably at some date in 1779, when he wandered through Switzerland seeking a position as a tutor in wealthy households or as an employee in the printing shops of Geneva, Lausanne, Yverdon, and Neuchâtel. His narrator follows this itinerary in the novel and finally lands a job as a tutor in Le Locle, a center of watch-making in the Jura Mountains above Neuchâtel.

14. Bellona: goddess of war, and also a reference to Brissot's name de Warville. Clavière: mountainous district of the Vaud, as well as Etienne Clavière, Representative leader defended by Brissot.

15. Charles Gravier, comte de Vergennes, was the French foreign minister who masterminded the repression of the *Représentants*.

16. Jean-André Deluc (1727–1817), an eminent physicist from Geneva who had settled in England. The colonel Tissot who is mentioned in the same sentence could have been a relative of the well-known doctor, Simon-André Tissot of Lausanne. Deluc reappears in the Pilgrim's narrative as barometer-maker and reader to Queen Charlotte.

17. At this point, Pelleport identifies the monk whose peregrinations he has been narrating as "the Very Reverend Father Rose-Croix," a pseudonym he had adopted while translating a tract by the English radical David Williams: *Lettres sur la liberté politique, adressées à un membre de la Chambre des Communes d'Angleterre, sur son élection au nombre des membres d'une association de comté; traduites de l'anglais en français par le R. P. de Roze-Croix, ex-Cordelier* (Liège, 1783). In the notes he added to this text, Pelleport included some violent criticism of the French monarchy, and in his preface, speaking as Roze-Croix, he said that he wanted to make radical English work available to French readers in order to wake them up from the apathy instilled in them by their government. The preface identified Roze-Croix as the "auteur du *Boulevard des Chartreux* et de bien d'autres petits ouvrages en vers." One copy of the *Boulevard des Chartreux, poème chrétien* (à Grenoble, De l'Imprimerie de la Grande Chartreuse," 1779) has survived in the Bibliothèque de la ville de Grenoble. It contains attacks on monasticism similar to those scattered through *Les Bohémiens*, and it celebrates liberty in the same spirit (p. 21): "Liberté, *libertas,* vive la liberté/ Plus de cagoterie et point d'austérité." Why Pelleport chose "Rose-Croix" with its suggestion of Rosicrucian-

ism is not clear, but from here on his narrative again becomes autobiographical. "Liberty, Libertas, long live liberty/ No more hypocrisy and no austerity."

18. Telichi: Fortuné-Barthélemy Félice, a defrocked Italian monk, who set up a printing shop in Yverdun in order to produce a corrected and expurgated version of Diderot's *Encyclopédie.*

19. Jean-Léonard Pellet, an important publisher in Geneva. Pellet was never imprisoned in the Bastille, but three volumes of a folio edition of the *Encyclopédie,* which he printed for the Parisian publisher Charles-Joseph Panckoucke, were confiscated by the police and kept in the Bastille as "prisoners," according to the term used in Panckoucke's correspondence. Pelleport may be alluding to that mishap. He evidently wrote such a eulogy after Rousseau's death in 1778.

20. The following description of a poor writer trying to sell his manuscripts—in fact, the text of *Les Bohémiens* and various poems—to Parisian publishers provides the most vivid account of author-publisher relations available anywhere in the literature of eighteenth-century France. Although obviously tendentious, it is highly realistic and describes actual *libraires (éditeur,* the modern term for publisher, had not yet come into general use) at three levels of the trade, from the wealthiest to the most marginal. At the same time, it expresses an imagined relationship between the author and his reader. Pelleport pictures his reader as a nouveau riche who began as a miserable tax collector (*rat de cave*) at the bottom of the tax-gathering administration (*ferme générale*) and rose to wealth through cheating and peculation. By casting the reader in this role, he picks a fight with him—and he will continue to provoke, quarrel, and make up with an imaginary reader throughout the novel.

21. The dialogue, set in Panckoucke's headquarters at the Hôtel de Thou, rue des Poitevins, describes France's most powerful publisher directing his press empire, which included the *Mercure de France* and speculations on many large-scale works, of which the *Encyclopédie méthodique* was the most important. Part of Panckoucke's correspondence, preserved in the archives of the Société typographique de Neuchâtel, shows that he did indeed fire off vollies of letters every day, combining and dismantling gigantic enterprises and recruiting the most famous authors to produce the copy for them. The title page of *Les Bohémiens* indicates that it was printed "â Paris, rue des Poitevins, hotel Bouthillier." This could be a false address meant to satirize Panckoucke; Robert Darnton cannot find traces of any other printing shop in the short rue des Poitevins.

22. Here Pelleport represents himself trying to sell *Les Bohémiens* as a "roman moral."

23. A quintal is 100 kilos (220 pounds).

24. He probably was the successor of Nicolas-Augustin Delalain, who had printed the *Almanach des muses* since 1765. In *Le Petit Almanach de nos grands hommes* (1788), Antoine Rivarol satirized the plethora of obscure poets trying to make their way in an over-crowded republic of letters. Pelleport, who composed a great deal of verse, located himself in this population. Here he is trying to sell *Les Bohémiens,* now described as a "roman philosophique," and the publisher's wife, infuriated at the notion of publishing a novel, threatens to pummel him with copies of Marmontel's *Les Incas,* which were sitting unsold on her shelves.

25. Jean-François Marmontel (1723–1799) is best known for his *Contes moraux* (*Moral Tales*), first published in the *Mercure de France,* of which he was an editor. He also wrote poetry, tragedies, and comic opera. *Les Incas* (*The Incas, or The Destruction of the Peruvian Empire,* 1773) is a philosophical work attacking the religious fanaticism of the Spanish conquest. Louis Sebastien Mercier (1740–1814) wrote descriptions of Parisian social and political life in his *Tableau de Paris* (published 1781–1788); he proposed utopian reforms as early as 1770 and also wrote popular patriotic and bourgeois dramas. Barnabé Farmian Durosoy (1745–1792) wrote journalism, essays, plays, and novels; in 1789 he would found the *Gazette de Paris.*

26. Pasquin: A "pasquin" can be a satirist, a talker with an evil tongue, or a manservant; here the author is doubly cuckolded as an author-satirist. A pasquinade is a satire, named for a statue onto which Romans pinned messages of personal attack.

27. Edme-Marie-Pierre Desauges, who kept a boutique behind the Palais de justice and had indeed been imprisoned twice in the Bastille. Desauges swindled Brissot while functioning as the Parisian dealer for his books. He could well have been a secret agent for the police, as Pelleport claimed. The police permitted small-time, semi-underground book dealers to sell illegal works, provided they supplied information about authors and suppliers. This time Pelleport refers to *Les Bohémiens* as a forbidden book ("mon prohibé").

28. Henry and Receveur were two police inspectors. Receveur was the secret agent of the Parisian police in London whom Pelleport pilloried in *Le Diable dans un bénitier.*

29. Godefroy Sellius, an adventurer-writer involved in the original plan for the *Encyclopédie,* died in Charenton in 1767.

30. Perhaps an allusion to La Fontaine's fable "The Sun and the Frogs," in which Aesop shows that even frogs realize the folly of drinking a tyrant's wine to drown one's cares (VI, 12).

31. In resuming his narrative and placing "le révérend père Rose-Croix" in Geneva, Pelleport gives a sardonic account of two potential sources of support for indigent writers who cannot sell their wares: patronage, which leads to humiliation rather than to a solid income, and political pamphleteering—in this case for the Négatif party, which is more than Rose-Croix can bear and therefore leads to his expulsion from Geneva.

32. Colin Muset was a medieval troubadour whose songs were about poetry as well as love.

33. Daniel Roguin, a Swiss from Yverdon, befriended Rousseau in Paris in 1742 and sheltered him in Yverdon when he fled from the French and Swiss authorities in 1762. Pelleport may have confused him with his nephew, Colonel Georges-Auguste Roguin, who also was a friend of Rousseau.

34. As explained above, Pelleport published *Le Boulevard des Chartreux,* a thirty-one-page poem, in 1779. Like all of his works, it was anonymous, but his authorship can be identified by allusions that he scattered throughout other texts.

35. The Vénérable Classe des Pasteurs in Neuchâtel often applied pressure on the town's executive, known as the Quatre Ministraux, to suppress offenses against orthodox Calvinism.

36. Because of Juno's anger, Delos was the only island of the Aegean that allowed Leto or Latona, daughter of the Titans, to give birth to Apollo and Artemis, who had been fathered by Jupiter.

37. The text has *piété* (piety), an apparent typographical error for *pitié* (pity).

38. A letter from Jean Diedey to the Société typographique de Neuchâtel, found by Robert Darnton, suggests that he was indeed a wealthy inhabitant of the nearby town of Le Locle. Apparently at the recommendation of Pierre Alexandre DuPeyrou, Rousseau's protector in Neuchâtel, Diedey employed Pelleport as a tutor for his son. The idyllic description of the Diedey household and of Le Locle corresponds to a happy period in Pelleport's life, when he settled in Le Locle with his new wife, a former chambermaid to Madame DuPeyrou, who bore him at least two children.

39. Penates: In Roman mythology, household gods.

40. *Le Boulevard des Chartreux, poème chrétien*, 1779, "Grenoble, de l'imprimerie de la Grande Chartreuse," 34 pp. Bibliothèque municipale de Grenoble, Section d'études et d'information o.8254 Dauphinois. A satire of monastic orders.

41. The Temple of Artemis at Ephesus (now in Turkey) was burned down in 356 B.C.E. by Herostratus, who wanted his name to be remembered forever as the arsonist, since he had no other source of fame.

42. Valeria Messalina (22–48 C.E.) was a prostitute before becoming the promiscuous third wife of the emperor Claudius.

43. Pelleport uses the term "gardien," a title for father superior in the Capuchin order.

44. Pelleport expresses this hedonistic version of the golden rule several times in *Les Bohémiens*. Despite the skeptical "riénisme" that he turned against philosophical systems earlier in the novel, he seems to have subscribed to the naturalistic morality defined at the beginning of Chapter 4 by the president of the Bohemians: pursue pleasure and enjoy liberty to the fullest, provided that you do not harm your fellow man. The place of women in his credo appears problematic, and Pelleport does not make much of the fact that all the Bohemians lived by Mordanes's plundering and therefore were complicit in it.

45. Tiresias, who was given in Greek legend the ability to understand the song of birds, could as an augur interpret their flight patterns to predict the future. His interruption of snakes copulating caused Hera to transform him into a woman, thus the warning to the presumably male reader who cherishes his masculinity.

46. By invoking pity, the fundamental sentiment on which society is built according to Rousseau, Pelleport links his Rousseauistic convictions to his celebration in the preceding pages of a sexual force that permeates nature and that he will identify, later in the book, with the basic element of fire, or phlogiston. At the same time, he makes Mordanes (Morande) into the embodiment of evil, for Mordanes murders the copulating chickens and by doing so stifles the sentiment of pity in Tifarès. Once initiated into this evil ethos, Tifarès becomes Mordanes's apprentice in a career of immorality that violates the social as well as the natural order: they support themselves by stealing poultry and livestock from

peasants, just as Morande lived by betraying his colleagues and destroying the reputations of others in his libels.

47. Saint-Côme d'Olt, in the Armagnac region, was considered a village of the Knights Templar.

48. The third hour after sunrise, by canonical reckoning.

CHAPTER 7. AFTER WHICH, TRY TO SAY THERE ARE NO GHOSTS . . .

1. George Knox (1765–1827) was an Irish member of Parliament. St. Francis Xavier (1506–1622) established Jesuit missions in India, Malay, and Japan. Maurice Benyowsky (1746–1786) was a Hungarian who led the establishment of a French colony in Madagascar in 1774. A friend of Washington, Franklin, and Pulaski, Benyowsky published his memoirs in 1783, and was later the subject of a play by Kotzebue.

2. An allusion to Pelleport's military service in Madagascar and India. Evidently, he sailed from Saint-Malo in a ship commanded by captain Patrice Astruc in 1774 and crossed the equator twice, but the autobiographical allusions in the following parody of zoological description—zoologists and botanists often accompanied captains on long-distance voyages—cannot be confirmed by other evidence.

3. The "line" was defined as the twelfth part of an inch.

4. Nicolas Barthélémy (1478–c. 1535), a Benedictine, wrote Latin epigrams and idylls, and a treatise "On Active and Contemplative Life" (1523). "Squaring the circle" was a term for the problem of finding the area of a curved space before the use of calculus; Pajot d'Osembrai developed a theory of "magic squares" for even numbers.

5. The abbé Pierre-François Guyot Desfontaines, editor of the *Journal des savants* and notorious for his quarrels with Voltaire, was imprisoned for sodomy and died in 1745. In citing Desfontaines's theory of narrative, Pelleport ironically invoked a view that directly contradicted his practice in *Les Bohémiens*.

6. This episode from Félicité's "memoirs" is one of the "sources" the narrator will later claim he has used as a basis for the novel, though he suggests in Chapter 9 that this "extract" was "published" by Felicity, not discovered in a London attic like the fragment copied in another girl's hand.

7. "And the LORD opened the mouth of the ass, and she said unto Balaam, What have I done unto thee, that thou hast smitten me these three times?" (*KJV* Numbers 22:28).

8. Sabbath: a witches' "Sabbath." Descriptions of Sabbath rituals included descriptions of older women or "hags," feasts, and the presence of Satan or his minions.

9. Jansenist sympathizers in the poor neighborhood around the church of Saint-Médard in Paris believed they could be miraculously cured of disease by contact with the grave of a saintly Jansenist priest, François Pâris, who died in 1727 and was buried in the churchyard. They were known as "convulsionnaires," because they often fell into convulsive fits. Linguet was the son of an eminent Jansenist; here Lungiet defends the cures as genuine miracles, although they were derided by the *philosophes* and sophisticated Parisians.

10. A *fier-à-bras* is someone who is trying to make himself look brave, a bully or brag-gart. The term comes from the name of a Saracen giant in medieval lore. It is also a term used by Cervantes for the "balm" in *Don Quixote*, to which Pelleport will allude later.

11. Ægipans: Forest-dwelling, goat-like demons or men with horns and tails.

12. The *Courrier de l'Europe* was a biweekly newspaper published in London and Bou-logne. The *Gazette d'Amsterdam*, also called the *Gazette d'Hollande,* was one of the main sources of political news during this period.

13. The Rubicon River in northern Italy that Caesar crossed decisively in 49 B.C.E., after which there was no turning back.

14. Charles Geneviève Louis Auguste André Thimothée (1728–1810), chevalier d'Eon de Beaumont, the notorious French adventurer and secret diplomat in London, pretended to be an Amazon-like lady, unbeatable in dueling.

15. The narrator conflates two episodes. In Book I (416–567) of Ovid's *Metamorphoses,* Apollo kills the Python. In Book III (1–130), Cadmus slays a dragon and follows Athene's advice by sowing his teeth into the earth (not sea) as seeds for a crop of armed men who suddenly rise from the ground.

16. Cervantes's lovesick Cardenio, the Ragged Knight of the Sickly Countenance, is so annoyed to have his narrative interrupted by various listeners' reflections and, in particular, Don Quixote's views on the fidelity or adultery of Queen Madásima, that he "picked up a stone that he found by his side, and struck Don Quixote such a blow on the chest that he tumbled over backwards" (tr. Rutherford, 203). Like the Bohemians, Cardenio carries his writings in a bag as he travels.

17. The first-century Alexandrian mathematician and physicist Heron invented a hy-draulic miniature machine that recycled water.

18. For the difficulty of getting a place in balloonist Blanchard's char-volant, see chap-ter 5, n. 24.

19. Evangelista Torricelli (1608–1647) invented the barometer. J. A. Deluc used the barometer, together with the mercury thermometer, in developing an accurate way to mea-sure heights. See chapter 6, n. 16.

20. Georges-Louis Leclerc, count de Buffon (1707–1788), known for his *Histoire na-turelle, générale et particulière* (1749–1778), suggested that species evolved over time, and contradicted the biblical narrative of the origin and age of the earth (*Les Epoques de la Nature,* 1788).

CHAPTER 8. THE DENOUEMENT

1. The town of Avioth is in French Luxembourg, near Belgium; a statue of Mary in the church was believed to work miracles.

CHAPTER 9. NOCTURNAL ADVENTURES THAT DESERVE TO SEE THE LIGHT OF DAY, AND WORTHY OF AN ACADEMICIAN'S PEN

1. This is a reference to Linguet's *Annales politiques, civiles et littéraires du dix-huitième siècle.*

2. The "Brutiens" (French *"Bruces"*) are the Prussians, and the "Galles" are the French.

3. Prussians. The following detailed account of a battle won against the French by Frederick II (Frederick the Great, 1712–1786) probably is a description of the Battle of Rossbach on November 5, 1757. While in the Bastille, Pelleport consulted a work on military tactics. He may have intended to describe the art of war as well as zoology, chemistry, and other sciences in order to give an encyclopedic turn to his novel, which is a collection of essays as well as a compendium of plots and subplots.

4. Emperor of the Germans, meaning Joseph II of Austria (1741–1790), although he did not become Holy Roman Emperor until the death of his father in 1765 and was only sixteen in 1757. "Kan" was a term used for emperor in French *romans à clef* such as *Mémoires secrets pour servir à l'histoire de Perse* (1745).

5. Frederick II.

6. Evidently the prince de Soubise, commander of the French army, an incompetent general who failed to exert effective discipline over his troops. "Borcas" is an anagram for Rossbach, the site of the Prussians' defeat of Charles de Rohan, prince de Soubise (1715–1787). Soubise was a childhood friend of King Louis XV and a favorite of his mistress, Madame du Barry.

7. Another reference to Frederick II, reputed to be a homosexual.

8. A reference to Frederick II as the son of Frederick William I.

9. Here Pelleport expresses the widespread resentment of his caste, the old feudal nobility, against upstarts from the recently ennobled bourgeois, especially financiers, who bought their way into the upper ranks of the army.

10. Prince Henry of Prussia (1726–1802), also a great general. However, it was not he but General von Seydlitz who commanded the crucial cavalry attack at Rossbach.

11. Here begins the most obscene part of the novel, an account of an orgy supposedly taken from Félicité's memoir but narrated in a burlesque classical manner, as if it were an epic battle directed by two deities from Olympus—on the one hand Love (Cupid, Amour), who promotes straightforward lust and presides over the union of Bissot and Félicité, on the other hand Luxuria (Lewdness), who stimulates perversion and disorder. Other deities, notably Jealousy and Discord (Zizanie), join in the scene, which degenerates into a wild brawl. The other narration taken from Félicité's memoir relates her rape by Mordanes and the trick she plays on him, which might fall into a category not approved by "Love."

12. This allusion seems to be one of the many private references or in-jokes that Pelleport scattered through the text, probably for his own amusement. The common nickname also occurs, however, in *Le Diable dans un bénitier*: an Englishwoman named "Sally" who might have become the mistress of a king is identified as living in Paris with a protector,

subsidized by gambling and the money given her by the young queen to pay her off (p. 42).

13. The marquis and marquise de Villette: she was Voltaire's "belle et bonne" adopted daughter, and he received guests in his bedroom in their Rue de Beaune house. Sugar-water was still served with a golden spoon in the bedroom in France when Elizabeth Gaskell visited there in the mid-nineteenth-century: "indeed, we have a little tray in our bed-room, on which is a Bohemian glass caraffe of water, a goblet with a gold spoon, and a bowl of powdered sugar" ("French Life," *Fraser's Magazine,* 1864). A Pinto cannula is a pointed tube or syringe used to inject fluid into a body cavity.

14. Luxuria: a medieval name for Venus.

15. Morion: a high-crested open helmet worn by soldiers in the sixteenth and seventeenth centuries.

16. Possibly a reference to Jacques Callot (1592–1635), a graphic artist whose famous and detailed series of etchings *The Miseries and Misfortunes of War* documented scenes relating to the Thirty Years' War.

17. Daedalus constructed an artificial cow within which Pasiphaë, daughter of the Sun and wife of King Minos, offered herself for sexual intercourse with a bull sent by Poseidon's curse; the labyrinth was designed, also by Daedalus, to house their offspring the Minotaur. Jealousy (Invidia) was personified as a minor Roman goddess.

18. The torch and dagger are features of the frontispiece of Pierre Manuel's *La Police de Paris dévoileé* (see Robert Darnton, *Scandal,* ch. 3, in which the enlightening torch-bearer is identified as the author Manuel himself, while the wielder of the dagger represents a tyrannical force oppressing enlightenment. Pelleport's discordant Zizanie represents both sides; "zizanie" is a term for discord, rivalry, or feud; in eighteenth-century French usage, a figurative expression used for a mixture of bad grain or tares among good grain. (Compare the contrary English expression "separating the wheat from the chaff.")

19. This fictional, burlesque treatise about men's unlimited rights to women typifies the "phallocratic" character of *Les Bohémiens.* It would be wrong to conclude that Pelleport subscribes to this doctrine himself, however, because he attributes it to Séché (Saint-Flocel) and the physiocratic view of property, reduced here to an absurdity.

20. F. Becket: T. Becket was one of the publishers of Laurence Sterne's *Tristram Shandy* in London (vols. 5–9, 1765–1767). Archbishop and Catholic saint Thomas à Becket (1118–1170) was murdered in the Canterbury cathedral by knights of King Henry II after years of serious conflict.

21. The maréchal de Richelieu was notorious as a Don Juan who seduced plebeian women as well as those from his own class, a theme emphasized in *Vie privée du maréchal de Richelieu* (1791). The chevalier Antoine de Bertin became famous for his dedication to the cult of love after the publication of his *Les Amours, élégies en trois livres* (1780).

22. "Habit does not make for passion."

23. "C.Q.F.D." is the French version of "what was to be demonstrated." Pelleport italicizes the Latin term "crater," cup or wine-bowl. I use the Greek term to suggest his eroticized choice of a classical word.

24. Robert Darnton has not been able to locate any publication under this title, but Pelleport's anecdote, despite its facetiousness, suggests that the agents of Joseph II were occupied in the same way as the police of Paris with missions to repress libel industry in London.

25. St. Vincent of Saragossa or Huesca's forthright speech aroused the anger of Diocletian's governor, and he was put to death on a gridiron (304 C.E.); he is Spain's first martyr and the patron saint of winemakers.

26. Shakespeare was not much admired in France at this time.

27. Lungiet follows Cervantes in describing this restorative balm, apparently as if it were a proprietary remedy sold by one Fierabrás: "the Balsam of Fierabras, for but one drop of it would have saved us both time and medicine" (tr. John Rutherford; New York: Penguin, 2003, I, x, 79). Lungiet's model for the anecdote is the general melee that begins after Don Quixote is beaten by a muleteer (the "enchanted Moor"); then "the muleteer thumped Sancho, Sancho thumped the girl, the girl thumped him, the innkeeper thumped her and they all thumped each other at such a rate that there wasn't a moment's rest for any of them" (I, 16, p. 128). But Lungiet is mistaken in the order of events; Sancho concocts the balm after the melee because the inexperienced Quixote has forgotten to bring any (I, 10). Sancho's concoction consists of "a little rosemary, oil, salt, and wine"; Quixote drinks "a couple of pints" remaining in the pot, vomits, sweats, and sleeps so well that "he firmly believed he'd hit upon the recipe for the Balsam of Fierabras" (tr. Rutherford; I, xvii, 132). Compare Pelleport's use of the term as applied to Mordanes the bully.

28. Our Lady of Joy. The Liesse basilica was a site of pilgrimages to its statue of the Virgin and Child, destroyed in the French Revolution. (For Avioth, see chap. 8, n. 1.)

29. The Counts of Joyeuse were also counts of Grandpré, in Alsace. The monastery of the Premonstratensians or Premonstrants, also called White Canons, was in the nearby Ardennes; they are sometimes known as Norbertines because their order, dedicated to preaching and pastoral work, was founded by St. Norbert.

30. The gold louis d'or coin, introduced in 1640, bore a picture of the king; it was to be replaced by the franc in the Revolution.

31. Pyrrhonism: a school of complete philosophical skepticism named for the philosopher Pyrrho (360–270 B.C.E.). Pyrrhonian skeptics differ from dogmatic skeptics because they suspend judgment even of the proposition that we cannot know anything.

CHAPTER 10. THE TERRIBLE EFFECTS OF CAUSES

1. Notre Dame de Mont-Dieu is a Carthusian priory in the Ardennes.

2. *Remedia Amoris* ("remedies for love") is the title of a poem by Ovid (Publius Ovidius Naso, 43 B.C.E.–17 C.E.), suggesting ways for the reader to fall out of love by discounting the beloved.

3. "The Lord be with you." In the Catholic liturgy, this initiates a response from listeners invoking the "spirit": "Et cum spiritu tuo" (and with your spirit).

4. *Lex talionis*: the law of retaliation, an eye for an eye, presumably a comic reference to equal justice. *Maréchaussée*: Under the Ancien Régime, the Maréchaussée police were responsible for vagabonds, foreigners of no fixed domicile, and thefts on the open highway.

5. Apophysis: a protuberance on a bone. Epiphysis: such a growth on the end of a bone.

6. *Lavabo*: The phrase *Lavabo inter innocentes manus meas* is said by priests in the ritual washing of hands: "I will wash mine hands in innocency" (*KJV* Ps. 26:6).

7. *Ad usum*: according to experience, custom.

8. During the eighteenth century legal divorces in England were granted by private Acts of Parliament rather than the archbishop of Canterbury; Women initiated them very rarely.

9. Pelleport gives archbishop and saint Thomas à Becket (1118–1170) as the ancestor of the printer of *Counts-Monopole* (see Chapter 9).

10. *Futuum*: Susannah's legalese for semen, her nonesuch word from Fr. *Foutre*.

11. Châlons: A mocking reference to Brissot and the Academy of Châlons. Piélatin: In Chapter 22, the Pilgrim refers to his friend the famous violinist and composer Piélatin in London.

12. *Aqua regia*: mixture of nitric and hydrochloric acids.

13. The Trinitarians or Order of the Holy Trinity were a Catholic mendicant order, founded near Paris in 1198.

14. Busiris, Egyptian king associated with Osiris and believed by the Greeks to be the son of Poseidon, sacrificed humans annually on an altar to liberate his land from famine; he was slain by the hero Herakles. Pelleport's narrator conflates Busiris with another son of Poseidon, Procrustes, who chopped down or stretched strangers to Eleusis so that they fit on his bed; he was slain by the hero Theseus.

15. The Greek god of ridicule and carping, the patron of criticism. As he is the son of Night, his bonnet may be a nightcap.

16. Pope Clement XIV had issued a Bull abolishing the Society of Jesus in 1773.

17. A magic wand. (See Chapter 4, n. 5; *KJV* Genesis 30:41–42.)

18. A phlogistic is an inflammatory substance.

19. *Amatrice*: feminine form of amateur, lover or appreciator of the arts and sciences.

Chapter 11. Uncivil Dissertations

1. This long parody of Linguet's views may seem overdone or out of place to the modern reader, but Linguet provided an ideal target for Pelleport's satire. He was the most famous figure among the French expatriates in London, notorious for his extravagant views and the paradoxical character of his arguments. In a series of historical works beginning with his *Histoire du siècle d'Alexandre* (1762), he justified the tyranny of Nero and other rulers as less disastrous for ordinary people than the slaughter produced by wars. He went on to defend slavery and serfdom in the same way: they inflicted less misery on the masses

than did modern varieties of liberty such as free trade in grain, the favorite measure of the physiocrats, which could force prices up to a starvation level. At the same time, Linguet inveighed against the French attachment to wheat and white bread, claiming that rice was more nutritious. He advocated a single property tax, which would fall equally on all land-owners and would replace the inequitable system of taxation that weighed so heavily on the poor. Linguet also argued for increasing the power of the king, particularly by eliminating the independence of the parlements. And to reinforce royal power, he insisted that no re-ligion should be tolerated except the established religion of the state. A vitriolic polemicist and master of self-dramatization, he heaped scorn on encyclopedists, physiocrats, the parle-ments, the legal profession (he was expelled from the Paris bar at the height of his brief but flamboyant career as a lawyer), the Académie française, and the most eminent writers of his time, all except Voltaire, whose works he proposed to rewrite, purged of their irreligion.

2. Marcus Curtius, a Roman citizen, rode into a chasm that had opened in the Forum (362 B.C.E.) because seers predicted that it would not close until Rome's most precious pos-session was thrown into it; Rome's proudest possessions were said to be her citizens.

3. Garlande family: Guillaume de Garlande (1055–1120), a popular figure, was chan-cellor of France; his second son, Étienne de Garlande, archdeacon and seneschal after the death of his older brother Guillaume II, quarreled with King Louis VI. Abbot Suger (1081–1151), adviser to Louis VI, considered the king as protector of the middle class and peasants. Louis VI (1081–1137) limited the powers of barons, granted communal charters and fiscal advantages to bourgeois citizens, and gave some cities the right to self-administration.

4. The legal right of the bishop and canons of Saint-Claude, near Besançon, to hold their lands in mortmain had been unsuccessfully challenged in 1770 by the local peasants, who were, in effect, serfs; their cause was supported by Voltaire and other philosophers. Serfdom was not entirely abolished in France until 1789, the estimated number of serfs depending on the definition. In Poland and Russia, serfdom was practiced until the mid-nineteenth century.

5. The Count de Saint-Germain (1707–1784?), a favorite of Louis XV, was an adven-turer of unknown birth, mysterious talents, and occult inclinations; he claimed to be three hundred years old. He may have been arrested as a spy in London.

6. Linguet favored the repressive measures of Etienne-Charles Loménie de Brienne, the dominant minister in the French government in 1788. Brienne attempted to destroy the political power of the parlements but aroused such opposition that he was forced out of office on August 25, 1788. The "red" Musketeers were companies of armed guards attached to the king's household.

7. Clovis, already mentioned (Chapter 1, n. 4), converted to Catholicism and ruled over the Alemanni, Burgundians, and Visigoths, as this burlesque history claims. Legends include the Saint Chrême, an ampulla of holy oil carried down by the Holy Ghost in the form of a dove for his coronation.

8. Wisdom of Solomon (Apocrypha), ch. 2: "the breath in our nostrils is as smoke."

9. Pierre-Louis-Claude Gin was the author of several works on law and government, including *Les vrais principes du gouvernement français démontrés par la raison et les faits*

(1777). The palace guards of the Pope were Swiss mercenaries. St. Stephen I, who asserted papal supremacy as pope (254–257), corresponded with St. Cyprian of Carthage. René Nicolas Charles Augustin de Maupeou (1714–1792), chancellor of France, tried to reform the system of hereditary offices in judicial parlements so as to increase the power of Louis XV, but was dismissed by Louis XVI in 1774.

10. Louis the Debonair or Pious (778–840) was made king of Aquitaine at the age of three; he reigned as emperor for twenty-six years and appointed the child of his wet-nurse to be archbishop of Reims.

11. A villein was a serf who was entirely subject to his lord, with no restrictions.

12. In Greek mythology the Titan Geryon possessed a herd of fat red cattle, captured by Herakles as his tenth labor.

13. *KJV* Exodus 21:20–21. Pelleport gives both Latin and French; in giving the Latin, he marks his omission of the word "criminis" from the first line. The second ends in the Vulgate "vel duobus non subiacebit poenae quia pecunia illius est."

14. The Lex Visigothorum or Liber Judiciorum was an adaptation of Roman law promulgated in portions of the late Roman empire for Romans and Visigoths. Book IX, 2 deals with subjects who refuse to go to war.

15. For Louis VI (known as "the Fat") see note 3 above. St.-Maur-des-Fossés, originally an abbey, was a chateau from which the Edict of Saint Maur was issued in 1568, proscribing all religions in France except Catholicism.

16. I have translated Pelleport's inventive wordplay on halberd and hatchet; Fr.: the marquis de la Hauberaldiere and the marquis de la Hacherie.

17. Villeinage: a legal term for the tenure of lands held by villein serfs (see n. 11).

18. *Filii belial guerratores variorum*: Sons of Satan who are warriors from various parts. This Latin expression for these "Grandes Compagnies" is associated with the "Great Companies" of fighters from various countries in Charles Jean François Hénault's *Nouvel abrégé chronologique de l'histoire de France* and Christian Friedrich Pfeffel's *Nouvel abrégé chronologique de l'histoire de du droit public d'Allemagne* (1776). Among other sobriquets for these fighting sons of the devil, Pfeffel lists "Routiers" or travelers who, like the Bohemians, lived off the land and ravaged farms and villages.

19. Balm of Fierabras: see Chapter 9, n. 27.

20. Doucon: in French, literally sweet-cunt; in Latin, "dulci conis" puns on "cunnus." Guines-la-Putain is a town near Paris, northeast of Melun, "putain" means prostitute. Bandeville's name implies that he is an outlaw to his own village. *Si villaneus . . . sicus [sic] catulos*: if a villein of our lord of the city erection has sons or daughters with one or more female serfs of Lady Doucon, let the lord and lady divide these children between themselves, as in the case of puppies.

21. Saint-Flocel published his *Journal des princes ou examen des journaux et autres écrits périodiques relativement aux progrès du despotisme* from London in 1783. Apparently it did not survive beyond three issues, which defended the abstract principles of natural law and liberty but failed to produce the promised digest of the contemporary press.

22. *Ab ovo*: from the egg. In his *Ars Poetica*, Horace (65 B.C.E.–8 B.C.E.) advises against

the poet's beginning "ab ovo," starting with the egg from which came Helen, the cause of the Trojan War.

23. The art of acrostics—traditionally from prophecies, psalms, and ciphering—was a learned practice as well as an entertaining parlor game.

24. In this speech, the following comic place-names are nonsensical, so I have translated them: *Piaillerie* as Squealhaven, *Vitenflasque* as Fiasco, and *Tire-encoin* as Thrust-Corner.

25. For unmonastic behavior of Carthusians and Capuchins: Linguet's *Histoire impartiale des Jésuites* had spoken of attempts by both Capuchins and Carthusians to assassinate Henri IV. A coadjutor is a bishop's assistant. Dom Hachette may have been a friend of Pelleport's who became a Carthusian monk.

CHAPTER 12. PARALLEL OF MENDICANT AND PROPRIETARY MONKS

1. The following essay on monasticism, a favorite topic at the time, echoes many of the themes in Pelleport's anti-monastic poem, *Le Boulevard des Chartreux*. Mendicant orders were hated by established proprietary monasteries.

CHAPTER 13. VARIOUS PROJECTS HIGHLY IMPORTANT TO THE PUBLIC WEAL

1. An allusion to Linguet's *Mémoire sur les propriétés et privilèges exclusifs de la librairie présenté en 1774* (1774). Linguet's *Annales* were widely pirated, and he often protested about the inability of authors to protect themselves from piracy and to obtain adequate compensation for their labor. The burlesque royal edict that follows is testimony to the desire of authors at the end of the Ancien Régime to profit from what they perceived to be a huge expansion of the reading public. Pelleport's reference to the spread of commercial lending libraries (*cabinets littéraires*) confirms the view that they had become important institutions well before the nineteenth century.

2. At the invitation of Holy Roman Emperor Charles V (1500–1558) and with his explicit support, learned Catholic clerics condemned the declared heretic Martin Luther in the Diet at Worms (1521), and he continued to support the clerics' verdict in their Confutation of 1530. This confrontation had ultimate political as well as theological consequences in the rebellion of Protestant princes, widespread dissension, and Charles V's abdication in 1555.

3. Bulls of the Crusade, first granted by Urban II in 1089 to those who fought against Muslims and other infidels in Spain and the Holy Land, sold indulgences for various sins, commutation of some vows, and permission to eat eggs and meat on certain fast days. Voltaire, who notes the "remarkable" Crusade Bull given by Julius II in 1509, claims in this context that the sale of a later bull included forgiveness for theft if one did not know the owner of stolen property (*Essai sur les Moeurs*, ch. 102). Pelleport's fictional "bull" would confer borrowing rights.

4. This remark confirms the view that booksellers often sold books in loose sheets or stitched (not sewn) in paper covers, leaving it to their clients to have them bound in whatever manner was desired.

5. St. Bruno (c. 1030–1101), born in Cologne and canon of Reims, teacher and scholar, was the founder of the Carthusian order.

6. Persius (*Satire* III, 85): "hoc est quod palles?" Is *that* the reason why you grow so pale? In his prologue to these satires, the Stoic Aulus Persius Flaccus (34–62) represents himself as an outsider among poets, inspired to write by the need to feed his own belly. The half-line Pelleport cites continues with his misquoted word "cur" and a sentiment he echoes elsewhere: "cur quis non prandeat, hoc est?" (Is *that* any reason to go without one's dinner?).

7. Sillery is a Champagne region known for sparkling and still wine; the town is near Reims.

Chapter 14. On Hospitality

1. The Greek goddess Hestia, or Roman Vesta, associated with the fires of the hearth and home, is often linked with domestic hospitality as well as with public ritual. The Vestal priestess Rhea Silvia was the mother of Romulus and Remus, twin founders of Rome.

2. The Italian proverb "Chi va piano va sano" may be translated "He who travels slowly, travels well."

3. The bishop of Soissons was the senior suffragan of the Reims diocese.

Chapter 15. Morning Matins at the Charterhouse

1. The best-known St. Serapion, Patriarch of Antioch (190–211), preached and wrote against various forms of heresy; Pelleport may have given Lungiet "Sérapion" as a comic sobriquet to harmonize with Séchant and Séché, who form a trio with him in this scene.

Chapter 16. Panegyric of the Clergy

1. The following sermon parodies Linguet's sympathy for the dominance of the clergy during the Middle Ages, similar to his earlier apology for serfdom.

2. A reference to Jean Chardin, *Voyages de M. le chevalier Chardin en Perse et autres lieux de l'Orient* (Amsterdam, 1711; first edition under a different title, 1686). Mahomet is a French variant of Muhammad (570–632); "mullah" (lord) is an honorific once given to sultans as well as religious leaders.

3. Levites: Descendants of Levi were responsible for the priesthood; descriptions of their priestly duties can be found in Exodus, Leviticus, and Numbers.

4. In his war against Achish, Saul calls the dead Samuel: "God is departed from me, and answereth me no more, neither by prophets, nor by dreams; therefore I have called thee, that thou mayest make known unto me what I shall do"; the prophet speaks in favor of Achish and David (*KJV* 1 Samuel 28:15). Ezra, "the priest, the scribe, even a scribe of the words of the commandments of the Lord," was told by King Artaxerxes to regulate "statutes and judgments," magistrates, and financial matters for the people of Israel "whatsoever Ezra the priest, the scribe of the law of the God of heaven, shall require of you, it be done speedily" (*KJV* Ezra 7:11, 21). Caiaphas presided over the first trial of Jesus in an assembly of the "chief priests, and the scribes, and the elders of the people" (*KJV* Matthew 26:3).

5. The English translation of Matthew 5:17 uses the verb "fulfil," which is often glossed as to "perfect": "Think not that I am come to destroy the law, or the prophets I am not come to destroy, but to fulfil." The reference to Caesar is *KJV* Matthew 22:21.

6. Phi*** and his wife: Ananias and Sapphira keep back part of the price received for the sale of a possession. The apostle Peter judges them, determines guilt, and executes judgment both husband and wife give up the ghost in fear ("behold, the feet of them which have buried thy husband are at the door, and shall carry thee out"; *KJV* Acts 5:1–10).

7. Constantine I (280?–337) was the first Christian emperor, giving financial privileges and exemptions to the clergy and promoting its range of influence in the interests of imperial power and stability. Protesters were frequently persecuted for disobedience to anti-Christian as well as financial edicts of the Roman emperor Diocletian (244–311, abdicated 305), his predecessor. Constantine's nephew Julian (332–363, emperor from 361), who renounced Christianity in favor of paganism, was called "the Apostate" by Christians and "the Hellene" by Jews.

8. Clovis was affiliated with the Arian heresy before his conversion to Catholicism. He acknowledged the property and rights of the clergy, who served as his advisers. Pelleport has already mentioned the Saint Chrême, an ampulla of holy oil carried down by the Holy Ghost in the form of a dove for his coronation, a ceremony that also included a flag to which this "flag" may refer. (See Chapter 1, n. 4.)

9. Charlemagne (747–814) was crowned Emperor of the Romans in 800 by Pope Leo III, who had sought his protection from physical violence and accusations of misconduct.

10. Emperor Charles II "the Bald" of France (823–877), Charlemagne's grandson, was supported in his accession, rule, and war against Emperor Lothair by Archbishop Hincmar of Reims (806–882) and other bishops. He was given a share of his father Emperor Louis's lands at the Aix-la-Chapelle assembly in 837.

11. Hugh Capet (938–996, king from 987) made Arnulph Archbishop of Reims in 988 but had a synod of bishops depose him three years later in favor of Gerbert d'Aurillac. The bishops refused to reconsider their decision as commanded in the message delivered by Pope John XV's legate. Half-brothers Lothair and Charles the Bald (with another brother) fought each other for control of the Holy Roman Empire.

12. Pope Innocent III (c. 1160–1216) developed a theory of papal monarchy that expanded its temporal authority. King John of England swore fealty to the Pope and made England a papal fief in 1213.

13. The Valley of Josaphat or Jehoshaphat is mentioned in the Book of Joel: "I will gather together all nations, and will bring them down into the valley of Jehoshaphat and I will plead with them there for my people, and for my inheritance Israel, whom they have scattered among the nations" (*KJV* 3:2).

14. The Latin phrase translates as: "Against which I will adduce proof and contend."

15. Seneca (c. 5–65) was a Roman writer and Stoic philosopher who recommended alternating solitude and company. The donkey has read only the second half of Seneca's advice that solitude cures us of hating the crowd; the crowd cures the tedium of solitude ("odium turbae sanabit solitudo, taedium solitudinis turba"; *De Tranquillitate Animi* 17.3).

16. The Licée de Londres was the meeting place of philosophers and writers that Brissot attempted, unsuccessfully, to found in London. Here Pelleport shifts the narrative to the voice of Félicité, though the manuscript is apparently transcribed in the handwriting of an unknown Claudinette.

CHAPTER 17. A MOUSE WITH ONLY ONE HOLE IS EASY TO TAKE

1. The obscene *bon mot* in this chapter's title occurs in several libertine novels and libels from the eighteenth century.

2. The French proverb is: when you speak of the wolf, you will see his tail (*quand on parle du loup, on en voit la queue*).

CHAPTER 18. HOW LUNGIET WAS INTERRUPTED BY A MIRACLE

1. Another reference to Brissot's law degree.

2. The witch Canidia and her companion were trying to cast a spell on Priapus, but his emphatic fart drove them away (Horace, *Satires*, 1.8).

3. Regarding the miracle of the loaves and the fishes, all four gospels agree that Jesus fed five thousand men, women, and children on "but five loaves, and two fishes" rather than three (*KJV* Matthew 14:17). The Fête-Dieu celebration of the Eucharist on the first Thursday after Holy Trinity is also known as Corpus Christi, The Feast of the Body and Blood of Christ.

4. Benoît Joseph Labre, born in Amettes near Boulogne-sur-Mer in 1748, died in Rome after performing miracles and living in the most austere poverty as a beggar. He was already celebrated as a saint when Pelleport wrote, although he was not canonized until 1881. He will reappear in connection with another burlesque miracle in Chapter 21.

5. On the feast of Saint Louis, the occasion of its most important annual ceremony, the Académie française traditionally awarded prizes for eulogies of great men. The following are standard cracks at professions made by wits and writers under the "trees of Cracow" at the Palais-Royal and the Tuileries.

CHAPTER 19. WHICH WILL NOT BE LONG

1. Pelleport takes the obscene play of words on Beaumont-le-Vicomte from *Le Compère Mathieu ou les bigarrures de l'esprit humain* (1766) by Henri Joseph Dulaurens, a libertine novel that seems to have provided a model in some respects for *Les Bohémiens*. The "m" and "c" reversed references to cunt and erection; Mercury is often considered the god of concord as well as eloquence.

2. The reference to Stenay, Pelleport's birthplace, provides a transition to the last part of the novel, which is a fictionalized autobiography of Pelleport.

CHAPTER 20. A PILGRIM'S NARRATIVE

1. Pelleport substitutes "Fanchette" for Félicité. "Fanchette," a popular name for a soubrette, was the name of the bookshop owner's flirtatious daughter; here it may be a description of Félicité's admiring tone, or perhaps refer to another "Bohémienne" not previously named (there are more than two women). "Sérapion" is Lungiet, as before.

2. Jean Mabillon (1632–1707), Benedictine monk and paleographer, was a scholar of medieval manuscripts and a founder of the *Académie des Inscriptions et Belles-Lettres*. According to medieval legend, England was settled by Brut, great-grandson of Aeneas, and other descendants of the Trojans.

3. Dagobert I was king of the Franks (603–639).

4. Probably an organmaster; "rossignol" keys produce a birdlike sound. See also the advertisement concocted by the London charlatan Ashley.

5. Another typically oblique autobiographical reference—"Pelleport" has nine letters. Mademoiselle le Maure was a famous singer during the early years of Louis XV. François Robert Marcel was an admired eighteenth-century dancing-master, founder of a school with his father and brother, and much cited in manuals of the period.

6. Pelleport's stepmother, who detested the children born to the first wife of her husband, arranged for him to sell an office he owned so that she could distribute the money to her own children by him.

7. Bisanus—two-anused. Cadmus of Miletus, who may have been a sixth-century B.C.E. historian, was sometimes credited with the invention of the alphabet.

8. Both *musa* (song) and *mensa* (table) are first-declension Latin nouns used in standard exercises.

9. An allusion to Edme Jany Mentelle (1730–1816), professor of history and geography at the École Militaire, where he taught Pelleport. Mentelle was a friend of Mme Dupont and provided lodging for her daughter Félicité in Paris. It was in the literary circle that gathered in Mentelle's house that Pelleport met Brissot.

10. Evidently an allusion to Louis-Auguste le Tonnelier, baron de Breteuil (1730–1807), who was forced to resign from the government on July 24, 1788. As minister of the king's

household, which included the department of Paris, Breteuil had authority over the Bastille and refused Pelleport's pleas to be released from confinement.

11. Possibly Albert-Louis baron de Pouilly et de Chauffour (1731–1795); the barony of Pouilly was near Stenay. *Ex professo:* proficiently, with skill.

12. In French, "the spirit of God" moving over the face of the waters is translated as a hovering "breath": "le souffle de Dieu planait à la surface des eaux" (Genesis 1:2).

13. *Artamène, ou le grand Cyrus* (*Cyrus the Great*) was a ten-volume novel by Madeleine de Scudéry (1607–1701), a member of the "precious" circle of Mme de Rambouillet.

14. *Inde mali labes*: why and when this evil occurred.

15. The word "livre" can mean both book and a unit of money (twenty or twenty-five sous, depending on where it was minted). The Pilgrim's illiterate father has requested for money but receives a book; I have tried to suggest the French wordplay.

16. By explaining that *Don Quixote* (probably in one of the chapbook versions popular among domestic servants) provided his initiation into literacy, Pelleport points to another model for *Les Bohémiens*. He also made the point clear at the end of the first chapter, when he described Bissot and Tifarès setting off from Reims as if they were Don Quixote and Sancho Panza.

17. Minden, a cathedral town in Westphalia, was near the site of a disastrous defeat for French troops by British and Hanoverian infantry and artillery (1759).

18. Like Pelleport, the pilgrim is literate, but also fit for the army.

19. Don Quixote battles with a barber and takes his shiny basin for Mambrino's legendary golden helmet, altered by "a person who did not understand or appreciate its value" (*Don Quixote*, tr. Rutherford I, xxi, 168). Cervantes's allusion is to the story of the Moorish king Mambrino in Matteo Boiardo's epic *Orlando Innamorato* (1495).

20. Parapharagaramus: like English "Abracadabra," an expression recited by magicians. Triston is a variant name for the knight Tristan; the Arthurian enchanter was Merlin. Tales from Greek mythology include Phaedra's passion for her stepson Hippolytus as well as her involvement in Ariadne and Theseus's adventures with the Minotaur; in French, Jean Racine's tragedy *Phèdre* (1677).

21. This ironic account of Pelleport's education as a boarder in the Académie d'Amiens underscores his love of the classics, which is also apparent from his frequent use of Latin citations and Homeric metaphors.

22. Numa, the second king of Rome, established religious institutions and a religious calendar. Marcus Junius Brutus (85–42 B.C.E.), Roman senator and praetor, participated in the assassination of Julius Caesar and fought against his heir and nephew Octavian. Horace (65–8 B.C.E.) wrote lyrics, satires, epodes, odes, and the *Ars Poetica* on friendship, politics, and the art of poetry.

23. Jeanne de la Motte-Guyon (1648–1717) was a quietist imprisoned in the Bastille for seven years; her *Short Method of Prayer* (*Le Moyen Court*) was placed on the Index as heretical and associated with Molinism. *La Journée du chrétien* contained preparatory exercises and prayers. *Suspendatur a sacris*: set apart from consecration.

24. The Jansenist convent of Port-Royal des Champs was closed and razed, but Jansenists were not burned.

25. The Almanac of Liège, published from 1625, supposedly by a Matthew Lansbert or Laensberg, contained political as well as personal predictions; it was therefore prohibited by Louis XIII.

26. According to his dossier in the police archives, Pelleport was imprisoned several times by *lettre de cachet* at the request of his family for "atrocious offenses against honor." A sacred chicken (or *pullarius*) was kept by the Roman army; victory was predicted if the chicken ate the grain.

27. Fabert Abraham de Fabert d'Esternay (1599–1662), a printer's son who became the first commoner to be named Marshal of France, distinguished himself for leading the siege of Stenay in 1654, during the Thirty Years' War. Voltaire's *Philosophical Dictionary* refers to Fabert's reputation for sorcery in the "Possessed" entry: "The devil twisted Marshal Fabert's neck. Every village had its sorcerer or sorceress . . ." Voltaire, *The Works of Voltaire*, Vol. 6, *Philosophical Dictionary* (Part 4, "Possessed" entry [1764], trans. William F. Fleming; New York, 1901).

28. "So those servants went out into the highways, and gathered together all as many as they found, both bad and good: and the wedding was furnished with guests" (*KJV* Matthew 22:10).

29. Cinq-Ton: possibly Five Senses.

30. Lauterberg remains unidentified, but the context suggests that he was the Liégeois publisher of an almanac and that he hired Pelleport to write the astrological predictions for the coming year that were standard fare in almanacs. Such, it appears, was Pelleport's humble beginning as an author. From this point on, he relates his career as a hack writer: thus the reference in the next sentence to "le révérend père Rose-Croix" and to Pelleport's use of that pen name in his translation of David Williams's *Letters on Political Liberty* (1783).

31. John Goy, a French expatriate in London who worked on the *Courrier de l'Europe* until he was fired in 1783 for collaborating with Receveur, the secret agent of the Paris police. Pelleport, who had contributed often to the *Courrier*, probably was hired by its editor, Antoine Joseph de Serres de la Tour, to take Goy's place. Goy's brother Pierre, who remained in Paris, where he cut quite a figure, was known as "milord Goy."

32. Colombo extract was a medical ingredient. Ferry boats owned by Samuel Burton of Brighton were advertised as carrying passengers several times a week. Thomas Evans was an English attorney who countered Linguet in *A refutation of the Memoirs of the Bastille, on the general principles of laws, probability and truth; in a series of letters to Mr. Linguet* (1783). For *dragées*, see Chapter 2, n. 6.

33. Pelleport refers to a protest by the marquis du Crest, chancellor of the duc d'Orléans, against a letter published in the *Courrier de l'Europe* that criticized the pedagogical writing of his sister, Mme de Sillery, comtesse de Genlis (1746–1830). Evidently, Pelleport had written the letter and therefore nearly lost his job, because du Crest complained to Samuel Swinton, who owned a two-thirds share of the *Courrier*. Arnaud Berquin, who was also

insulted by the letter, was known—like Mme de Genlis—as an author of moralistic tales for children. Mascarilla (or Mascarillus) was a stock valet figure in Italian comedy.

34. Following his father's death, Pelleport left London for Paris in late 1783. This ended his employment on the *Courrier de l'Europe*, exactly as recounted here.

35. De milito: the usual expression is *de mortuis nil nisi bonum (dicendum)*: Say nothing but good about the dead, or in this case, the military.

36. "These things not even boys believe, except such as have not yet had their penny bath." Juvenal, *Satires* (II, 152, trans. G. G. Ramsay; London, 1918). Small boys did not have to pay a coin to enter the Roman baths.

37. The battle of Malplaquet (1709), near the Belgian border, a bloody and hard-fought battle in the War of the Spanish Succession; the French, who were defeated, lost eleven thousand men, while the Allied forces led by the Duke of Marlborough lost nearly twice as many.

38. King Aeolus's sons the winds disrupt the Trojan ships to please Juno, who is jealous of Aeneas's mother Venus; but Neptune rises from his ocean realm and sends the insolent winds back to their cavern (Virgil, *Aeneid*, I, 12–222).

Chapter 21. Continuation of the Pilgrim's Narrative

1. In November and December 1783, Pelleport was in Paris, trying to collect his inheritance while hiding from the police. In a side trip to Reims, he acquired four thousand livres worth of Champagne, which he intended to ship to London, calculating that he could sell it to Antoine Joseph de Serres de La Tour, who planned to establish a French import business after retiring as editor of the *Courrier de l'Europe*. But La Tour had not commissioned him to make the purchase and refused to pay for it. Pelleport also speculated on other French goods—including muslins and ten thousand livres worth of books—that he planned to sell to London merchants. As payment, he wrote bills of exchange that he planned to redeem from his inheritance. Meanwhile, however, his stepmother used legal maneuvers to cut him and his brothers out of any claim on their father's estate, which went to her and to her own children by Pelleport *père*. Therefore, at the end of 1783, Pelleport found himself unable to pay the bill of exchange for four thousand livres that he had written on La Tour, burdened by even greater bills of exchange that were soon to mature, and incapable even of financing his journey back to London. These circumstances form the background for the next section of the autobiographical novel-within-the-novel.

2. The year 1783 would not have been a bissextile or leap year, but 1784 would have had the extra day in the Julian calendar.

3. A reference to a businessman named Larrivée, who was in charge of Brissot's affairs in Paris and who tried to help Pelleport untangle the legal obstacles to the collection of his inheritance. Larrivée's letters in Brissot's papers in the Archives Nationales and the transcription of Brissot's interrogations in the Bastille provide the main source of information about Pelleport's life at this critical point.

4. A Spanish charlatan claimed to walk across the Seine in 1785 and was admired as a funambulist in Grimm's *Correspondance littéraire* (vol. 14, pp. 259–60; see Robert M. Isherwood, *Farce and Fantasy, Popular Entertainment in Eighteenth-Century Paris*; Oxford 1986, 211. Isherwood explains his wooden shoes functioning as a two-part boat).

5. The nymph Amalthea, one of Zeus's foster mothers, herded a nanny goat that suckled Zeus; in some versions, she is shown as the actual goat.

6. As explained in Chapter 18, n. 4, Benoît-Joseph Labre was already being celebrated as a saint at the time of his death in 1783. Pelleport may have drawn information for his sardonic description of Labre's miracles from a hagiographic *Vie de Benoît-Joseph Labre* (1784) or from local mythology. The text suggests that he had a thorough knowledge of life in Boulogne-sur-Mer, where Samuel Swinton, the publisher of the *Courrier de l'Europe*, kept a house and printed the edition intended for consumption within France.

7. Capuchins are New World monkeys, so named because their coloration reminded Europeans of Capuchins, with white faces surrounded by dark habits, and the dark tops of their heads as the caps or cowls.

8. Mount Tabor in Israel, the site of a series of monasteries, was sometimes identified as the "high mountain apart" on which the transfigured Jesus appeared to three disciples in radiant form: "his face did shine as the sun, and his raiment was white as the light" (*KJV* Matthew 17:1–2). The pilgrim quotes Virgil's *Aeneid* (III, 567) "*ter spumam elisam et rorantia vidimus astra*" but substitutes "effixam" for "elisam" and "rotantia" (whirling) for "rorantia" (dewy): we saw three times the waves crash and the stars bedewed. Aeneas is describing the whirlpool Charybdis: "Three times [. . .] she hurls / the waters high, lashing the stars with spray" (trans. Allen Mandelbaum, *The Aeneid of Virgil*, III, 549–52; New York, 1961).

9. Mme Dupont, Brissot's mother-in-law, earlier presented as Voragine, reappears at this point as the widow Catau des Arches. From a prominent bourgeois family in Boulogne-sur-Mer, Mme Dupont continued her husband's trade as a merchant after his death. She loaned Pelleport enough to pay for his journey back to London at the end of 1783 and also advanced money to help cover his speculations on Champagne and other goods, which came to about 14,500 livres. When the merchandise arrived in Boulogne, she stored it in her warehouse and forwarded it to London. But she insisted on being repaid, and her firmness apparently led to a bitter quarrel with Pelleport. Moreover, in July 1784, as soon as she learned of Brissot's imprisonment in the Bastille, Mme Dupont hurried to London to break the news to Félicité. Then she returned with Félicité to Paris and, along with her close friend Edme Mentelle, helped in Brissot's defense—a matter of attributing all the responsibility for the libels to Pelleport in order to clear Brissot from the charge of collaborating on them. These imbroglios probably explain the hostile treatment of Mme Dupont and everyone connected with her throughout *Les Bohémiens*. "Catau" may suggest Mme Dupont's given name, Marie-Catherine; "des Arches" may suggest Dupont (bridge).

10. The shepherd Celadon is the amorous hero of the novel *L'Astrée*, by Honoré d'Urfé (1568–1625), a long pastoral romance that set a fashion for preciously detailed description and dissection of the characters' affections (published in parts, 1607–1627/8).

11. Horace, *Odes* (I, 27) "A miser / Quanta laboras in Charybdi": "Miserable man,

how you suffered in Charybdis." Charybdis was the giant whirlpool in which Odysseus was nearly lost.

12. The legendary St. Julian the Hospitalier is a patron saint of travelers.

13. This son-in-law represents Brissot, who now reappears as an old-clothes dealer—an allusion to his recycling the works of other writers in his ten-volume *Bibliothèque philosophique du législateur, du politique, du jurisconsulte* (1782–1785). Mme Dupont had four daughters. Pelleport refers here to the youngest, Marie-Thérèse, who apparently accompanied him to London at the end of 1783 or the beginning of 1784, then took up residence in the Brissot household with her older sister Nancy. Captain "Cornu": horned devil or cuckold.

14. Another reference to Morande, author of *Le Gazetier cuirassé* (1771), who edited the *Courrier de l'Europe* for Swinton after 1783, replacing La Tour. "Cuirassé": wearing armor.

15. Troll-madam or "trou-" is a name used for various games of the period, including one played by striking balls into nine holes on a table with a semi-circular end.

16. Payn was the family name of proprietors of the York Hotel in Dover.

17. "*Moning houland*," perhaps an imaginary newspaper, translated here as "Morning Halloo." Giovanni Andrea (known as "Sir John") Gallini, married to a daughter of the Earl of Abingdon and author of *A Treatise on the Art of Dancing* (1762), opened the Hanover Square Concert Rooms in 1774; one of his partners was Johann Christian Bach. The rococo Rotunda of Vauxhall Gardens (erected 1743) could hold over a thousand people; the pleasure gardens, open to the public for an entrance fee, offered concerts, refreshments, walkways, masquerades, and sometimes occasions for sexual opportunity.

18. In this burlesque version of a debate in Parliament, Pelleport mentions several of the most important politicians of the day: Charles Gordon Lennox, Lord March; Charles James Fox; Frederick, Lord North; William Pitt the Younger; and David Murray, Lord Stormont. Charles Lennox, duke of Richmond and earl of March (1735–1806), became a Tory and joined the ministry of William Pitt the Younger in 1784. Charles James Fox (1749–1806), was a Whig opponent of the King, an ally of North's from 1783; he supported the Prince of Wales during the king's ongoing illnesses and was in favor of American independence, reform of the East India Company, abolition of the slave trade, and (later) the French Revolution. His unlikely ally Lord North (1732–1792) had been the Tory minister during the American Revolution, resigning when Cornwallis was defeated. The younger William Pitt (1759–1806), prime minister from 1783, had a majority of only one vote in early 1784; Parliament was dissolved, but after elections confirmed Pitt, he raised taxes to pay the national debt, in part caused by the cost of the American Revolution. The King's illnesses prompted continual crises; he prorogued Parliament in 1788. Lord Stormont (1727–1796), later the second Earl of Mansfield after the death of his uncle the Chief Justice), was ambassador to France during the early years of the American Revolution until 1778, when diplomatic relations were severed as a result of the Franco-American alliance; after returning to England, he continued to serve as a diplomat and a critic of government policy.

19. Relations between Parliament and the East India Trading Company, which oper-

ated as a government agency as well as a commercial monopoly, were the subject of the Regulating Act of 1773 and Pitt's India Act of 1784.

20. Horace, *Satires* (I, 3, 100): mute and filthy beasts.

21. Dr. Matthew Maty (1718–1776) founded the *Journal Britannique* in 1750, a successor to the *Bibliothèque Britannique* review that publicized and discussed English books for a European audience. He later became principal librarian to the British Museum, but died before the date of this 1784 "review."

22. The following mock-scholarly debate on noses is in the tradition of Rabelais and Sterne. Tristram Shandy's father Walter theorizes that men should have large noses, and the narrative includes a concocted tale in Latin and English about a man with an enormous nose, by the fictive "Hafen Slawkenbergius" (*Tristram Shandy*, v. 4). Here the classical references are to the *Iliad*, the *Odyssey*, and the *Aeneid*; Aeneas's enemy Turnus has characteristics of "violentia" and "furor" that may identify him as ferocious. The Shakespearean plays are *King Lear*, *The Tempest*, and *Othello*. Origen (185–c. 254) was a Greek Neo-Platonist theologian and biblical commentator whose views were declared anathema in the sixth century; the *Hexapla* are a synopsis of the Old Testament. St. Jerome or Hieronymus (347–420) was a learned hermit whose Vulgate translation was based on Hebrew text. Sanchoniathon, said to be an ancient writer on Phoenician cosmogony, was known from fragments cited by Philo. Berosius was the author of a cosmographical work reprinted in 1536 with the "Planispherium" of Ptolemy.

23. In "The Nose" episode, Voltaire's hero Zadig tests his bride's fidelity by making her believe he is dead and that her new suitor, lying ill, needs his nose as a remedy. Azora takes a razor to cut off Zadig's, but is stopped in time (*Zadig or Destiny, An Oriental Story* (1747).

24. Horace, *Ars Poetica* (191) "And let no god be introduced, unless there is a knot worthy of such a vindicator" (trans. H. R. Fairclough; Cambridge, Mass., Harvard University Press, 1926), 467. The vindicating "god" onstage would be introduced as a *deus ex machina*.

25. The periodical-writers' catalogue of Romans commemorated on medals includes Julius Caesar, conqueror of Gaul and dictator of the Roman republic, whom Marcus Junius Brutus, senator and praetor, conspired to assassinate in 44 B.C.E.; generals Lepidus and Mark Antony, members with Octavian of the Second Triumvirate; assassinated military leader Germanicus and his imperial family: uncle Tiberius, son Caligula, and grandson Nero; Antonine emperors Antoninus Pius and Stoic Marcus Aurelius; emperor Hadrian, who promoted Greek culture in the empire and unified its administration; Julian "the Apostate," the emperor who rejected Christianity for paganism. Gordian II is known as "Africanus" on his medal; he co-ruled for three weeks with his father until his death in battle and Gordian I's suicide. Valerius Licinius both persecuted Christians and issued an edict (313 C.E.) allowing them religious toleration. The deposition of the usurping emperor Romulus Augustulus in 476 C.E. is considered to mark the end of the Roman Empire.

26. Joseph Priestley (1733–1804), the philosopher-scientist and author of *An History of the Corruption of Christianity* (1782).

27. David Williams (1738–1816), a well-known deist and political radical. As already

explained, Pelleport translated his *Letters on Political Liberty* (1783), adding fierce attacks on the monarchy in the footnotes.

28. The liberal Honoré Riqueti de Mirabeau (1749–1791), whose family estates were in Provence, was trying to find work as a journalist in London in the mid-1780s; "escapee from Provence" (*échappé de Provence*) plays on his having been an *échappé de prison* (escapee from prison) and also estranged from his famous father, physiocrat economist Victor Riqueti de Mirabeau (author of *L'ami des hommes*, 1756), who had had him imprisoned by *lettre de cachet*. Mirabeau had written against arbitrary misuse of power with reference to the reign of Louis XV, the late king (*Essai sur le despotisme*, 1776), and was involved in various disputes about authorship. In 1784 his anti-Austrian *Doutes sur la liberté de l'Escaut*, published in London by Faden, enraged the French minister Vergennes by taking the Dutch side in a controversy with Holy Roman Emperor Joseph II about control of contested portions of the Scheldt or Escaut River. An émigré French cartographer, M. de la Rochette, supported Mirabeau's argument (Jean-Paul Desprat, *Mirabeau: L'excès et le retrait*; Paris, 2008, p. 307). Linguet took the opposite position.

29. The English word 'pal' had criminal connotations, as for a highwayman, in the eighteenth century.

30. Jean-Paul Marat (1743–1793) belonged to the population of French writers in England during the 1770s, but he wrote scientific treatises and a radical work on politics, *The Chains of Slavery* (first published in English in 1774), not libels. He returned to France in order to pursue his career as a doctor in 1777 and became a close friend of Brissot a few years later. Pelleport may have known him through Brissot.

31. "Guerreville": Brissot de Warville. He and Félicité were partisans of the Quakers.

32. Great St. Helens or Helene Street, in the financial district of east London, near Bank, was the site of a synagogue in the style of Inigo Jones.

33. An allusion to Théveneau de Morande's denunciation of Pelleport as the author of *Le Diable dans un bénitier*.

34. In the following references to notorious charlatans: Dr. James Graham claimed that he could help couples conceive through the use of his electric fertility bed. Graham (1745–1794) opened his "Temple of Health" in the Adelphi buildings in 1780, then moved in 1781 to the spectacular "Temple of Hymen" in Pall Mall, with its twelve-foot electromagnetic moving bed, organ music, fragrances, and dancers. "Naso" is a Latin sobriquet for a large-nosed person, but it is also part of Ovid's name, P. Ovidius Naso. Other names include "Rossignol" (or nightingale); as "rossignol" organ keys imitated birdsong, this could suggest an organ–trumpet duet. "Katerfiette" is possibly a transliteration of English catfight.

35. De Serres de La Tour, editor of the *Courrier de l'Europe*, was more attached to gardening and cooking than to journalism. See ch. 2, n. 6.

36. Desforges d'Hurecourt, a musician, was the financial backer of Brissot's *Licée de Londres*. Pelleport persuaded him to withdraw his funds from the Licée and to invest them in a journal that Pelleport planned to establish, thereby touching off a quarrel between Brissot and Desforges.

37. Jean-André Deluc, the Genevan physicist who emigrated to England, became

reader to the Queen in 1773; see ch. 7, n. 16. The *Letters to a German Princess* (1761) by mathematician Leonhard Euler (1707–1783) included topics of general interest related to physics and astronomy.

38. Mary Assheton, Lady Harbord (1741–1823), was the wife of a long-standing member of Parliament, Sir Harbord Harbord, created Lord Suffield in 1786.

39. The beautiful Georgiana, Duchess of Devonshire (1757–1806), a powerful political hostess, led a Whig circle that included the Prince of Wales, later Prince Regent and then George IV.

40. François Henry La Motte, who was hanged as a French spy in London in July 1781.

41. Capes Gris-Nez and Blanc-Nez (gray and white), near Calais, form the rocky promontory of mainland France closest to England.

42. An allusion to Morande's denunciation of Pelleport as the author of *Le Diable dans un bénitier*. Here again, Pelleport represents Morande (Thonevet) as the wickedest libeler in the colony of French expatriates.

43. Jean-Baptiste Lefebvre de La Boulaye was Secrétaire du Roi de la Grande Chancellerie de France from 1778 to 1788 and might have been this patron-poet.

44. The Pilgrim's two allusions suggest both elements of his despair over loss of fortune and ignominy caused by others' malevolence. In La Fontaine's fable, milkmaid Perrette loses all her hopes of fortune when she breaks her jug (*Fables*, VII, 9). The curate associates Don Quixote's cart with malevolent envy "'for he is indeed travelling on this cart under a spell, not for his crimes and sins but because of the ill will of those who are annoyed by virtue and infuriated by valour'" (*Don Quixote*, Rutherford, I, xlvii, p. 437).

45. Coming to the denouement of the Pilgrim's autobiography, Pelleport brings together his enemies: Madame Dupont (Catau des Arches), Brissot (here Bissoto), Brissot's brother Thivars (Scaramouche), Félicité (Pernelle), Samuel Swinton, and Théveneau or Thevenot de Morande (Thonevet)—and he provides an accurate description of the events that led to his own imprisonment in the Bastille. Morande denounced Pelleport as a libeler, while Swinton lured him to Boulogne-sur-Mer with an offer to let him use the presses of the *Courrier de l'Europe* to produce a new work—one that he would write himself, as he indicates by the use once more of his pseudonym, the "très révérend père de Rose-Croix." In fact, this publication was to be a new journal, modeled on the *Courrier de l'Europe*. The trap for Pelleport's arrest was set by Morande, Swinton, and a secret agent of the French embassy named Buard de Sennemar, who accompanied Pelleport to Boulogne on June 30, 1774. Eleven days later, Pelleport was in the Bastille. Meanwhile, Brissot had been in Paris all this time trying to find new funding for his Licée. Pelleport describes that mission as a rag-gathering expedition. The reference to America as the market for Bissoto's recycled rags (compilations of old articles) is an allusion to Brissot's plans, never realized, to emigrate to the United States. The police arrested Brissot on July 12 under suspicion of helping Pelleport market his libels. Brissot had indeed aided in their distribution, but he convinced the police that he had not collaborated in their composition and was released from the Bastille on September 10. Pelleport dispatches

him from the narrative by sending Bissoto to his death in Bicêtre, a particularly nasty prison for the lowest sort of criminals.

46. The preparations for Labre's canonization had indeed begun by 1783, when his followers in Rome compiled a list of his miracles, but the canonization did not take place until 1881.

47. *La Police de Paris dévoileé* (II, 23) says Pelleport's father later married "en secondes noces la fille d'un aubergiste de Stenay nommé Givry, fille de la mère du sieur à Némery." Pelleport quarreled with his stepmother, so he may here be making a characteristic in-joke to praise her father's competition, a rival cabaratier.